LOVE, REMEMBER ME

LOVE,
REMEMBER ME

—

Bertrice Small

BALLANTINE BOOKS
New York

ISBN: 0-345-37392-8

Cover design by Kathleen Lynch
Cover illustration by Elaine Duillo
Manufactured in the United States of America

To Barbara Bretton, with love

PROLOGUE

HAMPTON COURT

Autumn 1537

*T*HE *queen was dead.* She had been safely delivered of a strong, healthy son on Friday, the twelfth day of October, at two o'clock in the morning. The king, at Esher when the queen birthed the prince, rode with all haste to Hampton Court to see his son. The child was sturdy of limb and fair-haired. Henry Tudor was overwhelmed with his joy. At last he had a male heir! He could even feel benevolent toward his two daughters, sallow Mary, overpious and always looking at him sidewise, and wee Elizabeth, Nan's girl. The less said about her the better. The wench was far too pert and knowing for a baby-maid of three. Yet Jane, God bless her, loved both his girls. She wanted them with her here at court; Mary for a companion, and Bess to raise with their son.

"You have done well, sweetheart," the king told the queen. He placed a kiss upon her brow, and patted the little hand reaching out to him. "He's a fine lad, and we'll have a few more to keep him company, eh Jane?" He beamed lovingly at her. "Three or four lads for England!" Ohh, he felt triumphant and justified now. God was but approving his behavior of the past few years by finally giving him a son.

Jane Seymour smiled wanly at her husband. She had had a long and a very hard labor, almost three days of it, but the matter of her son's name must be settled. "What would you call him, my lord?" she asked her husband. She did not want to think of three or four additional births just yet, as the memory of her pain was still strongly with her. If God had made men capable of childbirth, she thought secretly, would they be quite so enthusiastic about large families?

"Edward," the king said. "My son shall be named Edward."

The royal heralds were sent out to every part of the country to give the people the glad news that King Henry VIII and his young queen, Jane, were the parents of a goodly lad. The church bells in the city of London began a happy pealing that lasted the whole day long and into the following night. *Te Deums* were sung in every church in England to celebrate Prince Edward's arrival. There were bonfires everywhere. The Tower of London was practically ringed in blue smoke as its guns thundered two thousand times in honor of the newborn prince. Housewives hung garlands above their doorways and prepared food for the celebratory feasts that would follow the happy birth. Gifts and good wishes began to pour into Hampton Court at a great rate. Who knew where or whom the king's benevolence might touch in light of his pleasure. All of England rejoiced with Henry and his queen at the news of Prince Edward's birth.

On Monday, the fifteenth of October, Prince Edward was christened in the Chapel Royal at Hampton Court. The celebration began in the queen's private apartments. The king had decided, and the queen had meekly agreed, that Archbishop Cranmer, the Dukes of Suffolk and Norfolk, and his eldest daughter Mary would act as their son's godparents. Nan's brat was also allowed to take part in the festivities. Softhearted Jane had absolutely insisted.

So the Lady Elizabeth, carried in the arms of the queen's brother, Lord Beauchamp, held the chrism tightly in her little hands, extremely conscious of the importance of the event and her own part in it. She was not certain what pleased her most—being included in this great spectacle, or the marvelous rich-looking gown she had been given. After Edward was baptized, Elizabeth returned to the queen's chambers holding the hand of her elder sister, Mary.

The queen blessed her son, as did the king. Then, having been admired all around, the baby was taken off to his own apartments by the Duchess of Suffolk, who was entrusted with his care for now.

The king, remembering past difficulties with the sons borne him by the Princess of Aragon, ordered that Prince Edward's apartments be kept scrupulously clean. Every room and connecting hallway had to be scrubbed down with soap and water daily. Every chamber had to be swept daily. Anything that Edward touched, or wore, or needed, must be clean. Such fanaticism was unheard of with regard to cleanliness, but Henry

Tudor was obeyed. The two royal wet nurses were healthy country girls, free of disease and wholesome. One had borne a dead child. The other gave her daughter to her sister-in-law to nurse. The royal infant would not share his food supply with any other child, for another, not as well cared for, could become ill and infect the prince. This child would live to succeed his father. Every precaution was taken to ensure it. Edward Tudor was a most important child.

The day after the prince's baptism, the queen fell ill. She seemed recovered by evening, but then grew quite sick during the night. The physicians attending her agreed that she had contracted puerperal fever. During the night the queen sank deeper toward death. Her confessor, the Bishop of Carlisle, was about to administer extreme unction to Jane Seymour the next morning when she suddenly appeared to rally. By Thursday she seemed to be recovering quite nicely, to everyone's relief. Then late Friday the queen's fever rose dramatically once more. She fell into a coma. There was no doubt now that her death was near, but no one dared to voice it aloud.

The king had intended to return to Esher for the hunting season, which was scheduled to begin on Tuesday, the twenty-third of October. He could not, however, bear to leave his sweet Jane. It was obvious even to him that the queen was dying. He wept bitter tears, to the surprise of all about him. Few could ever remember having seen him cry. Henry Tudor remained by his wife's bedside throughout the night. Just after midnight the Bishop of Carlisle entered the bedchamber to administer the last rites to the queen. This time there would be no miraculous recovery. Having done his duty, the bishop did what he could to comfort his master, but the king was inconsolable. At two o'clock in the morning, the very same hour in which she had birthed her son twelve days prior, Queen Jane died quietly. The king immediately departed for Windsor, and a period of seclusion. It was considered ill luck for a king to remain long in the same vicinity as death.

The queen's funeral was, of course, a most magnificent one. Her slender body was dressed in gold tissue, her lovely blond hair combed loose, a bejeweled crown set upon her head. She lay in state in the presence chamber of Hampton Court while masses were sung around the clock for the good of her sweet soul. Queen Jane was then moved to the Chapel Royal, where her ladies kept vigil for a full week.

Mary Tudor was the chief mourner. She had loved and respected this gentle, pious stepmother who had lovingly eased her back into her volatile father's good graces. Few people had been kind to Mary Tudor since her mother's fall from grace, and the reign of Anne Boleyn had been hell on earth for her. Jane Seymour, however, had always been kind.

On the eighth day of November, the queen's coffin was removed to Windsor, where she was to be buried on Monday, November twelfth. The king was yet in a depression, but he had already decided to take a fourth wife. One son was simply not enough to guarantee the continued survival of the House of Tudor. His sweet Jane was dead, but he was young enough yet to sire several more sons on a fecund female consort. *The queen was dead, but the king was very much alive.*

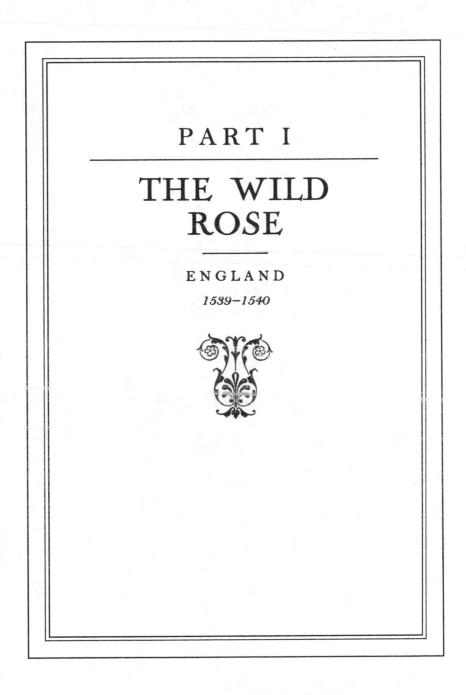

PART I

THE WILD ROSE

ENGLAND

1539–1540

CHAPTER 1

"WELL, he did say that he might visit *RiversEdge* one day," Lady Blaze Wyndham, the Countess of Langford, said to her husband. "You know he did. You heard him yourself."

"I thought he was being polite," the earl responded, aggravated. "People always say that they'll visit you someday, but one never really expects that they will come, and usually they do not. Did you honestly expect to ever see the king here? *In our home?* I know that I did not." Anthony Wyndham ran an impatient hand through his dark hair. "We are not a great house, Blaze. How long is he to stay? How many will be with him? Is it really possible for us to entertain the king well?" He glared at his wife, who was certainly, because of her long acquaintance with the king, responsible for this disruption of his life.

Blaze laughed. "Oh, Tony," she said soothingly, "it is not an official visit that Hal makes us. He is merely hunting nearby. When he realized that *RiversEdge* was in the vicinity, he decided to come and see us. He will arrive with no more than half a dozen companions to break his fast in the noonday hour." She patted her husband's hand. "It will be all right."

"There's not enough time to prepare properly," the earl grumbled. "How typical of the king to give us so little notice."

"Indeed, my lord, and when did my household become your province?" Blaze demanded sharply. "The king comes tomorrow. There is more than enough time for *me* to prepare to receive him. You need do nothing more, Tony, than be your charming self." She kissed his cheek in an attempt to mollify her handsome spouse. "By the way, my love, I have sent to my parents in Ashby to come to meet the king, and to my sisters as well."

"All of them?" her husband asked nervously. Blaze was the eldest of eleven children, eight of whom were female.

"Only Bliss and Blythe," she reassured him. "Mother may bring my brothers Henry and Tom, though. Gavin's wife is too near her time. He will not leave her, I know. After all, it is their first child."

The Earl of Langford felt relieved at the knowledge that he was not to be inundated with all of his wife's relations. Of his sisters-in-law, he knew best Bliss, the Countess of Marwood, and Blythe, Lady Kingsley. They were nearest in age to his wife. The fourth sister, Delight, had been swept off to Ireland by her husband, Cormac O'Brian, the Lord of Killaloe, years ago. They rarely heard from her. The next of his wife's siblings, Larke and Linnette, had been married to twin brothers, the sons of Lord Alcott. They were content to be country wives as long as they remained together. Proud Vanora, the next-to-youngest sister, had married the Marquis of Beresford, and the last of the Morgan sisters, Glenna, not to be outdone, had wed the Marquis of Adney. The daughters of Lord Robert Morgan were all famed for their beauty and their extraordinary ability to bear healthy offspring.

"This is really the most wonderful opportunity," Blaze said to her husband, who was drawn back to reality by hearing *that* tone in her voice.

"Opportunity for whom?" he demanded. "And for what, madame?"

"Our children, Tony! Nyssa, Philip, and Giles. Now that the king has ceased mourning Queen Jane and is betrothed to the Princess of Cleves, his mood should be very good—particularly if the hunting is excellent tomorrow morning and the repast I serve him is particularly to his taste."

"What is it you are planning, Blaze?" the earl asked her.

"I want places at court for Nyssa, Philip, and Giles, Tony. They need the polish, and we have settled no matches on any of them yet. I think Nyssa can attract a good husband at court. Perhaps the boys will appeal to certain fathers; not the high and mighty, of course, but good families looking for good matches. Philip will be the next Earl of Langford, and I have given Giles my manor of Greenhill with its comfortable income. Our two eldest sons are most eligible catches," she finished with a smile.

"I do not know if I like the idea of Nyssa going to court," the Earl of Langford said. "The boys, yes, I agree with you there, but not Nyssa."

"Why not Nyssa?" she pressed him. "There is no one hereabouts to whom we would marry her, nor is there any who takes her fancy. The Princess of Cleves is, I am told, a most gentle and refined lady. If Nyssa could find a place among her maids, she would be protected, but she would also have the opportunity to meet the eligible young men she otherwise would not meet. If the king still harbors tender feelings for me—and I know he does, for Hal is a sentimental man who remembers what pleases him through a rose-colored mist—then he will be willing to do us this kindness, and place the children at court. Ohh, Tony! We will never again have such an opportunity to advance the future of our children. And the people they meet at court may be of help to our other sons when they are old enough to go to court. The others, not being propertied, will need all the help they can obtain."

"Richard may take holy orders one day," the earl said. "What need will he have of a visit to court?"

"The archbishop goes to court," Blaze returned with a smile. "What a fine contact for our son!"

Anthony Wyndham laughed. "I had forgotten how resourceful you can be, my darling Blaze. Ohh, very well, make your plans. If God wills it, then so be it. Nyssa, Philip, *and* Giles will go to court, and Richard will one day meet the archbishop." Reaching out, he patted her very distended belly, for Blaze was in the final days of a pregnancy. "And are you certain that this is a son also?"

"You only seem to sire sons on me, my lord," she said with a smile. "Five fine boys I have had by you."

"And Nyssa," he said.

"Nyssa is Edmund's child," she answered him softly. "You have been a good father to her, Tony, but she is Edmund's blood."

"My blood as well," he insisted, "for were not Edmund and I related? He was my uncle. I loved him well, Blaze."

"He was more a brother to you," she said. "You were but a few years apart in age, and your mother, his elder sister, raised you both."

"My mother! God's blood, Blaze! Did you send to Riverside for her? She would want to pay her respects to the king."

"The messenger going to my parents stopped at Lady Dorothy's home first," Blaze said with a chuckle. "Poor Hal! He knows not what awaits him when he pays his little call tomorrow."

T HE king arrived late the following morning. His mood was a most jovial one. He had personally taken two does, plus a stag with a set of antlers unequal to any his companions had seen before. His successes made him feel young again, but he was not young. It had been over three years since Blaze had seen him, and she was shocked by his appearance. The king had put on a great deal of weight. His girth strained the seams of his garments visibly. His once fair complexion was now florid. Sweeping him a deep curtsey, her apple-green silk skirts spreading gracefully about her, the Countess of Langford strove to remember the virile, handsome man who had once been her lover. It was not easy.

Henry Tudor took her hand and drew her to her feet. "Get up, my little country girl," he said, the familiar voice taking her back in time. "I know you are ever my most loyal servant." The royal eyes twinkled at her with the memory of a shared but private jest.

"My dear lord!" Blaze answered him, smiling up at him, standing upon tiptoes that she might kiss the kingly cheek. "It is good to see you once again. Our hearts and our prayers are ever with your majesty, and Prince Edward. You are most welcome to *RiversEdge*!"

"May I echo my wife's sentiments, Your Majesty," the Earl of Langford said quietly, stepping forward.

"Ahh, Tony! You shall hunt with us this afternoon," the king said. He turned to his companions. "Why did no one think to invite my lord of Langford this morning? Must I think of everything?" His blue eyes narrowed irritably.

"I shall be honored to join your majesty," Anthony Wyndham said quickly, attempting to forestall Henry Tudor's ire. "Will you come into the hall now and break your fast? Blaze sets a fine table."

The Countess of Langford slipped a hand through the king's arm. "Come, Hal," she said, using his nickname, as she had always done. "My parents and Tony's mother have come to meet you. They await your majesty within the hall, and I've a fine side of beef waiting for you. And there is partridge pie too. As I recall, it was always a favorite of yours. I've made it with a wonderful red wine gravy, tiny shallots, and new carrots as well." She smiled up at him again, and led him into the house.

"Will you join us, gentlemen," the earl invited the king's companions, and they followed after him as he conducted them into the Great Hall.

There the earl found his wife already introducing the king to her parents, Lord and Lady Morgan, and his mother, Lady Dorothy Wyndham. His brothers-in-law, Owen FitzHugh, the Earl of Marwood, and Lord Nicholas Kingsley; and their wives, Bliss and Blythe, also greeted his majesty. Lord Morgan presented his two youngest sons, Henry and Thomas, who were young men of sixteen now.

The king was in his element, for he very much enjoyed the adulation of his subjects. He greeted each of them graciously, praising the Morgans for the fine family that they had raised; asking Lady Dorothy why she had not come to court of late. "There is always room at court for another pretty woman, madame," he said, chuckling.

Lady Dorothy, now sixty-five, replied, "Alas, sire, my son will not let me go. He says he fears for my virtue."

The king guffawed loudly. "Indeed, madame, and he is probably right." He turned back to Blaze. "And where is your fine brood, my little country girl? The last time I heard, you had four lads and a lass."

"We've five sons now, my lord. Our Henry was born two years ago this June past, and named in honor of your majesty," Blaze told him, "and as you can see, I shall shortly deliver an eighth child."

"There is nothing like a good English wife," the king said meaningfully, and his companions grew visibly uncomfortable. "How I miss my sweet Jane."

"Come and sit down, Hal," Blaze invited him, leading him to the place of honor at the high board. She could see that he was favoring one leg over the other, and realized he would be more comfortable seated. "I shall have the children brought into the hall since you wish to meet them, but I did not want them to intrude upon your visit."

"Nonsense!" the king boomed. He lowered his bulk into the chair. "I would see them all, even the littlest."

A servant immediately put a large goblet of wine into the king's hand, and he quaffed it thirstily. Blaze signaled for her tiring woman, Heartha, and instructed her to fetch the children at once. From the minstrel's gallery high above the hall, light music began to be heard. The king leaned back in his chair, visibly relaxed now.

The Wyndham offspring came into the hall with Lord Philip Wyndham, the heir, leading the way, and Lady Nyssa Wyndham, the eldest, bringing up the rear, her baby brother in her arms.

"May I present my children to your majesty," Blaze said formally. "This is Philip, our eldest son. He is twelve. And Giles, who is nine; Richard, eight; Edward, four; and Henry, just two."

Each of Blaze and Anthony's sons bowed elegantly, including the littlest boy, when he was set down upon his feet by his sister.

"And this is my daughter, Nyssa. Although Tony has raised her like his own, she is the child of my first husband, Edmund Wyndham," Blaze said.

Nyssa Wyndham curtsied to the king, her deep pink silk skirts billowing prettily about her, her eyes lowered modestly as she rose to stand before her sovereign.

"As fair an English rose as I have ever seen," the king said in complimentary tones. "How old is the lass, madame?"

"Nyssa is sixteen years of age, sire," Blaze answered him.

"Is she betrothed?"

"No, my lord," Blaze replied.

"Why not? She's pretty enough, and an earl's daughter. She has a goodly dowry, I have not a doubt, madame," the king said.

"There is no one with whom we would match her hereabouts, Hal," Blaze told him. "Her dowry is indeed a very good one. It includes Riverside, a fine house, and the lands that go with it. Nyssa is a well-propertied and -dowered girl. Actually, I should like it if she could go to court for a time." Blaze smiled sweetly, but looked pointedly at the king.

He began to chuckle, wagging an admonishing finger at her in mock reproach. "Madame," he growled, "you are shameless, but then I always knew that. You seek a place for your little wench, don't you? Do you know that every family with an unmatched daughter, indeed *any* daughter, is importuning me right now for a place in my bride's household? Great names and small ones too plead for my ear." His glance swung to Nyssa. "And you, my pretty lass, would you come to court to serve the new queen?"

"Aye, and if it please your majesty," Nyssa said pertly, looking straight at him for the first time.

The king noted that she had her mother's beautiful violet-blue eyes.

"Has she ever lived anywhere but her home?" he asked.

Blaze shook her head. "Like me, Hal, she is a country girl."

"She would be gobbled up whole by the rakes at court," he said. "It would be poor repayment for your friendship, Blaze Wyndham."

Bliss FitzHugh, Countess of Marwood, who had been listening, now spoke up uninvited. "I have been told that the Princess of Cleves is a most chaste and good lady, sire. I believe my niece would be safe within her household. Then too, my husband and I are returning to court this season. I should be there to watch over Nyssa for my sister."

Blaze threw her sister a grateful look even as the king said to her, "Very well then, madame, I will appoint your daughter one of the new queen's maidens as long as my lady FitzHugh is there to act in your stead. Is there anything else I may do for you?" he concluded dryly.

"Appoint Philip and Giles as pages to the Princess of Cleves's household," Blaze said daringly.

Henry Tudor burst out laughing at her audacity. "I do not think I shall ever play cards with you again, madame," he chortled. "As I recall, you always beat me. Very well, I will accede to your request. They're pretty lads, and mannerly too, I can see." Then he grew serious. "When you were with me, Blaze Wyndham," he said quietly, "you never asked anything of me. I remember there were many who called you a fool for it."

"When I was with you, Hal," she replied in equally soft tones, "I wanted for nothing, for I had your affection and respect."

"And you still do, my little country girl," he said. "I look at your fine brood, and I wonder if they would have been mine had I taken you for my wife instead of the others."

"Your majesty has a fine son, I am told, in Prince Edward," she answered him. "You want the best for him even as I want the best for my children. I ask now for them. You know I would not presume upon your generosity otherwise."

Reaching out, the king patted her slender hand with his fat one. "I never knew any woman, nay not even my sweet Jane, whose heart was as pure and good as yours, my little country girl," he told her. "My new queen will be pleased to have your children in her service." He looked to Blaze's sons. "What think you, Master Philip and Master Giles? Will you be happy to serve us, and our queen?"

"Aye, Your Grace!" the two boys chorused brightly.

"And you, Mistress Nyssa? Will you be as content as your brothers?" He chuckled and went on without even waiting for an answer. "She will have all the young men eager, I'll vow. You will have your work cut out for you, my lady FitzHugh, watching over this English rose."

"I am quite capable of looking after myself, Your Grace," Nyssa said. "After all, I am the eldest of my mother's children."

"Nyssa!" Blaze was scandalized by her daughter's impudence, but the king laughed good-naturedly.

"Do not scold her, madame. She reminds me of my own daughter, Elizabeth. Nyssa is of the same ilk. An English rose, but a wild rose, I am thinking. It is a relief to know she is a strong girl. She will need that strength at court, as well you know, Blaze Wyndham. Now, am I to be fed? I have agreed to your requests." He chuckled. "There is no need to starve your king into submission."

Blaze signaled her servants, and immediately they began to hurry forth in a line bearing the kitchen's best efforts to please their sovereign. As the Countess of Langford had promised, there was beef; a great joint of it, which had been packed in rock salt and roasted until its juices began to seep through its saline armor. There was a large country ham, sweet and pink; trout, broiled with lemons and served upon a bed of fresh raw spinach from the garden; and of course, the partridge pies, six of them, their crusts oozing gravy, wine-scented steam coming from the decorative vents cut into their crusts. There were several ducks, well-roasted, sitting in a sea of plum sauce upon a silver salver; and a platter heaped high with tender baby lamb chops. Bowls of peas, roasted onions, and dishes of carrots in a marsala and cream sauce were offered. There was freshly baked bread, newly churned butter, and a fine small wheel of sharp cheddar cheese.

The king had always been a fine trencherman, but his increased appetite astounded Blaze. He helped himself liberally to the beef and ham, ate one whole trout, a duck, a partridge pie, and six lamb chops. He seemed to enjoy the roasted onions particularly, smacking his lips with pleasure. He devoured a loaf of bread, a great deal of butter, and at least a third of the cheese by himself. His cup was never allowed to grow empty, and he drank with as much gusto as he ate. When one of several apple tarts was presented for his inspection and approval, the king nodded happily.

"I'll have it with clotted cream," he ordered the servant holding the large tart, and when it was readied to his satisfaction, he ate it with obvious pleasure. " 'Tis a fine repast you have served me, madame," he complimented his hostess. "I shall not be hungry until dinnertime surely." Loosening his belt, he belched softly.

"If I had eaten that much," Lord Morgan murmured to two of his sons-in-law, "I should not be hungry until Michaelmas next."

As the king was about to take his leave to return to the hunt, the Countess of Langford went into sudden labor, to her great surprise.

"The child is not due for another few weeks," she gasped, horrified to have spoiled the king's departure.

"Surely, Blaze," her mother, Lady Morgan, replied dryly, "you have had enough babies to know that they come when they are ready; not a moment before, not a moment later." She turned to the king. "Go back to the hunt, Your Grace, and take my lord Wyndham with you. This is woman's work. I've never known a man to be worth anything when his wife is laboring to bring forth their child."

"Because the man does his labor first, madame," the king said with a grin.

The men tramped forth as ordered, and helped by her mother, her mother-in-law, and her sisters, Blaze gained her bedchamber. There, after a relatively brief labor of some two hours, she birthed twin daughters.

"I cannot believe it!" she said, astounded. "I thought Tony only good for lads, and here he has given me two little lasses."

"They are identical in face and form," her mother said with a chuckle. "I was wondering if any of my girls should one day bear twins, as I have four sets of my own. You are the first one to do so, Blaze."

"I shall ride out and tell Papa," Nyssa said. "He will be thrilled, I know." She peered down at the new babies. "They are sweet!"

"Now," said Lady Morgan, "you will have these two dear little girls to raise, and will not miss Nyssa so much when she goes to court."

"No, Mama," Blaze replied, "Nyssa shall always be dear to my heart wherever she may be. She is all I have left of Edmund Wyndham. I must see her happily married else I have not done my duty by him, and he was the best of men, as you must surely remember."

"He was that," Lady Morgan agreed, and Lady Dorothy Wyndham, who had been Edmund Wyndham's half sister, nodded. "Without him your sisters would not have been able to marry so well, nor would your father been able to repair our fallen fortunes. I bless the day when he first came to Ashby. I pray for his good soul each night."

The new mother was made comfortable, and her babies swaddled. Heartha, Blaze's tiring woman, bustled in with a nourishing posset for her mistress. When Blaze had drunk it down, she was left alone to rest.

The women gathered back in the Great Hall of *RiversEdge,* chatting companionably while they waited for Lord Wyndham and the other gentlemen to return home, as all of the men but Lord Morgan had joined the king's hunting party.

"I wonder what she will call them?" Blythe, Lady Kingsley, said.

"Ah, yes, Mama, I wonder if she will have your flair for feminine names?" Bliss, Countess of Marwood, chuckled.

"Nyssa is unique," their mother noted.

"But Edmund named her," Lady Dorothy told them. "Blaze chose Nyssa's Christian name in honor of Edmund's first wife, Catherine de Haven, but it was Edmund who said his daughter should be called Nyssa, which is Greek for 'a beginning.' Edmund bragged she was to be the first of many children. He could not know it would be my Anthony who would father the Wyndham line, and not he. I miss him even now, though he is dead these fifteen years past."

"Blaze has given her sons very sensible names," Blythe said.

"But these are girls, you silly creature!" sharp-tongued Bliss said to her identical twin. "Blaze will choose wonderful names for them, I am absolutely certain! How can she not, given the example set by our dear mama? Ohh, I cannot wait to learn what she has chosen!"

"Our daughters have sensible names," Blythe countered.

Bliss threw her twin a disgusted look.

Lord Wyndham returned, and to their immense surprise, the king was with him.

"I must go and congratulate my little country girl," he said, his eyes misting with sentiment. He turned to Anthony Wyndham. "May I offer you my congratulations, sir, on your fine family!" He shook Anthony Wyndham's hand heartily.

Blaze awoke to find the king at her bedside beaming down at her. She blushed, remembering a time past when his visits to her bed had been of a more intimate nature. Henry Tudor's eyes twinkled back conspiratorially, but his words were of a most proper nature.

"I am pleased to see you looking so well after your travail, madame," he told her, and he kissed her hand.

Blaze smiled up at him warmly. "There was little travail, Your Grace. I am like an old tabby cat. I've birthed my babies quickly in recent years. Still, it was good of you to return to see me."

"I have looked on your lasses, Blaze. They are as pretty as their mother. What will you call them?"

"With your permission, Hal," Blaze said, "I should like to call the firstborn Jane, after her late majesty. The second I will call Anne, in honor of the Princess of Cleves, who will soon be your new queen and helpmeet. It seems fitting, as you were here this day, the day my little girls were born into the world."

The king, a sentimental man who enjoyed his role as a benevolent monarch, grew teary. Whipping a large square of white silk from his doublet, he dabbed at his eyes. Then turning to Lord Wyndham, he asked, "Have you a priest in the house, Tony?"

The earl nodded. "Fetch him, then," the king commanded. "He is to baptize your daughters this day, and I will stand godfather to them both. This is my desire, my little country girl," he said to Blaze. "Now I shall always have you and your good family in my life."

"Oh, Hal, you honor us so greatly," Blaze said, near tears herself.

A servant was sent to fetch Father Martin. The priest had been with the family since the time of Edmund Wyndham, and had grown old in the service of the Earls of Langford. When he was told that the countess had delivered twin daughters that very afternoon, and that the king himself would stand godfather to them, and that the baptisms were to be performed immediately, he hurried to find his best vestments, telling the servant, "Find Master Richard, and tell him to light the altar candles. I will expect him to serve."

"Aye, Father Martin," came the respectful reply.

Blaze was carried to the family's private chapel on a litter, that she might see her daughters christened. Bliss rolled her eyes in disgust, and Blythe was hard put not to giggle when they were asked by the priest to

name the infants now being held by their third godmother, their elder
sister, Nyssa.

"Jane Marie," Blythe said sweetly.

"Anne Marie," Bliss almost snapped.

The king beamed effusively, and taking each baby in turn from Nyssa,
handed it to Father Martin for baptism.

When the sacrament had been completed, the Countess of Langford
was returned to her bedchamber, where a health was drunk to the newest
of the Wyndham offspring. The king then took his leave.

"A messenger will be sent to tell you when Mistress Nyssa is expected
at court, my dear little country girl," the king told Blaze. "I will want her
to come early that she may be familiar with her duties before my bride
arrives. She must know where to go, and what to do, and who is who, if
she is to be of true service to Princess, ah, Queen Anne. I expect the lady
late this autumn. You will not have a great deal of time to prepare your
daughter, but I promise you, I will see no harm comes to her in my care,
or my queen's. She will be safe, Blaze Wyndham."

She took his hand up and kissed it respectfully. "I thank you, Hal, for
your kindness to us all," she told him, and then, exhausted, fell back
against her pillows asleep.

Smiling, the king arose from her bedside and, returning to the Great
Hall, took his farewell of the Wyndhams and their kin. "I shall look
forward to seeing you at court, Mistress Nyssa. Your brothers too. Serve
the queen well, and you will always have my friendship." He then departed
RiversEdge.

"What a day it has been!" Lady Morgan exclaimed with a gusty sigh.
"Who would have expected such a day when it began so simply? Three of
my grandchildren off to court, and two more granddaughters than I had
when the sun arose." She settled herself into a large chair by the fire, and
turning to Bliss, said, *"And just when was it decided that you go back to
court?"*

"Indeed, madame?" Owen FitzHugh said mildly. "I was most amazed,
nay, surprised, myself, to hear you say it, though I should not have
contradicted you before the king. We had not discussed it, Bliss. It has
been years since we went to court. I am not certain we belong there now."

"Oh, Owen, do not be such an old fuddy-duddy," his spouse returned
airily. "It is the most fantastic opportunity for Nyssa. She will be seventeen December thirty-first, Owen, and she is not even betrothed yet! She
is going to be an old maid if something is not quickly done. Court is a
perfect place for a young woman of Nyssa's background, and wealth, to
find a good husband. Besides, with Philip and Giles having been appointed

pages to the new queen, Blaze will need a surrogate for her children. We will take our young Owen and Blythe's Edmund with us! It will be such fun!"

"*What?*" her husband said, startled.

"*Take Edmund?*" Blythe cried.

"Of course," Bliss replied. "Philip Wyndham, young Owen FitzHugh, and Edmund Kingsley have been friends their whole lives. They were all born the same year, within months of each other. They've never been separated, and even though Philip will have his duties, there will still be time for him to be with his cousins. They'll have an absolutely wonderful time," Bliss finished, smiling broadly at her relations.

"I think it an excellent idea," Lord Kingsley agreed, his eyes twinkling merrily. " 'Twill be good seasoning for the lads."

"What you mean," his brother-in-law said pointedly, "is that you shall get rid of that young hell-raiser of yours for a few months!"

"They are not going to embarrass me, Aunt, are they?" Nyssa fretted. "Philip and Giles going to court is one thing, but if you are to bring Edmund and Owen as well, Uncle Owen is correct. Together those three scamps are really quite wicked. I cannot have them teasing me like they do here at home. Ohh, why did Mother ask for places for the boys too!"

"Do not be selfish, Nyssa," Lady Morgan chided her granddaughter.

"Ohh, Grandmother, you are always taking the boys' part! You know how hard it is for me to put a bridle on my temper. A queen's maid of honor must show dignity, and decorum. If I am constantly being hounded by my brothers, and my cousins, how can I maintain such traits?"

"Why do you assume that they will tease you?" her grandmother asked.

"Because they are little savages," Nyssa declared heatedly. "They have spent their lives torturing me."

"If you were not such fun to torture, sister dear," young Philip Wyndham said, grinning at her, "we should have stopped long ago."

Lady Morgan laughed indulgently. "You are such a naughty boy, Philip," she murmured. "You really must show some respect for your elder sister. Hers is the most important position a woman in our family has ever held. To be a queen's maid is a great honor."

"I would have thought to be a king's mistress was a greater one," the heir to Langford said blandly.

Lady Morgan paled. "*Where* did you ever learn such a thing?" she demanded, scandalized. "Who has been telling tales?"

"Oh, Grandmother," Nyssa said, "we have known forever about Mother's little adventure at court. She always said if she did not tell us, that someday someone else would; and depending upon what they wanted from us, they would put an unhealthy slant upon it. Papa agreed. Because we know the truth, we can never be hurt by the fact that mother was King Henry's mistress for a few months. There were no bastards, after all, and no harm has ever come of it. Indeed, had the king not felt he owed our mother a debt, we should not be going to court. After all, the Wyndhams of *RiversEdge* are hardly an important family."

"Well!" Lady Morgan said. *"Well!"*

"Oh, Mother, do not fuss so," the Countess of Marwood said. "Nyssa is absolutely correct, and very practical in her thinking, it seems to me. As soon as it is known who her mother is, the gossip will begin, and Blaze's tenure in the king's bed be relived in minute, and probably incorrect, detail. It will be a great deal easier for Nyssa, Philip, and Giles to know the truth than to fall prey to cruel gossip. There is very little to do at court for those not involved with the powerful. They gossip more to pass the time than to be deliberately unkind. It is a way of life for them."

"And you would return to such a life, and leave your children behind to servants?" Lady Morgan said dramatically. She had never been far from her home, and had not even seen London.

Bliss laughed. "I've given Owen three sons and a daughter, Mother. He promised me that we would go back to court when the children were able to manage without me, and they certainly can."

"And I will always be there for them," the countess's identical twin sister said. Blythe was ever the peacemaker.

"Am I to have new clothing?" Nyssa asked. She was somewhat irritated by her grandmother and her aunts. She was to go to court! Yet here they sat by the fire arguing back and forth over nothing, as far as she could see. Aunt Bliss's children would be fine without her.

Blythe immediately understood her niece's anxiety, and turned the conversation to Nyssa's advantage. "I should think an entire new wardrobe would be in order for Nyssa. Her gowns are those of a country girl, and not a young woman of the court. What think you, Bliss?"

Bliss, the sisters' fashion expert, nodded emphatically. "She'll need everything from the skin out," the countess declared, "and we do not have much time either. The new queen will be here within the next two months, and the king did say he wanted Nyssa at court beforehand. We must start tomorrow if we are to have Nyssa properly rigged out for court."

"I'm not very good with my needle," Nyssa admitted, shamefaced.

"Neither was your mother." Her aunt Blythe giggled. "When she married your father, most of what was in her hope chest had been made by us. Do not worry, Nyssa. You will have a fine wardrobe in time. We will help, and your mother has always kept a seamstress in her household. There will be plenty of fabric in the storeroom for our use."

The following day, while her mother recovered from the birth of her new sisters, Nyssa, with the help of her aunt Bliss, chose the fabrics from which her court clothing would be made. In her sixteen years she had never traveled beyond the bounds of her extended family's estates.

"Surely not these, Aunt," she protested as Bliss put aside several bolts of rich, heavy fabrics. "They are far too elegant for me."

"They are exactly right," the Countess of Marwood told her niece. "Everyone at court is dressed to the teeth, my dear." She peered closely at the girl. "You have excellent skin, Nyssa. It is fair and clear. You've inherited your mother's violet-blue eyes and her heart-shaped face, which is to the good. It is surprisingly attractive with your dark brown hair. That you have from your father."

"Mama says my hair is a bit lighter than my father's was," Nyssa noted. She could not remember Edmund Wyndham at all, for he had died when she was not even two years of age. His nephew, Anthony, who had later married her mother, was the only father she had ever known.

"You do have rather attractive golden lights in your hair," her aunt told her. "Your father did not."

"I do look like him, Heartha says," Nyssa noted. "Sometimes I stand before his picture in the gallery and just stare, but he seems a stranger, Aunt. Still, I can sometimes see the resemblance I bear to him."

"He was a wonderful man," the Countess of Marwood said. "You can be proud that you were born of his loins, Nyssa, and thank God you have his nose, not that little retroussé one of your mother's."

Nyssa laughed. "Mother's nose is sweet," she said, "but I agree with you, Aunt. I like my nice straight nose quite well."

The Countess of Marwood chose fabrics of velvet, taffeta, brocade, silk, satin, and damask weaves for her niece's gowns. Some were plain, and others woven with metallic threads. Lengths of black, gold, and white lace were selected to trim the gowns. There was silk, wool, cotton, and linen for undergarments. Nyssa's hose would be of silk, or wool, cut and sewn for a perfect fit. She would have cloaks of silk, wool, or linen, some lined in fur. There would be delicately embroidered nightrails of linen and cotton; nightcaps, caps, and hoods of velvet. Her newly made shoes and boots were of the best leather, and to her great excitement, some of her shoes were decorated with real jewels. She would have jewelry not only sewn to her apparel, but jeweled ribbons, necklaces, and rings of her very own as well.

"I have never had such magnificent clothing!" she exclaimed when at last her wardrobe was completed. "Do people at court really dress like this all the time?"

Blaze, who had recovered from the twins' birth, laughed. "You will be a little sparrow amongst peacocks, my darling," she told her eldest child. "It is not required, however, that you outshine the mighty. You are a beautiful young girl, Nyssa, and your clothing is exactly what it should be, thanks to your aunts' kindness."

"Ohh, Mama!" Nyssa told her mother, "I am so confused! One moment I am excited to be leaving *RiversEdge* for court, and the next moment I am absolutely terrified over the prospect. I've never been anywhere in my whole life. What if I make a mistake before the king? What if I disgrace the family by my actions? Perhaps I should not go." Nyssa was suddenly pale.

"Did you know that your aunt Bliss took me to court when I went for the first time?" Blaze told her daughter. "Your father had died in late autumn. I loved him so much. His death and that of your infant brother were a terrible shock to me. Your aunt, however, decided I must not mope about. Shortly after New Year's I went with Bliss and your uncle Owen to Greenwich. The farthest from Ashby that I had ever been was *Rivers-Edge*. I cried. I was very frightened. I felt awkward and quite gauche, despite the fact I was a widow, not a maiden. I just wanted to hide, but your aunt would not let me.

"Bliss had taken to court after her marriage to Owen FitzHugh like a busy duck takes to a millpond. It is her natural milieu. She will guide you safely through the maze of manners and morals there. If you are wise, Nyssa, you will trust her, and listen well to what she has to say."

Blaze put an arm about her daughter. "There is one piece of advice that I must give you, however, my dear. Guard your reputation carefully. Your virginity is the greatest treasure that you possess, Nyssa. The gift of it is yours alone to give, but I would hope you should give it to the man you will marry one day, for he will appreciate it far more than any other. Because I was the king's mistress for a short time, there will be fools crass and coarse enough to believe that you are an easy prey. Remind them sharply, for I know you will not have to remind yourself, that you are the virtuous daughter of the Earl of Langford, not some common drab. You are not to be trifled with by any."

"Was the king in love with you, Mama?" Nyssa asked. She had never before dared to voice the question.

"He was *enchanted* with me for a brief time," her mother replied, "but I do not believe he was ever really *in love* with me. We became friends, however, which was to the good, Nyssa. I have ever been the king's most loyal servant. So I hope you will be as well."

"I had always heard it said, Mama, that the king was the handsomest prince in Christendom, but I do not think him handsome. He is quite fat, and the stink from his sore leg the day he visited us was quite dreadful. I do not imagine even a crown could make me want to marry such a man. I do not envy the Princess of Cleves, poor lady. Yet I could see the king thinks himself quite grand. I cannot believe you loved him."

Blaze smiled. The young were apt to be quite harsh in their judgments of their elders. "The king has gained a great deal of weight since our time together, Nyssa. He was in his youth a very handsome man. Time, I fear, has not been particularly kind to him. We do not see ourselves age as others see us. In his own mind the king still thinks himself as a very dashing gentleman. It would be wise for those about him to treat him as such. No one enjoys getting older, my daughter, and even a king is not safe from the ravages of time."

"I shall miss you, Mama, and Papa too!" Nyssa told Blaze.

"I shall miss you also, my darling," the Countess of Langford replied, "but it is time that you began your journey into life. Court will offer you wonderful opportunities. You are certain to find a husband there, Nyssa. He might be a man of stature, or perhaps the brother of a friend that you will make. There is so much ahead of you!"

"I will only marry for love, Mama," Nyssa said.

"Love often comes after marriage, my dear," her mother replied. "I laid eyes on your father only once, and quite briefly at that, before I married him. I didn't even know him, but Edmund was so good. I very quickly fell in love with him. He was an easy man to love."

"But what if you hadn't fallen in love with him?" Nyssa said with firm logic. "It would have been horrible for you! I think I should rather love the man before I marry him, and not leave such things to chance, Mama. Mistress Fortune can be a fickle creature."

"As long as he is a suitable match," her mother said. "It must be a proper marriage that you make, Nyssa."

"But I will first love him," Nyssa insisted.

Blaze smiled at her eldest child. "He will be a very lucky gentleman," she said.

CHAPTER 2

THE king was planning a gala Christmas wedding. His mood was gayer than many had ever seen it. The festivities would be held at the monarch's favorite palace of Greenwich. There would be twelve full days of joyous celebration following the marriage ceremony. The new queen would make her formal entry into the capital city of London on the first day of January. Her coronation was already tentatively planned for February second, the feast of Candlemas. Westminster had been chosen as the site for the coronation ritual.

The king was currently at Hampton Court. Each day he issued more orders regarding his wedding and the convivial days that would follow it. Henry Tudor had thrown himself wholeheartedly into the preparations. Several times each day, and always in the presence of others, he would draw Holbein's miniature of the Princess of Cleves from his tunic, where it nested against his heart, gaze dramatically upon it, and sigh gustily like a young lad seriously involved with a woman for the very first time. The king fancied himself in love again. This Anne, he declared to his intimates, would be far different from the other Anne. This Anne would be gentle, wise, and loving. She would ease his old age when it finally arrived in some far distant future. Perhaps he would even have more children by this pretty German princess with her sweet face. That would be to the good, he assured them. Some among the court wished the king well in this new marriage. Others silently thought him a fool that he continued to believe in romantic love at his age.

A messenger arrived at Hampton Court on the fifth day of November. The Princess of Cleves had departed her brother's ducal seat at Dusseldorf, and would arrive in approximately three weeks, or by the end of the month at the latest, according to all reports. She traveled with a large, stately retinue of 263 people, along with 228 horses. There were coaches for the ladies, and over fifty baggage carts. The progress of so great a retinue was very slow, however. The king finally sent to Calais for news of his bride's arrival when word came that she was overdue. Now it was believed she would reach Calais by the eighth of December. The king's brother-in-law, Charles Brandon, Duke of Suffolk, and the lord admiral, the Earl of Southampton, Sir William FitzWilliam, departed for Calais to escort the bride across the Channel to England. The Duke of Norfolk and the king's chief minister, Thomas Cromwell, were ordered to stand by to greet Anne of Cleves at Canterbury.

Thomas Howard, Duke of Norfolk, was not pleased by the match. Most, including Bishop Gardiner, believed it was because the bride was a German Protestant. Actually, Duke Thomas hated Cromwell, and equally disliked being out of the intimate power structure surrounding the king. The Duke of Norfolk was England's premier noble. He was used to being part of the decision-making process of the Privy Council. He had opposed this marriage from the start, for it was Cromwell's great plan. It would be Cromwell, responsible for lifting this German princess from obscurity, who would influence this new queen, not Thomas Howard, whose foolish niece, Anne Boleyn, had once worn England's crown. If Anne had but taken his advice, she would yet have her crowned head.

He sighed deeply. Was it not bad enough that he had seen Anne replaced by that whey-faced Jane Seymour? That he had been forced to endure the arrogance of Jane's two brothers, Edward and Thomas Seymour, those upstarts from Wolf Hall? That he had seen a Seymour succeed where a Howard had failed? At least this bride was royal. It was his only consolation. That, and the fact he had miraculously managed to retain his position as Lord Treasurer, despite his family's failures and the king's displeasure.

The retinue from Cleves did not reach Calais until December eleventh. They were escorted into the town with much grand celebration, but once there, they were detained for the next two weeks by storms of horrendous proportions that were wracking the coasts of France and England. It was simply not possible until December twenty-sixth to make the comparatively brief crossing from Calais to Deal.

Anne whiled away her time learning to play cards. She did not know how, but quickly picked it up. Her teacher, the Earl of Southampton, had told her that the king loved to play cards. Anne was eager to learn all things that would endear her to her husband. The court of Cleves had been a somber one. Cards and music and dancing were considered frivolous. Anne wondered about it. She found gaming, particularly for money, most stimulating.

THERE had been hundreds of applications for the designated places in the new queen's household. More were disappointed than pleased by the king's appointments. Nyssa Wyndham, arriving at Hampton Court on the fifteenth of November, could scarcely contain her excitement. It fortunately overwhelmed her nervousness, which had grown with each passing mile that took her from *RiversEdge*. She watched her aunt Bliss carefully, aping her every move; and refused to be disconcerted by her young male relations, who found her new behavior hilarious, to say the least.

Knowing that there would not be room for them at the palace, Owen FitzHugh had rented a small house in the village of Richmond. Decent lodgings were at a premium. He had had to outbid several others to obtain it. When he and Bliss had been younger and very much involved with the court, it had been different. There had always been a place for them. It had been years, however, since they had been a part of all of this. He grimaced. Court was too damned expensive these days, it seemed to him. Not only had he had to rent lodgings for them here in Richmond where Hampton Court Palace was located, but he had had to rent a house near Greenwich as well. At least his two brothers-in-law had contributed generously to the expenses he would incur with all of this. After all, he would not have come had it not been for Nyssa and the lads.

"Will we live here while the court is here?" Nyssa asked her uncle as they arrived in Richmond-on-Thames.

"You will live at court," Bliss answered before Owen even had the chance to think. "Philip and Giles will live there as well, but our young Owen and Edmund Kingsley will live here with us."

" 'Twill not be easy," the Earl of Marwood told his niece. "You'll be lucky to have a bed, and will probably share one with another girl. You'll have little space for your possessions, and will have to leave most of them here with us. You'll be on call to the queen 'round the clock, and have little time to claim for your own. You'll eat and sleep on the run. Your brothers too. 'Tis not easy to be in the royal service."

Nyssa paled slightly, her look plainly asking why no one had told her all this before. Being a maid of honor suddenly sounded awful! She wished now that she had stayed at home.

Bliss, divining her thoughts, said, " 'Tis hard, I'll not deny, my child, but ohh, the advantages to being here at court! *Everything* happens at court. 'Tis where the power and the excitement lie, Nyssa. *And the gentlemen.*" Bliss drew her hood up, and taking the hand proffered by the footman, stepped from their carriage. She looked hard at the residence her husband had rented for them. "Surely this cannot be right, Owen. It is practically a cottage, my lord. Are you certain this is the house that you obtained for us?" Nyssa had alighted from the vehicle, and took her aunt's hand in hers. Bliss gave her a quick smile.

"We are fortunate to have any lodgings at all," the Earl of Marwood replied testily. "Coming to court under normal circumstances is not easy. Coming to court when the king is about to remarry is impossible, madame! I know several who fought over accommodations in barns. Perhaps you would prefer to share your quarters with the cows?"

Nyssa giggled. Uncle Owen could be so forceful when he chose to be. Usually he pretended to allow Aunt Bliss her way in all things, not fully realizing that Bliss had wrapped him about her little finger years ago. The young girl strove to ease the situation. "I think the house sweet. I have never lived in town."

Bliss, finally realizing the situation, said, "I am certain that you have done your best, Owen, but why are we standing in the street? Let us go and see exactly what it is we do have."

Inside, Bliss found the house not quite as bad as she had anticipated, but certainly not as good as she had hoped for. They stepped into a narrow hall to ascend equally narrow stairs up a flight to the first floor of the house.

"The library is in the front, a family hall in the rear," the earl said quietly. "On the lower floor there is a kitchen, although most of our meals will come from the public cook house nearby. On the next floor up are three bedchambers, and the top floor will house the servants. A garden and a stable come with the house as well. 'Twas the best I could do under the circumstances."

Bliss nodded. "We'll be going to Greenwich shortly," she told them hopefully. "It isn't as if we had to live here forever."

"The house in Greenwich is larger," the earl said with a smile. "Someone had already rented it, but there was a near-death in the family, so of course they could not come to court. I arrived at just the right time to snap it up. I rented it through April. Even if we have to go up to London, the Greenwich house will be convenient for us. It sits in its own little park, my dear. Did I tell you that?"

"No, you did not, my lord," Bliss answered him slowly. "Your description, however, will make our time here in Richmond easier."

They had moved into the small family hall as they talked. A cheerful fire was burning in the paneled room, lit by the house's caretaker, who had been expecting them. The furnishings were plain, but everything seemed clean, which was a relief to Bliss.

"When are we to report to court, Aunt?" Nyssa asked nervously.

"Not until tomorrow," her aunt reassured her. "Sir Anthony Browne's wife will be supervising the maids of honor, I am told. She is very strict, but fair, I have heard. The pages too will be in her charge, I believe." She fixed her Wyndham nephews with a stern look. "You two will have to behave," she warned them. "You, in particular, Philip. As your father's heir, you must not disgrace the Langford earldom. The king has done your mother a great favor in placing you in Queen Anne's household."

"I have certainly been taught the social graces, Aunt," Philip Wyndham said loftily. "I know well what is expected of me. I would hardly disgrace myself, or my family's name."

"And you shall make us all proud," Owen FitzHugh said heartily, clapping his nephew on the back and avoiding his wife's outraged look.

Bliss, however, was not to be thwarted. "You must be more careful, Philip, and think before you speak," she chided him.

A wink from his uncle encouraged young Lord Wyndham to hold his tongue. "Yes, madame," was all he replied.

It was now late in the day. Bliss ordered a simple meal served, that her brood might retire early. "Even though the Princess of Cleves has not yet arrived," she warned them, "this will likely be the last full night of sleep you have for some time."

The four male cousins were to share one of the bedchambers. Nyssa would have a small room barely large enough to contain a bed and her baggage. The little serving maid who had come with her from *RiversEdge* was to sleep on the bed's trundle.

"It ain't much, Mistress Nyssa," the girl, who was called Tillie, said plainly. "Me dad's dogs have more room in their kennel." Tillie's father was the head gamekeeper at *RiversEdge*. She was an outspoken girl, small of stature, with a pleasant but plain countenance. Her flaxen hair was neatly plaited into a single braid that hung down her back, and her brown eyes were sharp with a look of intelligence.

"We won't be here for very long, Tillie," Nyssa promised.

"The countess's woman says you will be going to court first thing in the morning to pay your respects to the king and meet the mistress of the maids. We'd best decide what you're to wear now. There will be precious little time come morning, I'll warrant."

Nyssa nodded. Tillie was a sensible and practical girl. She had been in Nyssa's service for ten months now, having been chosen by her mother's own beloved tiring woman, Heartha, who had personally trained the girl in her duties. Tillie was Heartha's niece, and had been raised at *Rivers-Edge*. She was the same age as her mistress.

"Now we'll want to make a good first impression," Tillie said thoughtfully, "but we don't want to look bold, do we?" She shook her head, answering her own question. "The burgundy? Nay. The apple-green? 'Tis not quite right, I'm thinking."

"What about that lovely violet-blue that matches my eyes?" Nyssa asked her maid. " 'Tis very flattering, Tillie."

"Aye, but you'll attract too much attention in it, being a newcomer, I'm thinking. 'Tis not the kind of impression you'll want to be making, mistress." She furrowed her brow in concentration, and then suddenly it cleared. "The peach velvet!" she said. " 'Tis just the thing! You'll wear it with that wonderful cream and gold damask underskirt, Mistress Nyssa. I'll unpack them right away and get the wrinkles out. You'll look as you should, a beautiful, well-to-do young lady. You get into bed and go to sleep. We have an early start before us. You'll have to bathe in the morning, and I must do your hair. Here, let me help you to undress, and then I'll be about my business preparing your gowns and petticoats for the morrow."

Nyssa didn't think she could sleep. She was far too excited, yet the moment her head touched the pillow, she was off. When Tillie awoke her in the morning, it was yet dark, and the room, without a fireplace, was freezing. She snuggled beneath her coverlets, protesting as Tillie fussed at her to get up.

"I've got a tub ready and waiting for you, Mistress Nyssa," Tillie said. "The water will not stay hot in this place for long. You had best hurry, or 'twill be as icy as the room itself."

"I don't care," Nyssa muttered defiantly, and burrowed deeper beneath the down. It was so cozy in her bed. She shrieked as Tillie yanked the covers from her. *"No!"* She struggled to grab them back.

"Into the tub with you," Tillie said firmly. "You'll not be disgracing the

Wyndhams of Langford by coming before the king and his grand court with the stink and stain of the road upon you, mistress! Why if my aunt Heartha learned of it—and believe me, that gossiping Maybelle who serves Lady Bliss would be quick to tell her—Aunty would tan the hide right off of me. You wouldn't want that to happen, Mistress Nyssa, would you?" she wheedled. "Lord knows I try to do my best by you."

Nyssa laughed. "And you do, Tillie," she assured the servant. Climbing from her bed, she pulled off her nightgown to get into the small, round, oaken tub. She sat down in the warm water, shivering slightly. Sometimes Tillie sounded like Heartha, and far older than her years, but at other times she was such fun.

"I've got to do your hair," Tillie warned her apologetically. " 'Tis filled with dust from the road." Before Nyssa could answer, Tillie poured a small bucket of warm water over her mistress's head. "You do the rest, and we'll be done the faster," she said.

"Hurry!" Nyssa said through chattering teeth. The room was terribly cold, and with wet shoulders, she felt it all the more. Taking up the small cake of hard-milled soap, she quickly washed herself, gasping as Tillie poured another bucket over her head to rinse the first washing away.

Tillie scrubbed her lady's head a second time, rinsed it vigorously with her bucket, then finally ordered, "Quick, get out, mistress!" She wrapped a large towel about Nyssa and began to vigorously dry her hair with a second towel.

Nyssa rubbed herself with the rough fabric until her skin began to glow. Then at Tillie's suggestion she climbed back into bed to get warm once again.

Tillie handed her the smaller towel. "Keep getting that water from your hair, mistress," she said. "I'll go downstairs and see if I can find you something to eat before we must dress."

Nyssa pulled the coverlets as high up as she could, trying to ward off the chill of the room. She rubbed her long dark hair until at last most of the bathwater was gone and her hair was merely damp. Across the small room her bodice, gown, and petticoats were spread neatly over a chair. There wasn't a wrinkle in them. Tillie must have been up half the night, Nyssa thought guiltily, pressing them out so that her mistress would make a good first impression at court. What a treasure the maidservant was. Her mother had always said a good tiring woman was invaluable, but Nyssa hadn't given it much thought until now.

Tillie bustled back into the room with a tray. "Well, I didn't have much hope when I went downstairs," she said matter-of-factly, "but lord bless me if there wasn't a one-eyed old woman in the kitchen who said she was the cook for this place. She gave me a nice bowl of oat porridge, some bread fresh from her ovens, butter, honey, and mulled, watered wine for you, mistress." Tillie placed the tray on Nyssa's lap. "Now you eat it all up. From what Maybelle tells me, you'll be lucky to get fed the rest of the day. They don't eat much at court, she says."

"What about you?" Nyssa asked her servant. "Did you get something for yourself to eat, Tillie?" She spooned porridge into her mouth.

"I'll eat when you've gone, mistress," Tillie told her. "Maybelle says you'll probably be back here for the next few nights since the new queen ain't arrived yet. The maids with family nearby will usually come home to rest. Once the queen has come, though, 'twill be a different thing, Maybelle says."

"I'm glad Maybelle is such a font of information," Nyssa said, her eyes twinkling with humor.

"Pea-green with jealousy, she is." Tillie giggled. "Oh, her mistress is a countess, but at court countesses are a ha'penny a pound. Lady Bliss ain't never served a queen, but *my* mistress will be serving a queen. Poor old Maybelle is torn between envy and her natural inclination to tell me what to do because I'm just a girl like yourself, mistress."

"Glean what knowledge and gossip you can from her, and any others you may become friends with," Nyssa instructed her serving maid. "I'm not very wise in the ways of the world, Tillie, as you well know. I think I will have to become so to survive at the court. Mama has said this is such a wonderful opportunity for me. I cannot disappoint her."

Tillie nodded her head sagely. "Don't you worry, Mistress Nyssa. We're going to do just fine here at court. Now, finish up your breakfast before your aunt is in here scolding us both for being late."

Nyssa swallowed the last of her bread and wine then climbed from her bed. The room was still cold, but she felt better now that she was clean and fed. Tillie helped her into a soft linen chemise with a standing collar edged in lace. Then she slipped a pair of delicately knitted stockings on her mistress's legs, gartered with silk rosebuds. Next came a satin corset and several petticoats over which was set a shakefold, a delicate wire frame with stiffened pads. Her cream satin underskirt, which was embroidered with gold thread dragonflies and daisies, fell over the little hoop, spreading itself out smoothly. Next came the peach velvet divided overskirt, which displayed the underskirt to its best advantage. Finally Tillie fitted a peach velvet bodice embroidered with gold thread, pearls, and tiny, glittering topaz over her mistress's corset. The bodice had a low neckline and wide bell-like sleeves turned back at the lower edge.

It was the fashion for young girls to wear their hair parted in the middle and loose. For neatness' sake, not to mention elegance, Tillie fitted Nyssa's long hair into a pretty gold caul. Then the maidservant bent to fit narrow, round-toed shoes of cream-colored kid upon the girl's feet.

Tillie stood up to survey her handiwork, and nodded, pleased. "I'll just get yer jewelry casket, mistress. 'Tis all that's needed now to supply the finishing touch to your garb."

When Tillie returned with the jewel case, Nyssa chose two beautiful strands of pearls of a creamy hue. One was longer than the other, and they hung below the neckline of her gown. She slipped two rings, one a pearl, the other a topaz, on the fingers of her right hand, and then closed the box. "Put it away, Tillie," she said. "I have what I need for today. It is not too much, is it?"

Tillie tucked the box back into her mistress's trunk, saying as she did so, "Nay, Mistress Nyssa. 'Tis just right."

There was a knock upon the bedchamber door, and Maybelle stuck her head in. Her eyes widened at the sight of Nyssa. "Ohh, and don't you look pretty, little mistress," she said admiringly. "Yer aunt is awaiting you downstairs. They're ready to go."

Tillie picked up a light brown velvet cloak lined in rabbit's fur for her mistress, and handed Nyssa her gloves. "Come along, my lady," she said briskly, moving so swiftly that Maybelle was forced to give way at the door. Tillie winked at Nyssa as Maybelle, swept aside, sputtered irritably, running behind them to catch up.

They moved quickly but carefully down the staircase. Nyssa took in every elegant bit of her aunt's attire. Bliss was, at thirty-three, still an outrageously beautiful woman. Her deep blue velvet gown, embroidered with gold and silver threads as well as pearls, matched her sapphire-blue eyes. In defiance of fashion, Bliss wore her daffodil-blond hair in a chignon, held by gold pins at the nape of her neck.

"I see no reason to hide my beautiful hair beneath those ugly headdresses," she often said. Then she would turn and smile at her doting husband. "Owen would not like it," she would finish, as if his opinion in the matter were really of great import to her.

This morning she carefully scrutinized her niece with critical eyes. Finally she smiled approvingly. Both Tillie and Nyssa let out a collective breath.

"Very nice, my child. You look absolutely pure perfection. Elegant, but not gaudy. A young woman of means and good family; not some opportunistic little wench come husband-hunting to court, eager to attract the attention of some foolish gallant."

Nyssa's eyes twinkled. "I thought I *had* been sent to court to find a husband," she teased her aunt, and her uncle Owen guffawed.

"You have come to court to serve the queen," Bliss said in smooth tones. "Now, if you should just happen to find a gentleman who takes your fancy, steals your heart, and pleads for your hand in marriage, *and* if he is suitable, that is an altogether different matter, child."

Nyssa laughed. "Is that how you caught Uncle Owen's fancy, at court?"

"I met your uncle in your father's house," Bliss replied primly.

"It was your mother's sixteenth birthday," the Earl of Marwood said, taking up the story. "Bliss and Blythe and your aunt Delight came to *RiversEdge* to celebrate the occasion. One look at your aunt, and I was lost to her, just as Nick Kingsley was as taken with Blythe."

"You fell in love at first sight?" Nyssa had never heard the story, but it sounded so very romantic.

"At first sight," her uncle said softly. His eyes swept to his wife. "Did I not, puss?"

Bliss had a look in her eyes that her niece had never before seen. "Aye," she drawled. Then, remembering herself and where they were, she snapped, "Why are we standing here in this draughty hallway? We are due at court shortly." She turned to Tillie. "You've done well, girl. I'll give my sister a good account of you when I write her next. Heartha has trained you well and can be proud."

"Thank you, m'lady," Tillie responded, bobbing a little curtsey. Then she put the cloak over Nyssa, settling it smoothly and turning her mistress about to fasten the gold frogs that held the garment shut.

"Where are the boys?" Nyssa asked as they exited the house.

"Awaiting us in the coach," her aunt replied. "Edmund and my Owen will ride with the coachman. 'Tis not far."

Her two cousins scrambled from the carriage and climbed atop the coach box with their driver as the two women reached the vehicle's door. Nyssa saw her brothers, seated with their backs to the coachman. They were more elegantly dressed than she had ever seen them. Philip was dark-haired and light-eyed like their father; Giles, fair like their mother. They wore haut-de-chausses of black velvet, the slashings in the fabric showing white satin beneath. Their stockings were striped black and white, and their black leather shoes had rounded, narrow toes. Their doublets were of black velvet, embroidered with pearls, over which they wore identical sleeveless jerkins of white doeskin with shoulder puffs. The jerkins hung to their knees. Each boy wore a small gold neck chain from which hung a medallion with the family's coat of arms. Small jeweled daggers hung from their girdles, and each wore a flat bonnet of black velvet with ostrich tips atop his head.

"You both look very fine," she complimented them, surprised.

"As do you, sister," Philip Wyndham told her in return.

"Look, Nyssa," Giles said excitedly. "I have my own dagger!" He proffered the bejeweled weapon for her to see. It was studded with garnets, tiny diamonds, and seed pearls.

"You must never draw it in the king's presence," she warned him. "Or the prince's either. Remember, Mama told you that was treason."

Giles nodded, his blue eyes wide. "I won't forget," he said.

Philip, however, looked irritated at his elder sister's admonition. "If you tell me once," he said archly, "I remember. It is not necessary to repeat it, Nyssa."

"Your apologies, my lord," she mocked him, settling her skirts about her. "I don't know why I always forget how wise you are, Viscount Wyndham. How terribly remiss of me to have done so."

Giles giggled, and even Philip was forced to smile at the barb.

"There must be no squabbling amongst you," Bliss warned.

Nyssa folded her hands meekly and became instantly silent, as did her two brothers. The coach pulled away from the house and headed down the road to Hampton Court. Soon the traffic was very heavy. Nyssa found herself fascinated by it all. Other coaches surrounded theirs, some of them even more elegant and rich-looking. There were ladies and gentlemen mounted upon fine horseflesh wending their way amid the carriages. Everyone was going, it seemed, in the same direction—to Hampton Court.

Hampton Court had been erected by Cardinal Wolsey, the king's counselor. It had been built on land acquired from the Knights Hospitalers of St. John in 1514. The Order of St. John, however, would not sell the cardinal the land. They rented it to him instead for ninety-nine years, at a nominal fee of fifty pounds. Building had begun in the spring of 1515. Although the king and Katherine of Aragon were entertained there in May of 1516, the palace was not completed for several more years.

It was built around three courts: the Base Court, the Clock Court, and the Cloister Green. The buildings were of red brick, decorated with blue-black patterns in a diamond shape. All the turrets were crowned with lead cupolas. The exterior walls of Hampton Court were decorated with the cardinal's coat of arms, as well as a set of terra-cotta roundels which had been a gift from the pope. There was a long, windowed gallery where the cardinal walked on inclement days, and a garden where he would sit each evening. The palace had a thousand rooms, of which 280 were guest chambers. There were two kitchens, and in a room between them sat the master cook, garbed as elegantly as any courtier, directing his underlings grandly by word and the waving of a wooden spoon, his badge of office.

Bliss explained this all to her niece and two nephews as the coach slowly traveled along the crowded road.

"Mama met the cardinal once," Nyssa told her aunt.

"I know," Bliss replied. "He was a man to be feared in his heyday. He climbed long, and high. His fall was swift."

"Mama always said he was a loyal servant of the king. Why was he executed?" Nyssa wondered aloud.

"The king grew angry with him because he could not seem to get the pope to agree to a divorce for him from the Princess of Aragon. The cardinal knew that the king wanted to marry Anne Boleyn, and the cardinal did not like her. He wanted the king to marry Princess Renee of France. It is possible the Princess of Aragon might have given way to a princess of France that the king have a male heir; but Wolsey had no intention of her giving way to Tom Boleyn's girl.

"The cardinal had many enemies. Very powerful men always do. They saw this rift between the king and the cardinal as a chance to pull Wolsey down. The cardinal's rather extravagant way of life was suddenly questioned quite vocally. A rather scurrilous rhyme was circulated. It set the king to wondering who was really in control of his realm: himself or the cardinal. The king does not like being eclipsed."

"I know the rhyme!" Nyssa said excitedly. " '*Why come ye not to court? To which court? To the King's Court or to Hampton Court? Nay, to the King's Court! The King's Court should hath the excellence but Hampton Court hath the preeminence.*' "

"The author had to seek sanctuary at Westminster," the Earl of Marwood told them. "The king was very angry, and became even more so when a Franciscan monk visiting court saw the magnificence of Wolsey's court and asked, 'Have they not in England a king?' I heard it myself, as did those who were quick to report it to the king himself. Poor old Wolsey! The king's vanity was sorely pricked. He called the cardinal to him, demanding to know why he had built so magnificent a house for himself at Hampton Court. I will give Wolsey credit, for he as quickly answered the king, 'To show how noble a palace a subject may offer to his sovereign.' He then turned the place over to the king, lock, stock, and barrel," Owen FitzHugh finished.

"You mean lock, stock, tapestries, and carpets," Bliss said with a laugh, and then she explained to the others, "The cardinal had a passion for tapestries. One year he ordered one hundred and thirty-two of them. As for carpets, he had all kinds. Foot carpets, table carpets, window carpets. In one shipment from Venice there were sixty carpets alone just for Cardinal Wolsey. How he loved beautiful things!"

"Mama says he was going to be tried for treason," Nyssa said. "What treason did he commit?"

"None, child," Bliss told her, "but never repeat it. Wolsey simply made too many enemies. When he fell from favor, he was exiled to York, where he was archbishop. Had he lived quietly, and piously, perhaps he would have escaped his detractors, but the cardinal was not capable of it. He once again set up a sumptuous court. The king heard of it, and allowed himself to be persuaded that Wolsey might be in league with foreign powers. After all, the cardinal had always been able to gain the king what he desired, until now. With regard to the king's divorce from the Princess of Aragon, he seemed helpless. Or was he? He was arrested at Cawood Castle, and died in Leicester Abbey on the road to London."

"The king wields great power, doesn't he?" Nyssa said softly. "I think I am afraid of him now, and I was not before."

"You are wise," her uncle told her, "to fear Henry Tudor. He can be the best of friends, kind and generous; yet he is a deadly enemy, Nyssa. Your mother survived her tenure at court because she was clever. She never allowed anyone to draw her into a faction, nor did she flaunt her privileged position while she held it. You would be wise to model your behavior after hers."

"Perhaps I would be better off going home," Nyssa said, and her brothers groaned in disgust at her cowardice.

"Nonsense!" Bliss said. "You have an envied appointment, Nyssa Wyndham. As a maid of honor to the queen, you will be sought after by many eligible gentlemen. Once you find a husband, you will marry and live happily ever after. That is the whole purpose of your coming to court. I am ashamed that my sister's daughter would be so weak-livered as to want to run away. You will be seventeen at the end of next month, Nyssa. Need I remind you you are practically considered too old for a first marriage? Blaze does not need you mooning about RiversEdge. She does not need to worry about you when she has your two little sisters to get safely through their infancy, and your younger brothers to bring up and find rich wives for, child. You, Giles, and Philip have been sent to court to find your destinies. To flee home is unthinkable!"

Philip and Giles Wyndham looked as if they wanted to burst into laughter, but they did not. Instead they watched as their elder sibling grew pink with embarrassment and outrage at her aunt's words.

"I am not weak-livered!" Nyssa said angrily. "This is all very new to me. Please remember, Aunt, that when you first came to court, you came with your husband. You came to play. I, however, have been asked to serve a queen. I have no experience in the court. I am terrified lest I shame the family, but I am not weak-livered!"

"No, you are not," her uncle agreed. "I remember when I first came to court as a lad, Nyssa. I was to be a page to Prince Henry, now our king. I was only six, and I had never before been away from home. It was a terrifying prospect. I know just how you feel, but do what I did. For the first few days be very mannerly, and watch, and ask. Do not be afraid of seeming stupid. Better you ask than make an embarrassing error later on. Besides, the new queen has not yet come, and will not arrive for a few weeks yet. You have plenty of time to learn your new duties. The Mistress of the Maids will help you. Your good performance reflects well upon her. She will want you to learn."

"Thank you, Uncle Owen," Nyssa told him. "I am glad you understand my fears." She glared angrily at her aunt, but Bliss was not affected by it.

Their carriage had now arrived at the palace, and footmen in royal livery ran forward to open the doors to the vehicle so that its occupants might quickly dismount, and the coach be parked in order that room for the next carriage be made. As Bliss stood shaking the wrinkles from her gown, there was a nearby shriek of delight.

"Bliss! Is it really you? I cannot believe it!" A plump woman with dark hair, a pretty face, and lively brown eyes flung herself at the Countess of Marwood and hugged her enthusiastically.

"Adela? Adela Marlowe? Why indeed, it is you!" Bliss responded.

Adela Marlowe laughed. "I've grown as plump as a shoat with childbearing, haven't I? *But you!* You look the same as ever!"

"Only a true friend would say such a thing," Bliss said, laughing in return. "I'm not quite the slip of a girl I once was, Adela."

Adela Marlowe swung her gaze to Nyssa. "Is this your daughter?" she asked, obviously assessing the girl. *Young. Innocent. A good dowry.*

"Nay, 'tis Blaze's eldest daughter," Bliss answered. "This is my old friend, Lady Adela Marlowe," she told her niece. "This is Lady Nyssa Catherine Wyndham, Adela. She is to be a maid of honor to the new queen. Blaze's two eldest boys have places as pages." She nodded to her nephews. "Philip, Viscount Wyndham," she said, "and Giles Wyndham." To her absolute delight, both boys bowed elegantly, impressing Adela Marlowe.

"Are you betrothed, child?" Lady Marlowe asked Nyssa.

"Nay, madame, I am not," was the soft response.

"Ahh, then, you must meet my son Henry," replied Lady Marlowe.

"What a fine idea!" Bliss enthused.

"Bliss, my dear," her husband interjected, "we had best present Nyssa to Lady Browne. She is expected, and should not be late. That would not, I fear, make a good impression upon the lady." He took his wife's arm in a firm grip.

"Owen is correct," Bliss said regretfully, and then she kissed her friend upon both cheeks. "We'll see each other later, Adela, and catch up on all the gossip," she promised with a smile. Then her attention was caught by her son. "Young Owen, you get right down off that coach box! Where is Edmund Kingsley? Have we lost him already? Ohh, perhaps it was not a good idea to bring all these lads to court after all."

Her husband smiled archly. "They are your responsibility, puss," he said wickedly. "You did volunteer to bring them."

Bliss glared at her husband, but with a smile he turned to go, and she was forced to quickly gather her brood and follow him.

Lady Margaret Browne was the wife of Sir Anthony, a gentleman-in-waiting, and the King's Master of the Horse. Her husband stood very, very high in the king's favor. He was a hardworking man whose sole interest was the king's interest. He never involved himself in the political infighting that went on among the different factions of the court. His loyalty was to Henry Tudor alone, and his wife echoed his sentiments. Sir Anthony's behavior had recently been rewarded by huge tracts of land in Surrey, formerly in the possession of Chertsey Abbey, Merton Priory, St. Mary Overey in Southwark, and Guildford Priory. His wife had been appointed the new queen's Mistress of the Maids, a most coveted position.

Lady Margaret's apartments were near those that would belong to the new queen. She greeted the Earl and Countess of Marwood cordially.

"It seems only yesterday that you came to court a bride, Lady FitzHugh," she said to Bliss. "You do not, I think, suffer time too greatly. How many children living have you?"

"Three sons and a daughter, madame," Bliss replied.

"Are these they?" Lady Browne asked, peering myopically.

"Only one is mine, madame. Young Owen, make your bow," Bliss commanded her son; smiling, pleased, when he did so. "Allow me to present Edmund Kingsley, the eldest son of my sister Blythe, and her husband, Sir Nicholas Kingsley. And these two lads are Philip, Viscount Wyndham, and his brother Giles, the sons of my eldest sister, the Countess of Langford. The king has appointed them pages in the new queen's household. I was told to bring them to you, madame."

The three boys bowed in turn as they were introduced, and Lady Browne nodded, obviously delighted by their good manners. "And the lass, Lady FitzHugh. Who is she?"

"This is Lady Nyssa Catherine Wyndham, madame. The daughter of the Earl and Countess of Langford. She is to be a maid of honor."

Nyssa curtsied prettily.

"*A maid of honor?*" Lady Browne exclaimed, and her face registered her distress. "Oh, dear, not another one! Every young woman of good family has come to court to be a maid of honor. There are simply not enough places! I wish I could help you, Lady FitzHugh, but I cannot."

"I have not made myself clear," Bliss said in an apologetic tone, but her husband recognized the iron beneath it. "Nyssa has already been appointed to her position by the king himself, when he visited Nyssa's home last October and stood godfather to her newborn twin sisters. Nyssa is the daughter of Blaze Wyndham, Lady Browne. We are here today because she was summoned to court by the king. Nyssa's appointment is not a tentative one, madame." She smiled, but there was determination in her eyes. No one would take this position away from Nyssa!

"*Oh!*" Lady Browne answered. "I did not know. Blaze Wyndham's daughter, you say? The name is familiar, but I cannot quite place it." The girl was pretty and had good manners, but she was a total nonentity. There were fully a dozen families petitioning her for places; families of much more importance, who would be willing to show her their gratitude in most substantial ways. The king had probably already forgotten his appointment of this pretty creature. She had to be put off.

"My mother was called the 'Quiet Mistress,' madame," Nyssa said suddenly. She had seen the look in Lady Browne's eye, and reacted instinctively to it. "Mama's tenure was brief, but I am certain you will remember her. She remains to this day the king's most loyal servant, *and friend.*"

"You must not be so forward, child," Lady Browne said sternly, but when she sighed, both Bliss and Nyssa knew she was beaten. "Have you ever been to court before?" Lady Browne asked, but knew Nyssa's answer even before she spoke it. "Well, then, you have much to learn, and precious little time in which to learn it, I fear. Beginning tomorrow you will report to me after mass each day that we are here at Hampton Court. You will have to sleep at your family's lodging temporarily, as it is impossible to find accommodations right now in the palace. The Maidens' Chamber is filled with guests, since it is not needed for the new queen's use presently. When we move on to Greenwich, however, that will all change. You must then remain with the queen unless she gives you permission to go elsewhere."

"Yes, madame," Nyssa said, and she curtsied.

Lady Browne nodded then turned to Bliss. "The same instructions apply to the pages as well, Lady FitzHugh. They have not been from home before either, I imagine. I hope they will not become homesick, and weep about it. I cannot be bothered with weeping boys."

Both Philip and Giles looked extremely indignant at her words.

"Come, children," Bliss said. "We shall show you about the palace, for you will need to know where everything is."

"An excellent idea!" Lady Browne approved. "Do not forget, Nyssa Wyndham. First thing after mass in the morning!"

"I shall not forget, madame," Nyssa replied, and she curtsied again.

When they were safely away from Lady Browne's chambers, Bliss said, laughing, "If she could have frightened us off, Nyssa, she would have."

"I wonder if we should not have let her," Nyssa said thoughtfully.

"Nonsense!" Bliss replied sharply. "This is a wonderful opportunity for you, Nyssa Wyndham. Your mother would be furious if you came home with your tail between your legs. Besides, it would take more than Lady Browne to frighten us off. She was only thinking of what she might gain from others, eager to place their daughters as maids of honor. Anything can be bought and sold, child. Your mother paid for your position in full many years back. The king owed her a debt and he knew it."

Nyssa was silent for the brief time it took to make their way into the public rooms of the palace. There, Lord and Lady Marlowe were waiting for them. Indeed it seemed to Nyssa as if Lady Marlowe had deliberately planned to meet up with them again as soon as she might. With the Marlowes was a young boy with a blotchy face, who shifted his feet nervously and looked extremely uncomfortable. He flushed, embarrassed, as his mother trilled out,

"Over here, Bliss! Here we are!"

While Lord Marlowe and the Earl of Marwood renewed their old acquaintance, Lady Marlowe proudly introduced her son Henry to Bliss. It was quite clear that she had a match between her son and Nyssa in mind. The male Wyndhams and their cousins were highly amused.

Owen FitzHugh decided to take matters into his own hand, saying to Lord Marlowe, "I say, I was just about to take my lads to see the tiltyards and the tennis courts. Why don't you and young Henry come along with us?"

"Excellent!" Lord Marlowe enthused, even as his son eagerly agreed.

"How old is Henry?" Bliss asked her old friend as the gentlemen departed. "He is a quiet boy, much like his father, I think."

"Twelve," Lady Marlowe said, and sighed deeply. "Aye, he is like John. Even more so, I fear."

"Nyssa will be seventeen on the thirty-first of December," Bliss said, and then went on to gently deflate her friend's hopes. "We mean to make a good match for her here at court. There is none yet to have engaged her heart. She is a considerable heiress, you know. She has her own estate, Riverside; lands from her late father; and her stepfather has settled a goodly sum on her. She is the apple of his eye, and to be frank, the only father she remembers, her own having perished before her second birthday. She is quite a headstrong girl, I fear, and will need the firm hand of an older husband to guide her."

They were speaking as if she were not even there, Nyssa thought irritably. She said in her own defense, "Why, Aunt, were you not headstrong in your youth? I do seem to remember hearing stories from Mama."

"Headstrong? Me? I do not recall being headstrong at all," Bliss replied, but her friend and her niece laughed at her denial.

They had found a quiet spot in which to settle, and the two women seated themselves.

"Tell me about your family," Adela Marlowe said. As they began to catch up on each other's lives over these past years, Nyssa grew restless.

Seeing them well-engaged, she slipped off, threading her way carefully through a noisy throng of chattering courtiers. Through the windows Nyssa could see a garden, and when she spied a small door in the same wall, she opened it, stepping out into the crisp morning air. Although it had been cloudy and gray earlier, when they had come to Hampton Court, the skies had finally cleared. The heavens were blue now, and the sun shone brightly down. She drew a long, deep breath. Court was very crowded. Her nose told her that not all the elegantly garbed ladies and gentlemen peopling it were as scrupulous about bathing as she was. It was good to be outdoors, away from them.

Nyssa began to walk slowly about, exploring her surroundings. The garden was filled with many small ponds, each one ringed with heraldic stone beasts set upon pillars. The wood railings edging the flower beds were painted green and white, the Tudor colors. They were empty now of blooms, but neat, and ready for the spring, when it finally would come again. She quickly discovered she was not alone in the garden. A young boy came toward her smiling, and bowed before her.

"You are new at court, lady," he said, and then he grinned mischievously. "I know all the pretty girls. I am Hans von Grafsteen. I am the ambassador from Cleves's personal page." He swept his velvet bonnet off his blond head and bowed again most politely.

She curtsied to him. "I am Lady Nyssa Wyndham, sir, come to court to serve the new queen. The king himself has appointed me a maid of honor."

"She vill like you," Hans said. "You are young, and not so stuck-up as many of these ladies are."

"Two of my brothers have come with me to be pages in her majesty's household," Nyssa volunteered. This young boy was not as intimidating as all the other people she had seen inside. "How old are you?" she asked him. "I think you are close to my brother Philip's age, but not quite as old as he is; yet you are older than Giles."

"How old are your brothers?" he countered.

"Thirteen and nine," she said.

"I am eleven," he told her. "The ambassador is my uncle. He is my mother's eldest brother, and that is how I obtained my place. Who are your people, my lady Nyssa?"

"I am the daughter of the Earl and Countess of Langford," she answered him. She did not think it was necessary to explain that Anthony was her stepfather.

"That is not a great name, I think," Hans said. "How did you obtain such a coveted appointment as maid of honor to my lady Anne?"

What on earth am I going to tell him? Nyssa wondered briefly. Then a little voice inside her said, *Tell him the truth.* "My mother was the king's mistress many years ago," she answered him "They have remained good friends. When she asked him for this appointment, the king gladly complied." She was relieved to see that Hans von Grafsteen did not seem in the least shocked by her bold revelation.

Rather, he asked frankly, "Are you the king's get, lady?"

Nyssa blushed to the roots of her dark hair. "Ohh, no, sir! My father was Edmund Wyndham, the third Earl of Langford. I am trueborn. My mother was a widow when she came to court to meet the king." She would now have to explain everything. "My mother afterward married my father's nephew, who was his heir. The only father I can remember is my stepfather."

"Ahh," Hans said, smiling. Now it made sense to him.

"Tell me about the lady Anne," Nyssa said. "I am told she is fair of face and kind of heart. I am pleased to have been chosen to serve her. What is she really like? What language shall I speak to her?"

The boy looked amused, and then he said, "Do you speak High Dutch, my lady Nyssa?"

"High Dutch?" She looked puzzled. "Why, no," she replied.

"Then you vill not be able to speak to the lady Anne, for it is the only language she knows. In Cleves, vomen, even highborn vomen, are not educated as you English educate your vomen. God and the house; that is vhat the vomen of Cleves know, my lady Nyssa."

"How will she speak to the king?" Nyssa wondered aloud.

"I think it vill not matter," Hans said frankly. "She comes to cement an alliance, and to haf babies. She need not speak for that."

"Oh, you are wrong, I fear, Hans," Nyssa told him. "My mother always told me how greatly the king values an intelligent woman; a clever woman; a woman of wit. He loves music and dancing and cards. Any woman hoping to please him must conform to these standards. Beauty is not enough for the king, although he appreciates a pretty woman."

"Then my lady Anne is doomed on all accounts," the boy said. "She is not really pretty, and knows neither music, or cards. She cannot dance, for dancing and many other such pastimes are thought to be frivolous by the court of Cleves."

"Ohh, dear," Nyssa said. "What will happen to the poor lady if the king is not pleased with her? Hans, you must teach me some words and phrases of High Dutch, so I may help the lady Anne learn to acclimate herself to her new country, and to our ways."

How kind she is, the boy thought. None of the other women appointed to the lady Anne's new household had thought to inquire if there was a way they could make their new queen comfortable. Well, he would help Nyssa Wyndham. He had been at the English court for several months now, and he had quickly decided that his poor princess would have a very difficult time of it. Her upbringing had been so strict and sheltered. The English court was going to be a shock to her. "I vill help you to learn my language, lady. Vhat other languages do you speak?"

"Just French and Latin," Nyssa admitted, "although I can read Greek. I was raised in the country, you see, and never thought to come to court."

"Vhat else did you learn?" he asked, curious.

"Simple sums; I read and write a legible hand; and I know some history." She smiled at him. "The languages came easily. The sums were harder, but Mama says a woman must know enough to be sure that she is not being cheated by her servants or the tradesmen."

He laughed, his bright blue eyes crinkling at the corners. "Your mama sounds like a practical voman. In Cleves ve like practical vomen. The princess is a practical voman."

"She will need to be, I fear, if the king does not like her," Nyssa said. "Poor lady. It cannot be easy coming from so far away to a strange land with all new customs, and a new language. Do you think she will be able to learn English, Hans?"

"She is not stupid," Hans replied, "and although it vill be hard for her at first, I think she vill like England, and its many freedoms. My uncle, who knows her vell, says she is a high-spirited voman, although they haf tried to beat it out of her. A voman should be meek and modest in her behavior."

Nyssa giggled. "Not an English woman," she told him.

He stared at her. "You are very beautiful vhen you smile," he said seriously. "Alas I am too young, and of not high enough stature for an earl's daughter. Still, ve can be friends, can ve not?"

Nyssa was startled by his frankness, but she managed another smile. He was really very sweet, and she felt safe with him. "Aye, we can be friends, and I will introduce you to my brothers. Perhaps you can teach them some of your language as well, so they may be of true help to the princess, ah, the queen. She is to be the queen, and we must think of her that way, Hans von Grafsteen."

"Come," he said, and he offered her his arm. "I vill escort you back into the palace. It is becoming vindy, and you must not get sick, or another vill leap forvard to steal your place."

"Indeed she will," Nyssa agreed, taking his arm. "Lady Browne tried to frighten me off when I reported to her this morning, but I have come to serve the queen, and serve her I shall, as loyally and as dutifully as I know how."

When they reentered the palace, Nyssa found her aunt and Lady Marlowe still engaged in conversation. She had not even been missed. She introduced the ambassador's page to them, but Adela Marlowe, it seemed, already knew of Hans, and gently corrected Nyssa.

"*Baron* von Grafsteen, my lady Wyndham," she said with an arch smile. "Am I not correct, sir?" She beamed at him.

He nodded, annoyed. He did not like being a baron, but his father had died two years before, and he was the eldest son. There was no help for it. He wished that automatic wealth had at least come with the title.

"Hans is to teach me High Dutch. The lady Anne speaks no other language," Nyssa informed them. "I must have lessons with him every day until the queen arrives. I will be more of a help to her if I can at least communicate with her. Do you not think so, Aunt?"

"Indeed," Bliss said, pleased with Nyssa for her quick thinking. She would wager none of the other girls appointed maids of honor would bother to learn the queen's tongue. She patted her niece's hand approvingly.

The Earl of Marwood returned with Lord Marlowe and the young gentlemen. They were introduced to Hans von Grafsteen, and immediately the youngsters became friends. Nyssa felt very much out of place. Her brothers and cousins seemed already at ease in their new surroundings; and her aunt had settled in as comfortably as if she had never left the court at all. Perhaps when the queen came, and she was able to do something other than just stand about, she would feel better. Then suddenly she felt eyes upon her. Looking up, she saw she was being stared at from across the room by a richly clad gentleman. He made her most uncomfortable, and she felt her cheeks grow pink with the heat of embarrassment. She tugged at Lady Marlowe's sleeve.

"Who is that gentleman staring at me?" she asked her.

Adela Marlowe looked quickly across the chamber, and then she too blushed. "God's bones! 'Tis the Earl of March. He's one of Norfolk's grandsons, though born on the wrong side of the blanket, I'm told. He's notorious, my child! A dreadful womanizer! Do not look back lest he believe you to be encouraging him. No maiden of good reputation wants to be seen with Varian de Winter, and a girl seen alone in his company is ruined!"

"He is very handsome," Nyssa said softly, and she didn't think he looked like a villain.

"Indeed he is," Lady Marlowe admitted, "but he is a dangerous man. Why, I'm told most reliably that . . ." She lowered her voice and whispered to Bliss so that Nyssa could not hear them.

Bliss paled. "Holy Mother!" she exclaimed.

"I do not suppose you want to tell me," Nyssa said with some humor.

"You are too young," her aunt said emphatically.

"I'm old enough to find a husband," Nyssa teased her.

"There are some things a woman is always too young to know," Bliss said firmly, "and this is one of those things."

The two women went back to their gossiping, and Nyssa snuck another look at Varian de Winter. He was now speaking with a distinguished gentleman, and fortunately did not notice her. He had a hawklike face with strong features. His hair was very black, and she wondered what color his eyes were. Unexpectedly, he turned his head and looked directly at her. Placing his fingertips to his lips, he blew her a kiss, his smile wicked. Nyssa gasped and quickly turned away, her cheeks burning. Ohh, he was bold! She did not dare to gaze back again, to see if he was still looking at her, but the hair on the back of her neck felt all prickly.

D URING the next few days she came to Hampton Court each morning after mass and reported to Lady Browne. Nyssa was introduced to the senior ladies-in-waiting chosen for the queen's household. Two, Lady Margaret Douglas and the Marchioness of Dorset, were the king's nieces.

The Duchess of Richmond was his daughter-in-law, being married to Henry, Duke of Richmond, the king's bastard son by Elizabeth Blount. There were two countesses, of Hertford and of Rutland; and Ladies Audley, Rochford, and Edgecombe, plus sixty-five other women of lesser rank. Nyssa was presented to the Earl of Rutland, who had been appointed Lord Chamberlain of the new queen's household. The management of that household would be his responsibility. She met Sir Thomas Denny, to be the queen's chancellor, or chief secretary, and Dr. Kaye, the kindly cleric appointed the queen's almoner, or chaplain.

There would be a dozen maids of honor, of which only the Bassett sisters—Katherine and Anne, who were the daughters of Lord Lisle, Governor of Calais—and Nyssa Wyndham could be certain of their appointments. There was a list from which the other girls would be chosen, and of course, the new queen would have maidens with her. Most of them would eventually return to Cleves, making places for other English girls, but certainly one or two would remain with Anne. As the available places were so scarce, there was some grumbling about the appointment of a girl unknown to the court.

The king silenced the carping by greeting Nyssa effusively her second day at court. Spying the girl with Lady Browne, Henry called to her, and Nyssa dutifully came forward to make her curtsey to the king. Henry raised her up himself, kissing her on both cheeks.

"So, my young lady Wyndham, you have arrived safely. What think you of this court of ours? Is it unlike anything you have ever seen?"

"Indeed, Your Grace, it is! I have never been anywhere as grand. Lady Browne is working hard to teach me all I must know to be of true use to our gracious queen. I am even learning High Dutch!"

The king beamed with obvious pleasure. "Is she not every bit as sweet as her dear mother, my friends?" he demanded of his companions. "You remember Blaze Wyndham, my little country girl? This is her daughter, Lady Nyssa Catherine Wyndham. She is my personal choice to serve my new queen. I have promised her mother that I would keep her safe here among us, for Blaze was most reluctant to let her go." He patted Nyssa's slim hand. "Run along now, my sweet child, back to Lady Browne."

Nyssa curtsied once again beneath the king's approving gaze.

"Well," murmured Lady Rochford to Lady Edgecombe, "that's one place that is well-secured. He has made it quite plain to us all, has he not?"

"Assuredly," Lady Edgecombe agreed. "I fear it shall quite pique Lady Browne. Twelve places to fill, and at least half will be from Cleves. Margaret had hoped to benefit from the other six, and here the king has filled three of them with girls who cannot be overruled."

"I can see places for the Bassett girls," Lady Rochford said. "After all, Anne served in Queen Jane's household, and Katherine with the Duchess of Suffolk, but this Wyndham chit is a nobody. Just because her mother was the king's plaything all those years ago . . ." Lady Rochford's dark eyes grew round with speculation. "You don't think the king is interested in the daughter now, do you?"

"Don't be ridiculous," replied Lady Edgecombe. "He's about to be a bridegroom again, and is already enamoured with the new queen's portrait. He has no time right now for another woman. Besides, the chit is young enough to be his daughter."

"The new queen is also young enough to be his daughter," Lady Rochford noted meanly. "She is but five months older than Princess Mary."

Lady Edgecombe looked horrified. "You are mad to voice such a thing aloud!" she said. "Are you not satisfied to have been restored to favor despite your unfortunate connections?"

"Connections by marriage only, and I am widowed now," Jane, Lady Rochford said. "Remember that I am related to the king himself on my mother's side, although being related to Henry Tudor is certainly no guarantee of personal safety."

Winifred Edgecombe paled. "You will end up without your head one day, Jane," she warned. "As for Lady Nyssa Wyndham, the king has remained friends with her mother. And the girl, I am told by Lady Marlowe, is an heiress."

"So, the chit has something to recommend her besides her beauty," Lady Rochford noted. "Still, only the highest born should serve the queen. It was that way in Queen Jane's time . . . *and before.*"

She was referring to her late sister-in-law, Anne Boleyn. Jane Rochford had had an unhappy marriage to Anne's brother, George; but Anne, who adored her sibling, could see no wrong in George. In the end, Jane had had her revenge on them both. They were dead, and she was in favor again. Lady Rochford smiled coldly. She gazed across the room at Nyssa Wyndham. She was young, and beautiful, and rich; but it took a great deal more than just those attributes to survive at court. You will have to be clever, little one, she thought. If you are not clever, you will not survive. Yes, you will have to be most clever, I think.

CHAPTER 3

T HE six English maids of honor had finally all been chosen. They included the Bassett sisters, Anne and Katherine; Kathcrine Carey, the daughter of William Carey, and his wife, Mary Boleyn; Catherine Howard, the niece of Thomas, Duke of Norfolk; Elizabeth FitzGerald, called the Orphan of Kildare, the late Earl of Kildare's child; and Nyssa Wyndham. To Lady Browne's pleasure, the king had ordered her to fill the other six places.

"We will send the maidens from Cleves packing in short order," he told her. "If my bride is to be Queen of England, then she should be served by English women, should she not, Lady Margaret?"

"Yes, Your Grace," the smiling lady replied, her good humor restored. Lady Browne no longer minded that the king had chosen the first six maids. She would profit handsomely from the other appointments.

Nyssa and the Bassetts were the eldest of the maids chosen, but the sisters were clannish, and enormously proud of the fact that their father was the royal governor of Calais. Anne, the elder of the two, had been the cause of gossip when the king had presented her with a horse and saddle in early summer. There was nothing to the chatter, but the talk had erupted anyway. The sisters, however, had always been a part of court life in one way or another, and Nyssa found their superior airs very annoying.

"Pay no attention to them," little Catherine Howard said, and she laughed. "They're naught but a pair of babbling magpies."

"It's easy for you," Nyssa told her. "You're a Howard. I'm just a Wyndham of Langford, and am yet ignorant of court ways."

"Fiddlesticks!" Elizabeth FitzGerald said. "I've been practically raised here at court, and your manners are impeccable, Nyssa."

"Indeed they are," Katherine Carey agreed. "No one would guess you are newly come to court. Honestly!"

They were friendly girls, fifteen and sixteen years of age, and each of them prettier than the other. Catherine Howard had auburn curls and beautiful cerulean-blue eyes. Katherine Carey was a black-eyed blond. Elizabeth FitzGerald was black-haired and blue-eyed. They were also, Nyssa discovered, mischievous and full of high spirits. The gentlemen of the court were eager to be with them. Lady Browne had her hands full keeping her charges in order.

The Princess of Cleves finally arrived in Calais on the eleventh of December, but could come no farther. The weather simply refused to cooperate. The Channel was ferociously stormy for the next two weeks. It was soon apparent that there would be no gala Christmas wedding. The court, however, was at a fever pitch of excitement. Each day, more and more of the nobility arrived at Hampton Court, summoned by their king to pay their respects to the new queen, who remained stranded in Calais.

Then on December twenty-sixth the weather lifted briefly, and the Lord Admiral decided that if he did not sail immediately, another winter storm would roar down the Channel, making a crossing impossible until spring. They sailed at midnight. The crossing was fair and pleasant. At five o'clock in the morning the ships carrying the wedding party disembarked at Deal, where the Duchess of Suffolk, the Bishop of Chicester, and others were waiting to meet the new queen. Anne was lodged at Dover Castle, and almost immediately the weather turned foul once more. It began as sleet and quickly turned into a late December snowstorm. The winds were icy and blew without ceasing. It was colder than most remembered a winter being in many years.

Anne, however, insisted on pressing forward to London. On Monday the twenty-ninth she arrived at Canterbury, where Archbishop Cranmer greeted her, escorted by three hundred men in scarlet silks and cloth-of-gold. There Anne was housed in the guest house of St. Augustine's Monastery. On Tuesday the thirtieth of December, Anne departed Canterbury and rode as far as Sittingbourne. On New Year's Eve day she pressed on to Rochester. She was met on Reynham Down by the Duke of Norfolk and a hundred horsemen in green velvet coats decorated with gold chains. They escorted her to the Bishop's Palace, where she would remain for the next two nights.

It was there that Lady Margaret Browne and fifty of the new queen's ladies, including the six maids of honor, awaited Anne. Brought before the bride-to-be, Lady Browne attempted to conceal her astonishment and dismay. The woman before her was but barely recognizable as the woman in the Holbein painting that the king so admired. Lady Browne curtsied low, remembering as she did the scurrilous rhyme that had recently been making the rounds at court.

If that be your picture, then shall we
Soon see how you and your picture agree!

The gentle-visaged lady in the painting appeared to be one of medium stature, but the original was a tall woman with extremely sharp features. Why, she would be able to look the king directly in the eye! Her complexion was not pale, but rather sallow-hued. Her eyes were her best feature, Lady Browne decided; a bright blue, nicely shaped, and well-spaced. As Lady Browne arose from her curtsey, the lady Anne smiled. It was a kindly, sweet smile, but the Englishwoman knew in her heart that this woman would absolutely hold no appeal for the king. She was not at all the sort of woman Henry Tudor favored.

Margaret Browne and her husband had been part of the court for many years. She knew that the king, although a large man himself, preferred dainty, feminine women with clinging natures. This was a Valkyrie! A Rhine maiden! There was nothing helpless about her. And worse, her clothes were horrible. Totally unfashionable. Ugly! She wore an enormous elephant-eared headdress that hid her hair and gave the illusion of even greater height. It would have to go.

"Welcome to England, madame," Lady Browne said, remembering her manners. "I am Lady Margaret Browne, appointed by his grace, the queen's mistress of her maids. I have brought six of them with me, and would present them with your gracious permission." She curtsied again.

Young Baron von Grafsteen translated for the princess. He had now been assigned to her service by his uncle. When he had finished speaking, she nodded her head vigorously, the headdress swaying dangerously as she did so.

"Ya! Ya!"

Lady Browne signaled to another page by the door. Opening it, Philip Wyndham beckoned to the six English maids of honor to enter. The young girls, in their finest gowns, came tripping gaily into the chamber. They stopped at the first sight of Anne of Cleves, and both Bassett sisters gasped noisily. Lady Browne glared furiously at them, saying as she did, "Make your curtsies, maidens!"

The six young girls curtsied quickly.

"You will come forward as I present each of you to her grace," Lady Browne instructed them. Then she turned to Hans von Grafsteen and said, "I shall introduce these maids to the lady Anne, sir."

"Bring the lady Nyssa forward last, my lady," the young man requested. "Her highness vill be excited that Lady Wyndham can speak her tongue, even slightly. She vill vant to question her about England."

"Of course, sir," Lady Browne told the young boy, and then she introduced each girl to her future queen, pleased that in spite of their obvious shock, they had regained their equilibrium and displayed excellent manners. She presented Katherine Carey first, as the girl was a niece of the king. Catherine Howard was next. She was not particularly important of herself, but her uncle, the duke, was. Then came Elizabeth FitzGerald and the Bassett sisters.

Finally Nyssa made her curtsey to the Princess of Cleves. "I welcome you to England, Your Highness," she said slowly and carefully in the High Dutch that Hans had taught her.

A broad smile split the princess's face, and she burst forth into a stream of words of which Nyssa could only identify a few.

Hans von Grafsteen grinned, delighted with his creation, and said to the lady Anne, "She cannot understand you, Highness. She is just learning our tongue. I am teaching her. She thought that perhaps it would be difficult for you in a new country, with no one to understand you. If you speak slowly, and distinctly, the lady Nyssa vill comprehend."

The Princess of Cleves nodded at the boy, and then turning back to Nyssa, said carefully, "You are kind, my lady, to have thought of how I might feel. Do you understand me now?"

"Yes, madame," Nyssa said, curtseying again.

The princess turned to the page. "Who is she, Hans? Her family, I mean."

"Lady Wyndham is the daughter of the Earl of Langford. They are not an important family by any means, but many years ago her mother was the king's mistress. She was, I am told, a gentle lady of kind disposition and modest demeanor. She was known as the 'Quiet Mistress.'"

"Ahhhh," the Princess of Cleves exhaled. "Is it possible that this girl is *his* daughter, Hans?"

"Nay, madame, she is not. Nyssa was born before her mother ever came to court. She is not the king's bastard, but trueborn."

"Tell me, Hans," the princess said, "why do these ladies look at me so strangely? This Lady Browne's jaw dropped when she first entered my presence. What is it? My clothing, I know, is not English, and must seem strange to her, but it is more than that, I can tell."

"It was the painter, Holbein, Your Highness. He flattered you when he painted your portrait," Hans said frankly. "He made you seem smaller, and perhaps a bit softer than your features actually are. The king is most enamored of that portrait, I must warn you, my gracious lady."

"*Is he,*" Anne of Cleves replied. "Well, he will have to take me like I am, I fear; and after all, he is no longer in the glory of his youth, Hans, is he?" She chuckled. "He is lucky to get a royal bride at all. He has not the best reputation as a husband." She chuckled. "I shall, however, be as meek and modest as I can, for I have never in my life been more relieved to be away from a place as I am to be away from Cleves. My brother, the duke, has been insufferable since our father died."

Nyssa listened wide-eyed. She could not understand most of the conversation, for the princess and the page chattered too quickly for her to follow, but here and there a snatch of sentence or a word penetrated her brain. The princess, she realized, was a woman of humor, and she was not at all stupid. "I will help you to learn English, my gracious lady," she said boldly.

"Good!" the princess said with a smile. "Hans, tell Lady Browne I am most pleased by all the maids, but Lady Wyndham's kindness in attempting our tongue bodes well for my happiness."

The boy repeated his mistress's words, and almost laughed aloud to see the look of relief that passed over the older woman's face.

"Her highness is most gracious," she said. Gracious, yes, but a pretty young woman who would delight the king, no. Heaven help us all, Lady Browne thought. What will he do when he finds out? With another low curtsey to the Princess of Cleves, she shepherded her charges from the room. They followed after her like chicks after a hen.

"God's blood, she is appalling," Anne Bassett declared when they were safely back in their assigned chamber. "Gross and unfashionable!"

"The king will take one look and send her back," Katherine Bassett agreed in superior tones. "She is a great tall stork of a creature, and nothing at all like our gentle Queen Jane."

"Queen Jane is dead, and buried these two years past," Cat Howard said in practical tones. "Her greatest accomplishment in life was producing our darling Prince Edward. The king would have become bored with her eventually, and her Seymour relations are intolerable, my uncle, Duke Thomas, says. The king needs a new wife, and more sons."

" 'Tis true," Katherine Carey agreed, "but this princess, I think, will not suit him at all. Poor lady to have come so far."

"The king is hardly in the flower of his youth, and cannot expect a perfect young beauty," Elizabeth FitzGerald spoke up in her soft, lilting voice. "It is true that the lady Anne is not quite like her portrait, but she seems a good lady. I think her eyes are kind."

"It will take more than kind eyes to win over Henry Tudor," Lady Browne told them. "What do you think, Lady Wyndham? You spoke with her. What did she say?"

"I merely welcomed her to England, and she thanked me," Nyssa told them. "I offered to help her with her English. She appears willing and eager to learn, madame. I like her. I hope the king will too."

They were shortly to find out, for the king, eager to meet his bride, had galloped all the way from Hampton Court in order to, as he had told Cromwell, "nourish love" between himself and the lady he would shortly marry. He burst boldly into the presence chamber of the Bishop's Palace unannounced, clad in a great cloak, a hood obscuring his identity, clutching in his hand a dozen sable skins he intended gifting the lady with. But she, seeing the enormous, bulky figure in the long, swirling cloak, screamed with fright, and grabbing up a pillow, began to beat the intruder about the head. The king fended her off, backing away; it was not an auspicious beginning.

Hans von Grafsteen bowed to the king and apologized. "She does not know it to be you, Your Grace. Allow me to explain."

Henry nodded impatiently. "Be about it, lad! I have patiently awaited this lady's arrival, and am now anxious to make her acquaintance." He strove to make out the features of her visage.

The young page moved to the princess's side. "Your Highness, do not be frightened. It is the king himself come to surprise you."

"This great wild boar of a man is the king?" the princess said, the pillow dropping from her hands. She stared at Henry Tudor, then looked away, saying, "Gott in Himmel, what have I pledged myself in marriage to, Hans?"

"You must greet him, my lady," the boy told her nervously.

"If I must then I must," she answered him, and made him a deep curtsey, her head lowered.

How sweetly modest she is, the king thought, his good mood restored. Frightened by a strange man, and so brave, but then charmingly polite. What delicacy of manners, what . . . what . . . *what a big woman!* This was not the woman in the portrait! Henry Tudor was shocked when she arose to smile at him, meeting his gaze most directly. "Welcome to England, madame," he managed to say, manfully concealing his horror.

Hans von Grafsteen conveyed the king's greeting to the princess.

"Thank him for me, Hans," Anne of Cleves replied, distressed to see on closer inspection that her bridegroom was as fat as a well-fed hog ready for butchering. His clothing was magnificent, she could see when he tossed his cloak aside. Far more fashionable than anything she had ever imagined. Her own wardrobe would be most inadequate despite all the expense and preparations. It was certainly old-fashioned compared to her own attendants. She would have to remedy that, but as Queen of England that would be no problem.

His initial surprise over with, the king said, "Ask the princess if her trip was a pleasant one, Hans." The woman was too damned tall, and her nose was pointed to boot.

The page relayed the king's words.

"Tell him my welcome at Calais was more magnificent than anything I have ever encountered," she answered. "I am appreciative of the warm greetings of the English people. I have been well-treated." He is not happy with me, she thought silently, all the while smiling at him. I shall have to tread lightly with him else I end up without my head. Perhaps I can win him over, but do I really want to?

"I am touched by the princess's eagerness to reach me," the king said. Of course she was eager to get here, so she could bind herself to me in marriage. They have lied to me. They have all lied to me. Cromwell. He wanted this match to the exclusion of all others. He shall pay! And if there is a way I can extricate myself from this nightmare, by God's bloody bones I shall find it! I will not be shackled to this creature, though I cannot blame Holbein. He is an artist, and sees with his heart.

"Ask the king if he would like to sit, Hans. I can see he is favoring his leg, but do not say that. He will be sensitive about it. Old men are always sensitive about such things. Just say I would be honored if he would take a cup of wine with me, and if he accedes, then pour us some. He has ridden many long, cold miles, and as we can both see, he is not exactly delighted by my person, I fear."

"Courage, madame," the boy said, and then turning to the king, said, "The princess asks if you will take a cup of wine with her, Your Grace. She worries that you might catch a chill after your long, wet ride this day. She is a most thoughtful lady."

"Aye aye," Henry Tudor agreed. "A cup of wine would be good, lad.

Thank the princess for her solicitude." Well, the creature had a kind heart. That was something, but not enough, damnit!

The princess beckoned him to a comfortable chair by the roaring fire, and took her place opposite him. Her clothing was appalling. Her accent was thick. Ohh, they were all going to pay for this debacle; Cromwell in particular. Certainly he had lied when he said that Mary of Guise and Christina of Denmark had refused his overtures. What woman in her right mind would not want to be Queen of England? Cromwell obviously had some hidden agenda, but his plans would not come to fruition. I will not marry this woman! *I will not!*

The young page brought silver cups of wine for the king and the princess. He stood respectfully, translating the careful small talk between the two until finally the king arose stiffly and turned to him.

"Tell the lady Anne I must now go. I thank her for her very gracious hospitality. I will see her soon." But not too soon, I hope, he thought. Then he waited while the boy spoke in his own tongue to the princess.

"He can scarce conceal his eagerness to go, can he," Anne said wryly, but her face was devoid of emotion. "Tell his grace my heart is full with his warm welcome, and if you laugh, Hans, I shall smack you. The situation is serious."

Hans von Grafsteen gravely told the king, "The princess says her heart is full with your warm and loving welcome, Your Grace."

"Humph," the king grunted, and with a sketchy bow to his bride-to-be, he hurried from the room. Stamping out into the corridor, he found Sir Anthony Browne awaiting him. His temper overflowed at last, and he snarled, "I have been ill handled, my lord! There is nothing in this woman as has been reported to me. *I like her not!*" Then realizing that he was still clutching the sables he had brought with him, he thrust them at Sir Anthony. "Give them to the creature!"

"You do not like the Princess of Cleves?" Sir Anthony's voice quavered.

"Have I not said it," the king thundered. *"I like her not!* There is a story of a swan who came down the Rhine to impregnate two Princesses of Cleves. Her line is said to spring from those maidens. I expected the silver swan of Cleves. What I have been sent is a great Flanders mare! *I like her not!"*

Nyssa, coming into hearing range, paled as she heard the king's words, and gasped. Both men turned to her, and she shrank back frightened, somehow remembering her curtsey to the king. His face softened when he saw her, and he held out his hand to her.

"Do not let my righteous anger make you afraid, my lady," he told her.

"Ahh, Nyssa, be glad you are but an earl's child and not a king's. Kings may not marry where they please, but rather they must please their people." He sighed dramatically.

"Ohh, my lord, she is a good lady, the Princess of Cleves," Nyssa said earnestly. "I will soon teach her our tongue."

"Anthony! Anthony! Is she not sweet, the daughter of my little country girl? Her heart is a gentle and good one, as her mother's heart has always been." The king patted Nyssa's slender hand, and then to her horror he drew her against his massive gold-embroidered velvet chest, stroking her hair as he did so. "Dearest little Nyssa, may you never know the anguish of being forced to the altar, but nay! That shall not be your fate, my child. You will marry for love. I, your king, command it!" Then gently he set her back from him, and turning away from her, walked slowly off down the corridor.

"You will hold your tongue, girl," Sir Anthony warned Nyssa grimly. "This is more than a disappointed bridegroom."

"I am aware of the political ramifications involved, my lord," she replied seriously. "Though I be young, and new to the court, I have been educated, and understand that the marriage of a king is no simple thing. Besides, I would not hurt the lady Anne. I like her."

"So," the seasoned courtier said slowly, "you are not quite the little country mouse the king believes you are."

"Nor was my mother, sir," Nyssa said boldly. "She survived the court, and so I intend doing as well." She curtsied and then hurried into the bishop's presence chamber, where the princess still sat.

"She knows he does not like her," Hans von Grafsteen burst out as Nyssa closed the door behind her.

"Hush!" she warned him. "Sir Anthony Browne is outside."

"What will happen?" the boy asked her. "Will he kill her?"

"For what cause?" Nyssa demanded. "Because he is disappointed that she is not quite as Holbein portrayed her? 'Tis not her fault. She is a pawn on the political chessboard of Europe."

"Then what will happen to her?" Hans said, lowering his voice.

"He is the king, so I do not know; but a simple man would try to find a way to void the betrothal. I suppose it will be the same for the king. He will want Cromwell and his council to give him a means of escape; but he will not want to appear at fault, you understand. Henry Tudor is not a man to easily admit a fault. My mother warned me of that lest I inadvertently offend him. Is there anything that could be used against the princess, Hans?"

"There was talk of a betrothal with the son of the Duke of Lorraine when the princess was a child, but it came to nothing. No contracts were drawn, or signed. She was completely free to contract this marriage."

"What are you saying?" the princess asked Hans.

He quickly told her, saying, "Lady Nyssa is sympathetic to your cause, my princess. She would help if she could, but has no power to do so."

"You must tell the princess to behave with dignity and composure," Nyssa interrupted him. "She must behave as if everything is perfectly all right and she has not the least suspicion that the king is disappointed in her. She must go out of her way to please him both publicly and privately. The king is not a man to hide his feelings, and once the different factions that people the court learn of his dissatisfaction, your mistress will become a hunted animal. She must pretend she is unaware of her position, Hans. That will be the key to her survival."

The page translated her words to the princess, who nodded most vigorously. "Ya! Ya! She is right, my liebling. She may be unfamiliar with the court, but she is a clever little girl. Do you think the king will keep his pledge, and marry me?"

Hans asked the questions of Nyssa, who said, "Unless the council can find a legitimate reason to void the marriage contract, the king will have no other choice than to marry the princess. I do not think they will find such a reason, and that is why I advise her to do everything in her power to please the king. She must begin music lessons immediately. Mistress Howard is a very fine musician. Have the princess ask her to teach her to play the lute, and the virginals. And she must learn to dance, Hans. We can all teach her to dance. The king loves to dance."

Hans relayed Nyssa's advice to his mistress.

"That great hulk of a man dances?" Anne of Cleves said, astounded. "I cannot imagine it. Why, the very floor must shake when he prances about in his elegant finery." She chuckled at the thought.

"He is a fine dancer, and very graceful despite his size," Nyssa said when Hans had told her the princess's words.

"Ya? So, I must learn to be as facile and as graceful, then. Ya! I shall be the very model of a wife for King Henry."

Nyssa giggled when Hans told her what the princess had said. Then she grew serious again. "The princess must defer to the king at all times, and in all things, but she must not be so weak-kneed as to be thought spineless, or taken advantage of by others. He is not afraid of women with intellect. He just prefers to be superior to them."

Anne of Cleves burst out laughing as Hans translated the girl's words. "Ya! 'Tis true of all men. My brother and King Henry would get on most famously, I think. Still, cannot one consider that the Lord God, having created man first, possibly acknowledged an error, and created woman? It is something to ponder, eh, my friends?"

The princess and her retinue moved on to Dartford while the court departed for Greenwich on the second day of January. *I like her not!* became a catch phrase among witty courtiers who quickly learned of the king's unhappiness with the Princess of Cleves. As expected, however, the painter, Holbein, escaped the royal wrath. His New Year's gift to his outraged master, a portrait of the two-year-old heir apparent in a red satin gown and bonnet, gained him instant pardon, particularly as the little boy's resemblance to his father was most pronounced.

To almost everyone's delight, the king was furious with his chief minister, Thomas Cromwell. Back in London's Whitehall Palace, before the council, the king roared, "You deceived me, you wily devil, and I would know why! I might have had a French or Danish wife, but no! Only the match with Cleves would suit you. *Why?* Her skin is sallow, and her features are sharp. She is tall, and though not fat, she is big. A Flanders mare! Well, 'tis one mare this royal stallion will not mount, sir!"

The council snickered as Thomas Cromwell paled. Still, he was not yet beaten. He turned to the Lord Admiral and demanded angrily, "You saw her, my lord, and yet you did not warn the king of her unsuitability. I could but rely on the reports of her. You were the first Englishman to see her, and you did not tell us that she would not do."

"It was not my place to do so, my lord," the admiral said indignantly. "The match was made. I assumed this woman was to be my queen. It was not my place to criticize her. Perhaps she is not quite the lady Master Holbein portrayed her as, but she is pleasant and good-hearted. It was not my place to find fault in her."

The king rounded on Cromwell. "He is correct, Crum! You did not investigate this woman thoroughly enough, and now I am left to be wed and bedded with her. *I like her not! I like her not!*"

"It is an advantageous match for Your Grace," Cromwell took another tack. "This marriage you have so wisely contracted to balances the alliance between France and The Holy Roman Empire."

"Surely there must be another remedy for Your Grace," the Duke of Norfolk said softly.

"There is no remedy," Cromwell said bluntly. "There is absolutely no excuse the king can offer for crying off of this match. There is no precontract with any other. There is no consanguinity. She is not a Lutheran, but rather like Your Grace follows the doctrine whereby the Church yields its authority to the state."

"I have not been well-handled," muttered the king dourly. "She is nothing as was reported to me; and had I known it, she would not have come to England, my lords. Now I must needs put my neck in this noose you have fashioned for me. Nay, I have not been well-handled!" He glared around the table at them, but his hardest look was reserved for Thomas Cromwell, and the Lord Chancellor's enemies knew then and there that his days were numbered. The butcher's son had finally made a mistake.

Cromwell arose and said, "On what day will you be pleased to have the queen crowned, Your Grace? Will it still be Candlemas as we discussed?"

The king glowered at him. "We will talk on it when I have made her my queen," he said grimly.

Cromwell winced, but continued. "We will have to leave soon to welcome the princess to London, Your Grace."

Without another word Henry Tudor arose and departed the room.

"Your time grows short, Crum," the Duke of Norfolk said boldly.

"I am a more loyal servant of the king's majesty than you are, Duke Thomas," Cromwell replied. "I am not gone yet."

The king left London for Greenwich with a great party of nobles in his retinue. They would meet Anne of Cleves and her escort at Shooter's Hill near Blackheath, and the king would accompany his bride into London. Henry Tudor came down the Thames from London by barge. All the vessels accompanying him were decorated gaily with bright silk streamers that fluttered in the cold light breeze. The Lord Mayor of London and his aldermen had their own barge, and they traveled behind the king's royal barge.

Anne rode from Dartford, where she had been resting for the past few days. Only a hundred of her people from Cleves remained with her for the present. Two of her native maids of honor spoke English. They were Hans's elder sister, Helga von Grafsteen, who was thirteen, and her cousin, Maria von Hesseldorf, who was twelve. Although ignored by the Bassetts, they were welcomed into the group of younger English maids. Both girls easily picked up the lute, which delighted Cat Howard. She had been most discouraged in her efforts to teach her new mistress.

"She has no ear for music," Cat said, shaking her auburn curls. "If the king hears her efforts, he will be even more displeased with her than he already is, I fear."

"But she is quickly learning to dance," Nyssa said with a smile. "She is very graceful. And her English has been improving in just these past few days. I think the king will be pleased with her."

"She tries so hard," Kate Carey said. "It should not matter that she is not quite what her portrait made her seem."

"God's blood!" Cat Howard swore softly. "What kind of a ninny are you, Kate, that you have not realized that men will be taken by a woman's looks before all? For many of them nothing else matters."

"Surely all men are not like that," Nyssa said.

"You will not have to worry about it," Cat replied. "You are the most beautiful of us all. Do you look like your mother?"

"I have her eyes," Nyssa answered.

"They say the king was mad for her in her day," Cat continued.

"You know more than I do," Nyssa said quietly. "I was but an infant, and not even at court then."

They had brought their finest gowns with them for the official reception of Anne of Cleves into London. Nyssa had chosen to wear her burgundy velvet. The underskirt was a brocade of gold on wine velvet. Her gown was trimmed with rich marten at its hem and sleeves. Her cape matched her gown, and both the hood and the hem were richly furred, but she did not wear the hood. Her long dark chestnut-colored hair was neatly gathered in a gold caul. Her hands, sheathed in soft kid riding gloves, rested lightly on the reins of her gray mare. The other girls were as richly garbed, remembering the late Queen Jane, who had once sent Anne Bassett home until her bodice had more pearls sewn upon it. A queen's maid of honor must reflect her royal mistress's station. She could not appear shabby.

The Princess of Cleves was conveyed down Shooter's Hill to the cloth-of-gold pavilion that had been set up to receive her. About it several smaller pavilions were clustered. She arrived at the foot of the hill at precisely noon, and was received by her Lord Chamberlain, her chancellor, her almoner, and the other officials of her household. Dr. Kaye addressed the assemblage in Latin. He then formally presented Anne to all those who had been sworn to serve her. The ambassador from Cleves replied to Dr. Kaye's speech on behalf of the princess.

The ladies of the new queen's household were now officially presented. Each stepped forward to appear before the princess, curtsied, and then moved on. The maids were last, and Anne smiled warmly at them all. She was greatly appreciative of their efforts to help her adjust to her new life. It was cold, and the princess was frankly relieved when she was able to alight from her decorated chariot and retire to the pavilion with her ladies, where they might warm themselves by the braziers with their scented fires.

"Ach du lieber, mein girls," the good lady exclaimed, pulling off her gloves and handing them to Elizabeth FitzGerald, "is it cold!"

"*It is cold,* Your Grace," Nyssa gently corrected her mistress.

"Ya, Lady Nyssa," Anne replied with a smile, nodding. "It is cold, ya? Is better?"

"Much better, madame," Nyssa said, smiling back.

"Bring a chair for the princess," Cat Howard said aloud, and it was instantly done.

Anne of Cleves sat down before the brazier, holding out her hands and sighing gustily. "Hans! Vhere are you?"

The page hurried forward and bowed. "I am here, madame," he answered her in their native tongue.

"Stay close by me, Hans. Nyssa is willing, bless the girl, but she is not as facile in our language as she desires to be. I will need you. Where is the king?"

"He is on his way from Greenwich now, madame," the boy said.

Young Viscount Wyndham slipped next to his sister. "You're getting on well with her, aren't you?" he said. "She's not really quite like her portrait, is she? The king is furious, I hear."

"More the fool he, then, little brother," Nyssa said sharply. "The lady Anne has both charm and dignity. She will make a good queen if our sovereign liege lord will but remember he is nearing fifty and is no prize catch himself. He must give her a chance. He will find she is a good companion, and will make a good mother."

"For God's sweet sake, sister, do not say such as you have said to me to others," Viscount Wyndham murmured low. "If it is not treason, it is near treason; although," he amended with a mischievous smile, "you should probably not lose your head, but just be sent home in deep disgrace. Then who should want to marry you, my lady Nyssa?"

"I shall not marry but for love, Philip," she told him.

"I am much too young for love," he said, "and I thank God for it. Master Culpeper, who is Mistress Howard's cousin, is most smitten with her. When the king was being fitted for his wedding clothes, he offered Culpeper some velvet for a doublet, and he begged another piece for Mistress Howard, I am told. She had the very gown she wears today made from it. The fool has next to nothing, and would have done better to keep the extra material for himself for another doublet. Love. Pah!"

"I think it most romantic of him," Nyssa said with a smile, and then turned at the sound of the princess calling her younger brother's name. Giles came forward with a goblet of hot spiced wine for his mistress. "She is very fond of Giles," Nyssa noted.

"Aye," Philip concurred. "The little turniphead seems to have a knack for being a courtier without being arrogant."

Brother and sister both watched amused as the princess fondly pinched their little brother's rosy cheeks. Giles was the only one of their siblings who was a blond, and with his light blue eyes he looked like a cherub. It was obvious that the Princess of Cleves doted on him, much to his embar-

rassment, but Giles was far too clever a boy to show anything but his good
side to his mistress. Still he squirmed under the lady Anne's fingers,
murmuring, *"Madame!"*

It needed no translation, and she laughed, saying to Hans in her own
tongue, "He is a little angel, and I cannot resist him."

Hans translated, and Giles flushed at the giggles that erupted from the
maids of honor. Cat Howard blew him a kiss, and the pretty Elizabeth
FitzGerald winked at him. He was saved from further teasing by Dr.
Kaye, the queen's almoner, who came to announce that the king was near.

"Her highness must change into the dress she is to officially greet the
king in," Lady Browne said. "Come, maids, you are far too idle. Fetch the
princess's gown and jewels."

The dress was of red taffeta embroidered with raised cloth-of-gold. It
was made in a Dutch fashion with a round skirt and no train, but it was
nonetheless pretty and elegant. A serving woman sponged Anne's arms,
chest, and back with warm rose water. It had already been noted that the
Princess of Cleves had a slightly stronger than usual body odor, and her
women, knowing how fastidious the king was, sought to overcome her
unfortunate difficulty as best they could. Once the gown was settled upon
her, Nyssa brought forth a beautiful parure of rubies and diamonds. There
was a necklace and pendant ear bobs. A caul held her thick blond hair in
place, and on her head she wore a velvet cap encrusted with magnificent
pearls.

"The king is in sight, madame," Kate Carey said.

The princess was escorted outside, and she blinked at the sunlight after
the dimness of her pavilion. She was helped onto a snow-white palfrey
which was richly caparisoned with a cloth-of-gold and diamond coverlet,
and a saddle of finely tooled white leather. Her own personal footmen
were mounted, and liveried in rich clothing embroidered with the Black
Lion of Cleves. Young Hans von Grafsteen led them, carrying a banner
with that same lion on it.

Anne rode to meet her future husband, and the king, seeing her approach, stopped and waited for her arrival. When she had reached him, he
doffed his bonnet gallantly to her with a brilliant smile, and for a moment
Anne of Cleves saw him as he once was: the handsomest prince in Christendom. She smiled back at him as Hans translated his official words of
welcome. Some of those words, she realized to her surprise, she had
actually understood.

"I will greet his majesty first in English, Hans, and then you may act the
part of translator," she said.

"Yes, madame," the boy replied.

"I thank his majesty for his goot velcome," Anne said. "I vill try to be a goot vife to him, and a goot mutter to his kinder."

The king raised an eyebrow slightly at her thick but understandable speech. "I was told the Princess of Cleves did not speak any language but her own," he said to no one in particular.

"Her highness is trying hard to learn your tongue, Your Grace," Hans explained. "Lady Nyssa Wyndham is teaching her, and the other maids of honor as well. The princess is eager to please Your Grace."

"Is she?" the king said dryly, and then remembering the cheering crowds about them, he leaned forward and embraced his bride, to the delight of the people. Together they smiled and waved as they returned to the magnificent pavilion, the trumpeters going before them; the Privy Council, the archbishop, and all the great lords both English and from Cleves, following them. *"A Flanders mare,"* the king murmured beneath his breath. *"I am to be mated to a Flanders mare."*

The royal couple shared a loving cup before the pavilion, and then the princess was transferred into a carved and gilded chariot for her processional journey to Greenwich. With her sat Mother Lowe, Anna's old nurse and now appointed mistress of her Clevion maids, and the Countess Overstein, the ambassador's wife. The ducal arms and the Black Lion of Cleves were carved upon the sides of the chariot. Behind Anne came less ornate open chariots carrying the ladies of the future queen's household and all of her personal servants. An empty litter draped in crimson velvet and cloth-of-gold was also carried in the procession. It was a gift from Henry to his new queen. Bringing up the parade were the Princess of Cleves's serving men, all in black velvet and silver, riding identical large bay horses.

The citizens of London crowded their route, and where it wound along the river, the Thames was filled with barges and small boats of every description, some seeming unfit to float, and all filled to overflowing with people anxious to get a look at their new queen. All the London guilds had barges, newly painted, and decorated with the royal arms of England and the ducal arms of Cleves. The guild barges carried minstrels and choirs of young children singing the royal praises and welcoming Princess Anne to England. The king and his bride stopped to listen and praised the performers greatly.

When Anne alighted in the inner courtyard of Greenwich Palace, the guns of the tower sounded a salute. The king kissed his bride and welcomed her to her new home. In the Great Hall the king's guard all stood at attention as the royal couple entered, and they tipped their lances in greeting as they passed by. Henry then led Anne to her own apartments, where she was to rest until the banquet that night.

Anne, though she appeared serene and regal to those watching her, had been astounded by the warm and spontaneous welcome she had received from the English. "They are good people, Hans, are they not?" she said for the third or fourth time. "Still, for all the king's outward good manners and apparent affection toward me, he does not like me."

"How can you be certain, madame?" the boy asked her.

Anne smiled sadly. "I have no experience with a lover, Hans, but I know men well enough to be certain that when they cannot look you directly in the eye, there is something wrong. The painter Holbein has made me something I am not. The king fell in love with Holbein's portrait, but me, nein, he does not like. He marries me for political reasons, and nothing more. Were it not that he wished to tweak the noses of the French king and the Holy Roman Emperor, I should not be Queen of England."

Henry Tudor would have been very surprised to know Anne of Cleves's thoughts. He was miserable over his impending marriage. The princess was not at all what he had imagined, and he did not see himself as others saw him. In his heart and mind he was still young, handsome, and vital. After the banquet that night he again sought out Cromwell, but Cromwell just sighed and sought to put a good face upon the matter.

"She is most regal, Your Grace. The people like her," he said.

"The lawyers have found nothing?" the king demanded, ignoring Cromwell's attempt to ameliorate the situation.

Cromwell shook his head. He was becoming more and more anxious about his personal safety and that of everything he had built up over his years of service to England. He remembered his former master, Cardinal Wolsey. Wolsey's failure to obtain the Princess of Aragon's cooperation in the king's Great Matter had cost him his life. He would have been executed had he not died on the road to London, summoned from exile in York.

Wolsey had tried hard to placate Henry Tudor, but even his gift of Hampton Court Palace had not soothed the royal ire. Now Henry once again had that same look in his eyes, but this time his wrath was directed at Thomas Cromwell, and for the first time in his life Cromwell did not know what to do. Henry was a man capable of patience where revenge was concerned. A quick execution would be preferable, Cromwell decided.

The king went to his bedchamber and angrily sent his gentlemen fleeing for safety. Pouring himself a large goblet of red wine, he sat himself down in a chair and sipped slowly, glowering fiercely.

"You are like a lion with a thorn in its paw, Hal," his fool, Will Somers, said quietly, coming to sit at the king's knee. Will's wizen-faced little monkey, Margot, was cuddled in the crook of his arm. She was very old now, and bald. Her dark fur was streaked liberally with gray and white. She chittered softly, looking up at Will for reassurance.

"Keep that beast away from me," the king growled.

"She has few teeth left, Hal," Will said, stroking the monkey gently.

"If she had but one, it would still find my fingers," the king grumbled. He sighed deeply. "I have been badly handled, Will."

Will Somers did not dissemble with his master. "She is not like her portrait, Hal, I will admit. There is a slight resemblance, but that is all. Still, she seems a fine lady, and most royal."

"If there was a way out of this marriage, I would take it, Will," the king said. "She is a damned gross Flanders mare!"

"The lady Anne is taller than you are used to, Hal, but perhaps being able to look a woman in the eye will prove a novelty you will enjoy. She is big-boned, aye, but she is not a fat woman. You must remember that you are not in the full flush of youth yourself, Hal. You are fortunate I think to have such a fine princess for a wife."

"Were this charade not so far gone, I should send her home," Henry Tudor said grimly.

"That would not be like you, Hal," his fool chided. "You have ever been the most elegant and genteel of knights. I have always been proud to serve you, but I should not be proud if you were unkind to this poor princess who has done you no harm. She is far from her homeland, and lonely of heart. If you send her away, who will have her to wife? The shame would be unbearable, and besides, her brother, Duke William, would be forced to declare war on you. France and the Empire would laugh themselves sick at your expense, Hal."

"Will, Will," the king said pitifully, "you are the only one who speaks the truth to me. I should have sent you to Cleves, except that I could not get on without your company." He sighed deeply, and draining his large goblet, arose heavily. "Help me to my bed, fool, and then stay with me. We will talk on other, happier times. Do you remember Blaze Wyndham, Will? My sweet little country girl?"

"Aye, Hal, I remember her well. A gentle and good lady." Will Somers allowed the king to use him as a crutch, and led him to his bed, where he lay down. The fool and his monkey sat at the foot of the royal bed.

"Her daughter is at court now, Will. A sweet girl, but not at all like her mother. Lady Nyssa Wyndham is a wild English rose. She is one of the Princess of Cleves's maids of honor. Her mother asked me for her appointment."

"Which girl is she?" the fool asked his master. "I know little Kate Carey, Bessie FitzGerald, and the two Bassetts. There are two I do not know. Mistress Auburn Curls, and a beauteous dark-haired wench."

"Nyssa is the dark-haired girl. Her eyes are her mother's, though. The other little wench is Catherine Howard, Norfolk's niece." He chuckled. "Mistress Auburn Curls. It is most apropos, Will. Mistress Howard does have rather charming curls. She is a very pretty girl, is she not? God's foot! Any one of those maids would suit me far more than the Princess of Cleves! Why did I listen to Crum? I should have looked about my own court, and taken an English wife. Was not my own sweet Jane an English rose of good stock?"

"Ah, Hal, have you lost your taste for variety?" the fool gently teased the king. "I do not believe you have ever had a German. At least not in my time with you. Did you have one before I came to serve you, Hal? Is it true what they say about German women?"

"What do they say?" the king demanded suspiciously.

"I do not know." The fool chuckled. "I have never had one."

"Nor will I," the king said. "I do not think I can bring myself to couple with her, Will. God's blood, I should have married Christina of Denmark or Marie of Guise instead of this Flanders mare!"

"Hal," his fool admonished sternly, "how convenient your memory is. Marie of Guise was so anxious to wed with you that she hastily pledged her troth to James of Scotland when she learned you were seeking a wife. I suppose she prefers the Scots summers to ours. As for the beauteous Christina, she told your ambassador that had she two heads, one would be at your disposal, but as she had not, she preferred to mourn her late husband another year or two. You are not as fine a catch as you once were, Hal. The ladies are wary of your treatment of your past wives. You are lucky to have the Princess of Cleves, although I am not so certain she is lucky to have you."

"You tread dangerously, fool," the king said in a low voice.

"I speak the truth to you, which is more than those about you will do, for they fear you, Henry Tudor."

"And you do not?"

"Nay, Hal. I've seen you naked. You are but a man like I am. But for an accident of birth, Hal would be the fool and Will the king."

"I think I am a fool," Henry Tudor said, "that I allowed others to choose a wife for me, but there is no help for it now, is there, Will?"

Will Somers shook his grizzled gray head. "Make the best of it, Hal. The lady Anne may surprise you yet." He slipped off the bed, Margot clinging to his neck, and pulled the fur coverlet up over his master. "Go to sleep, Hal. You need your sleep, and I do too. Neither of us is as young as we once were, and the next few days will be full of pomp and circumstance, and too-rich food, and too much wine. You never do anything by halves, and so you will outeat and outdrink us all, and then you will suffer for it on a grandiose scale."

The king chuckled sleepily. "You are probably correct, Will," he said, smiling, and then his eyes closed.

The fool sat quietly until the king began to snore. Then he crept from the room, telling the gentlemen of the bedchamber who awaited outside the door that Henry Tudor was finally, to everyone's relief, asleep.

CHAPTER 4

The sixth of January dawned cold. A weak sun glittered in a mother-of-pearl sky. The wind off the Thames was biting. By six o'clock the king was awake, but he lay quietly abed for half an hour more. It was his wedding day, but he was unwilling yet to begin it. Finally realizing he had no other choice, he called for his gentlemen, and they entered, chattering and smiling, carrying his wedding garments. The king was helped from his bed. He bathed and was barbered. Then he donned the finery prepared for this charade he must participate in this day. What a waste, he thought, tears coming to his eyes. I am not so old yet that I cannot appreciate the joy of a fair maid in my bed.

The royal wedding garments were quite magnificent. There was a gown of cloth-of-gold edged in rich sable and embroidered with silver flowers. The coat was scarlet satin, every bit as richly embroidered, and was fastened with large round diamond buttons. There was a gold collar about his neck. His footwear was of red leather, in the latest style with the toe narrow and rounded. Each shoe had an ankle strap and was studded with pearls and diamonds. On each of his fingers he wore a jeweled ring.

"Your majesty looks most fine," young Thomas Culpeper said.

The others murmured and nodded in agreement.

"Were it not to satisfy my realm," the king snapped, "I should not do what I must this day for any earthly thing!"

"Cromwell is a dead man," Thomas Howard, the Duke of Norfolk, said softly.

"Do not be too certain," Charles Brandon, the Duke of Suffolk, whispered back. "Old Crum is a wily fox, and may yet escape the royal wrath."

"We will see," the Duke of Norfolk returned, and he smiled, a thing he rarely did. It was a smile of triumph.

"What mischief are you up to, Tom?" the Duke of Suffolk asked. Charles Brandon knew that Thomas Howard was closely allied with Stephen Gardiner, the Bishop of Winchester. The bishop had supported the king in his rejection of papal authority over the English Church, but he was a strong opponent of the doctrinal changes championed by the archbishop, Thomas Cranmer, a man Cromwell supported.

"You overestimate me, Charles," Norfolk replied, but he was still smiling. "I am the king's most loyal servant, and always have been."

"If anything, I underestimate you, Tom," Suffolk replied. "Sometimes you frighten me. Your ambition is a fierce thing."

"Let us get this travesty over and done with," the king growled at his gentlemen. "If I must marry her, then let it be done."

The king, escorted by his nobles, moved through the palace to the Princess of Cleves's apartments. There Anne awaited him calmly. She too had lain abed as long as she dared. When finally she was forced to arise, she had had to be coaxed to bathe her entire body in perfumed water. Despite her upbringing, which taught her that personal cleanliness was a vanity and sin of pride, she had enjoyed it.

"I vill do this every day," she declared to her ladies. "Vhat is da smell in da vasser, Nyssa Wyndham? It is nice."

"It is oil of damask rose, Your Grace," Nyssa replied.

"I like!" Anne declared, and her maids giggled. Their mirth was not directed at their new mistress, but rather, they were pleased to have made her happy. There was not one of them who did not know of the king's displeasure. Only Anne's lack of knowledge regarding English customs and the language protected her from deep hurt. She might not love Henry Tudor any more than he loved her, but she was a woman, and had her pride.

Her wedding garments were brought forth, and exclaimed over by all. Her gown was of cloth-of-gold. It was embroidered with flowers made of pearls. Cut in the Dutch fashion, it had the rounded skirt but no train. On her feet she wore slippers of gold kid with virtually nonexistent heels, to temper her height next to the king. Her blond hair was loose, declaring her virginity, and atop her head was a delicate gold coronet encrusted with gemstones, and golden trefoils resembling bunches of rosemary, a symbol of fertility. Mother Lowe placed a necklace of large diamonds set in gold about her mistress's neck, and then fastened the matching belt about Anne's slim waist. There were tears in the old woman's eyes, and when several escaped down her brown cheek, the princess gently wiped them away with her own hand.

"If your mama could but see you, my darling," Mother Lowe said.

"Is she all right?" Lady Browne inquired of Nyssa.

"She mourns the fact that the princess's mother is not here to see her married to the king," Nyssa answered. A good thing she is not, the girl thought silently to herself. A mother would see the king's unhappiness with her daughter; but perhaps that will change.

Told that the king was awaiting her, the bride stepped from her apartments. With the Count of Overstein and the Grand Master of Cleves escorting her, she followed the king and his train of nobles to the Chapel Royal, where the archbishop waited to marry them. Anne's face was serene, belying the fear she felt. He didn't want her, and she didn't want him either, yet they would marry for expediency's sake. She felt sorry for them both.

She was given in marriage by the Count of Overstein. She understood little of what the kindly faced archbishop was saying, but when Henry Tudor grasped her hand and jammed the heavy red-gold ring onto the appropriate finger, Anne of Cleves knew without a doubt that she was finally married to England's king. As Thomas Cranmer concluded the marriage ceremony, she painstakingly made out the words engraved upon her ring. *God send me well to keep.* It was all she could do not to laugh.

Now the king was grabbing at her hand and practically dragging her into his private chapel. She almost stumbled in her effort to keep up with him, and felt angry that he should so embarrass her on their wedding day. Whatever either of them might think, she was his wife. With effort she calmed herself, managing to get through the mass that followed. And afterward the bridal party was served hot spiced wine.

It was a day of unending ritual. Following the wedding ceremony, the king went to his private apartments to change clothing again. He put on a gown of tissue lined in embroidered red velvet. As soon as he had changed, a procession formed, and the bridal couple led their guests into the wedding banquet. In the afternoon the new queen departed the feast for a brief time to don fresh garments, choosing a gown with sleeves that gathered above her elbow. Her women also changed clothing, picking gowns decorated with many pretty golden chains, as was popular in the German states.

Cat Howard was filled with gratitude to Nyssa Wyndham, for she really had not the means to be a maid of honor. Her uncle, Duke Thomas, had obtained the position for her; but he was not so generous with his gold as he was with his influence. She had few gowns, and was forced to mix and match those she had, but even so, she was not as well dressed as the other girls. She and her sisters and three brothers were orphaned. What little their father had left, and it was indeed little, was reserved for her eldest brother. So as the queen's wedding had approached, Cat Howard had despaired of how she could afford another gown, particularly one that had to be lavishly decorated with chains.

"Let me give it to you as a Twelfth Night gift, Cat," Nyssa had said. "My allowance is more than I can spend even after having a new dress made." She shrugged. "What good is gold if you cannot share it with friends?"

"Oh, I cannot let you do such a thing," Cat Howard protested weakly, but it was obvious her heart was not in her words.

"Why not?" Nyssa inquired politely. "Is there some rule of court etiquette that I have not been told that forbids gifts between friends? If there is, I shall defy it, for I have gifts for you all!"

The others all giggled, and Lady Browne said, "Nyssa Wyndham is most generous, Mistress Howard. You are fortunate to have such a nice new friend. Of course you must accept the gift she offers. To do otherwise would be impolite, I fear, and Duke Thomas would be angry."

"In that case," Cat Howard said with a mischievous smile, "I must accept, which I do with thanks, Nyssa Wyndham."

Lady Browne nodded approvingly. "Prettily done," she said.

"I have nothing I can give you," Cat Howard told Nyssa softly, "but I do not forget a good turn done me, even as I do not forget a fault. Someday I will find a way to repay your kindness, for it is indeed kindness you do me. I am as poor as a church mouse, yet you have never made me feel inferior, as do the proud Bassetts. Eventually I shall have a chance to do you a good turn, Nyssa, and I will, I promise you."

When they returned to the banquet that afternoon in their fresh gowns, the new queen and her ladies were greeted with applause. The ladies received many compliments on their costumes. There was a program of masques and pantomimes. There was dancing. With ill-concealed grace the king led the new queen out onto the floor. But to Henry's surprise, Anne proved an excellent partner. She had learned well from her ladies. When he swung her up in the air, and she laughed down at him, he considered that perhaps she was not quite as unattractive as he had originally thought. Mayhap they could come to an arrangement.

"Nyssa?"

She turned at the sound of her name. There stood Cat Howard with . . . with . . . *with him!*

"This is my cousin, Varian de Winter, the Earl of March," Cat said. "He is without a partner. I thought perhaps you would take pity upon him. I know how you love to dance."

His eyes were green. Dark green. Dark water-green like the river Wye when it settled in sunlit ripples in the shallows where the river rushes grew by her home.

"Madame." He made her a most courtly bow. His face was grave.

"Sir." She curtsied, even as a shiver rippled up her back. His voice was deep and musical. There was a mysterious quality to it. His stern, handsome face set her heart to racing.

"Oh, do dance with Varian, Nyssa," Cat begged. Then she was gone to find her own partner.

"It is said you are not a gentleman, my lord. I am told by Lady Marlowe that to even speak with you endangers my reputation," Nyssa said boldly, regaining her composure.

"Do you believe her?" he asked dryly. She could hear the amusement in his wonderful voice. Still, his face remained serious.

"I think that Lady Marlowe, who is my aunt's dearest friend, is a gossip who thrives on scandal," Nyssa answered him slowly. "Yet within every scandal there is a grain of truth. Still, if we are in a public place, and surrounded by the entire court, I cannot quite see how you might compromise my reputation. Therefore, my lord, if indeed you are asking me to dance, I accept. To refuse you would be unthinkably rude." She curtsied to him again.

He took her hand, and she felt the warmth of his grasp pulse through her. They joined the lively country dance already in progress. A second dance followed, but when the music had finally ceased, Nyssa's uncle, Owen FitzHugh, was suddenly at their side.

"Nyssa, my dear, your aunt wishes to speak with you." He took her arm in a firm grip. "You will excuse us, my lord?"

The Earl of March bowed, a faint, sardonic smile upon his handsome face. "Of course, my lord," he said softly, "if you insist." He then turned and walked away.

"How could you!" Nyssa demanded of her uncle, stamping her foot for emphasis. "You have embarrassed me before the entire court!"

"My darling girl, I have full faith in your ability to handle your own life, but your aunt, egged on by Adela Marlowe, has not. Save your outrage for Bliss and her bosom friend."

"I will," Nyssa said ominously, and pulling away from her uncle, hurried across the floor to where the two older women sat.

"Nyssa!" Bliss said before she might even speak. "Have you not been warned about *that* man? Why, if Lady Marlowe had not seen him dancing with you, I can but imagine what would have happened."

"Nothing would have happened!" Nyssa retorted. "Little harm can be done to my reputation in a banquet hall full of people. You have embarrassed me greatly. I was introduced to the Earl of March by his cousin, Mistress Howard, one of my fellow maids. I could scarce refuse his invitation to dance under the circumstances, could I?"

"Dear sweet child," Adela Marlowe said, "an innocent such as you cannot possibly know the sort of man Lord de Winter is. Remember that you have been sent to court to find a suitable husband. No gentleman of good breeding will want to enter into a match with a woman of dubious repute." She smiled in what she believed was a kindly manner, but it seemed more supercilious to the younger woman.

"Madame," Nyssa said, her eyes dark with anger, "how dare you presume to lecture me on morality and manners? You are my senior in years only. I outrank you both by birth and position. Were I as foolish a peahen of a creature as you seem to think me, perhaps your interference would be of some value. I am not foolish, however, and I am mortally offended that my aunt would have been so influenced by you as to forget that I am my mother's daughter. I know well how to behave in polite society. You allude to some unsavory scandal in Lord de Winter's past, yet you do not elaborate. As far as I am concerned, the Earl of March is a pleasant gentleman, and an excellent dancer. As for me, I am a maid of unblemished virtue. If you have anything else to say on the matter, then do so. If you have not, I will thank you to rein in your wild imagination and not interfere in my life again!"

"She must be told!" Adela Marlowe declared dramatically to Bliss. "My conscience will not allow it otherwise."

"What must you tell me?" Nyssa demanded, her tone almost mocking.

"This man you insist upon defending, *and* with so little true knowledge of his history," the older woman said, "this man is an admitted debaucher of innocence. He seduced a young girl, and when she found herself with child, he would not own up to his responsibilities. The poor young creature killed herself. Will you defend such a man now, my fine young lady?"

Nyssa was shocked, but worse, she felt like a total fool. Yet how could she have been aware of such a terrible thing?

Still, she was irritated at Adela Marlowe, who now looked at her with the light of righteous triumph in her eyes, a small smile of victory upon her lips. Nyssa wanted to wipe that smile from the woman's face.

"You, madame," she said in scathing tones, "are the most vicious gossip I have ever encountered." She was pleased to see the woman wither beneath her assault.

"*Nyssa!*" Even Bliss, noted for her temper, was astounded at her niece's outburst. "You must apologize to Lady Marlowe this instant!"

"Rather I think Lady Marlowe should apologize to me," the girl snapped. "And you also, Aunt Bliss." Then she turned on her heel and hurried away to find her friends. Her heart was beating violently in her breast. It was not that she was enamored with Lord de Winter, for until this moment she had known virtually nothing about him. But she bitterly resented being treated like a child by her aunt and Lady Marlowe. She was seventeen now!

Adela Marlowe took several minutes to recover from her shock. She was white about the lips. "Never in my life have I been spoken to in such a fashion," she gasped. "If that girl were my charge, I should beat her black and blue, and then send her home to her parents. She is totally out of control, Bliss, and will come to a bad end, mark my words!"

"Nyssa was rude, I agree, Adela, but 'twas you who encouraged me to be overprotective of her. I forgot that she is not that kind of a girl. She is intelligent, and has quickly learned the ways of the court. She knows the stakes involved, and will not allow her reputation to be ruined. Besides, she loves the new queen, and delights in serving her."

"I suppose her large dowry will smooth over any tittle-tattle," Adela Marlowe said nastily.

THE time had come to put the king and queen to bed.

"Fifteen hours of night," Henry grumbled. "The next time I wed with an ugly woman, it shall be a midsummer's eve wedding, on the shortest night of the year instead of a long winter's night."

"*The next time he weds,*" murmured the Duke of Norfolk meaningfully to Cromwell.

"The night has only begun," Cromwell answered. "By the dawn the king may be a happier man, my lord." He smiled with a confidence he was not truly feeling, and the duke smiled back. Norfolk's smile was a knowing and superior one. Thomas Cromwell felt an icy premonition slither down his backbone. What was the duke up to?

The queen was divested of her wedding finery by her ladies, and the maids of honor were kept busy running to and fro fetching this item and the other. Anne was a tall, big-boned woman with slender limbs and a narrow waist. She had small pear-shaped breasts, which were entirely out of proportion for a woman of her stature. The queen's ladies silently eyed one another and shook their heads in despair as they helped the queen into a simple white silk night shift. Still, her lovely blond hair was long and thick as they brushed it out.

Mother Lowe, the queen's old nurse, and now comistress of the maids, said to Anne in a soft voice, using their own language, "What will you do with this great bear you have married, child? He does not like you, as we both know—thanks to young Hans, who listens to the foolish men who ignore him because he is a boy, and chatter in his presence. Your mother, I know, has told you nothing of what transpires between a man and his wife; but I have enlightened you. Will you try to win him over, child? I am fearful for you."

"Do not be," Anne reassured the old woman. "I do not know what I shall do yet. It depends upon this king, my husband. Perhaps if I give him an excuse to annul our marriage, he will think more kindly of me. If he had had an excuse to break the betrothal, to avoid the marriage ceremony today, I do believe he would have done so. He is not, I am told, a man who likes being denied his will. We are just married. He has no cause for divorce, yet he wishes to rid himself of me. If I do not give him just cause for an annulment, then he must kill me. I did not come to England, Mother Lowe, to lose my head, but rather to gain my freedom from that boring court of my brother's." She smiled and patted her old servant's hand. "Pray for me that I make the right decisions."

The sound of revelry came from the queen's antechamber, and then the door to her bedchamber was pushed open. All the ladies in the room curtsied as the king, in a velvet robe and nightcap, reluctantly entered, followed by his gentlemen and the archbishop. Without a word the king climbed into the bed next to the queen. Archbishop Cranmer then droned a prayer for the marriage's success and the couple's fertility.

When he had finished, the king growled to them, "Get out! I want to get this over and done with. Out! *All of you!*"

The ladies and gentlemen of the court departed, chuckling, and casting sly looks at one another. The door closed behind them with an ominous sound.

The bride and groom sat silently side by side. Finally Henry turned and looked at his new queen. He could barely repress a shudder of distaste. It was not that she was really ugly; she wasn't. But her features were stronger than Holbein had painted them, and she was so damned big when he compared her to Katherine, the first Anne, and his sweet Jane. Her blue eyes were intelligent, however, and they regarded him cautiously now. Best to get the thing over with. He reached out and fingered a strand of golden hair. It was soft, and somehow that pleased him. At least there was something about the woman he liked.

"You do not like me," Anne said suddenly, her voice clear in the tense silence.

He remained silent, surprised, and curious as to what else she would say to him.

"You vould not haf ved me, but you not haf . . . haf . . . ach! I do not know the vord!" Her accent was thick, but he fully understood her words.

"Excuse," he supplied gently.

"Ya! You not haf excuse to . . . to . . ."

"Reject," the king offered.

"Ya! Reject me!" she concluded triumphantly. "If I gif you excuse, vill you let me stay here in England, Hendrick?"

He was amazed. She had been in England but eleven days, yet she was already speaking the language, a clear indication of her intellect; *and,* she had quickly grasped the situation with regard to his feelings. Was he making a mistake? No. He would never love this woman. He could not. Not even for England's sweet sake.

"What excuse?" he demanded of her, his blue eyes narrowing with speculation. "It must be foolproof, Annie. They tell me my reputation with wives is not the best, but 'tis not true. I am misunderstood."

He had spoken very slowly, that she might at least grasp some of his words, but it seemed that his bride understood more than she could say. She laughed aloud, and he saw she had big teeth.

"I understand Hendrick vell," she told him. "Ve no make luf, and you haf excuse to reject me. Ya?"

It was simple and absolutely brilliant, Henry Tudor thought, and then he realized that it must be he who could not make love to her, not she who refused him. Either way, he thought, he would be embarrassed, but he would be less embarrassed if he blamed her unattractive person for the problem. She had to understand that.

"We need Hans to talk for us," he said, "but not tonight. In secret. Tomorrow. Yes?"

"Ya!" she nodded, and then swinging her legs off of their bed, she stood up and asked him, "Ve play cards, Hendrick?"

Henry Tudor laughed. "Ya!" he told her. "We play cards, Annie." She wasn't the sort of woman he wanted for a wife, or for a lover, but he had a strong feeling that she was going to become a good friend.

The king was up early the following morning. They had gambled until well after midnight, and his Flanders mare had won heavily off of him. At any other time he might have been angered to be beaten so thoroughly, but his new queen had been a good companion. Gaining his own bedchamber by use of a private passage, the king greeted his gentlemen dourly. It was all part of the plan that had formed in his head the previous night. He must continue to appear dissatisfied from the very start with Anne of Cleves. He would not be believed otherwise.

Cromwell met the king on his way to mass. "What think your grace of the queen now?" he asked low. "I trust your night was pleasant."

"My night was not pleasant, Crum. Not pleasant at all. I have left the queen as good a maid as I found her. I cannot for the life of me bring myself to consummate this marriage, though my dreams were of a most sensuous nature, I admit. At least twice I soiled myself with the passion of them, but I am not happy, Crum."

"Perhaps your grace was tired with all the pomp and excitement," Cromwell offered weakly. " 'Twill be better tonight when you are better rested."

"I am not tired!" the king snapped. "Bring me another woman, and I could perform the act eagerly, *but not this woman!* She fills me with repulsion, Crum. Do you understand me?"

Cromwell understood all too well. Unable to get out of the marriage before it was formally celebrated, Henry Tudor was now going to seek another route by which to rid himself of this unwanted new wife. He had gotten the king into this situation, and he knew for certain that his very life would be forfeit unless he got the king gracefully out of it.

Cromwell's peace of mind was shattered irretrievably when the king personally told every influential gentleman at court of his inability to perform the marriage act with the new queen. When Henry Tudor spoke with his personal physician, Dr. Butts, Cromwell found himself growing dizzy with anxiety. Across the room the Duke of Norfolk smiled.

On the eleventh of January a tournament was held in the new queen's honor, although the court wondered why. Henry Tudor was making no secret of his deep dissatisfaction with his bride. Anne, on the other hand, remained charming and dignified. Her English was improving at a rapid pace, and on the day of the tournament she wore an English-made gown in the latest London style with a delightful little French hood. The common people were impressed with her, as were many at court, despite the king's feelings, but the power brokers would have been astounded if they had known the scheme hatched by their new queen to allow the king his freedom.

The day after the wedding, the queen had called Hans to her privy chamber. The king had entered the room directly by means of a secret passage. There, an agreement had been hammered out between Henry and Anne, with young Hans acting as translator so there would be no misunderstanding between the two parties. Henry and Anne would not consummate the marriage just celebrated. Henry would blame his inability to perform with his wife on Anne's appearance, which was unappealing to him. In return Anne would pretend everything was all right between them as far as she was concerned. There were already rumors that the alliance between the French king and the Holy Roman Emperor was deteriorating. England would shortly not need the goodwill of Cleves. When that rumor became fact, an annulment would be suggested due to the king's inability to consummate his marriage. It would, of course, be granted.

In return, Anne of Cleves would be given two homes of her choice. Since she was new to England, she would need to visit the royal residences in order to make her decision. The king would settle a goodly allowance upon her, and she would be called his *sister*. Only a new queen would take precedence over her at court. She would also assure her brother that this change in her status was entirely satisfactory to her, and that she had been treated with kindness.

Both Henry Tudor and Anne of Cleves were content with their secret agreement. It would just be a matter of time. Still, Henry was curious as to why his bride was so damned restrained. Was she not a virgin, and feared his discovery of the fact? He shuddered. He was not curious enough to find out for himself. Or perhaps, he considered, she was afraid of her fate were she not reasonable with him. He frowned. His conduct toward the Princess of Aragon, and that witch, the first Anne, had been entirely correct. No one could fault him, although he knew there were those who had tried.

Henry Tudor stared at Anne, silently questioning her easy acquiescence, and was suddenly tempted to ask her true feelings. She wouldn't tell them to him, of course, but neither, he realized, would she lie. She was far too clever a woman. Henry Tudor shook himself like a large dog coming in from the rain. The first Anne had been clever, and her daughter, wee Bess, was showing signs of being clever as well. God deliver him from clever women! Best to leave well enough alone and be glad that Anne, his princess wife from Cleves, was such a discreet lady with a temperate disposition. The king's thoughts slid away to more pleasant matters.

On the twenty-seventh of the month the king gave a great feast for Anne's attendants from Cleves. They were then all sent home with many gifts and the royal couple's good wishes. Only Helga von Grafsteen and Maria von Hesseldorf remained from among Anne's maids. Mother Lowe, who had been the queen's nurse, also remained with her mistress, as did young Hans von Grafsteen. To Lady Browne's great annoyance, the king personally told her that eight maids of honor were enough for Anne. No more appointments would be approved.

On the third of February orders were given for a reception to be held for the new queen in London. If some thought it strange that the king had not yet planned the queen's coronation, they did not dare say so. The following day the royal barge came down the river from Greenwich to Westminster. As they passed the tower, the guns sounded a salute. The riverbank was lined on both sides with the cheering citizenry. The king and queen were escorted by barges filled with members of the court and the London guilds.

Anne was very touched by her new subjects. She was almost sorry she would not be their queen for very long, but if Henry Tudor did not want her for a wife, she certainly did not want him for a husband. A friend, yes. He was going to become a very good friend, but a husband? Never! However, for the sake of appearances, when the king's barge landed at Westminster, Henry and Anne walked hand in hand to Whitehall Palace, where they would be staying overnight.

The Earl of March attempted to single out Nyssa while they were at Whitehall, but the scurrilous gossip surrounding him made the girl have a special care for her reputation. She did her best to avoid him.

"My duties with the queen leave me little time for myself, my lord," she told him firmly when he sought to invite her for a ride. "And when I do have time for myself, I prefer the company of my family." Varian de Winter was disappointed, but he vowed to himself that he would try again to win her favor at a more opportune moment.

It wasn't long before the ladies of the queen's household knew for absolute certain that their mistress was a wife in name only, and would remain that way. Anne, in an effort to support the king, played the innocent. In a court rife with intrigue, sexual promiscuity, and adultery, it was unbelievable that the queen should be so innocent, and yet it appeared she was. One winter's afternoon as Anne sat with her ladies, the queen even remarked how thoughtful the king was of her.

"Vhen he comes to bed each night, he gifs me a tender kiss and says,

'Good night, sveetheart,' and vhen he leaves me in the morning, he kisses me again and says, 'Farevell, sveetheart.' Is he not the best of husbands? Bessie, my girl, fetch me a cup of malmsey, please."

The queen's ladies looked astounded, and finally after several long moments Lady Edgecombe said, "We hope your grace will soon be with child. All the country will rejoice when we have a Duke of York joining Prince Edward in the royal nursery." She smiled weakly.

"I am not vith kinder," the queen said blandly, and she accepted the goblet of wine Elizabeth FitzGerald brought her. "Thank you, Bessie."

"I think your grace may still be a maid," Lady Edgecombe said daringly, and her companions paled at her impudence. They knew she would not have said such a thing to another woman, but this queen was so good-natured, and unfailingly kind, she rarely took offense.

"How can I be a maid, and yet sleep vith mein Hendrick each night, Lady Vinefred?" She chuckled. "Dot is foolish."

"To be a true wife in every sense there must be more, madame," Lady Edgecombe said gently. *"Is there no more?"*

The queen shook her head slowly, adding, "But I am contented that I know no more. Hendrick is a goot husband to me." There, she thought. I have, thanks to the nosey Lady Edgecombe, corroborated the king's word regarding the nonconsummation of our marriage. The queen then arose and said, "I vould rest, ladies. You are all dismissed but Nyssa Vyndham, who vill attend me." She arose from her chair and walked slowly into her bedchamber with Nyssa hurrying behind her.

"Poor lady," the Duchess of Richmond said. "She truly does not understand. What a shame the king does not like her. I wonder what will happen to her? He certainly cannot accuse her of adultery, like the other one, nor claim consanguinity, as he did with the first."

"It will probably be an annulment," the Marchioness of Dorset said. "What other excuse does he have?"

Nyssa closed the door to the queen's bedchamber firmly behind her. She turned to the queen, whose face was strangely contorted, and said sympathetically, "Do not let them distress you, dear madame."

To Nyssa's surprise, Anne burst out laughing, and when Anne had finally managed to regain control of herself, she said to the girl, "I vant to tell you something, Nyssa, but it is a great secret. If you cannot keep such a secret, you must tell me now, and I vill not tell it to you at all, but I vould like to tell you. The others, they are not my friends. They are too overcome vith their own importance, and the other maids not mature enough. I need a friend, Nyssa Vyndham. Ya! Even a qveen needs a friend.

Hans, he is a friend, but he is also just a lad, for all his responsibility. I vould have one of my own sex to talk vith."

Nyssa came and knelt by the queen, who had seated herself by the fireplace. "I am proud to serve you, dear madame, and I will keep your secrets. I should be honored to be the friend of a queen."

"I shall not long be your qveen," Anne said.

"Oh, madame!" Nyssa cried. Distressed, she looked up at her mistress. "Do not say it, I beg you!"

"Listen to me, Nyssa Vyndham. Hendrick Tudor does not like me. I saw it from the first. The king vould not haf married me if he could haf found a way out of our betrothal, but he could not. On our vedding night ve made an arrangement between us. He vould not consummate the marriage, claiming my person repelled him; and I vould not contest an annulment when the time came. Today that silly, vell-meaning, but curious Lady Edgecombe gave me an opportunity to confirm the king's claim."

"But his grace is so courteous of your person," Nyssa said, confused. She had heard the rumors, but had ignored them as idle gossip.

"As a vife, Hendrick cannot abide me, Nyssa, but as a friend, vell, that is a different matter. Ve play cards each night vhen ve haf retired to the bedchamber. I usually beat him, for he is not very clever, poor Hendrick. I vonder that people fear him."

"Oh, madame, he is much to be feared. He is pleasant with you because you have given him his way, but when he does not get his way, he is like a surly beast. Make no mistake, the king can be dangerous."

"Your mother, I am told, vas his mistress," the queen said.

"For just a few months before he became enamored of the first Queen Anne. Mama was a widow, and my aunt, the Countess of Marwood, dragged her to court to help her overcome her grief. The king was instantly taken by her, but Mama hid behind her mourning. She was very frightened by the king, and had never known any man but my father. The king, however, told Mama that on May Day she would become his. She wanted to run away, but she could not, for the king threatened to take me away from her."

The queen's blue eyes widened with surprise. "So," she said slowly, "Hendrick can be ruthless vhen he vants to be."

"Aye, madame, he can," Nyssa said softly.

"So your mama became Hendrick's lover on May Day, ya?"

"Yes, and for several months after, she was his. She grew to love him, and she understood him quite well. Then came Mistress Anne Boleyn to court, and everything changed. My stepfather came to court too, and the king arranged that he should marry Mama. He was my father's heir, and had loved Mama from afar, though he never dared to give voice to his passion while my father lived. So they were married in the king's own chapel, and then returned to *RiversEdge*, our home. Mama, however, has always remained the king's most loyal servant. She returned briefly to court twice at his request; once to intercede with the Princess of Aragon, and a second time when Mistress Anne was executed. She has never been back since."

"Vhat is it Hendrick calls her?" the queen asked.

"His little country girl," Nyssa replied with a smile.

"And are you a country girl, Nyssa Vyndham, or do you like this court? I think it is very exciting. My brother's court vas so dull, and serious. No cards or dancing, or pretty gowns."

"The court can be exciting, Your Grace, but I think, like my mother, I prefer the country life," Nyssa answered. "Still, I am honored to serve you, and my aunt hopes I will find a husband here."

"You haf no one at your home?"

"Nay, madame. I am quite the despair of my family. I have attained my seventeenth year, and there is no gentleman, suitable or unsuitable, who catches my fancy or appeals to my heart," Nyssa told the queen. "If you are not to be queen long, I wonder what will happen to me. Do you know when the king will seek this annulment, madame?"

"I tink it vill probably be in the spring sometime. Hendrick is not a man to go long vithout a voman. Already his eye begins to roam. Haf you not noticed it? He smiles upon Mistress Anne Bassett, upon Mistress Howard, and upon you. You do not see it?"

"*Upon me?*" Nyssa was horrified. "Oh, madame, surely not upon me? The king was my mother's lover! He is old enough to be my father!"

She grew pale and near to fainting. The queen put a comforting arm about the girl. "Nyssa Vyndham," she said, her voice filled with laughter, "Hendrick is old enough to be my papa too. Perhaps I haf listened to too much gossip. Perhaps the king's kindness to you is because of the affection he bears your mama."

"Aye!" Nyssa said, able to draw a breath again. "I am certain that his grace looks upon me as he would the lady Mary or the lady Elizabeth."

Still, the queen's words disturbed her, but she could not speak even to her aunt about it. To do so would violate the trust that the queen had put in her. What would happen when the marriage of Anne of Cleves and Henry Tudor was dissolved? The king's ministers would insist he take another wife, a wife who could give him more sons. The king had, of late, begun to speak on the virtues of Englishwomen as wives as opposed to foreigners. Nyssa was suddenly very aware that she was being studied by certain important members of the Privy Council. Her virtuous behavior and her loyalty to the queen became even more pronounced. It was the only shield behind which she might hide.

In March, Henry Tudor informed his council that consummation of his marriage to Anne of Cleves would be absolutely impossible. The Privy Council realized that they were being commanded, as subtly as Henry Tudor was capable of being subtle, to find a way out of his marriage for him. The king insisted to his ministers that he was *certain* that there was a precontract between Anne and the son of the Duke of Lorraine.

"We will certainly reinvestigate the matter, Your Grace," Thomas Cromwell assured his master, and the Duke of Norfolk almost laughed.

The king thanked his council and left them to their debate.

The members of the Privy Council looked to Cromwell.

"There was no precontract," Cromwell said bleakly. "Before the king's marriage contract was even signed last autumn, we sent to the current Duke of Lorraine. He was the bridegroom proposed for Anne of Cleves when they were children. He has since inherited his father's dukedom, and he swears that there was no precontract. He sought among his father's papers. He even spoke with his father's confessor. There was no evidence of a precontract. The late duke's priest says a betrothal was but casually discussed once, and then never pursued. The king cannot dissolve this marriage by means of that excuse."

"He will be rid of her, Crum," the Duke of Norfolk said. "His juices are already flowing, and he is eager for a woman in his bed. I am told his eye is happily wandering among the prettier women of the court. He will not bed this Flanders mare, but I believe him still capable of siring a child. One prince is not enough, gentlemen! We must have a nursery full of little princes for England."

"I agree," Bishop Gardiner said silkily.

"Yet the queen is a good woman," the Archbishop of Canterbury interjected in kindly tones. "We should not be responsible for harming this faultless creature. It is unworthy of us as Englishmen. If this marriage is to be dissolved, it must be done through annulment. The queen must be gently treated, and given a generous portion in return for her cooperation. I think you would all agree to that, gentlemen."

"What if she is like the Spanish bitch, and will not cooperate?" the Duke of Norfolk demanded. "After all, the fault is his grace's. Has he not told everyone who would listen that he cannot consummate the marriage? What if she will not give way? We'll have to find another way, and what way is there other than . . ." He made a slicing motion across his own long throat. His face was grim.

"Thomas, Thomas," the archbishop chided the duke softly. "This lady is nothing like the Princess of Aragon. She can be reasoned with, and I will reason with her myself. What think you, Crum? An annulment?"

Thomas Cromwell nodded. "It is the only way, my lords."

"Then you must propose it to the king, and see what he says," Archbishop Cranmer told him. "With his grace's permission, I will deal with the queen. She cannot be mistreated. She is of a royal house."

"So was the Spaniard," muttered the Duke of Norfolk.

"This is a different matter altogether, Thomas," was the archbishop's patient reply.

"The king may not wish to be held up to public ridicule," fretted Cromwell. "What man wishes to admit to his kind of problem?"

"He has no other choice," Bishop Gardiner replied practically. "If he would be rid of this lady, then he must make some sacrifice."

"This is not a simple man we are speaking of," Cromwell said irritably. "This is Henry Tudor himself!"

"We will support you in this, Crum," the Duke of Norfolk assured the chancellor. "Partisan politics must be put aside for England's good. Are we not agreed there, gentlemen?" He looked about the table.

"Aye!" the others said with one voice.

"I am not certain of your reassurances, my lord," Cromwell replied, "but it would seem that I have no choice in the matter other than to approach the king with regard to an annulment. It will be done this very day. Waiting cannot help us."

The chancellor departed the Privy Council to seek out the king. The other men began to drift away as well. Bishop Gardiner sidled up to the Duke of Norfolk and said, "We must speak, Tom."

"Come with me," the duke answered.

The two men moved out into one of the royal gardens, deserted on this rather chilly day. Spring was near, but not quite at hand. Walking among the green maze they would be unobserved, and unheard. It was the perfect spot for plotting.

The Duke of Norfolk looked at his companion. The bishop was a tall man with a long face ending in a round chin. His nose was big and his lips fleshy. His dark eyes were unfathomable. He wore his graying hair cropped close just below the top of his ears. He was a very difficult and arrogant man, but like the duke, he was conservative both politically and religiously. And like the duke, he had been kept from court in recent years by Thomas Cromwell. Neither man had any love for the chancellor.

"Now that the matter is practically settled," Stephen Gardiner said low, "we must consider the matter of a new marriage for the king."

"There isn't a woman of rank in Europe who would have him," the duke said harshly, "but that is all to the good, isn't it, my lord bishop? The king will find his new bride right here in his own garden. He will choose from among English roses, not from among foreign flowers."

"Have you a lady in mind, my lord?" the bishop asked slyly. "For all his great size, he prefers dainty women of some beauty who can flatter him into believing that he is still the handsomest prince in all of Christendom. A lady who loves music, and dancing. A lady who is young enough to bear children, and to flatter his always burgeoning ego. Yet what young girl would want to ally herself in marriage to that great, hulking mound of flesh with his stinking abscessed leg? A man who has cast off three of his four wives—and one must ask oneself, would Queen Jane have survived to live a long life had she not died of the complications of childbirth? In retrospect he fashions her the perfect wife, but would she have continued to be so, or would his eye have begun to wander again? What maid of good family would sacrifice herself to such a man, Thomas?"

Norfolk regarded the bishop evenly. The duke's long, lean face, set with high cheekbones, was calm, his eyes serious. He was the premier noble in all of England, but even his own wife, Lady Elizabeth Stafford, had warned Thomas Cromwell not to trust Thomas Howard, who could speak as fair to his enemies as he could to his friends. Not that Cromwell had needed the warning.

The Duke of Norfolk was a schemer, but he was also ambitious and highly intelligent. His first wife had been Anne, the daughter of Edward IV, sister to Henry VII's wife. She had given him one son, Thomas, who had died young. The lady Anne had not lived a great deal longer. His second wife had given him a son, Henry, who was the Earl of Surrey, and a daughter, Mary, who had been married to Henry Fitzroy, the Duke of Richmond, the king's beloved illegitimate son. There had been times the Duke of Norfolk dreamed of seeing his daughter on England's throne, but Henry Fitzroy had died, and Queen Jane had produced the desired legitimate heir.

Now another plot was forming in his mind, and he answered the Bishop of Winchester quietly. "What maid, you ask, my lord bishop? Why, my niece, Catherine Howard, my deceased brother's daughter. She is young, and pretty, and most malleable. Already the king eyes her, for she serves the queen as a maid of honor. Why, only the other day he called her a rose without a thorn. She is a perfect choice."

"He eyes others as well," the bishop said. "There is the Bassett girl, to whom he gave a horse and saddle last autumn, and another maid of honor, Nyssa Wyndham, whom he calls a wild English rose. Your niece may have competition for the royal marriage bed, and however you scheme, Duke Thomas, the king will have his way this time. Last time he left the choice to others, and it will cost him dearly to right the matter, both in prestige and worldly goods. Remember that well as you plot."

"The Bassett girl is of no import, Bishop. He had her once, so I am told, and neither of them thought a great deal of the experience. He rewarded her good nature with a minor gift, and thinks kindly of her, but he would never marry her now. He wants in marriage a woman he can have no other way. He will have my niece only when he slips a wedding band on her dainty little finger. The game has not yet begun, Bishop, but it is about to, and I will personally instruct my niece in her behavior. We will have no debacles with Catherine as we did with Anne Boleyn, that foolish head-strong creature who lost her head for her alleged adulteries."

"But what of the other girl?" the bishop asked.

"Lady Nyssa Wyndham?" the duke replied. "Her mother was the king's mistress some fifteen years ago. Perhaps you remember her. Her name was Blaze Wyndham."

"Is the girl the king's get?" the archbishop wondered. "As I recall, her mother left court rather suddenly, did she not? Is that why you are not worried about this girl? She is the king's daughter perhaps?"

"She is not the king's daughter," the duke said. "Her father was Edmund Wyndham, the third Earl of Langford. She was already two years old when her mother, then widowed, came to court."

"Then why," demanded Stephen Gardiner, "do you not fear this young woman, my lord? You know what a romantic fool the king can be. It would be just like him to choose this girl over all others in a desperate attempt to recapture his youth. As I recall, her mother allied herself to no one. Her loyalty was solely for the king. This girl could be dangerous to us, my lord."

To us. The duke masked his triumph. Gardiner was with him. "If I feel the Wyndham girl is becoming a threat to our plans, my lord bishop, I will see that she is discredited in the king's eyes. You know how he dislikes being disappointed by someone in whom he has placed his trust. With your help, our little Catherine will be England's next queen."

"It is to be hoped she will not go the way of your other niece, Anne Boleyn. You managed to survive her, but if this girl is not all you make her out to be, you might not survive the disaster that will follow in the wake of the king's anger and disillusionment."

"Catherine Howard is nothing like Anne Boleyn. Anne was very sophisticated by virtue of her years at the French court. She was older, and willful. Catherine is but sixteen, sweet, silly, and pliable. She has had a hard life, being orphaned early and placed in my mother's care. Why, had I not obtained her place for her at court, I cannot imagine what would have happened to her. She will be grateful to be queen, and to have everything she has ever wanted. Putting up with the king and his little foibles is a small price to pay for such a glittering prize as a throne. She can take comfort in the knowledge she will surely outlive her husband. She will do as I tell her."

"You are certain that she is everything that the king would want in a bride, my lord? There are no little secrets? No ugly flaws?" the bishop pressed.

"None," the duke told him in positive tones. "She has lived like a nun down at Leadinghall in my mother's care. She is a skilled musician, and she loves to dance. She is nothing more than a frivolous piece of pretty fluff. She is just what the king needs."

"Then so be it," the bishop said. "We will encourage our sovereign liege lord in his pursuit of Catherine Howard. We will not be queenless long, once he has freed himself of Anne of Cleves. But Cromwell? What of Cromwell? Will he not try to stop us, my lord?"

"Cromwell is finished," the duke said, his triumph evident. "He has failed the king in the worst way possible. All of Henry Tudor's embarrassment and difficulties in this matter have been laid at old Crum's doorstep. The king will never forgive him. We need not worry about his foiling our plans, my dear bishop. Thomas Cromwell will be too busy trying to save his miserable life. It is astounding that one of such low birth could have climbed so high, but then these are very modern times, are they not? I do not like modern times. I am a man who prefers life the way it has always been, and when finally we are rid of Cromwell, it will be that way once again." He smiled a wintry smile, and then without another word he turned and left the bishop standing in the middle of the green maze.

CHAPTER 5

IN the early spring of 1540 the abbeys of Canterbury, Christchurch, Rochester, and Waltham were finally surrendered to the king's majesty. Thomas Cromwell had completed his dissolution of the monasteries. His great usefulness to Henry Tudor was almost at an end. Much of the wealth that had belonged to these abbeys was funneled directly into the king's treasury, but some of it was distributed to those nobles loyal to the crown. It was a ploy to draw these men even closer to their sovereign. They would certainly not oppose the religious reforms being put in place while profiting from them.

The French ambassador, Charles de Marillac, wrote to his king that Thomas Cromwell was tottering. Yet Henry Tudor suddenly created his chancellor Earl of Essex. The king was possessed of a mean streak that was even now exhibiting itself.

When the Duke of Norfolk discreetly sounded the king out as to the honor bestowed on Cromwell, the king smiled wolfishly and said, "I but soothe poor Crum's fears, Thomas. A frightened man does not think clearly, and right now we need old Crum's cleverness if I am to be completely and unequivocally free of this unfortunate misalliance in which he has entangled me. I think it only fair that having arranged this royal marriage, he dissolve it."

"Then there is no hope?" the duke said.

"For my marriage?" the king demanded. "It has been but a marriage in name only. Not that the lady Anne isn't a good woman. She is. But she is no wife to me. And never has been. Nor will she ever be."

"What of the Duke of Cleves, my lord?" Thomas Howard said. "Will he not be offended that you cast his sister off and sent her packing home to Cleves? She is, after all, a princess."

"The lady Anne will be treated generously, Norfolk. You need not concern yourself. As for Cleves, can it stand against the might of England? I think not. It has served its purpose for us. France and the Holy Roman Empire are both seeking our friendship once again." The king grinned at the Duke of Norfolk. "I'll have me another bonnie English rose like my sweet Jane, eh Thomas?"

"Would not a princess be a better choice, Your Grace?" the duke murmured softly. "A simple English woman lacks prestige, think you not?"

"*Lacks prestige?* You're a snob, Thomas, and you always have been. There isn't an English lass who would not outshine the most perfect of foreign princesses. No more royalty! I want a flesh and blood woman to love. A good bedmate. A mother for my children. And as God is my witness," the king said, his voice rising, "*I shall have her!*"

"And has any particular lady taken your majesty's fancy?" the duke inquired.

The king bellowed with laughter, and poked the duke in his ribs with a fat finger. "You'd like to be the first to know, you old slyboots, wouldn't you?" he chortled, tears of mirth running down his face. "Well, I've not quite made up my mind yet. So, you'll not know before I know, my lord, and that's an end to it!"

But the Duke of Norfolk, like everyone else at court, had seen the king's eyes upon his niece, Catherine, and upon the Wyndham girl, Nyssa. Thomas Howard had spoken to young Catherine the same day he had had his conversation in the maze with Bishop Gardiner. As he had a spy in the queen's household, he knew his niece had free time that afternoon, and he had sent for the girl. She came, looking particularly lovely in a velvet gown of light yellow-green. It suited her coloring, and he complimented her.

"It is a gift from my friend, Nyssa Wyndham. She says it does not become her, and she has too many dresses. I think she is just being kind to me because I am poor, Uncle. Still, it is good to have such a friend, is it not?"

"How would you like to never have to worry about having enough gowns again, my child?" he asked her. "How would you like to have all the pretty gowns and beautiful jewelry that your little heart desires?"

Her blue eyes grew wide. "I do not understand, Uncle," she said.

"I have a marriage in mind for you, Catherine. But first you must promise me that you will not discuss with anyone, even your friend, Nyssa, what I am about to reveal to you. Do you promise me?" His cold eyes bored into her.

She nodded solemnly, her rising excitement evident. Thomas Howard was almost as powerful as the king himself.

"I mean it, Catherine," he warned her. "This is a deep secret between us. Should you reveal it, it might mean your very life. You do understand me, do you not?" He looked hard at her.

Her pretty mouth made a little O, and then she said, "I will do whatever you want me to do, Uncle, and no one shall know of our conversation. What is the marriage you propose for me?"

"How would you like to be the Queen of England, Catherine?" he questioned her. "Think on it, my child. *Queen!*"

"Then I should have to marry the king," Catherine Howard said slowly, "and he already has a wife. How could such a thing be, Uncle?"

"The lady Anne will soon no longer be the queen," Thomas Howard told his niece. When her pretty face registered deep distress, he reassured her. "No harm will come to the lady Anne, my child, I swear it, but the king is seeking an annulment. You know, as does everyone at court, that he has not had the stomach to consummate his marriage to this lady. England needs more legitimate heirs. The king must have a young wife who can give him those children. He looks upon you with great favor, Catherine. I think you can be the one to make him a happy bridegroom, and a devoted husband. What think you of this?"

She pondered for a long, long moment, thoughts racing through her head. Henry Tudor was old enough to be her father. He was fat, and the thought of him touching her turned her stomach, for she was a fastidious girl and loved beautiful things. His abscessed leg, when it flared up, stank and ran pus, *but he was the King of England.* What were her chances for another good marriage? She was one of six children, the eldest of three daughters. Both of her parents were deceased. She depended upon the charity of this powerful uncle of hers for her very bread. He was a tight-fisted man, and would not dower her to any suitor save a rich one. Rich men did not marry poor girls no matter their powerful connections. A convent was no longer an option. She could become a rich man's mistress, or . . . What choice did she really have?

"I am afraid, Uncle," she told him honestly.

"Why?" he demanded fiercely. "You are a Howard, Catherine!"

"My cousin Anne Boleyn was a Howard. She lost her head on Tower Green. The king is easily displeased, and only the lady Jane ever really satisfied him. I wonder had she lived if she would have continued to satisfy him, or if he would have grown bored with her too? His grace has wed four women. One has died, one he divorced, one he executed, and now he wishes to annul this latest marriage. You ask me would I like having beautiful clothing, and jewelry. I tell you, aye, I would! But how long will I keep them before the king finds an excuse to rid himself of me, Uncle? This is why I am afraid."

Thomas Howard then did something he rarely did. He softened his attitude toward his niece, and actually put an arm around her. "If you will do exactly as I tell you, Catherine, you will never bore the king so much that he wishes to be rid of you. More is involved here, my girl, than just finding the king a good wife. The king, though Catholic in his own worship, allows the Lutheran element more and more freedom within the Church. Archbishop Cranmer, of course, is behind it. We must stop it. The key to stopping it is selecting a wife for the king who follows the old traditions, and who will be guided by those wiser than she. It has been decided, Catherine, that you are that girl; and our cause is helped by the king himself, who shows you obvious favor." He dropped his arm from about her slender shoulders and demanded, "I ask you once again, niece, would you like to be queen?"

"Aye, Uncle," she said low, telling him what she knew he wanted to hear. What other options did she really have? These were powerful men dealing in matters far too complicated for her to understand. She was just a helpless girl. At least the king was clever, and he loved music as she did, and when his leg was not paining him, he was an excellent dancer. She must concentrate upon the positive elements of this matter. Perhaps if she could learn to soothe and dress his leg when it pained him, she would endear herself to Henry Tudor. She could not be squeamish about it, no matter her own delicate sensibilities.

"I am pleased with you, Catherine," the Duke of Norfolk told her. "I am going to teach you how to ingratiate yourself with the king. You must be a bit more helpless with him, yet always gay and amusing. Defer to his judgment both publicly and privately, for it will please him. Most important of all, my child, is that you keep his lust at bay until he has put his wedding ring upon your finger. If he can have what he wants of you without that ring, you are as ruined as any maid who lets the stable boy fumble her in a dark barn. Do you understand me? A chaste kiss, a tiny cuddle, *but nothing more,* Catherine, even if he begs it of you, or grows angry with your refusal. Fall back upon tears then. You are a virtuous maid. Remind the king of that when he importunes you for more than you are willing to give him. Your virginity is the only real dowry you have to bring him."

"Yes, Uncle," she obediently answered him. "I will do all you say. You have but to guide me, and I will obey, I swear it!"

"Now, I will tell you another secret," the duke said to her. "Lady Rochford is my spy in the queen's household. You may trust her, but never completely, Catherine. She is an unhappy woman. Her guilt over her husband George Boleyn's death weighs heavy on her. She gives me her loyalty because I have secretly seen to her support since his death. The Boleyns, of course, disowned her, as did her own family. As for Nyssa Wyndham, my girl, you must immediately sever your friendship with her."

"Nay, Uncle, I will not! She is the first true friend I have ever really had. Besides, if I cut her, will not people wonder why, when we have become so close in the queen's service? I would certainly think it strange of another."

"Perhaps you are correct, Catherine," he said, surprised at her astute insight. He had not thought her capable of such reasoning, but then she was a Howard. "Aye, very well, my girl, you may keep your friendship with Lady Wyndham. Yes, it is better that you do, I think upon reflection. That way no one will really be certain which of you the king will choose until we want them to know. But remember, girl, you cannot tell your friend what we have planned. Do you understand? No giggling girlish confidences in the Maid's Chamber at night."

"I understand completely, Uncle. I am not dim-witted," she answered him calmly. "If you are to succeed in placing me above all others in the king's affections, you need a clear path."

Again he was pleased, and he told her so. She was not quite as silly as he had previously believed. She had a sharp little mind, but her kind heart worried him. It could be her undoing. Time, he hoped, would take care of that weakness in her character. He dismissed her from his presence, and sent her on her way feeling quite satisfied with the afternoon's work.

He had placed one Howard on England's throne. If she had but heeded him, she might still be there with her head intact; but Mistress Anne had been overly willful and headstrong. Now he had, to his great amazement, been given a second opportunity to be the power behind a queen. This wench would not fail him. His family was about to climb higher than it had ever climbed, and would soon be the most powerful in all of England. The Seymours would fall back into the obscurity from which they came.

If Catherine would give the king another son, who knew what would transpire?

THOUGH deferential to the queen, the king now appeared to be openly paying court to two young women. Catherine Howard giggled and smiled up at the king with melting glances; but Nyssa Wyndham was more circumspect in her behavior. She was not quite certain exactly what the king's attentions meant. His open kindness of her had to be because of his long-lived affection for her mother. It could surely be nothing else. Yet the sly glances of the court made her very nervous. Even her aunt was disturbed.

"My God, Owen," Bliss declared to her husband in a soft voice one afternoon as they watched the king showing Nyssa how to notch her bow with just the right arrow. "He cannot possibly be romantically inclined toward her. It's horrifying! She is but a child!"

"So even your ambition has limits," her husband replied.

"Oh, Owen, do not scold me! It was different with Blaze," Bliss said. "It was entirely different!"

"Aye, the king only wanted Blaze for a mistress, as he had a wife. Now he still has a wife, a different wife to be certain, but he considers our niece for the next queen. Well, Tony did not want her to come to court. If you had not volunteered so gaily to chaperone Nyssa, she should not now be in this dangerous predicament," the Earl of Marwood severely reminded his wife. He had heard talk among the gentlemen of his acquaintance that Nyssa's coolness was far more challenging to the king than the little Howard girl's charms. He knew not how much truth there was to the talk, but he dared not tell his wife.

"Ohh, Owen, what shall we do?" Bliss said desperately.

"There is nothing we can do, my dear. Not now. It is all in the king's hands, I fear, and those hands are reaching out eagerly for a new sweetmeat. Perhaps he will favor the Howard girl over Nyssa."

"Nyssa is far lovelier!" Bliss said in defense of her niece, and her husband laughed till his sides ached.

"Madame," he told her, "you are mad, I think!"

They turned at the sound of the king's voice. He was smiling down at Nyssa, and to their surprise, he gave her a kiss on the cheek. "Very good, my sweet wild rose! What an archer she is, gentlemen. She is a veritable Diana, Goddess of the Hunt, is she not?"

His companions murmured their assent, smiling toothily.

"I do not think I could ever learn to shoot as well as Nyssa can," Catherine Howard said, smiling up at the king, and then she sighed. "I am not very clever, I fear, Your Grace."

"I do not believe that for a minute," Henry Tudor said. "Let me teach you to shoot, Cat. I believe there is little you cannot do if you but put your mind to it. You are a rose without a thorn, my dear." The king turned to his page. "A bow and quiver for Mistress Howard."

Once again the court was perplexed as to which one of the young women the king favored. Henry Tudor was obviously enjoying keeping them in suspense. As the terms of the dissolution of the king's marriage to Anne of Cleves were slowly being worked out, he was obviously preparing for a long sweet summer of sport.

The Bishop of Winchester sought out the Duke of Norfolk. "We cannot take a chance that he will choose the Wyndham girl," Stephen Gardiner said nervously. "Once he is free of Cleves, anyone can catch his fancy. We must act quickly to solidify your niece's position."

"Aye," the Duke of Norfolk agreed. "He is becoming like a young stallion let loose in a meadow full of pretty mares. We must fix his attentions upon Catherine, and Catherine alone."

"And how will you do that?" demanded the bishop.

"By discrediting Mistress Wyndham in his eyes," the duke said.

"By all accounts Mistress Wyndham is a virtuous young woman," the bishop replied. "Even I can find no fault with her, or her behavior. There is no gossip attached to her name, nor has she permitted any gentleman to single her out. Her manners cannot be faulted, and her loyalty to the queen is to be commended. She would appear to be the perfect gentlewoman."

"Yet, if she were found naked in the bed of an equally naked gentleman, my dear bishop, what do you think the king would say?" the duke answered with a small smile. "Appearances are often deceiving."

"God's blood, my lord, you cannot mean to destroy the maid's reputation? She has come to court to find a good husband. If you do what you propose, her reputation will be in shreds, and no man of decency will have her. I certainly cannot be a party to such a scheme!"

"Calm yourself, Stephen," the duke said. "I can discredit her, and at the same time supply her with an excellent husband that even her family will approve of, I assure you. I will tell you no more lest I discommode your conscience, but I swear to you that no real harm will come to the Wyndham girl. I simply need to remove her from the king's attentions. This is the only way in which I may successfully do it. Henry Tudor will want no other man's leavings. He will order Mistress Wyndham's marriage himself, I guarantee you. You must trust me."

The Bishop of Winchester said nothing more, but he thought placing trust in Thomas Howard was like placing one's trust in a fox with the key to the henhouse door. There was nothing he could do, he decided, and besides, the fate of one young girl could not be allowed to interfere with their plans to see that the Church remained conservative and orthodox in its beliefs and in its centuries-old traditions.

The Duke of Norfolk watched as the bishop moved away from him. How sickeningly pious he is, the duke considered. He cared not what happened to the Wyndham girl as long as his own power was preserved. Oh, he did not want to be involved in what he considered an un-Christian and immoral act; but he would not protest the benefits of such an act. Then Thomas Howard searched among the courtiers for one particular person. Finding him, he called to his personal page, "Go to the Earl of March, boy, and tell him I would see him in my privy chamber."

The duke turned away from the archery field and walked slowly back to the palace. Inside, he made his way to his own private apartments. A servant came forward with a cup of wine for him as he entered. Taking it, he told the man, "The Earl of March is expected. Show him to my privy chamber when he arrives, and make certain that we are not disturbed while he is with me." The duke then entered the private room he maintained for special meetings, and settled himself into a chair by the fire. There was a good blaze going, for though it was April, the day had a chill to it. Thomas Howard was always cold, and though he was parsimonious in many ways, there were always fires burning wherever he was in residence. He sighed deeply and sipped at his wine. He was sixty-seven years old this year, and he was beginning to grow tired of always having to watch out for his family, but his son could certainly not be expected to handle matters as well as he. Henry was a poet, not a tactician. Well, at least he had a son to carry on the Howard name.

I have sired four children, the duke thought, and two are dead. The meanderings of an old man, he decided, shaking himself. He drank deeply of his cup. He had become a father for the first time when he was fifteen, and what an uproar his illegitimate daughter, Mary Elizabeth, had caused. Her mother had been his distant, orphaned cousin, Bess, and she had died giving birth to their child. Bess had been only fourteen, but she had been one of his best friends. Her death had somehow changed him. He never again gave away his heart. Their daughter was raised by the family, for he would have it no other way. He arranged a good match for her. Mary Elizabeth had been married at twenty, the same year in which his first legitimate son, Thomas, had been born to Anne of York, and had died.

It had not been easy finding a suitable husband for Mary Elizabeth Howard. But as his family was rich and powerful, and because his daughter was formally recognized, a bridegroom had finally been obtained. Henry de Winter, Earl of March, was an ambitious man. Marriage to a Howard, even one on the distaff side who had been born on the wrong side of the blanket, offered advantages he otherwise would have been unable to obtain.

His family had never been an important one. Although they were comfortable, they were not rich by any means. Henry de Winter had not expected to fall in love with his wife, but he had done so. Hence his grief at Mary Elizabeth's death in childbirth, two years after their marriage, had been great. He had not remarried, and been somewhat confused as to how to raise the infant son he had been left. Fortunately, his father-in-law had involved himself in the matter.

Thomas Howard's first wife, Anne of York, had died in 1513. He had married Lady Elizabeth Stafford three years later. Their son, Henry, had been born the following year. A daughter had been born in 1520. His wife had insisted upon naming her Mary, and he dared not protest. Mary Elizabeth had been dead these ten years past, and what difference did it really make? But he never forgot his wife's insensitivity, for she had known of that first daughter, as she knew his grandson, who lived in his house.

There was a knock upon the door, and Varian de Winter, Earl of March, entered the duke's privy chamber. "Good day, Grandfather," he said. "What mischief are you up to now?"

"Help yourself to the wine," the older man said gruffly, "and then come sit opposite me. Varian, I need your help in a small matter."

Varian de Winter lifted an eyebrow questioningly as he poured himself a generous goblet of wine. His grandfather kept a good cellar, and had taught him to appreciate a fine vintage. He was obviously not so far off the mark. The old man was up to something. He sniffed at his wine, smiled, satisfied, and took a swallow even as he settled himself across from Thomas Howard. "Very well, my lord, I am listening."

He's got my long face and eyes, the duke thought, but the rest of him looks de Winter. How deceiving, for he is pure Howard in his thinking. "The land that was part of your mother's dowry," he began.

"The land you somehow never remembered to turn over to my father?" the earl said, his tone amused. "Aye, I know it."

"Would you like it if I signed it over to you, Varian?"

"At what price, my lord?" the earl said softly.

"Must there necessarily be a price between us, Varian?" the duke asked his grandson, his tone just faintly pained.

"Do you remember the first lesson you ever taught me, Grandfather?" the earl said. "You taught me, that which you can have for nothing, is worth nothing. That everything desirable has some price attached to it."

Thomas Howard laughed. "You learned well, Varian; certainly better than your uncle Henry. Very well, there is a price, but first I would know if you have pledged yourself to any woman."

"Nay," the earl said, growing more and more curious. "Why?"

"I have a match in mind for you, but it will involve a slight bit of danger. That is why I am willing to give you your mother's dowry lands in payment for this small deed. The girl I have in mind is an heiress with lands close to yours, in fact just across the river from you."

"What is it you want me to do, Grandfather?"

"I want your cousin, Catherine, to be England's next queen," the duke said quietly. His grandson's eyes widened just barely, but he remained silent, and Thomas Howard continued. "The king has recently begun to show her great favor. His marriage to the Flanders mare will soon be annulled. When it is, Catherine Howard must be the king's choice for a bride. One small thing stands in her way, however."

"Lady Nyssa Wyndham," the earl said. "I am privy to all the same gossip, Grandfather. The king dances between these two maids like a lad of sixteen. Nyssa Wyndham could as easily be England's next queen as my cousin Catherine, could she not? What is it he calls her? His wild rose? Well, let me tell you, Grandfather, that rose has thorns. She is as proper a young woman as I have ever met, and devoted to the queen."

"Your cousin, Cat, the king calls his rose without a thorn," the duke said. "We must see that Henry Tudor chooses the gentler of these two English roses, who is, of course, our Catherine. Nyssa Wyndham must lose the king's favor. I have a plan."

"I had not a doubt about that," the earl said with some humor.

"If the king were to discover Nyssa Wyndham in a gentleman's bed, his disappointment would certainly be great. Such a discovery would make it impossible for him to marry her, and leave the field wide open to our own little Catherine. It is a foolproof scheme, Varian."

"Except for one thing, Grandfather. The king would be quite apt in his anger and disillusionment to lop off his rival's head. Surely you are not suggesting that I be that rival?" the earl said.

"It is precisely what I am suggesting, but you need not worry about losing your head, my lad. In the eyes of the world, the king is a married man. He may take a mistress, of course, but that mistress cannot be a

young girl of good family. Such a thing, as you know, would be unaccept-
able. Therefore, though we know he is half courting these two maidens
despite his married state, we look the other way, and say nothing. If you
were to even hint that he was courting these maidens beneath his lawful
wife's nose, *then,* my dear Varian, you would be in danger of losing your
head. The king is a prude. He believes himself a righteous and virtuous
man. Though he will try to seduce a married woman, he would never
seduce a maid. For Henry Tudor, Catherine Howard and Nyssa Wyndham are his romantic ideal of innocence. Either one is the perfect bride for
him. He has but to choose. I wish to make his decision a simple one.

"If he finds that the Wyndham girl is not what he believed, his choice
will naturally fall upon our Catherine. As for Nyssa Wyndham, her family
sent her to court to see if she might find a husband. Naturally the king will
insist that because you have dishonored her, you must marry her. I will
concur with his decision, and apologize profusely for your behavior. The
king will have Catherine for his next wife, and you will have a pretty
heiress for your wife. Her family cannot object, as you will make things
right, and their daughter will be the Countess of March."

"And if I refuse you, Grandfather?" the earl demanded. "This is not as
simple as you try to make it sound. The king is unpredictable in his
temper, as you know. He could send both the girl and me to the Tower."

"If you refuse me, I shall have to find another man to do this deed for
me. Are you refusing me, Varian? You have never refused me before. I
have always been able to rely upon you," the duke said.

"Aye, you always have, Grandfather, haven't you? I have always done
your bidding, even when I felt you asked too much of me. Like the time
my uncle Henry seduced the daughter of one of your farmers, and she
hung herself when she discovered she was with child, and my uncle would
not accept his responsibility. The girl had never named her lover, but to
say he was of the duke's get. You asked me to accept the blame for that
crime, and I did so. I understood, even if Henry did not, that Norfolk's
heir must be a man with a spotless reputation for honorable behavior.

"Your gratitude was heartfelt, Grandfather, but the gossip surrounding that incident has caused decent families to practically hide their daughters from me. I am thirty years old, and cannot find a bride of equal birth
to give me sons. Now you ask me to put my neck upon the executioner's
block so that that silly little girl, Catherine Howard, can have her chance
to be queen. Was not one Howard queen enough?"

"If you do this for me, Varian, you will have a bride of more than equal
birth, and one whose family is famed for healthy children. Do not refuse

me! I would rather give this prize to you than another, if you would but take it. The girl is pretty enough, and rich to boot!"

Varian de Winter shook his head wearily. He had not a single doubt that his grandfather would do exactly as he said. If Varian refused to help him, the duke would find another man who would. He thought about Nyssa Wyndham, and remembered the dances they had shared several months ago. The girl was not simply pretty. She was spirited and intelligent. He had wanted to pursue her, but he had seen the writing on the wall when her uncle had been sent to fetch her, and she had later put him off firmly. Yet had he not vowed to himself that he would eventually have her?

He had seen little of her since that brief winter meeting, for she was devoted to the queen. Across the Great Hall; in the chapel; walking in the Knot Garden. He had not again approached her, though he had wanted to, for the first time he had seen her, she had, unknowingly, captured his heart. Now his grandfather was proposing a monstrous scheme to discredit the girl in the king's eyes so his cousin, Catherine, could be the next royal bride.

If he did not aid his grandfather, who would be chosen in his place? Would he treat the girl gently? It was cruel that a stranger should be chosen for the unsuspecting maid's husband, and wrong that her family should have no say in the matter. The thought of any man but himself possessing her sent his blood to boiling, but these thoughts he had kept to himself. Nyssa Wyndham was to be sacrificed for the Howard ambition. He could do but one thing.

"Must I forcibly dishonor the lass?" he queried of his grandfather.

"Nay," the duke said. "The girl will be drugged and carried to your bed, Varian. You will be discovered by her side. Whatever she may say in her defense will not be believed. She will be assumed guilty. The king will be outraged. Her family will be outraged. I will be the most outraged of all, and will insist to the king that you marry her at once before a scandal ensues. He cannot refuse, as the girl's reputation will be at stake. He can hardly publicly admit to his own interest in his wife's maid of honor, can he?"

"You had best not be wrong about this, Grandfather," the Earl of March said, resigned. "I think your ambition for little Catherine madness, and this is a bad business with Nyssa Wyndham. I am ashamed that I would aid you, but I would not see the girl sacrificed to some lout."

"Do you know her?" the duke asked him, curious.

"I danced with her once, and then her uncle hurried to take her away. Remember, the world believes me guilty of driving an innocent girl, who was carrying my child, to her death. I am not considered a particularly desirable match. She had charm, Grandfather. I hope I shall be able to win her over. The rest of my life shall be hell if I do not. A man and his wife should at least be friends."

"You have odd ideas, Varian, and I cannot imagine where you ever got them," Thomas Howard said. "You did not learn such things from me. A wife for a gentleman should have a dowry consisting of both lands and monies. Her bloodline should be good. Nothing else is required of a good match but that. Nothing else."

The Earl of March did not respond. In many ways he was like his powerful grandfather. He could be ruthless and cold like Thomas Howard. But beneath the veneer of arrogance, he hid a soft heart. That much his father had given him, even if he had given him precious little else. Henry de Winter had died when Varian was sixteen. Until his death he had never ceased talking about his Mary Elizabeth. Though he had never known her, Varian de Winter felt he *had* known her because of his father's deep love for her. Her portrait, painted as a wedding gift, hung in the earl's bedchamber. As a little boy he had thought she was the prettiest mother any lad could have. Now he was struck by how young and vulnerable she had been; much like Nyssa Wyndham—and because of that, he had to help Nyssa, even in this roundabout way.

"When is this deed to be done?" he asked his grandfather.

"Tonight," the Duke of Norfolk said.

"So soon?" the earl replied. "Grandfather, could you not give me a few days to attempt to make friends with Nyssa Wyndham?"

"You have already told me that her family has kept her from you, Varian. They are not likely to change their minds about you now. Why would they? I shall tell you another secret. Cromwell's fall is very near now. He will soon be in the Tower waiting for his miserable life to come to a traitor's end. We have not a great deal of time in which to act."

"But the king has only just created him Earl of Essex!" Varian de Winter exclaimed. Then his brow lightened. "Ahh, of course! The king lulls him into a false sense of security, does he not, Grandfather? A frightened Cromwell will not be able to do his best to extricate the king from this most undesirable marriage into which he got him."

"Precisely!" the duke answered, pleased at his grandson's astuteness. It's a shame he is not a Howard by birth, the duke thought. Varian has a courtier's mind, but unfortunately he has a countryman's heart. He only stays at court to please me, but once he is married he will have to leave, for the king will be very displeased with him for the moment. I will miss him.

The Earl of March noticed his grandfather was drawing his furred, velvet robe about him. He arose and put another log upon the fire. "Tell me how you will go about executing your plan, my lord?" he said.

The duke wasted few words. "Lady Rochford will administer a mild sleeping draught to all the maids of honor tonight. Then she will admit two of my men to the Maidens' Chamber. They will bring Nyssa Wyndham to your bedchamber. Once I am told she is safely there, I will see the king knows of it. We will discover the two of you together. Be sure to take the girl into your embrace when you hear us outside the door, Varian. The drug administered to her is very mild. She will most likely awaken when you embrace her. Her movement in your arms will not be seen as the struggles of a frightened girl; to other eyes she will look as if she is party to the deed. Under the circumstances, the king will have no choice but to reject her, leaving the field clear for your cousin. You may be assured that I will show my gratitude to you shortly after your marriage, Varian. You are truly the only one I can trust with this most delicate matter. I have always been able to rely upon you."

He is brilliant, Varian de Winter thought. At an age when most men sat back to enjoy what remained of life, Thomas Howard continued in the thick of things, plotting and scheming, each plan well thought out and perfect to the last detail. "If you wish my cooperation in this matter," the earl told his grandfather, "you will deed that land over to me this very afternoon, my lord. Unlike my father, God assoil his good soul, I know better than to trust you."

The Duke of Norfolk laughed aloud, which was something he rarely did. "That is because you are clever like a Howard, and not trusting like a de Winter, my lad!" he said, chuckling. "Very well, the deed will be in your hands by sunset."

"If it is not, Grandfather, I will not be party to your plan," Varian de Winter said. "And I trust your wedding gift will be a most generous one, despite my wicked behavior."

"Aye," the duke replied. "Now get you gone, lad! I have other work to be about this day. Yours is but a small part in my efforts to make your cousin Catherine Queen of England. There is much more to it."

"I have no doubt that there is," the earl answered, and bowing to his grandfather, he departed his privy chamber.

Varian de Winter's own bedchamber was within the apartments of the Duke of Norfolk, the small prerogative of being Thomas Howard's grandson and in Thomas Howard's favor at the moment. He had lived with his father at their ancestral home of Winterhaven until his sixth birthday. He had seen his grandfather Howard several times in his young life, and he remembered standing next to his father's chair, in his father's library, as his fate was being discussed on the day the great duke came to take him away.

"It is time he took his rightful place," the duke had said. "He has spent six years among the rustics, and has the manners of a cowherd. He is, after all, my only grandson."

"But he is *my* only son," Henry de Winter replied quietly, with a rare show of spirit. "I agree with you, however, my lord. I am content here among the rustics on my land, having seen what I wanted of the world. Varian should know what life has to offer before he decides how he wishes to live. I can think of no better place for him to learn the ways of the world than with you, my lord. Take him, but return him home each summer that he does not forget he is a de Winter by birth, and that he has responsibilities here on his lands as well. He is all I have, and I shall miss him."

So Varian had gone to live with his grandfather, and was raised with the two children that resulted from his grandfather's second marriage, neither of whom was even born at that point. Henry Howard was born the following year, and his aunt Mary the year he was ten. When his uncle Henry was fifteen, he impregnated the daughter of one of the duke's farmers. When the girl's condition became apparent, her father beat her in an effort to learn who had seduced his daughter. There would, of course, have to be a marriage. All the girl would admit to was, " 'twere one of his lordship's."

Then she secretly appealed to her lover, Henry Howard, arrogant, inexperienced, and frightened of what his powerful father would say and do, ashamed to admit his lust to his mother, had turned the girl away. The farmer's daughter hung herself in her father's barn to escape her sorrow and her shame, thereby causing a terrible scandal among the duke's people. They could talk of nothing else.

The Duke of Norfolk was furious. For all his faults, he was a fair man. When he had impregnated his cousin Bess, he had stood by her, although he could not marry her, being betrothed to another. His son had not shown the same strength of character. But then his grandson had agreed to take the blame to protect his younger uncle. No one considered that Varian de Winter had been home on his estates the summer the farmer's daughter had been seduced. Instead they remembered that the Earl of March's mother had been the duke's bastard daughter. They spoke of his saturnine handsomeness, and the ladies secretly imagined what it would be like to be his lover. Several found out, and not only relished the experience, but whispered about it among themselves. Marriageable maidens were kept away from him. He was believed to be an unsuitable and a dangerous man.

He had wanted a wife for some time now. Being the last of his line was a responsibility he did not enjoy bearing. He wanted sons and daughters, but the damned scandal would not die. No family of good lineage would discuss giving a daughter in marriage to a man who so callously had dismissed his obligations to a lover and their child.

It was only in retrospect that the Earl of March realized that he should not have taken the blame for what his fifteen-year-old uncle had done. Henry Howard's youth would have earned him forgiveness within their social strata, but Varian de Winter had been past twenty-one. It was believed a man of his years should have known better, particularly given his mother's history. Even his grandfather agreed now that they had made an error. But it was too late. Well, by the morrow he would have a wife, but he could not help feeling his method in obtaining that wife a shabby one.

Entering his bedchamber, he called to his body servant, who came from the dressing room where his clothing was kept. "When did we last change the sheets on this bed, Toby?" he demanded of the man.

"Entertaining tonight, are we, my lord?" Toby said with a chuckle. "Well, them sheets ain't been changed in two weeks or more. 'Tis past time, and if the lady is special, we should. I'll go to the duke's housekeeper and fetch some nice clean linens for ye."

"And I'll want a tub, Toby," the earl told his man.

"Aye, this one must be special." Toby chortled.

Toby, the earl thought, was fortunate to be a simple man. He had no idea how complicated life could be when one was not only a courtier, but the Duke of Norfolk's grandson. *Special.* Aye, Nyssa Wyndham was special. Even she, poor lass, could not even begin to imagine how special she was considered to be. God's blood! Varian grimaced. I hope Henry Tudor does not lop off both our poor heads.

No matter what his grandfather had said, the earl knew the king to be a volatile man. If Nyssa Wyndham was the woman the king really wanted for his next queen, there was going to be merry hell to pay. Even his pretty cousin Catherine would not be able to soothe the king's ire.

Why had he agreed to help Thomas Howard? Why had he not attempted to talk him out of this scheme? Had the debacle of his cousin Anne Boleyn not taught the duke anything? Nay, it had not. He had managed to keep his position as Lord Treasurer while the other men involved had lost everything, even their lives. The Duke of Norfolk loved power. It was both his weakness and his strength.

Varian de Winter knew why he had promised to help his grandfather. It was Nyssa Wyndham. The thought of her in another man's bed had shaken him greatly. *Why?* He didn't even know the wench, yet she had haunted his dreams since the first time he had seen her. He was in love with her. He shook his head in wonderment. How could he love a girl he barely knew? Yet he did, and somehow, some way, he was going to make her love him!

Nyssa, unaware of the consternation she was causing in the heart and mind of the Earl of March, dined with her aunt and uncle that day. Although she was due back at court by nightfall, she had spent her entire day with them. The lease on their Greenwich house would be up at the end of the month, and they discussed renewing it.

"I do not think you should," Nyssa said. "It is no secret any longer. Even the queen knows, though she pretends not to, that her marriage to the king will soon be a thing of the past. There will be an annulment, or divorce, whichever is decided. I will no longer be needed here at court. Go home, Aunt Bliss. I shall soon follow."

"Not if the king decides he wants you for his wife," Bliss said seriously. "His favor toward you is most marked. I believe that we should stay on so that you may have the counsel of your family."

"For once I am in agreement," Owen FitzHugh said.

"He favors Catherine Howard too," Nyssa said, "and her family is far, far more important than mine is. Besides, remember my mother's place in the king's life. He would never seek me out for such an exalted position because of the consanguinity involved, Aunt."

"Mary Boleyn was his mistress, and yet he married her sister," Bliss reminded her niece. "The Princess of Aragon was his brother's widow, and yet he had to have her for his wife. He is a man who seems to make the same mistake over and over again. Henry Tudor's relationship with your mother will not stop him if he desires you, Nyssa."

"Ohh, Aunt, I pray that you are wrong," Nyssa said. "I should rather die than be married to that old man! And how would my mother feel about such a thing? It would kill her, and my father too! Ah, did good Queen Anne not need me, I should ask her permission to go home this very day, but I cannot desert her, poor lady."

"I shall tell the landlord tomorrow that we wish to have the house through the end of June," Owen FitzHugh said. "You will not desert your mistress, Nyssa, and we will not desert you, my child."

Nyssa returned to court just as the sun was setting. There were no entertainments scheduled for that evening, and so she joined her friends in the Maidens' Chamber. The queen had retired early, the strain of her situation weighing upon her. The girls gossiped while playing cards.

"She is very sad that old Cromwell's fate should be so bleak because of her," Bessie FitzGerald said. "Her heart is very good."

"He would have fallen eventually," Kate Carey remarked with wisdom beyond her years. "Both he and Wolsey were of comparatively humble birth. Each climbed high, and gave their loyalty to no man save the king. Both incurred the jealous wrath of men like the Dukes of Norfolk and Suffolk. Such men, men without friends, have their fates sealed. Who is there to speak for them?"

"You would think the king would be loyal to those who are loyal to him," Nyssa said. "How can one expect loyalty when one does not give loyalty in return? Cromwell is a reptilian little man, but he has spent most of his life trying to make the king's life a happy one. This is his only failure. I feel sorry for him."

"It is too big an error in judgment for the king to forgive," Cat Howard said. "The king does not like those he trusts to make mistakes."

"I think I shall be glad to go home when this matter is finally settled," Nyssa said softly. "I miss my family, and my home. I want to see my parents. Like my mother, I am a country girl at heart."

"Perhaps you will not be allowed to go," Kate Carey said.

"Ohh, do not say it!" Nyssa cried, paling.

"Wouldn't you like to be a queen?" Cat Howard said slyly. "I know that I would! Imagine having everything you ever wanted, and the very least of your whims indulged at your demand, and the very people who have ignored you for months striving for your favor! The thought is very exciting. I should adore it!"

"Not I!" Nyssa said. "I would have a man to love me, and a home among the green hills of England, and a houseful of children! That is a dream far more to my taste than yours, Cat."

"But you haven't found a husband yet," Bessie FitzGerald said.

"No, I have not," Nyssa said with a small smile. "I have been so busy attending to my duties for the queen, I have had no time at all to seriously look the gentlemen over. But then few of them have even approached me. Perhaps they don't find me eligible enough."

"Oh, Nyssa, you are such a goose!" Cat Howard told her. "Have you not seen how my cousin, Varian de Winter, looks at you?"

"He is sooo handsome," Kate Carey sighed.

"My aunt, and her friend, Lady Marlowe, say he is a rogue, and that no respectable girl should associate with him," Nyssa said.

"Villains are far more fun than saints," Cat replied, and the others giggled at her witticism.

"Such happy maidens," Lady Rochford said as she entered the chamber, carrying a decanter and some small cordial glasses upon a tray. "What are you making merry about, or is it a secret?" She smiled, and Nyssa thought she looked like a ferret.

"We are speaking about the gentlemen," Cat said boldly.

Jane Rochford raised a slender eyebrow. "What naughty girls you all are," she said with an indulgent little smile. She looked about the room. "Where are the others?" she asked.

"The Bassetts are visiting their aunt overnight," Kate Carey volunteered. "Maria and Helga are sleeping in the queen's chamber this night. It is their turn. Her grace was sad this evening."

"Good," Lady Rochford purred. "Then there is no one to tell on me. Poor darlings! You strive so hard, and are all so good, and have so little amusement, I know. I have brought you all a little treat. Sweet cherry cordial, just made from French cherries, newly imported." She poured them each a small glass and offered her tray around. "Help yourselves, my maids."

"Are you not having any, Lady Rochford?" Bessie asked.

"Oh, child, I've already had two small glasses," Lady Rochford confided with a small hiccough. "If I drink any more, I shall be quite tipsy. It is really most delicious, is it not?"

They all agreed with her, eagerly sipping the fruit-flavored liqueur.

"It is late," Lady Rochford noted, "and you have all gossiped long enough. Ready yourselves for bed while you finish your cordial. I must take all the evidence of our treat away lest old Mother Lowe or Lady Browne come upon it and scold me for indulging you so." She smiled again. "It is rare for you to have such a quiet evening. You will want to catch up on your sleep, unless, of course, some of you are planning to slip out and meet your lovers?" She peered closely at them, and they burst into good-natured laughter at her teasing.

"Ohh, Lady Rochford," Kate said, "who among us has a lover, do you think? None, I fear!"

"Do not be so certain." Lady Rochford chuckled. "It is always the one you least expect, sweet Kate. Perhaps it is you!"

"Nay! Nay! Though I wish it were so, madame," the girl replied, laughing.

"Let me have a tad more of that cherry cordial," Bessie said. "Neither Lady Browne, who has gone to spend the night with her husband, nor Mother Lowe, who stays with the queen, is here to catch us."

Lady Rochford frowned. "Certainly not, Elizabeth FitzGerald," she said sternly. " 'Twas a treat, and you will be tipsy if you drink more. Now, be off with you, my maids." Lady Rochford shooed them to their beds saying, "There is no need to double up tonight, is there, with four gone? How nice to have a bed to one's self, even for a night."

Nyssa, who thought the cordial too sweet, had surreptitiously pushed her glass over to Bessie, who grinned conspiratorially. Nyssa had to agree with Lady Rochford about the sleeping arrangements. She could not get used to having to share a bed with another girl. She had always had her own bed her entire life. The others did not seem to mind, or if they did, they said nothing. Cat Howard had been raised in a dormitory for young girls at her grandmother Howard's house. Bessie had spent most of her life at court as the king's ward, and Kate Carey had a sister. Nyssa yawned. She was suddenly very sleepy, and so, it appeared, were the others. She drew the coverlet up over herself, her eyes closing even as she did so.

Lady Jane Rochford settled herself into a chair by the fire and waited, growing a bit sleepy herself with the warmth from the fire toasting her toes. An hour passed, and the girls were sleeping soundly. She arose and checked each of them individually. It was time. Taking a taper, she went to the chamber window that faced the courtyard and slowly waved the candlestick back and forth several times. Then she sat back down again in her chair to wait. Several minutes later she heard a soft scratching at the chamber door. Moving quickly, she opened the door and led the two men who entered to where Nyssa lay.

"That is the girl," she said softly. "Quickly now!"

One of the men picked up the slumbering girl, coverlet and all, and hurried from the Maidens' Chamber, the other going swiftly before him to be certain that no one saw them. Behind them Lady Rochford quickly closed the door. The two men moved swiftly through the dimly lit palace corridors, taking a roundabout route that was less likely to be patrolled by the king's guards, who would most certainly ask questions that they could not answer.

Nyssa's abductors were two of the most trusted of the Duke of Norfolk's men. They had been ordered to bring this girl to the Earl of March's bedchamber in secret. They had no idea what was afoot, nor would they have ever considered asking. They were servants, and servants, even those of long-standing, did not question their masters. Upon reaching their destination, they entered and deposited the girl upon the bed, as they had been ordered. There appeared to be no one else in the room, but the two men had completed their assignment, and so they left.

When the door closed behind them, Varian de Winter stepped from the shadows and walked over to the bed to look down at Nyssa. She was going to hate him, and he did not want her to hate him. He had wanted to court her, and win her honestly. He had wanted her family to consider him worthy of their daughter, but it was not to be. They would accept him because they would have no other choice. He would have to win them over. If only he could convince Nyssa not to hate him. Perhaps she would never love him, but he desperately did not want her to despise him.

She was wrapped in the coverlet that had obviously been on her bed. Carefully he untangled it from around her, and folding it up, hid it in the carved cabinet on the wall to the left of his bed. Opposite the bed a small fire burned in a tiled fireplace. The earl laid another log upon the fire, then drew off his velvet robe, throwing it over a chair. The flames played upon his long, lean body. Several of the women who had been his lovers claimed that he was like a piece of beautiful sculpture come to life. It both flattered and amused him.

Walking back over to the bed, he did what had to be done to make this charade convincing to Henry Tudor. He pulled the pink silk ribbons of Nyssa's chemise open, raised the girl halfway up and began to draw it off of her. She stirred restlessly. The flimsy little garment was soft. It slid easily down her delicate frame. He set her back to lie against the pillows. He struggled not to look too closely at her, but he had not the strength to resist. She was lovelier than any woman he had ever possessed. She had a long torso, and pretty, shapely legs. Her breasts were small but pert, and her skin looked as soft as the garment he had just divested her of a moment before. Her dark hair against her fair, fair skin made her look so vulnerable. If his conscience had plagued him before, it certainly ate at him now, but it was much too late to turn back. God help us all, he thought; me, and Nyssa Wyndham, and my poor cousin Catherine. No man is safe from the ambition of another man, and Thomas Howard is more ambitious than most.

Lifting her again, he slid her beneath the down coverlet and climbed into the bed next to her. She stirred once more, this time murmuring restlessly. The Duke of Norfolk would certainly be here at any moment with the king to discover Nyssa Wyndham lost in a moment of unbridled passion with the Earl of March. He raised himself on one elbow and gazed down upon his innocent victim. To his great surprise, Nyssa opened her violet-blue eyes. Her look was one of total confusion as she looked up at the velvet bed hangings and then at him.

"Am I dreaming?" she whispered, her heart beginning to hammer with fright.

"I wish I could say you were, sweetheart," he answered low.

Her eyes widened. Gasping, she clutched at the coverlet, peeping quickly beneath it. *"Ohhhh!"* Her shock was obvious as her cheeks reddened.

At that moment he heard movement outside the bedchamber door. Reaching out, he tangled his hand roughly in her hair and said, "Forgive me, Nyssa Wyndham!" Then his mouth came bruisingly down upon hers, even as the door to the room burst open and he heard his grandfather's voice say, "You see, Your Grace! I was not misinformed."

Henry Tudor could not believe his eyes. They bugged from his head. There she lay, a startled look upon her beautiful face, one perfect little breast exposed to his view, her ripe little mouth absolutely bruised with kisses. *Nyssa Wyndham!* His little country girl's daughter, as wanton a wench as her mother had been good and decent. It was patently obvious to him what was going on. It would have been obvious to anyone. "Madame!" he roared. "I would have an explanation for your disgraceful behavior, although I can think of no explanation that would excuse your lewdness!"

"Your Grace," Nyssa began, half sobbing. Where in God's name was she? How had she gotten here? The sensation of the Earl of March's leg against hers was exciting, but it shouldn't be.

"Silence, girl!" the Duke of Norfolk said. Then he turned his gaze to his grandson. "Varian, I am outraged that you would debauch an innocent maid of good reputation and family. You have gone too far this time, I fear. There is but one solution open to us to prevent a scandal and save this lady's heretofore good name."

"They're to go to the Tower! *Both of them!*" the king snarled.

"Wait, Your Grace," Bishop Gardiner said in conciliatory tones. He had been standing behind the duke, but now he moved forward with the Archbishop of Canterbury at his side. "There can be no scandal at this particular time in your court—particularly as it has been whispered that you favor this young woman."

"Favor Nyssa?" the king said. "Of course I favor her. She is the daughter of my friend, Blaze Wyndham. I promised Nyssa's parents that I would look after her as if she were one of my own daughters. God's blood, Gardiner! Certainly you did not think that I looked upon her with romantic intentions? If you did, you are a fool!" he shouted.

"No, no, Your Grace," the bishop said, nonplussed. The king had once again surprised him. Why was it he was always able to do that?

"I do not know how I came to be here," Nyssa cried out, but no one except the Archbishop of Canterbury heard her.

Thomas Cranmer saw the honest confusion on the girl's face. He noted the barely masked worry on the earl's handsome visage and knew instantly that there was some plot afoot. Since he could not imagine what it was, he kept his suspicions to himself. Lady Nyssa Wyndham's reputation must be protected. The girl was obviously innocent of any wrongdoing, although he would be hard-pressed to convince the king of it. Henry Tudor would only believe what he considered the evidence of his own eyes.

"Your Grace, there is but one remedy to this situation," the archbishop said in his soft, soothing voice.

The king looked questioningly at him.

"Lady Wyndham and Lord de Winter must be joined in matrimony this very night, before any word of this incident gets out. I am certain that Bishop Gardiner and the duke will agree with me, will you not, my lords?" The archbishop smiled gently, encouragingly, at them.

"Of course, of course, my lord," the bishop said.

"He's right, though 'tis not often I agree with the archbishop," the duke said. "We can silence the gossip by saying my grandson fell in love with the chit; that the king gave his permission for them to marry, and that because of your grace's own marital difficulty, they chose to be married by the archbishop quickly and quietly so they might continue to serve you and the queen during this difficult time for you both."

"If you were an animal, Tom, you would be a fox," Henry Tudor said grimly. He turned to the couple abed and said to the earl, "How long has this been going on beneath my very nose, my lord?"

"Lady Wyndham only came to my bed this night, Your Grace," Varian de Winter answered truthfully.

"And have you breached her defenses yet, or did we arrive in time, sirrah?" The king was very angry, but he was not certain which of them angered him more. He had certainly thought better of Nyssa Wyndham, but then these young women today were not like their mothers.

"I am a virgin!" Nyssa said furiously, glaring at them all. "I do not know how I came to be here, Your Grace, *but I did not come to his bed!* I do not know how I got here!"

"Madame," the king said coldly, "your mother never lied to me. I am sorry that you see fit to do so."

"I am not lying!" Nyssa almost wept.

"Madame, am I a fool?" the king roared angrily. "Is that what you think of your sovereign? I find you naked as the day your sweet mother bore you, in the bed of an equally naked man. Am I to believe that you came here by magic? If you indeed did not come here willingly, or under your own power, then how did you come here, Nyssa Wyndham? Answer me that? How came you to the Earl of March's bed?"

"I do not know!" she sobbed.

"Your Grace," the archbishop said quietly, "I think perhaps it would be wise to send for Lady Wyndham's aunt. Her guilt has obviously overcome her, and she is in need of female comfort. In the meantime, Bishop Gardiner and I will repair to the Chapel Royal to make our preparations for the wedding of these two young people. I know that they are both distressed to have caused your grace such acute suffering."

"Aye, go along, both of you. I want them married within the hour," the king said, glaring at the couple. "I will witness their nuptials myself, as will the duke. In the morning, Lord de Winter, I shall expect to see proof of Lady Wyndham's defloration. You will marry her, and you will remain married to her. There will be no excuse for an annulment. Do you understand me, my lord?"

"Aye, Your Grace, completely, but I assure you that I am eager to marry Lady Wyndham, and will endeavor to be a good husband to her in all ways. We will name our first son after you, will we not, sweetheart?"

"I will not marry this man!" Nyssa shouted. "I do not love him! I do not even know him! I will only marry for love!"

"You knew him well enough to creep into his bed!" snapped the king. "God's blood, wench! Who the hell do you think will marry you if not de Winter once this scandal is out, and it will get out, I assure you. The walls have ears, you may be certain. You are ruined, girl. I gave your mother my solemn word that I would care for you and keep you safe. You have made your bed, by God, and now you will lie in it. You will accept the consequences of your actions! There is no other choice, Lady Wyndham. You will marry Varian de Winter because I, your king, order you to marry him. To disobey my order is treason. Your mother has always been my most loyal servant, and I expect no less of you, Nyssa Wyndham." He sighed. "At least the man is of equal birth to you. I can but hope you are satisfied with your choice, girl, for you have no option in this matter now. You will be married to this man within the hour." So saying, Henry Tudor departed the earl's bedchamber in the company of the Duke of Norfolk.

For several long moments the silence within the room was thick. Then Nyssa said to the man by her side, "How came I here, my lord?"

"Not now, Nyssa," he said grimly.

"I have a right to know!" She did not look at him, and her voice was ragged with her emotion. "I went to sleep in the Maidens' Chamber. I awoke here to find myself in the center of a maelstrom."

"I promise that I will tell you, but not now," he said. "I know that under the circumstances I have not the right to ask it of you, but please, Nyssa, trust me. You will not come to any harm."

Now she turned to look directly at him. "Trust you, my lord? Why should I trust you? Your reputation is foul, and whatever has happened here tonight has done little to reassure me otherwise. No! I do not trust you. Indeed I think I could hate you for your part in this charade. My parents always promised me that I should choose my own husband. Now it seems that decision has been taken from me by strangers, and I would know why. I think you owe me that."

"And more," he agreed, "but I cannot tell you now. You will have to accept that, and be patient."

"Patience is not one of my long suits, my lord," she warned him. "You have much to learn about me."

"How old are you?" he asked her.

"Seventeen, the last day of December past," she answered. "How old are you, my lord? Are you very old?"

"I will be thirty the last day of this month," he replied, smiling at her. There was so much he needed to learn about Nyssa Wyndham.

He has a nice smile, she thought; neither too broad nor too thin. I could almost like him. *Almost.*

"Where do you live when you do not live at court?" she asked.

"My estates are across the river Wye from your house at Riverside," he said. "Until recently I did not possess the river frontage, but now I do. My house is on a hill a mile from the water. My estate is called Winterhaven. Your uncle, Lord Kingsley's lands, partly border it."

"Why have we never met before I came to court?" she asked him. She was surprised, nay amazed, at her calm.

"Because I have lived with the Duke of Norfolk's household since I was six years old. My father, Henry de Winter, the previous earl, died when you were just a very little girl. I come to Winterhaven only for a few weeks each summer to escape the court, and to be private. I have never entertained, or socialized with my neighbors there. Had I, we might have met before you came here. I hope you will not be disappointed, but I should very much like to leave the court and live in the country, Nyssa. I know this must be exciting for a young girl, but I am weary of it all."

"I had planned to go home once this business with the king's marriage was settled. My mistress will not need me when she is no longer Queen of England," Nyssa said. "I will not be unhappy to leave court." It was not calm she felt. It was cold. She suddenly realized she felt cold. Was she in shock? Or was she simply stunned with outrage?

There was a knock upon the chamber door, but before the earl might say "Enter," Bliss FitzHugh rushed in, her beautiful blue eyes wide at the sight of her naked niece in bed with the Earl of March.

"Ohh, Nyssa," she said, nearly weeping. "What have you done, my child? I have just received the most dreadful scolding from the king himself. He says you must marry immediately." She turned her gaze on Varian de Winter. "You are a scoundrel, my lord, to have seduced an innocent maid! At least this time you will not be able to leave her with child, to kill herself over the shame of your betrayal!"

"As we are to be related, madame," Varian de Winter said with as much dignity as an unclothed man might muster, "I will overlook your thoughtless remarks. You have been misinformed by that great gossip, Adela Marlowe, I am most certain. When we know each other better, I shall enlighten you with the truth. I assume you can recognize the truth, Lady FitzHugh."

Bliss gasped, and Nyssa could not help the little giggle that escaped her. It was not often that someone could set her aunt back on her heels so firmly and neatly.

"You dare to laugh, mistress?" Bliss said, outraged. "Your parents will be heartbroken when they learn of your behavior. Get out of that bed, Nyssa Wyndham! You are to be married at once, and I do not know what you can wear under such circumstances as these!" She snatched up Nyssa's little silk shift and threw it at her. "As for you, sirrah, get some clothing on this instant unless you intend to be wed to my niece in the altogether!" She glared fiercely at them both.

The Earl of March, sheepishly pulling the coverlet about his loins, climbed gingerly from his bed and slowly backed into the dressing room where his clothing was hanging. Nyssa pulled her shift over her head and climbed from the bed.

"Well," Bliss said, "he's handsome, I'll give him that. At least his blood is noble. *A Howard!* You've caught a big fish in your net, my child!"

"I did not catch him at all," Nyssa said irritably.

Bliss paid absolutely no attention to her niece. "What can you wear? Oh, lord! The king said you were to come immediately to the chapel. What are we to do? You cannot stand before the archbishop in your shift!" Her blue eyes suddenly lit up. "Of course! You can wear my cloak over your chemise. It's trimmed in fur, and the rose velvet is very flattering to you. Your hair needs brushing, Nyssa. My lord," she called out. "I shall need a brush to neaten Nyssa's hair." She fussed about her niece, settling her ermine-trimmed cape over Nyssa's shoulders, fastening it shut with the small gold frog closures. Bliss snatched up the brush that Varian de Winter handed her and vigorously removed the tangles from the girl's lovely dark hair. Then suddenly she began to weep. "Ohhh, your mother will never forgive me for letting this happen to you! And to not be at your wedding!

Tony will be simply furious, my child. You know how he dotes upon you. He did not want you to come to court."

Nyssa said nothing for the moment. She let her aunt babble on, for it would have been impossible to get Bliss to cease. I have imagined my wedding my whole life, Nyssa thought, but I could have never imagined anything like the reality I now face. Am I dreaming? She pinched herself, but she was not dreaming. This was truly happening. Her aunt's strident tones brought her back to the present.

"My lord de Winter!" Bliss's beautiful face was the picture of perfect outrage. "Surely you are not going to your wedding dressed in such a manner? This matter is scandalous enough as it is!"

"I do not choose to outshine my bride, madame," he answered her calmly. "To do so would be unforgivable. Unless Nyssa has some objection, I will remain as I am. What say you, Lady Wyndham?"

For the first time since this dreadful affair had burst upon her, Nyssa truly liked Varian de Winter. Whatever else he might be, he was a man with a sense of humor. He stood before her in a white silk nightshirt, over which he wore a deep green velvet robe trimmed with dark sable. His feet were as bare as hers.

Nyssa giggled, much to her aunt's mortification. "I am content with your garb, sir. It seems appropriate to this particular occasion." She curtsied to him, and he bowed in return.

Bliss sighed dramatically. "Then there is no help for it," she said, "and if we keep the king waiting much longer, all our heads will roll, I fear. Come along, both of you. We have a wedding to go to. Ohhh, Nyssa! I can but imagine what your parents will say! Hurry now! Your uncle is awaiting us outside the door. He did not want to come in for fear of embarrassing you, but you do not seem the least ashamed of your actions this night. I do not understand you at all!" She bustled from the room, her skirts flying about her.

"Is all of your family like that?" Varian asked Nyssa.

"You will shortly learn if they are," she responded. "I realize that we have both been trapped into this marriage, my lord. When it is finally fact, I will look forward to your explanation as to why."

CHAPTER 6

I SHALL hear Lady Wyndham's confession privately before I administer the sacrament of marriage," the Archbishop of Canterbury said calmly. "You, Bishop Gardiner, will shrive Lord de Winter."

"Can we not just get on with it," the king grumbled. The Chapel Royal was chilly at midnight, and his leg ached damnably.

"Your grace cannot think that I would allow these two young people to enter into matrimony without observing all the proprieties," Thomas Cranmer said, just the barest touch of censure in his voice. "Particularly under the circumstances that have brought us here tonight. I have, after all, waived the banns."

"Oh, very well!" the king consented irritably, "but do not dally." He glowered at Nyssa. "Remember, madame, you have far more important sins to tell this priest than the envy of another's gown, or an unkind word to one of your fellow maids. And be quick about it!"

Bliss clung nervously to her husband's arm. Ohh, why had she not listened to her brother-in-law and to her mother! If she had not insisted upon chaperoning Nyssa to court, none of this would be happening. Her family would never let her forget it, particularly her husband. From now on, whenever she decided upon a course of action that he disapproved of, he would surely bring up this incident. She peeped up at Owen to see what he might be thinking, but his handsome face was serene and without emotion. Damn him for a smug bastard!

The Earl of Marwood could feel his wife's great disquiet as she fidgeted by his side. He restrained a smile. It served her right! Bliss always wanted to have her own way in everything. Well, at least she would behave herself for a few weeks before she totally forgot her part in this affair. He himself would not have been half as calm as he now was had he not been inquiring discreetly about the Earl of March over the past few weeks. The earl's interest in Nyssa had not escaped him.

Varian de Winter had not quite struck him as a cad. Owen FitzHugh's interest had gained him the knowledge that although there had been one rather unpleasant scandal regarding the gentleman, there had been no other. He was in favor with his grandfather, the powerful Duke of Norfolk; he paid his gambling debts; and his few love affairs were limited to the kind of women who indulged in such affairs. It was said among the gentlemen that Varian de Winter would marry but for the fact that the ladies of the court would not allow his youthful indiscretion to be forgotten.

Owen FitzHugh knew that there was something far more sinister to this "discovery" of his niece in the gentleman's bed tonight, and the hasty wedding about to be performed. How had Nyssa been cajoled into that bed? The girl was not the flighty sort of flibbertigibbet who could be seduced. And how had the king known to seek her in Varian de Winter's bedchamber? He did not think Nyssa was a part of the plot.

The archbishop escorted the bride-to-be into a small private room off the chapel. She knelt respectfully before him. Taking her cold little hands in his warm ones, he said, "Now, my child, you are protected here by the law of the confessional. I shall repeat nothing of what you tell me, but on peril of your immortal soul, Nyssa Wyndham, I want the truth from you. How came you to the Earl of March's bed this night, and why?" His gray eyes bore into her eyes.

"My lord archbishop," Nyssa answered him, her gaze not flinching, "I swear to you that I know not how I came to be in the Earl of March's bed. I went to sleep in my own bed in the Maidens' Chamber. When I awoke, I was in the earl's bed and he was leaning over me. I swear to you that this is the truth. I swear it on my deceased father's honor!"

"Will you swear it on your eternal soul, my child?" Thomas Cranmer asked her softly. When she nodded vigorously, he said, "Tell me again exactly what you remember of this evening."

"There were only four of us tonight in the Maidens' Chamber," Nyssa told him. "Cat, Bessie, and Kate were with me. We gossiped and played at cards. Then Lady Rochford came in bearing a tray. It was a treat, she told us. A secret we must not reveal lest we get her in trouble. We agreed, and she served us tiny glasses of a most delicious cherry cordial. Lady Rochford would not give us more than a single serving for she claimed it was potent and had made her tipsy. Bessie wanted more, but she would not relent. When Lady Rochford wasn't looking, I let Bessie have the rest of mine, for I thought it was too sweet. Then we all disrobed and retired for the night. 'Tis all I remember."

"Nothing more, my child?" he gently encouraged her.

"Well," Nyssa said, "I can vaguely recall a feeling of floating, and when I opened my eyes, I saw velvet bed hangings above and around me. Our beds do not have velvet hangings in the Maidens' Chamber. Then I saw a man's face staring down into mine. I asked him if I was dreaming. He said I was not, and then he said, 'Forgive me, Nyssa,' and he kissed me. It was at that moment that the king burst in with the others," she finished. "There is nothing more, my lord archbishop, but I swear to you that I am no wanton to seek a strange man's bed! You must believe me!"

"I do, my child," he said, and indeed he did. Lady Jane Rochford. The Earl of March. There was a common denominator here, and it was Tom Howard. What mischief was the duke bent upon, and why had it involved ruining the reputation of an innocent maiden? This is a strange conundrum, the archbishop thought to himself. I will need time to puzzle it all out, but eventually I will learn the truth. "Kneel, Nyssa Wyndham, and I will absolve you of your sins," Thomas Cranmer said. Poor child, he said to himself as he blessed her. What have you become involved in?

The archbishop escorted the bride back out into the Chapel Royal, where, assisted by Bishop Gardiner, he quickly married her to Varian de Winter. Her uncle, the Earl of Marwood, acting in her father's stead, gave her away. Her aunt wept copiously. The Duke of Norfolk seemed too pleased with this situation, while the king continued to look furious.

When the two clerics had finished their task, the king said in surly tones, "You will no longer be considered a maid of honor, madame. Your marriage makes that impossible, as you must surely know."

"Of course, Your Grace," Nyssa said softly, "but I would ask your leave to remain in the queen's service for the present. She does need me now."

The girl is no fool, Henry Tudor thought, but then neither had her mother been a fool. Nyssa certainly knew the future Anne of Cleves faced, but she wanted to remain by her mistress's side until the end. He approved of her loyalty. His voice softened a trifle as he said, "Very well, madame. When you inform the queen of your marriage tomorrow, you may tell her I will allow you to remain in her service for the present."

"You are most generous, Your Grace," Nyssa said, curtseying.

"Aye," the king responded. "I am generous to you. I should not be, madame. Your shameless behavior this night does not merit my kindness. Still, for the sake of your sweet mother, I am prepared to be forgiving. Be as good a wife to your husband as your mother is to her husband. That will please me, Nyssa." He gave her his hand, and she kissed it, curtseying again as she did so. The king smiled briefly, then turned to the Earl of March. "Remember, I will expect proof in the morning that this marriage has been consummated, my lord," he said grimly. "If I have the slightest doubt, Dr. Butts will be called upon to examine your wife." Then he turned abruptly and left the chapel, followed by the two clerics.

"I do not know what to say to you," Bliss told her niece.

"Good night, Aunt," Nyssa replied. "Good night, Uncle."

Owen FitzHugh gripped his wife by the elbow and hustled her from the Chapel Royal before Bliss might recover her composure.

Now there were but three people in the king's chapel.

"You have done well, Varian," the Duke of Norfolk congratulated his grandson. Reaching out, he caught Nyssa's chin between his thumb and his forefinger. His cold dark eyes looked into her soft violet-blue ones. He was amused to find she would not look away. A brief wintry smile touched his mouth. "She is a beauty, my boy, and as you said, she has spirit. You'll get strong sons from her."

Nyssa pulled angrily away from his grasp. "*You*, my lord, are, I assume, responsible for this marriage," she said scathingly. "I think I am entitled to an explanation from you!"

"Take your wife to bed, Varian, and make a woman of her," the duke said coldly, and then he was gone.

"Ohhh, he is the most arrogant man!" she fumed.

"He is," her new husband agreed, "but he is also brilliant, and loyal to his family." He took her by the hand. "Come along now, sweetheart. We do not want to be discovered by anyone in our nightclothes wandering about the palace. There will be speculation aplenty about our marriage as it is. I know a shortcut back."

"Back to where?" she asked him as they hurried along, hand in hand.

"To my grandfather's apartments, where we have our bedchamber," he told her calmly. "I have some good red wine, and we will toast our union, as no one else has bothered to do so for us."

Nyssa suddenly realized that her feet were cold. They made a faint little slapping noise as she hurried along next to Varian de Winter. She wondered if his feet were cold too. *She was married. She was a bride. How had it happened? She had to know!* They reached their destination, and as the door closed behind them, she whirled about.

"Tell me now, my lord! Tell me how I came to your bed tonight, and why? There can be nothing between us until I know," Nyssa said.

"I will never lie to you, Nyssa," he said seriously. "The cordial Lady Rochford brought to the Maidens' Chamber tonight was laced with a light sleeping draught. It was believed that you were possibly too deep in the king's favor. Once his union to Queen Anne is undone, he will be required to marry again. It was feared that you might be his choice."

"Feared by whom? The Duke of Norfolk?" she demanded. "My dreams have been snatched from me, and I wish to know for certain who the thief is, my lord."

"You are right in naming my grandfather," the earl answered her. "There is another whom he thinks will make a more suitable wife for the king." Varian de Winter sighed deeply. "Thomas Howard is an ambitious man. Ambitious for himself, and ambitious for his family, Nyssa. I do not always agree with him, but I owe him my loyalty, and I love him despite all his faults. My mother was his bastard, yet he raised her lovingly, and saw to it that a good match was made for her despite her accident of birth. She died shortly after I was born, yet Grandfather did not desert me. He came every year to Winterhaven to see me. He always remembered my birthday and Twelfth Night with gifts. When I was six, he took me into his own household to raise. He is not always kind. Sometimes he is even cruel. But I love him even as he loves me. Can you understand that, sweetheart?"

"So because of Howard ambition," Nyssa said angrily, "I have had my dreams torn from me! All my life I dreamed of the man I would marry, and the wedding we would celebrate with our happy families in attendance. I would wear a gown of white satin, silver tissue, and pearls. There would be flowers in my hair. Papa would give me away in the same church where my father formally married my mother." She brushed the tears from her eyes.

"There would be a great feast on the lawns of *RiversEdge,*" she continued. "All my family would be there: my grandparents, my aunts and my uncles; my cousin, Mary Rose, would attend me, along with some of the littler cousins. We would dance, and Violet, my old nurse, would weep, foolish creature. And my bridegroom, my lord—he would be a man who knew and loved me. A man I loved. A man my family would respect. Now I will have none of that because your grandfather believed the king lusted after me. Thomas Howard has a more suitable candidate than Nyssa Wyndham for Henry Tudor's bed and crown. My reputation must be discredited in the king's eyes to serve Howard ambition. God damn you for it, Varian de Winter! And God damn your grandfather as well!" She burst into tears.

He reached out to draw her into his embrace, but Nyssa jumped back like a scalded cat. "Do not dare to touch me, my lord! I hate you! You and your family's overweening ambition have destroyed my life!" She angrily wiped the tears from her face with the back of her hand.

"Destroyed your life? How have I destroyed your life?" he demanded. "By marrying you? Who else would have had you under the circumstances, madame?" This was not going at all as he had anticipated.

"The *circumstances,*" Nyssa answered him coldly, "were not of my making, my lord. How easily you forget it."

Varian de Winter drew a deep breath, then said to her, "The day you came to Richmond, and I stared so boldly at you across the Great Hall at Hampton Court, I fell in love with you."

Nyssa gasped with surprise. Then she replied, outraged, "How dare you say such a thing to me! A man in love with a woman does not compromise her reputation as you have done mine."

"I love you enough that I allowed my grandfather to use me in this wild plot of his lest another be chosen to disgrace you, Nyssa," he told her. "Do you think the great Duke of Norfolk cared about what happened to you? My grandfather cared nothing for your fate. When he first brought this scheme to my attention, I tried to dissuade him. When I was unable to do that, I agreed to aid him when he threatened to choose another. I thought his design wrong for many reasons, but what if he had chosen a man of low degree to ruin you? Then your reputation would have been truly destroyed. Had you been caught with a guardsman, there would have been no one to marry you, despite your wealth. Instead, this sudden marriage between us will be but cause for good gossip which will shortly die away, particularly as I mean us to leave court. If we are not here, then something else will distract the gossips." There! Certainly he had explained it so that she would understand, and he had admitted his love for her. He held out a hand to her, but Nyssa slapped it away.

"Now I see the crux of it," she said scathingly. "Your grandfather has managed to forward his plans and gain you a rich wife in the bargain. I am not surprised, my lord, that you agreed to aid him in his wickedness.

Who else would have me? *Rather, who would have you?* Your reputation is so black that no decent parents would entrust their daughter in marriage to you, a man who deserted his mistress and caused her death. Only by deceit could you gain a respectable wife, sir!" Nyssa glared at him furiously. This was certainly not how she had imagined she would spend her wedding night; but then this was not how she had imagined she would be married either.

To his credit, he did not lose his temper, although it was near to boiling over. Yet she was correct in many ways, and he could not blame her for his past. "I told you that I would never lie to you, Nyssa. What I am about to tell you is the truth, but it must be kept secret, for so it has always been and must remain. Will you agree to keep what I say between us, madame?"

Nyssa nodded slowly. She was curious as to what he would reveal to her. Having had her say, she felt her anger beginning to drain away, for she was a practical girl. What was done was done, and there was nothing that could change it. "I will keep your secret, my lord, unless, of course, it is treasonous. If that is the case, it would be better not to tell me."

"There is no treason involved," he said quietly, and then he offered her his hand once again. "Come, madame, let us sit by the fire while we continue our discussion. I find I am growing cold, and surely you must be."

She nodded and slipped her fingers into the hand he offered, which then closed firmly over hers. Leading her across the room, he drew her down into his lap even as he sat himself in a large, tapestry-backed chair. Startled, Nyssa struggled a moment to regain her feet.

"Nay, madame," he told her, his grip upon her firm. "I have a tale to tell, but it will be told my way, and I would have you here in my arms as I tell it. Cease your attempts to escape me, or," he threatened softly, "I will be forced to take stronger measures."

"What measures?" she demanded.

"I shall spank you," he said calmly.

Outrage flooded Nyssa's being. "You would not!"

"Tempt me not, madame," he warned her.

"You are most hateful," she replied, but she was quiet in his lap now. "Spank me, indeed! I am not a child."

Varian de Winter restrained himself from smiling. Nay, he thought to himself, you are not a child, Nyssa. You are the most delicious armful I have ever held, and I long to possess you.

"Well, sir?" Her voice brought him back to reality.

"My tale," he began, his cheeks flushing as he wondered if she might have guessed his thoughts, "is a relatively simple one. When my uncle, Henry Howard, was but fifteen, he had a pretty lover. She was not his first, mind you. I, myself, had caught Henry beneath a hedgerow with a milk-maid when he was just twelve. This girl, however, found herself with child. When her family realized it, they sought to learn the father's identity. All the girl would say was that her lover was of the duke's family. She sought Henry out in secret and pleaded with him for help, but he was afraid of what his father would say. He sent the girl away. The poor little wench hung herself. When her outraged family came to my grandfather to demand remuneration for loss of their daughter, I accepted the blame for my uncle's crime. I did not want the boy saddled with that burden. He was so young."

"Not so young that he could not dip his wick in any honey pot conveniently offered to him," Nyssa said tartly.

"I should have allowed Henry to take his own punishment," Varian de Winter continued. "It never occurred to me that the scandal would not be allowed to die down after so many years."

She did not know whether she believed him or not. Were men in this day and age really that noble? Perhaps he was just lying to her in order to gain her sympathy. Did she dare to trust him? She wasn't certain. "How could your grandfather have allowed you to take the blame for his son's crime?" she asked him. "It was very wrong of him, my lord. Your uncle was but a boy. He would have eventually been forgiven, but certainly a grown man could not be. Only a true villain would do what you are alleged to have done. I am not surprised no decent families would allow their daughters to be associated with you."

"My grandfather," the Earl of March said quietly, "cares only for his family, and their advancement. He does what he believes he must do on their behalf. Still, for all his faults, he is a loyal Englishman."

"Who is the other woman?" she asked suddenly, changing the subject entirely. "Who is the woman the duke would make queen? The woman for whom I was sacrificed?"

"My cousin, Cat," Varian de Winter replied.

"Ohh, poor Cat!" Nyssa said softly as her eyes teared.

He brushed her dark hair away from her face, agreeing, "Aye, poor little wench, but if I tell you she is willing, will you be very surprised, for willing she is."

Nyssa shook her head. His soft touch had startled her. "Nay," she answered him. "I am not surprised. She has the Howard ambition, does Cat. Perhaps she will make the king happy, though."

"Are you still angry with me?" he asked her.

She turned her head so that she might look into his face, and was a bit nonplussed by how close his lips suddenly were. "I am not certain if I am yet angry with you, my lord," she told him honestly. "I think we both be victims of Howard ambition. When my service to Queen Anne is at an end, then we may go home and be done with Howard ambition. Your mother may have been a Howard, but you, my lord, are a de Winter. It is time that your ambitions were reserved for the de Winters, and not for the Howards."

All his life he had felt that there was something missing, and now he knew what it was. It had been a woman. Not just any woman, but a woman who would put his interests, and the interests of his family, above all else. That influence had never been there, and he hadn't even missed it until she had spoken so strongly to him. He had tried so hard for his grandfather's sake to be a Howard, but he was not a Howard. He was Varian de Winter, the fifth Earl of March.

Smiling down at her, he said, "My grandfather has thrown us together for expediency's sake, Nyssa, but he has done me the greatest kindness ever, and he does not even know it." His dark green eyes were suddenly warm.

"What kindness has the duke done you?" she asked him, shifting nervously in his lap. She could not break the gaze between them.

"He has given me you," Varian de Winter said low, and then he took a lock of her dark hair between a thumb and a forefinger, rubbing it between the two digits, enjoying the sensuous softness of it. Then raising that lock to his lips, he kissed it.

Her throat felt suddenly tight, and her heart beat a quick tattoo. She was very, very aware of their closeness to each other.

Slowly he reached up and unfastened the gold frog closures on the rose velvet cloak she wore, pushing the heavy fur-trimmed fabric back, exposing her chemise. His hand caressed her face, his fingers trailing lingeringly down the smooth, warm column of her neck. "The king has ordered that we consummate this marriage tonight, Nyssa. If it were in my power, we would get to know one another better first. I wanted to court you properly, the way a man courts a woman he admires and hopes to wed one day. When we first met, I hoped to have that opportunity, but your family was so protective of you. Now we are legally bound together as man and wife, and none of it is as I would have had it. The king will have proof that our union is made complete on the morrow nonetheless. If he does not get it we will end up in the Tower."

"How fortunate for Henry Tudor," Nyssa said sharply, "that the Duke of Cleves did not demand such proof of his sister's consummation from our hypocritical sovereign." She was beginning to grow a trifle frightened. Varian de Winter was handsome, and he was being most charming, but he was still a virtual stranger.

"Tell me what your mother has told you of passion between a man and his wife," Varian de Winter said as he tipped her gently from his lap and stood up. Taking her cloak from her, he laid it across the chair, then, undoing his own garment, he put it with hers, the dark green and rose velvets lying against each other, the sable and ermine furs mingling.

Nyssa stared at him, wide-eyed. "My mother thought no knowledge necessary until my marriage contract was settled," she said, recovering herself. "The women in the queen's apartments gossip, of course, but I know not what is truth and what is not. I fear, my lord, that I am woefully ignorant of such things as passion, having never before experienced it. I have never had a suitor."

She is a true virgin, he thought. Of course she would be. It was to be expected of a respectable maid from a good country family. When he had kissed her earlier in the evening, it had been for the benefit of the king. When their lips had briefly met at the command of the archbishop at their wedding, it had also been for the benefit of others. Now he tipped her heart-shaped face up, kissing her for their mutual benefit and pleasure. Her mouth softened beneath his. It was a good start.

She did not close her eyes when he kissed her, he saw, amused, as he opened his. "It is nicer when you close your eyes," he said.

"Why?" she wondered aloud.

He thought a moment, and then said, "I do not know, but it is, Nyssa. Would you like to try again with your eyes closed?"

In answer to his query, she closed her eyes and pursed her lips up at him. When he chuckled, her eyes flew open. "What is the matter?" she demanded of him. "Why do you laugh at me?" As if I were not nervous enough, she thought indignantly. He doesn't have to be so damned superior.

"I am not laughing at you," he swore to her. "But you are so absolutely adorable, sweetheart, you make me happy. Now, close your eyes again." When she did, he kissed her tenderly, pressing her against his chest. He struggled with himself that he not hold her too tightly. He recognized her own inner battle to stay calm in an unfamiliar situation, and for her, a possibly frightening one.

For the briefest time she felt dizzy, and she clung to him as his lips warmly met hers. She sighed deeply. It *was* nicer when you closed your eyes, although, like the earl, she could not have said why. In a sudden spurt of courage, she slipped her arms about his neck. He took her head between his hands, covering her face with soft, feathery kisses. His lips touched her fluttering, closed eyelids, her forehead, her cheeks, the tip of her nose, and finally her lips once again. His mouth pressed more firmly on hers this time, but Nyssa found it very pleasurable. She stood upon her tiptoes, straining to prolong his kiss. She was tingling all over, and had never before felt quite so . . . so . . . oh, why could she not find a word to describe how she felt?

His hands moved from her face, and clasping them about her waist, he lifted her up so that at first she was level with him, and their kisses deepened; and then he raised her up so that she was looking down into his face for a brief moment before he set her blushing back upon her feet. "You have never really been kissed before, have you?" he said, and not waiting for an answer, continued, "You learn quickly, sweetheart."

"Are you pleased, or displeased, my lord?" she inquired breathlessly. Her heart was hammering with her excitement.

"I am pleased you enjoy my kisses, and are so quickly expert in returning them," he told her, "but I am displeased you have not yet learned to say my name. We are husband and wife, madame, yet you do not speak my name. I love your name, Nyssa. It is Greek, is it not?"

"Aye," she said softly. He was so damned disarming, but disarming men were also dangerous men, she suspected. She did not truly know if he was a villain or merely maligned. Still, he was her husband now, and she frankly enjoyed his kisses.

"My mother named me before I was born," he said. "She told my father if she bore him a son, he should be called Varian, for men, like the wind, are variable creatures. So I was named as she wished me to be."

"Varian," she said low. "I like it, and I think I would have liked her. I am sorry that neither of us knew your mother."

"Say it again," he demanded, his voice intense.

"Varian. Varian. Ohh, Varian!" This last as he moved to unlace her chemise. She caught his hands and held them in her suddenly trembling ones.

"Do not forget," he told her. "I have already seen you naked. I disrobed you myself earlier, Nyssa." He raised her hands to his lips and kissed them. "You are very beautiful, sweetheart." He kissed each knuckle in turn, then clasped one of her hands against his cheek while, turning the other palm up, he pressed a warm kiss upon it.

Another flush suffused her fair skin, and she whispered so softly that he was forced to draw her even closer to hear, "Varian, I do not know what to do. You set my senses to reeling, but I am truly ignorant of lovemaking."

"For now, my sweet," he told her, loosing her hands and slipping her chemise over her shoulders, "you will do nothing but accept the homage of your besotted husband." His dark head dropped and he kissed a shoulder.

His lips were so warm, she thought, as they traveled back and forth across the column of her throat; lingering in the pulsing hollow of her neck; sliding softly to her other silky shoulder. She murmured a tiny half protest as he pushed the chemise down to reveal her young bosom. An arm cradled her while his free hand cupped a firm little breast. The gentle pressure of his hand had the most extraordinary effect upon her. Had it not been for his supporting arm, she believed her legs would not have held her. She watched, wide-eyed, as his thumb slowly rubbed against her nipple and it hardened to a tiny point.

"*Varian*," she cried low, and when their eyes met, she felt faint with a longing she could not understand. *Was this lovemaking?* It was but the beginning of lovemaking, she realized, but if this was the beginning, the rest must be too wonderful to even contemplate. *Wonderful and terrifying!* Another wave of weakness swept over her as he smiled. Then his mouth met hers once again. She let herself get daringly lost in his kisses, almost aching with the pleasure that they gave her.

Her fingers were kneading the back of his neck. He wondered if she realized it. He could not ever remember having been so filled with desire for any woman. She absolutely intoxicated him, yet he did not want to hurry them along the path of Eros. He wanted her very first experience with passion to be perfect, and damn the king for insisting they consummate their union this night. Ideally he would have waited for her to want him as much as he wanted her. Still, they had the night stretching out before them. He would move at as leisurely a pace as he could to ensure that she gained some pleasure her first time. *If he did not expire from wanting her so desperately first.*

He set her gently back a pace from him, his hands upon her hips, pushing the fabric of her chemise so that it slid with a soft hiss to the floor. With a single, swift motion he drew his nightshirt off and let it join her garment. Lifting her up, he pressed his face into the shadowed valley between her sweet little breasts. He could feel the rapidly beating pulse of her heart beneath his lips. Her eyes were tightly shut, for she dared not look at his naked form. Her fingers dug into his shoulders, and her little intake of breath assaulted his ears. Lowering her so that her feet touched the floor, he took her face between his hands once again, kissing her slowly and deeply.

Nyssa found suddenly that she couldn't draw a breath. She pulled away from him, eyes wide and frightened, face pale, whispering desperately, "I am faint, my lord!" Oh, Holy Mother! Did she really want this thing to happen between them? Her legs began to buckle beneath her. She was being assailed by a range of emotions she had no experience with at all. Why had no one told her how powerful passion was? Could one die from passion?

Sweeping her up into his embrace, Varian set her gently upon their bed and lay down next to her. Raising himself upon an elbow, he leaned over to look into her face. "Would you like some wine? Perhaps it would help to calm you, sweetheart."

"I am not afraid," she lied, embarrassed. "I was just not prepared for the intensity of lovemaking. Is it always so strong, Varian?" She had been unable in the brief moment he had stood by the bed to avert her eyes from him. His body was beautiful, yet it was also mysterious to her.

"It is stronger when two people truly love one another, Nyssa. What you feel at this moment is, I think, a mixture of lust and fascination with the unknown. That would be normal for a virgin entrapped in an arranged marriage with a virtual stranger. I can arouse your body, sweeting, with my touch, and with my kisses," he told her honestly.

"Are you thought to be a good lover?" she asked. "I am certain you have made love to many women." There was no jealousy in her voice, only curiosity.

"I have been told that I have the art of pleasing a woman," he answered her modestly. This was certainly the damnedest conversation I have ever had with a naked woman, he thought, a soft chuckle escaping him. He ran a single finger across her ripe mouth. "Do you always talk so much, sweetheart? This is, after all, our wedding night."

"There are things I need to know," she began seriously, but he silenced her with a quick kiss.

"If you grow frightened, you must tell me," he said, taking command again of the situation, his lips softly brushing the edge of her ear. "I do not want you to be frightened of me, Nyssa." He nuzzled her neck, and a shiver raced through her body. "Since we are now in bed, there is no danger of your falling," he continued. "If you grow dizzy, you need fear not." His teeth bit gently into the flesh of her shoulder, sending another shiver down her spine. "You are delicious," he declared huskily.

She was dizzy, but frightened? No. She did not think she was frightened of him. He was being very kind and gentle to her. Her instincts told her she was fortunate, for another man might have been less thoughtful. She lay silent as he explored her slowly and with great tenderness. It was all most curious, she thought, watching him through half-closed eyes as his lips wandered over her shoulders, down her arms, kissing each individual fingertip in turn, moving slowly across her upper chest. Her breath caught sharply in her throat once more when his mouth closed suddenly over the nipple of a breast. She knew infants suckled upon a woman's breasts, but she had never imagined that husbands did. He drew strongly upon her flesh, sending a jolt of pleasure deep into her very being. Was this behavior proper? She moaned low, stirring beneath the strong hands that lightly pinioned her, realizing she did not care if it was proper.

His head was whirling. He could not remember any time that making love to a woman had thrilled him so. He had, of course, never had a virgin before, not wanting the responsibility that went with a maiden's first initiation. Did she excite him so greatly because of her innocence, or was it because he loved her? His tongue slid over her perfumed skin, tasting her as he struggled desperately to maintain his control. He was so hot for her now that he was close to violence, but virgins, it was said, felt less pain if well-aroused. His mouth moved down her long torso and across her flat, quivering belly. Each place his lips touched pulsed wildly beneath his kisses.

No wonder some girls lost their reputations because of passion, Nyssa thought fuzzily. This was absolutely wonderful! No wonder mothers warned their daughters from it. If maidens knew how marvelous lovemaking was, parents would be hard-pressed to keep them from it! It was the most delicious of forbidden delights, but it was not forbidden to a married woman. She sighed deeply, enjoying the heavenly sensation of his warm tongue and his lips on her body. Her hands began a tentative exploration of his shoulders and long back. She kneaded and caressed him; shyly at first, then more boldly. Suddenly he was kissing her again, but more frantically. She tangled her fingers tightly in his dark, dark hair

"Open your mouth for me," he groaned against her lips.

When she did, he startled her by plunging his tongue deep into the warm cavity, seeking her tongue, finding it. Their two tongues entwined about each other in a wild dance of desire. She was all silky, sweet passion-fire. He could not get enough. His desire was nearly out of control.

"I want to touch you as you are now touching me," she whispered daringly against his mouth. She touched his face gently, caressing the line of it.

"You are a bold wench," he teased, intrigued by this sudden courage, curious to know how far she would go.

"Is it wrong for a wife to be bold with her husband?" Nyssa asked him. "Your touch gives me pleasure." She honestly admitted, "I would give you pleasure too." She let her hand slide down the length of his body to lightly touch his very taut buttocks. "I never thought that a man's skin could be so soft," she said wonderingly, "but you are very soft, Varian."

For a moment he could not breathe, his breath was caught so tightly. "What can you know of a man's body, sweetheart? I would not frighten you," he managed to grate out.

"I know that you are as excited by me as I seem to be by you," she answered him honestly. "Let me touch you, my lord! Please!" She caught his head between her two hands as he had earlier held hers, placing sweet little kisses all over his face. *"Please!"*

He groaned, helpless before her. Were all virgins like this? Rolling onto his back, he said, "Have your way with me then, you little vixen, but be warned that my patience with you is nearly at an end."

"What will happen when it ends?" she daringly inquired of him. Now it was she who was up on an elbow, staring down into his handsome face. His green eyes blazed up at her. She could almost smell the danger in the air. It was a precarious game she played with him, but realizing that only made it more exciting. Whatever fear she had felt was gone for the moment with the knowledge of this new power she had.

"When my patience ends, Nyssa," he said slowly, deliberately, "I shall mount you like a stallion mounting his mare, *and* I shall make you the woman you were meant to be." Then reaching up, he pulled her head down to his, and their lips met again in a searing kiss.

She seemed to draw strength from his passion this time, and pulling away, she smiled boldly down on him. Pushing his head to one side with her hand, she bent to kiss his ear, her tongue darting into its cavity to torment him. She did not know how she knew to do this, but it certainly had the desired effect. Still restraining him with her palm, she began to lick the column of his neck, sweeping down to his shoulders and chest. His skin tasted salty, yet there was an elusive fragrance to him that was not displeasing. She nuzzled at his nipples, and then bent to kiss his belly. It was then she saw *it*. Gasping, she turned to look at him. "What is that called?" she asked, awed. "And why is it so very big?" Reaching out, she touched it gingerly, briefly.

"I thought you had brothers," he said.

"They are younger than I am, and do not parade naked before me, my lord. Is this what the queen's ladies call a manroot?" She was intrigued by the thick, stiff piece of flesh thrusting up from his belly. It seemed to have a life all its own, moving about beneath her fascinated gaze.

"My patience is at an end," he said warningly.

"I am not ready yet," she replied, suddenly aware this was no game she played with him. A tingle raced down her spine as she seriously considered flight.

"How can you know?" he demanded, and with a quick motion he reversed their positions. "Now, my bold little virgin," he told her, "we will see if you are indeed ready to become a woman." His hand swept down her torso, pressing between her closed thighs. "Open your legs for me, Nyssa," he commanded her fiercely. "Do not deny us the pleasure that the joining of our two bodies will bring." His fist gently but firmly levered her thighs open when she instinctively resisted the order. His palm cupped her in a place she had never even touched herself. Leaning back, he looked into her blushing face, touching her lips with his. "I can feel the heat of you blazing through into my hand," he whispered. "Can you feel it too?"

She nodded, wide-eyed. Suddenly she was not in control of this situation any longer, but she was not afraid.

A single digit began to move against the cleft of her nether lips, exerting just the slightest pressure until it slipped between the soft folds. To her surprise, her flesh seemed wet and slippery there. A whimper escaped her.

"Your love juices have begun to flow, sweetheart," he said softly, kissing her ear as he spoke. "That is how I know you are ready for me." The tip of his finger found her tiny love button, and he rubbed it.

Nyssa gasped loudly. What was happening to her? It was too sweet, and with each touch of his finger it grew more so. "I do not think I can bear much more, my lord," she whispered desperately, and then to punctuate her argument, she cried out as something wonderful burst within her and she felt near to tears.

He covered her young body with his, simply unable to wait any longer. "I must have you, sweetheart," he told her low. *"I must!"*

Nyssa felt fear overwhelming her again. She struggled beneath him, but he pinioned her between his muscular thighs, capturing the little hands beating against his chest, securing them well above her head. Bending, he kissed her tenderly, covering her face with kisses to reassure her. "Don't fight me, sweeting," he begged her.

She pulled her head away from his. *"No! Please no! I want to love the man I marry. Ohh, please don't!"*

"Then love me! We are married," he ground out through gritted teeth. "You are my wife, Nyssa. We are bound to consummate this match tonight on the king's command. Damn, sweetheart, do not fight me now!"

Nyssa felt him penetrating her body, and she cried out. In a blinding flash she perceived what a manroot's use was. He was filling her full with it! She had a passage between her legs, and that was how a man locked his body to a woman's to create new life. She was not certain that she did not feel violated by his actions. Yet she could see that he was doing his very best to be gentle with her.

Despite her obvious terror, she began to open for him like a flower opening to the morning sun. His head swam dizzily as he slowly pushed himself into her tight, hot sheath. He did what he must now only in order to temper the king's ire, but dear God! He wanted this girl who was now his wife to love him as he loved her. Then suddenly his progress was blocked. He had reached the barrier of her maidenhead. She cried out and arched against him. There was, he knew, simply no gentle way to do this, for her maidenhead was firmly fixed.

"It hurts!" Nyssa sobbed. "Please stop!" she begged him.

In answer he drew back just slightly, then drove mercilessly into her fragile body, her scream piercing him to the heart. He saw the tears on her fair cheeks, and felt like a monster, but he could no longer help himself. He began to piston into her with smooth, deep strokes of his manroot, filling her full, driving as deep as he could go until he thought he would die with the pure, sweet pleasure of possessing her.

He was unforgivably cruel, Nyssa thought, sobbing as the burning agony swept up into her belly and down through her thighs. She fought him wildly, desperately seeking to elude the terrible torture he was inflicting upon her. Then, as suddenly as it had burst over her, the pain was gone. In its place was the distinct sensation of his strong body deep within her body. He pulsed and throbbed inside her hot passage until her head began to whirl. She was overwhelmed with a pleasure such as she had never known. She wept with the feeling, reveling in the sweetness until they both seemed sated with it, collapsing into each other's arms, exhausted, and to her utter amazement, wonderfully contented.

Varian de Winter rolled his weight off of Nyssa. Reaching out, he enfolded her in his embrace. Neither of them could say a word. His big hand stroked her tousled, dark hair gently, silently communicating his tender feelings for her. Beneath her cheek his heart beat wildly, slowing gradually, until finally it simply thudded rhythmically, comfortingly.

Nyssa was absolutely astounded by the passion that they had shared. She was also furious that her normally forthright mother had never even discussed these things with her. How could she? a saner voice in her head asked, and Nyssa honestly realized that there was no way Blaze could have possibly explained what just happened between herself and the Earl of March.

Was she all right? Would she ever forgive him for what had just transpired? Varian was almost sick with anxiety, and said low, "Are you

. . . are you . . . I know I hurt you, but it was the shattering of your maidenhead. It only happens once, Nyssa."

"I could not have begun to imagine it," she told him quietly.

"Then you forgive me, sweeting?"

She raised her head to look at him. "I know that you were both patient and kind, my lord. I apologize for my fear. I am not usually so cowardly." She touched his cheek with a single finger. "This passion is a most powerful thing, is it not? Is it always so?"

"Between people who desire each other, yes, my love," he told her, catching at her hand, turning it and kissing the palm.

She nodded gravely, and lay her head back down upon his chest. "Will the king be satisfied that we have done our duty?"

"Aye, Nyssa, he will," the earl told her.

She said nothing more. Very shortly he realized that she had fallen asleep. He lay awake for some time, listening to her slow breathing until, finally lulled by it, he fell asleep too, his arms wrapped tightly, protectively, about her.

They were awakened several hours later by a loud knocking upon their chamber door. Before he might arise and answer it, the door swung open and his grandfather entered the room. Varian de Winter drew the coverlet over his wife's nakedness.

"It will be dawn soon," the duke said without preamble. "Is the girl breached?"

He looked directly at Nyssa, but she was not in the least intimidated by him. She glared back, angered not merely by his intrusion, but by what she considered a great lack of delicacy as the old man ran an appreciative eye over her.

"Well, my lord? Is she breached?" he repeated. "She's fair enough to have aroused your lust."

"If you will leave the room," Varian said tightly, "I will obtain the proof for you that should satisfy the king, Grandfather."

"We have something to discuss first," Thomas Howard said bluntly. "Stop looking as if you would plunge a knife into my heart, girl," he ordered Nyssa. "What's done is done, but now we must have an explanation for your marriage to silence the gossiping tongues."

"You are so skilled at scheming, my lord," she answered him, "that I will leave it to you. What can you possibly tell people that they will believe? My virtue is well-known in a court not known for virtue. What will you say? That I was suddenly overcome with a reckless passion for your grandson, and he with an equal desire for me? *That we eloped?*" She smiled with false sweetness at the Duke of Norfolk.

"It has already been decided, madame," he replied coldly. "You have but to go along with the explanation. Your aunt and uncle see the wisdom of my plan, and have agreed to it. The king also agrees, for he will have no shame fall upon you for your wicked behavior of last evening."

"*My wicked behavior?*" Nyssa's voice rose dangerously. "Cease this charade, my lord, I beg you. I know how I came to be in the earl's bed last night. I know of your wretched plot to make poor Cat queen."

"*Do you?* Then you know enough to hold your tongue, girl, else you and your husband end your days in the Tower," the duke snapped.

"Were it not for my loyalty to Queen Anne," Nyssa said, "I should leave Greenwich this very day, sir!"

"You are free to leave, madame," he said.

"Nay," Nyssa answered him. "I will not leave my queen alone and defenseless, my lord. I will stay until the end. His grace has said that I may continue to serve her for the present."

"Then listen to what I tell you both. Last night Varian de Winter stole you from the Maidens' Chamber and raped you. You escaped him and fled to your relations. They protested to the king, who saw to your immediate nuptials. In this way your virtue remains intact, madame. You become the innocent victim in this affair," the duke said.

"Which I certainly was," she snapped back at him, "but I will not allow you to defame my lord husband in this manner! It is not right! Have you no heart, my lord duke, that you would blacken your own grandson's name further like this?"

"Considering his reputation," the duke told her, "it is the perfect explanation for what has happened. You, madame, will abide by it."

Nyssa opened her mouth to protest further; to tell him that she knew her husband's reputation was a false one, that he was innocent of the crime he had admitted to. But Varian suddenly squeezed her hand very hard beneath the coverlet. Nyssa's mouth closed abruptly. She turned to look questioningly at him. He put a warning finger to her lips and shook his head at her. For some reason he did not want her arguing further with his grandfather. She wondered again if perhaps his black reputation *was* deserved. Had Varian told her the truth or had he lied to win her over last night?

"I hope, at least," the earl said, attempting to inject some humor into the situation, "that you will claim I was driven by my passionate love for Nyssa, Grandfather."

"Considering the king's affection for me," Nyssa said wickedly, "will people not wonder why he has not clapped Varian in the Tower for this crime of passion he has committed against me?"

"The king is a married man for all intents and purposes," the duke said, discomfited by her continued show of spirit. "He could hardly admit to having loving feelings toward another lady, madame."

"He did toward your niece Anne, under similar circumstances," Nyssa answered him.

"Madame, you tread on dangerous ground," the duke growled at her. He turned to his grandson. "Obviously I have given you a viper to wife, Varian. Perhaps I should apologize to you."

"Aye," Nyssa returned angrily. "You should apologize to us both, my lord. You are a cruel man."

"Be silent, sweeting," the earl said softly to her.

"You know what you must do," Thomas Howard said coldly. "I shall wait outside for the proof, Varian. Be quick! The king will be awakening at any moment. I would have this over and done with." He turned and departed the room, closing the door behind him.

"How can you give him your loyalty?" Nyssa asked her husband when they were once again alone. "He thinks nothing of sacrificing your name in order to advance his ambition."

"This will be the last time he does so," the earl replied quietly. He loved his grandfather, but this was really too much. Sweet Nyssa knew not that much of the blame for his alleged rape of her would fall on her slender shoulders despite her reputation for virtue.

"I hate him!" she declared vehemently. "He is a wicked man!"

"But what other explanation could have been given for our sudden marriage, Nyssa?" he asked her. "We have hardly spoken to each other until last night. There was, I fear, no other way. I apologize for the pain and embarrassment it will cause you."

"Could he not have said seduced? I should rather be thought a foolish maid than you be called a villain. Why rape? It is disgusting, my lord! It makes you out to be an evil man, and I think you may not be one!" she cried. She was so confused! "Could we not have kept the marriage a secret from everyone for now? Would that not have been better? It was, after all, important only to the king," Nyssa said.

"What if our coming together last night produces a child? How would you explain your condition, Nyssa? It is better that our marriage be known. I will have no stain of bastardy on our firstborn." He tipped her face to his and kissed her lightly. "Now get up, madame."

"I have no clothing, my lord. I will need Tillie," she said.

"Tillie?"

"My tiring woman. You must send for her to bring me clothes," Nyssa told him.

"Wrap yourself in the coverlet for now," he said. "I need the bottom sheet from our bed for the king."

"Why?" she demanded of him, but she arose from the bed and carefully wrapped herself in the coverlet as he had advised her.

The earl pulled the top sheet away and pointed. "There, Nyssa, is the king's proof. The blood of your maidenhead staining the sheet." He yanked it off the bed. Going to the chamber door, he opened it and handed the bedcloth to his grandfather without a single word. Then he shut the door firmly and turned to his wife. "I will send my man Toby for your servant. Will she be in that small room the servants for the queen's ladies inhabit? What does she look like?"

"She is brown-eyed with a single flaxen plait, small of stature, and just my age," Nyssa told him. "Oh, please be certain that your Toby is discreet! There will be scandal enough, I fear."

The earl called for his own servant and instructed him most carefully. "I married this lady last night," he explained to the surprised Toby. "Do not believe the gossip you will hear as to why. Now go, and fetch my lady's tiring woman. Her name is Tillie." He described her.

"Tell her to bring me my clothes for today," Nyssa said to Toby. "I must attend the queen, and I can go nowhere until I have clothing."

"Yes, m'lady," Toby said, keeping his eyes well-averted from the beautiful girl wrapped in the coverlet. It was just all too much for him. He hurried off to find the woman called Tillie.

She, at first, did not believe the young man's story. "My mistress is in the Maidens' Chamber where she belongs," she said firmly.

"No, she ain't," Toby said low, struggling to keep his voice down. "She is in my master's bedchamber wrapped in a coverlet. She can't come out without her clothes, and says you are to fetch them to her. If you don't believe me, go and see for yourself, miss. I ain't much for jesting, as anyone who knows Toby Smythe will tell you. Look in the Maidens' Chamber if you will. Your lady ain't there."

Tillie did just that, and not seeing Nyssa about anywhere, ran to the little storage room where the maids of honor were allowed to keep their clothing. Quickly she gathered the garments needed, and also snatched up a hairbrush and shoes. "All right," she said to Toby. "Where do we go? And if I find you've made a fool of me, laddie, I'll see your master punishes you, and I'll get in a few smacks myself."

"You're a feisty one," he replied with a grin. "Follow me."

Tillie's eyes widened as they entered the Duke of Norfolk's apartments, but she said nothing. Toby knocked at a paneled door, and when it was opened, he waved Tillie through. She hurried past him, relief suffusing her features as she saw Nyssa. "Oh, m'lady! What has happened? Why are you here instead of in the Maidens' Chamber?"

"I am a married woman, Tillie," Nyssa said quietly. "Put down my clothing and send Toby to fetch some water for my bath. I will tell you everything, but I must reach the queen before the gossip does, if possible."

When Tillie had sent Toby off to do her bidding, she sat, at her mistress's insistence, upon the bed, listening while Nyssa told her the truth of what had transpired. A simple country woman, Tillie was shocked by the scheme fostered by the Duke of Norfolk, but she was relieved that Nyssa had told her of it. It would be easier to deal with the gossip knowing the real facts of the matter. She agreed to keep secret what Nyssa had said, fully understanding the necessity of it, for she was not a stupid girl.

"Yer mama and papa are going to be very angry," she noted when her mistress had finally concluded her tale. "They won't like it one bit that you've been forced into this marriage. I know they always promised you that you could make your own choice of a husband. I don't see how you can get out of it, though, the archbishop himself having performed the ceremony." She sighed, but then asked, "What is yer bridegroom like, m'lady? Is he handsome? They say he's a real devil with the ladies. At least," she amended, "that's the talk amongst the upper servants, but most of what they say is so much tittle-tattle, I find."

Nyssa thought a moment, and then said, "I do not know. Much about him is wrapped in gossip and dark innuendo. He has been kind to me, but I am not certain yet that I can trust him. Time will tell us that."

"Where are we going to live?" the practical servant asked.

"We will remain at court for the present," her lady said, "but you will be happy to learn that the earl's home is just across the river from my house at Riverside. We'll still be near our families and friends, Tillie. I think we will depart court in just a few more weeks. Lord de Winter prefers the country, he tells me."

"Well," Tillie pronounced, "he can't be too bad then, no matter what the others say about him."

Toby entered, struggling beneath the weight of a wooden tub. "Where do you want it, then?" he demanded of Tillie.

"By the fire, you dolt," she snapped at him. "Where else would I want it? Is my lady to catch her death of cold?"

"Yer pretty as a summer's day, miss," he told her, "but yer as mean as they come, I'm thinking." He plunked the tub down with a thump. "I'll be fetching the water now."

"You'd better have help," Tillie told him, not in the least discomfited by his backhanded compliment, "or it will take all morning."

With aid from several of the duke's footmen, the tub was quickly filled. Tillie shooed Toby from the room and locked the door behind him. Then she helped Nyssa bathe. The girl blushed silently at the sight of the dried blood on her thighs. Tillie said nothing until, toweling her mistress dry, she asked, "Where is yer husband, m'lady?"

"He has already dressed and gone," Nyssa said, although to be honest, she did not know where. He had not volunteered the information, and she had not asked him. Her main duty was to the queen. She grew silent again as Tillie dressed her. The rose-pink silk gown with its silver-embroidered underskirt was one of her favorites. Tillie brushed her hair, but instead of leaving it loose, befitting a maiden, she fashioned Nyssa's hair into a chignon set low on her neck. Over it she affixed a silver caul. Then she held up a looking glass, that Nyssa might see how the new fashion looked.

"I look so old suddenly," Nyssa told her servant.

" 'Tis a flattering style, m'lady," Tillie reassured her.

"I must go to the queen now," Nyssa said.

"Are we to live here for now, m'lady?" Tillie asked her. "What am I to do with your possessions now that you are no longer a maid of honor?"

"I will not stay here under the duke's rule while we are at court," Nyssa said. "Take my clothing and my other effects to the house my FitzHugh relations have rented. Toby can help you."

"What of yer husband, m'lady?" Tillie wondered.

"He may come, or he may stay," Nyssa replied. Then, unlocking the door, she hurried off to the queen's apartments.

Anne of Cleves was already awake. When Nyssa entered her apartments, the chatter was instantly silenced, and the queen's ladies stared hard at her. Her friends looked frightened. Lady Rochford had a distinctly smug air about her. So, Nyssa thought, they already know, or think they know, what has happened. She refused to lower her eyes.

Lady Browne hurried forward. "You can no longer serve the queen as a maid of honor, Lady Wyndham, er, Lady de Winter. The king has sent word." She looked distinctly uncomfortable.

"The king has promised me that I might remain in the queen's service, as she will need her friends in the days to come," Nyssa answered her quietly. "A married woman can hardly be a maid, madame, can she?"

Lady Browne flushed. "No, of course not," she murmured.

"I wish to see the queen now," Nyssa said firmly.

"Brazen hussy!" she heard someone say.

"I will tell her you are here," Cat Howard said loudly. None of the other women dared to stop her as she bustled off.

Nyssa swallowed back her laughter. So, not only did they know of her disgrace, they also knew in which direction the wind was blowing. It was amusing for the moment, but she did not really think she would like to live her life like this. It would be good to finally leave court.

Cat was back, her cerulean-blue eyes twinkling with amusement. "Her grace will see you immediately, my lady de Winter," she said sweetly, and curtsied politely to her friend, giving her a mischievous wink.

"Thank you, Mistress Howard," Nyssa replied loudly, moving past her into the lady Anne's privy chamber. She curtsied low before the queen. They were alone, much to Nyssa's relief.

"Ach, my friend, I am so sorry for your troubles," the queen said to her. "I vas no sooner awake than Lady Rochford told me." There were tears in her soft blue eyes.

Nyssa moved next to the queen's bed and said low, " 'Twas a plot by the Duke of Norfolk, madame, in order to discredit me in the king's eyes. I am certain you know the reason why. And I think you should know that Lady Rochford is in the duke's service. She spies for him."

Anne nodded. "I suspected it." Then she said, "But for the duke to haf his grandson rape you, my friend. 'Tis criminal!"

"I was not raped, madame. Lady Rochford drugged my bedtime drink." Nyssa quickly explained the facts behind her hasty marriage.

"Such plotting, and planning, and all for the privilege of vedding and bedding Hendrick," the queen said incredulously. "I do not know if I am sorry for Mistress Howard or not. Surely she must know vhat is in store for her, yet she seems a happy young maid."

"Her heart is good, madame, but she does have the Howard ambition. It seems to run hot and fierce in the veins of that family."

"And your bridegroom, Nyssa. Does he haf the Howard ambition too?" the queen asked her. "Vill you be happy vith him?"

"My husband is a de Winter, Your Grace. From now on I intend that he remember it. As for my happiness, Varian seems a good man, but I do not really know him. I hope we will like each other."

"You sound to me as if you might already like this man, Nyssa," the queen observed. "Had you ever met him before last night?"

"Once," Nyssa told her mistress. "We danced at your wedding, madame."

"Perhaps under the circumstances the archbishop vill gif you an annulment after the matter of my marriage is settled, and the king has taken himself a young and pretty English rose to vife."

"There are no grounds for annulment, madame," Nyssa said honestly. "The king was most insistent that the marriage be consummated, and demanded proof of such by this morning. The duke took him the proof."

Anne shook her head in wonderment. "Once," she said, "you told me that the king could be ruthless. I vas not certain you vere entirely correct, for Hendrick and I haf come so easily to our secret agreement; but his behavior in this matter is indeed heartless."

"He was very disturbed, madame; he had promised my mother he would keep me safe. Remember, the king is not privy to the duke's scheming. He felt my reputation had been compromised. So he took the only action he believed would restore my good name. He saw to my immediate marriage. He insisted upon the consummation, I realize now, to protect me from an annulment, or divorce later on. Remember that I am a considerable heiress in my own right."

"And the Howards are ambitious." The queen smiled.

"Aye, madame." Nyssa smiled in return.

"Vhen vill you leave the court, my friend?" Anne asked.

"Not until your grace is happily resettled. I have the king's permission to serve you until then in whatever capacity your grace wishes," Nyssa told the queen. "I could not leave you while you need me, dear madame. You have been so kind to me." She took up the queen's hand and kissed it.

Royalty did not cry, but Anne felt the tears welling up in her blue eyes. Since her arrival in England, she had met with great kindness from the common people, and from many here at court, but from young Nyssa Wyndham in particular. She squeezed the girl's hand. "Ya," she said huskily. "You vill stay vith me until everything is settled." She brushed her hand across her eyes. "I had best arise now, Nyssa. Call my ladies to come to me. I shall appoint you to personally oversee my jewelry until such time as I am no longer qveen."

Nyssa backed away from the queen's bed and curtsied to her. Then she went to fetch the queen's ladies-in-waiting to help their mistress get up and get dressed. When the women had hurried past her into the queen's bedchamber, the maids of honor crowded about her, all talking at once, demanding an explanation of her marriage.

"You have heard the official account, I am certain," Nyssa told them. "I can say nothing more, but you will be kind to the Earl of March. I think he may not be the man some would have you believe." The girls nodded, relieved.

"Is he a good lover, Nyssa?" Cat Howard demanded saucily of her.

"He says he is," came the serious reply.

The other girls giggled.

"But what do *you* think?" Cat persisted wickedly. "Did your toes curl up, and did you swoon with delight?"

"I have never had a lover before, Cat. I cannot make comparisons. I can only take the gentleman's word for it," Nyssa told her friend.

"I think he has been in love with you for some time," Elizabeth Fitz-Gerald noted astutely. "He was always staring at you when he thought no one was looking."

"You Irish are incurable romantics, Bessie," Nyssa told her. "Besides, how could you know he was staring at me? Were you staring at him?" she teased her friend.

"Aye," Bessie admitted, blushing. "Handsome men with dangerous reputations are always far more interesting than just ordinary handsome men, and we Irish are known to be reckless where such men are concerned."

"Will you leave us now?" little Kate Carey inquired.

"Nay, I have the king's permission to remain in the queen's service until such time as I am no longer needed. I will oversee the queen's jewelry," Nyssa told them.

"Then the remainder of your stay will be a relatively short one, I suspect," said Kate Carey wryly. "It will be back to the country for you, Nyssa. Why do I think you will not be sorry to go?"

Nyssa smiled at her young friend. "Because I won't. I have loved serving the queen, and making friends with all of you, but like my mother before me, I am a country girl in my heart. Varian's lands are across the river Wye from my own estate of Riverside. I will not be far from my parents, and we will be surrounded by my family."

"Will you learn to love the earl, I wonder?" Bessie mused.

"Whether I love him or not, we are bound together in matrimony," Nyssa replied seriously. "I think I can learn to like him." She smiled at them. "Do not fear for me, my young friends. You should save your pity for others less fortunate than I."

"I want to speak to Nyssa alone," Cat Howard said meaningfully. "Go in to the queen before the other ladies wonder where we are and come spying on us."

Bessie and Kate obeyed her without question.

"What do you want of me?" Nyssa said quietly. "I think I have already done enough for you, Cat Howard, don't you?"

Catherine Howard had the grace to blush at Nyssa's gentle rebuke. Then she said, "You have met Duke Thomas, have you not? Would you defy him? He is a formidable opponent. I have not the strength to oppose him, Nyssa. You know in your heart that he would not have allowed it. He wants another Howard on the throne, and I am that Howard."

"You could have told him no, Cat, but you did not because you like the idea of being queen. Henry Tudor is a dangerous man to wive—Queen Catherine divorced; your own cousin Anne, beheaded; Queen Jane dead of childbed fever; this Queen Anne to be annulled. What will happen when he tires of you, Cat? How will he rid himself of the next wife he takes when he grows bored with her, or another pretty face takes his fancy? You are putting your head in the lion's mouth!"

"Are you jealous?" Cat Howard asked her, curious.

The look Nyssa gave her was incredulous. *"Jealous?* God's blood, Cat! If the king had had a romantic interest in me, I would have died of fright! *But he did not.* Your uncle, the duke, made a miscalculation there in his eagerness to be a queen-maker. His grace favors me for my sweet mother's sake, and no more. She petitioned him for my place at court, and he promised her he would look after me as if I were his own, for my stepfather did not want me to come. Your uncle's overweening ambition has cost me the chance of marrying for love, as my parents promised me I could. I think little of him for that, and for other reasons as well. But nay, dear friend, I am not jealous of you. I have grown to love you as a sister. I fear for you, Cat."

"The king is in love with me," Cat Howard said softly. "He has told me so. I know he is old enough to be my father, but I think I can really love him. I have learned not to be repulsed by his bad leg when it swells and runs with pus. I can even dress it. He says my touch is healing. I know I can be a good wife to him, Nyssa. He will have no reason to cast me off. You need not fear for me. I will be all right."

"I pray it so, Cat, but what of your cousin, Thomas Culpeper, who professes his love for you? You have flirted with him for months now. Will he not be heartbroken by your match with the king?"

"Tom Culpeper is a fool," Cat said angrily. "He did not want to marry me, Nyssa. He wanted to seduce me, the rogue! Why, last Christmas he tried to bribe his way into my affections with some cloth for a gown with which he gifted me. In exchange he expected a romp in my bed. I quickly set him straight. Let his fickle heart be broken! I care not a whit for him. He will quickly find another gullible maid upon which to affix his affections."

Nyssa thought her friend's denial a bit too vehement to be believable. She thought perhaps Cat cared for Tom Culpeper, but Catherine Howard claimed she had what she wanted: a man who would love her, and make her a queen. And what have I got? Nyssa wondered. Who is this man I have been married to so precipitously? When good Queen Anne shortly ends her brief reign, I am going to have a lifetime to find out, she realized.

PART II

THE BRIDE OF WINTERHAVEN

Spring 1540–Spring 1541

PART II.

THE BRIDE OF
WINTERHAVEN

Spring 1580—Spring 1581

CHAPTER 7

I WOULD not be as brave as you in such circumstances," Anne Bassett said to Nyssa that afternoon. "I should want to hide myself away."

Nyssa, conscientious in her new duties, was carefully cleaning a diamond and gold necklace belonging to the queen. "What on earth do you mean, Mistress Anne?" she inquired sweetly.

Indeed she had some idea, having been subject all day to the stares, some hostile, some simply curious, of the queen's ladies. What hypocrites they were. They thought little of their secret meetings with their own lovers—most of which were not secret. Oh well, eventually something else would capture their fertile imaginations. She would be ignored again. Nyssa had no intention, however, of allowing the Bassett sisters to prolong her discomfort. She must bear the mild insults of the king's daughter-in-law and his niece, and the others of higher rank than she, but not of her former fellow maids.

"Ohh, come now, Nyssa Wyndham," Anne Bassett began with a knowing smirk upon her pretty face.

"De Winter," Nyssa corrected her. "Nyssa de Winter. Her ladyship, the

Countess of March, Mistress Anne." She rubbed with exaggerated diligence at the necklace.

"You undoubtedly invited your fate," Anne Bassett said waspishly. "No gentleman, even one with as unsavory a reputation as Lord de Winter, would rape a woman without a certain amount of provocation. That is a very well-known fact."

I will not slap her, Nyssa thought, struggling to control her outrage. Was Anne Bassett really one of those stupid souls who believed women invited their own rapes? *"What provocation?"* Nyssa demanded icily of her. "When was I even in the gentleman's presence that you can testify to, Mistress Anne? When have you known me to encourage *any* gentleman of this court? My reputation for virtue is above reproach."

"Certainly no longer, I would think," Anne Bassett replied meanly.

"My cousin, Thomas Culpeper, raped a gamekeeper's wife last year," Cat Howard said, coming to Nyssa's defense. "She was a very pretty girl. She rebuffed Tom on several occasions that I was witness to myself. I would hardly call that encouragement, but he raped her nonetheless. He waited until her husband was gone from their cottage one day. Then, with three friends holding her down for him, he had his way with her. Men do rape women without cause, Anne. Perhaps you had best beware, for you flirt far too much with the gentlemen for your own safety, I fear. Why, even the king, I am told, is prone to force on occasion." Cat Howard smiled brightly at the girl, but Anne was not yet beaten.

"A gamekeeper's wife is hardly a lady," she sneered, "and certainly cannot be compared with one. Besides, the girl had probably had her skirts lifted any number of times, and enjoyed it. She but taunted your cousin. As for the king, Cat Howard, beware! You speak treason when you criticize our sovereign lord. It is his right to do as he pleases."

"You are heartless," Nyssa told her. "No woman, no matter her station, should be thought fair game for violence by any man."

"Aye!" the others agreed, glaring at Anne Bassett and finally silencing her. The Bassett sisters were dreadful snobs, though Katherine was really the nicer of the two, particularly when her sister was absent.

In late afternoon the queen dismissed Nyssa. "You may haf the next two days for yourself, madame. Even a lady in the qveen's service should haf a honeymoon. Ya?" She smiled broadly, and Nyssa's friends giggled while the other ladies looked scandalized.

"Brazen hussy!"

Nyssa heard it as she prepared to leave the queen's apartments.

"Aye," was the reply. "She should be ashamed of herself, yet she holds her head high like a decent and virtuous woman, *the slut!"*

Nyssa whirled about to see who it was who would dare to pass judgment upon her, but the queen's ladies were silent now, though smirking. She could not tell who had spoken, for the voices, though plainly heard, had been unidentifiable. She walked over to the queen and curtsied low. "I thank your grace for her generosity and kind wishes," she said.

"Go! Go!" the queen answered, smiling.

Nyssa found her uncle dicing with several of his friends in one of the public rooms. "Will you take me to your house, my lord? The queen has granted me several days' rest, and I would retire now."

Owen FitzHugh nodded. "Do you want your aunt for company?" he asked her. "She is with Adela Marlowe, I believe."

"Nay, Uncle, I would be alone, I think," Nyssa said.

"What of your husband?" Owen FitzHugh replied.

"Tillie has told his Toby where I am. He may come or not as the spirit moves him, but I will not live under Thomas Howard's roof!"

"He is a bad enemy to make," the Earl of Marwood told his niece. "Be wary, Nyssa. Remember that your husband is his favorite grandson."

"If you knew what I did, Uncle, you would realize that I seek Varian de Winter's best interests, while his grandfather seeks only the best interests of the Howards. My husband is not a Howard. Besides, the duke does not think women of much import other than for marrying off. Varian's union with me is very much to his advantage. The duke will think me but a silly, temperamental wench for refusing to live beneath his roof. He will be glad when we shortly leave court. We are no longer important to his plans, and I am happy for that!"

Owen FitzHugh laughed. "You have your aunt's temper," he said, "but your mother's practical common sense, I am relieved to see. Very well then, Nyssa, I will escort you back to our house. It is fortunate, is it not, that I extended the lease through June, my dear niece."

Unlike the crowded little house in Richmond that they had rented, the house at Greenwich was a gracious and spacious dwelling set within its own green park. It was a relatively new building, having been constructed in the reign of the previous king, Henry VII. Nyssa had been given a large bedchamber with its own separate dressing room and even a small room for Tillie. From her windows she could see the beautiful park land about the house. She had scarcely used the room since their arrival at Greenwich, but she was pleased to have it now, for it meant she could be free of Varian's overbearing grandfather.

The walls of the room were done in a linen-fold paneling of richly polished oak. There was a large window with a cushioned window seat upon one wall, and a good-sized fireplace on another. The great bed with its heavy crimson velvet hangings was opposite the hearth. Next to the fireplace was a carved settle with a tapestried cushion. There was a large wood chest at the foot of the bed, and a single nightstand.

"I want a bath!" Nyssa said as she entered the room. "A lovely, hot bath, Tillie. Use the lavender fragrance in the water. It reminds me of home. We will soon be going home!"

"We'll be going to yer new home, m'lady," Tillie replied.

"Nay, first we are going *home* to *RiversEdge,*" Nyssa said. "My parents must meet Lord de Winter before we go on to Winterhaven. The news of my marriage will be shock enough."

"And who is to tell yer mother and father of this hasty wedding that the king has forced you into, I should like to know?" Tillie fretted. "Me aunt Heartha will surely find a way to blame me for it, I'm sure."

Nyssa laughed. "There is no way Heartha can hold you responsible for any of this, Tillie." Then she grew thoughtful. "As for Mama and Papa, I am not certain how they should be told of what has happened. I do not think they should learn of my marriage in a letter. It would be too much, and Papa would come raging up to court. I suppose I should discuss it with my aunt and uncle before I decide."

Tillie nodded. She agreed with her mistress that a letter would cause more consternation than was really necessary. "I'll see to yer bath," she said, and hurried off to marshal the footmen.

The large, round wooden tub was brought from the dressing room and set by the fireplace. Tillie stirred up the coals and added more fuel until there was a fine, hot blaze going. The footmen moved swiftly with precision in and out of the room with their buckets of hot water. Tillie filled an open kettle and placed it over the flames so she might pour it into the bathwater when it began to cool. When the last footman had finally left the room, she added a goodly amount of lavender oil to the steaming tub, and instantly the room was filled with its perfume.

Nyssa had been gazing out from her comfortable vantage point in the window seat. They were not on the river, but she could see it winding like a silver ribbon beyond the green willows. It made her long even more for her home on the Wye, in England's Midlands. She sighed deeply, and turning about, arose so that Tillie might help her off with her garments. The warm, perfumed water soothed her soul as she sank gratefully into it. Court had been very exciting. She had certainly accomplished her purpose in coming, although not at all in the way in which she thought she would. But oh, she was so relieved that in just a few more weeks she would be going home! Home to *RiversEdge. Home to Winterhaven.*

Winterhaven. It had a pretty ring to it. She wondered what it was like.

Would it be as beautiful as *RiversEdge*? Or her own house, Riverside? Poor old Riverside. Was it never to have a family in it again? Her father's half sister, Lady Dorothy, her stepfather's mother, had lived there, but she was now almost seventy, and preferred living with the family at *Rivers-Edge*.

It must go to my second son, Nyssa thought. Second sons have so little. What a startling idea! A second son? How could she be thinking of a second son already? There was no *first* son. She was still not at all certain she was satisfied with this marriage into which she had been so suddenly forced. Would there even be a first son? And what if she had only daughters? And should children be born of less than love? She did not love Varian, yet he said he loved her. Ridiculous! How could he love her? He did not even know her, nor she him. She flushed. Well, he had known her in a carnal sense, but only once, *and* he had said the words before he had taken her. He had said them because he was kind, Nyssa decided. Well, at least it was something in his favor.

Tillie, washing her mistress with cloth and soap, watched the play of emotions across Nyssa's face. What was she thinking about? Tillie wondered. Was she dreaming about that handsome new husband the king had given her? Ohh, how the gossipy servants had descended upon her this day, desperately trying to ferret out of her all the juicy intimate details of her mistress's situation. Men and women who had never before had time for her now attempted to draw her out. How long had her mistress been secretly meeting the Earl of March? Had she been a virgin when she came to court? Well, Tillie thought indignantly, she had sent them all packing. What could she possibly know that they didn't already know? she demanded of them. Did a fine lady like her mistress confide in a mere servant? Because most of them were overweeningly proud, and considered Tillie of low estate, she had been believed.

The upper servants had gone off disappointed, but May, Lady FitzHugh's tiring woman, had smiled approvingly at Tillie when they were alone. "Yer aunt Heartha would be proud of ye, girl!" she said, and Tillie realized that May had guessed the truth of the matter. Of course she would have, for like Tillie, she was *family* too.

The door to the bedchamber opened and both young women gazed up, startled, to see the Earl of March.

"Good evening, madame," he said quietly. "I understand that we are to domicile here until we leave court." He gazed about. "It is a most charming room. Is there a place for Toby?"

"I am certain my uncle will tell you where he may lodge," Nyssa said, not knowing what else to say to him. "I think, perhaps, the bedchamber next to this one would suit you, and your servant. You will need space for your clothing, and my dressing room is absolutely full, I fear. Uncle Owen can direct you."

"Tillie," the earl said with a smile, "will you go and speak with Lord FitzHugh for me. Then help my Toby find his way. We will call you when we need you," he told the startled servant. Tillie looked to her mistress for guidance.

"I will need Tillie with me to finish my toilette," Nyssa said.

"I will help you," he told her calmly. "I am a most expert maid, or at least I have been told so." He turned to Tillie. "Go along now, Tillie, and if you can help Toby get me settled, I should appreciate it."

"You are to remain, Tillie," Nyssa said firmly.

"Go, girl," the earl told her, putting a hand beneath her elbow and escorting her to the door.

"Stay, Tillie!" Nyssa commanded her tiring woman.

The earl opened the door to the bedchamber, and pushing Tillie out, closed the door behind her, locking it. He turned to meet the outraged gaze of his bride of less than a day.

"How dare you, sir!" she raged at him. "Tillie is my servant, and as such must answer to me first and foremost."

"Tillie is the servant of the Countess of March," he replied. "She is liable to me now, madame, as her master. Would you like me to help you from your bath? You must be finished surely."

"Get out!" Nyssa glared furiously at him. "I shall scream."

"And what, pray tell, madame, will that accomplish?" he asked maddeningly, taking the towel from its rack by the fire, opening it and holding it out for her. "I am your husband. Who will interfere with me even if I should beat you? Under the law, both God's and man's, you are mine."

"You are despicable, my lord," she told him tightly.

"If you will not get out," he replied calmly, laying the towel aside, "then I shall get in." Pulling his boots and hose off, beneath her startled eyes he stripped down to his shirt and breeches.

"You do not dare, my lord!" Nyssa said nervously.

He threw her an amused look and unfastened his shirt, drawing it off and laying it aside upon the settle with the rest of his garments. *"No?"* he drawled, his hand moving to his breeches.

Nyssa scrambled to her feet. "The tub is not large enough for us both. It is too full for two people," she cried. "The house is rented and must not be damaged!" Why was he staring at her? And then she realized that in her panic she had quite forgotten that she was naked. "Ohhh . . ." Her soft cry echoed in the room. Desperately she reached for the towel he had tossed aside, rosy with blushes, her eyes wide.

For a moment he couldn't breathe. His chest felt tight. His eyes hungrily ravaged her form. Wet, it glistened with the oily bathwater. He watched fascinated as a drop of moisture rolled between her pretty little breasts and slid down her long torso. She was all pink-gold in the firelight. Reaching out, he yanked her from the tub and pressed her wet body against him, kissing her deeply. He had never in his life wanted a woman quite so much as he wanted this one.

Nyssa's head swam dizzily with the sensation of his mouth against hers, with the heat emanating from his hard body. She knew so little of him. She certainly did not know him well enough to love him, but the feeling his actions engendered inside of her certainly was not fear. Raising her arms, she let her palms slide up his smooth chest. His very skin seemed to leap beneath her touch. It was then with wonder she realized that whatever it was he felt for her, she felt it also for him.

He slid his hand up to her head, pulling out the pins that had held her hair up from the water. Her dark mane tumbled free, caressing her shoulders. He kneaded her scalp, with his fingers turning her head this way and that, his mouth never leaving hers. His heart almost stopped as he felt her fingers unfastening his breeches, pushing them down along with his linen drawers. He stepped out of them, kicking them away, his arms still wrapped tightly about the girl.

Nyssa pulled her head away from his, gasping for air. Her eyes met his and she said tightly, "What is this I feel, Varian? What is it that makes me play the wanton with you? I do not understand. It cannot be love."

"It is lust you feel, sweeting," he said low. His big hand slid smoothly down the arch of her back to fondle her buttocks.

"The Church says lust is a sin," she whispered, unable to restrain her own body, which seemed to want to press itself into his palm. "Coupling between a man and his spouse is for the purpose of procreating children," she recited primly. "I have not heard it said that coupling should be an enjoyable thing, and yet I liked it last night when the pain was finally gone. Is it wrong for me to like coupling?"

"Nay, sweeting," he murmured against her lips, his finger rubbing sensuously against the very tip of her backbone. "And lust between a man and his wife is permitted, I swear it! The Church may not publicly say it, but they know it is so, and it is a good thing." With his palm in the small of her back, he pressed her closer to him.

Daringly she ran the tip of her tongue across his lips. She did not know why she had done it, but she had suddenly wanted to.

His nostrils flared, and then he was pressing his lips against hers again, his tongue wild in her mouth. To his surprise, she did not flinch, but met him kiss for kiss until his head was spinning. Slowly he turned her about so that her back was to him and they could see their reflections, dusky gold and nebulous, in the narrow pier glass she used to inspect her costume. He heard her sharp intake of breath as his hands slipped up to cup her young breasts. He felt her struggle to control the motion of her body.

Nyssa stared, fascinated by what she saw. She had never really gazed at herself naked in a mirror. Was it the firelight that made her body seem ripely lush? His hands were so big. Yet her small breasts seemed to fit nicely within the cups of his palms. She watched as he gently rubbed her nipples with the balls of his thumbs. Then bending, he kissed her shoulder softly, nuzzling the spot where it flowed into her neck.

"You are beautiful, Nyssa," he said low, "and you don't even know how beautiful, do you, sweeting?" While one hand remained clasped about her left breast, his other hand began to caress her belly.

She viewed him through half-closed eyes, tense yet relaxed. A single finger slid between her nether lips and burrowed itself deeply until it found her most vulnerable spot. She ground her bottom into his groin, and he groaned.

"You make me feel so naughty," Nyssa whispered to him.

She saw him smile in the glass. "I like you naughty," he told her, nibbling on her earlobe with sharp teeth. "I am going to teach you to be very, very naughty, sweeting, and you will like it, I promise you." His tongue swept up the side of her neck wetly while his finger began to tease at her insistently.

She wanted to close her eyes for this was too personal, but he would not allow it, and forbade her. She saw the subtle changes in her expression as he aroused her. Her face seemed to grow more wanton with each passing moment. Her body was afire with new and very powerful longings. She ached, but pleasantly so. She could see from his look that he did too.

"Let us couple now," she begged him.

"Not yet," he told her. He picked her up in his arms and walked to the bed. Instead of laying her lengthwise upon it, however, he placed her so that she lay sideways across the bed, her legs hanging over its edge. Shocked, but unable to move, she watched as he knelt between her outspread legs, his head pushing between her milky white thighs. She felt his fingers opening her, and then to her great surprise, his tongue began to play with her sensitive flesh.

"Ohhh, no! No! No! You must not," she protested feebly, but for the life of her she could not stop him. It was so delicious, but dear heaven, *this* had to be wrong! For a moment she struggled against him, but then the sweetness began to possess her and she couldn't fight him. *She just could not.* It was too wonderful. And then when she thought her honeyed flesh could bear no more of his torture, he rose before her, his great manhood rampant with his desire for her.

He stood, his legs pressing against the bed, and then leaning forward just slightly, he drew her forward, his fingers digging into the soft flesh of her thighs and buttocks until she was fully impaled upon him. His hands reached out to fondle her breasts; then, steadying himself, he began to slowly pump her with great majestic strokes of his manhood. He suddenly felt incredibly strong.

Her breasts ached and felt hard, yet his fingers dug easily into them, almost hurting her. She felt him filling her, and it seemed that now he was bigger and stronger than he had been last night. Without knowing why, she wrapped her arms and legs tightly about him, gasping as she felt him plunge even deeper within her body. A sound something like a moan came from somewhere in the back of her throat. It did not even sound human. Surely she had never made such a noise before? There was no pain this time, only an incredible tension very deep within her that seemed to be building and rising within her until she was certain that she could not bear it another moment, yet she did.

"Nyssa! Nyssa!" he half sobbed her name into her perfumed hair. "Dear God, sweeting, I have never desired any woman as I do you!" His thrusts became more and more frantic within her.

She heard his words, and then suddenly she was lost, caught up in a rainbow-hued vortex that was spinning out of control, taking her with it. She was a butterfly, soaring, trapped in a maelstrom of passion so great that she had no control at all. "Varian!" She cried his name even as the feeling of pressure building within her exploded in a starburst of incredible pleasure at the very moment of his own release.

He could feel his love juices gushing forth in a great discharge of sweetness that overflowed her womb. He fell forward atop her body, exhausted, yet filled with a contentment he had never before known. He struggled to raise his head, looking down into her beautiful face. She was pale and seemed to be scarcely breathing, but then she opened her lovely violet-blue eyes slowly, focusing upon him.

"I love you, sweeting!" he declared passionately, and his look was one of great tenderness toward her.

Nyssa burst into tears. "Do not say it!" she begged him. "I do not love you. I do not even know you! It is not fair! Fate has made us man and wife, but I do not know what love is. How can you love me, Varian? How can you love a woman you do not even know? Such things only happen in children's tales of old. It cannot, *does not,* happen in our time."

"I love you, sweeting. I told you so last night. The moment I first saw you at Hampton Court I knew you were the only woman for me, Nyssa. I do not understand it myself, but when my grandfather so coldly suggested giving you to another man, I knew I could not let that happen. I could not allow anyone else to have you, to kiss your sweet lips, to plow a furrow in your love fields, my darling. You are mine, Nyssa. In time I will teach you to love me, I swear it!"

He lay his head upon her breasts with a sigh, and Nyssa gently stroked his dark head. Can love be taught? she wondered. Her mother had certainly learned to love her father. Blaze had not even known Edmund Wyndham when she became his wife. And had not her stepfather Anthony secretly loved Blaze, even when she purported to despise him and held him responsible for Edmund Wyndham's death? Yet eventually her mother had come to love her stepfather deeply. This was the way of her world. Still, it seemed so strange that Varian should love her when she had not even considered him as a husband.

Suddenly she realized that she was hungry. She had not eaten since early that morning, and then she had had nothing but some bread and wine. "I am starving, my lord," she told him. "Have you eaten?"

He raised himself off of her and then drew her up onto her feet. "Has my love for you not satisfied your hunger?" He teased her with a smile. "Thou art a greedy wench, I find."

"My stomach is hollow, sir," she told him. "My aunt keeps a good table wherever she may reside. She has been here for months now, and the cooks are well-trained by her at last."

"Let us call Tillie and have her bring us a full repast," he suggested. "I find making love to you ravenous work, madame."

"Cover your nakedness, my lord," she told him, climbing back into bed and pulling the coverlet well up. "My Tillie is a good girl. You must not shock her."

He pulled his breeches back on before calling for their two servants. Then he instructed Tillie, who wide-eyed went to fetch them a good meal. Toby was instructed to empty the tub and refill it for the earl.

Tillie returned, two kitchen maids in her wake. The girls could not help but giggle at the sight of Lord de Winter in naught but his breeches, bare feet, and bare chest. Tillie rapped them both sharply on the back of their heads, admonishing them, "Mind yer manners!" She directed them to lay the food out on a long, narrow oak table which was set along the window wall. Then she placed a decanter of red wine and a pitcher of foaming ale upon the table, slipping the goblets from her apron pocket. With a curtsey to her mistress and new master, she quickly shepherded the kitchen maids from the bedchamber. Toby, having finished his task of emptying and refilling the bath, was already gone.

"Will you bathe first, or eat?" Nyssa asked her husband.

"The water is too hot," he said, perusing the contents of the table, and then he observed, "Your aunt does keep a good table. I hope you will do so as well, madame."

"You will not find me lacking in housewifely skills, my lord," Nyssa told him. "Is your home very grand?"

"Nay, 'tis but a modest house. I have scarcely ever lived in it. You may find it old-fashioned, but it is yours to decorate as you will, Nyssa. I want to spend the rest of my life at Winterhaven with you, and with our children. I often think how lonely my father must have been there. He waited until he was practically an old man to marry, and then he lost my mother in childbirth. From the time I went to live with my grandfather, I spent only Midsummer's Day until Mid-Lammas with my father. After his death I only came in September to hunt." The earl took his plate and heaped it high with beef, capon, raw oysters, bread, and cheese. Seating himself upon the bed, he asked her, "What was it like to grow up at *RiversEdge?* Your father's hospitality was famous. My father often remarked on what a fine gentleman he was."

"I do not remember Edmund Wyndham," Nyssa said quietly. "I was not quite two when he was killed. My stepfather, Anthony Wyndham, is the father I have known. Growing up at *RiversEdge* was wonderful. I wonder now why I ever left it. I have five brothers, and twin sisters born six months ago. I will hardly recognize them when we go home. They were but a few weeks old when I left for court. I had ponies, and later on horses, and of course dogs, to play with as a child. My cousin, Mary Rose, was my best friend. We ran barefooted in the summer months, and rode our horses upon the frozen river in the wintertime. There is nothing special about my growing up."

"You had a family about you, Nyssa," he told her. "A mother, a father, and a houseful of siblings. Your aunts and cousins live nearby, I know, for they are my neighbors too, and your grandparents also. You are very fortunate, my darling, in all your relations."

"Were you very lonely, Varian?" she asked him, suddenly aware of how hard it must have been for him, a small, motherless boy given over to his power-hungry grandfather to raise. There would have been no abiding love in the Duke of Norfolk's house, or even time for it. Even the duchess had separated from Duke Thomas, and did not speak kindly of him.

"Lonely?" Varian thought a moment, and then said, "Aye, I was lonely, Nyssa. People never thought of me as the Earl of March's son and heir. I was always the son of Duke Thomas's bastard daughter. Nonetheless, being brought up in my grandfather's shadow was an education in itself. I had no time to feel sorry for myself, sweeting. He is a hard man, but he is also an admirable one in many ways. Still, I am of no real value to him, I realize. I do not like the games he plays, and he knows it. Now that I have a wife, it is time I returned to Winterhaven and took up my own responsibilities. The estate is large, and has not been properly managed in years. I will have much to do." He looked at her. "You are not eating," he said. "You will need your strength, sweeting. I do not intend to let you off so easily as I did last night."

"Is that why you swallow oysters so greedily?" she demanded. "I have been at court long enough to have heard of their restorative powers. Is it true, my lord?"

He grinned wickedly at her. "You shall soon see, madame," he promised her. "I advise you to fill your own belly while you may."

She flung back the coverlet on the bed, and sliding from the bed, walked naked over to the table where the food was laid out. She smiled to herself, hearing his sharp intake of breath. It pleased her that she was able to affect him so. Taking up a plate, she took a piece of capon, a braised artichoke, some bread and butter. Setting her plate in the window seat, she turned back to him and said sweetly, "Wine or ale, my lord? Tillie has brought both."

"Ale," he managed to croak. Jesu Lord she was tempting, and he knew she was very much aware of it. He was suddenly amused.

She filled a goblet and brought it to him.

"I do not think I have ever been served in such a fashion," he told her, chuckling. "Will you always serve me thusly, madame?"

"If it pleases you, my lord," she answered him demurely.

"Eat your supper, Nyssa," he told her. "I am almost through with mine. I have another appetite that will shortly need satisfying."

"First you must bathe," she told him. Then she bit into the piece of capon's breast she had taken for herself.

"Only if you will wash me yourself," he teased her. "I have always wanted a wife who would bathe me. And then I will bathe you."

"You forget, sir, I have already bathed," she said, smiling at him. She was rather enjoying his teasing. She had never imagined a man and a woman would tantalize each other so. She finished off her capon and licked her fingers before picking up the chunk of bread she had taken for herself. Thoughtfully she smeared the butter across the bread with her thumb, then bit into it. She had certainly not realized that men, like boys, enjoyed playing games. These games, however, were surely of a more dangerous, though eminently satisfying, sort. She swallowed down her bread and then arose to pour herself some wine. He was watching her. She could feel his eyes upon her. It was exciting, and not just a little frightening. Nyssa wished now that she had not been so bold and had wrapped herself in the coverlet. Nervously she pulled the leaves from the artichoke and nibbled them.

What an adorable creature she is, Varian thought. Nyssa. *His wife.* He could scarce believe it. They had not even been wed a full day yet, and he wanted her more now than he had before. She bewitched him, fascinated him, consumed him not just with her beauty, but with a mixture of intelligence, wisdom, humor, and sensuality. He had not realized that a woman could possess all of these traits, but then, he thought to himself wryly, what had he really known of women other than their lovely bodies? In his own way he was as ignorant of women as she was of men. What a wonderful time they were going to have learning about each other. He wondered if Thomas Howard had really known what a magnificent gift he was giving his grandson, would he have given it? His grandfather was not noted for his generosity, even to those of whom he was fond, and they were few.

"I am ready to bathe you, my lord." Nyssa's voice broke the silence of the room. She looked anxiously at him.

Varian arose and slowly stripped off his breeches. He held back a smile at her blush. It was charming that she could still blush, considering their last and recent lusty bout with Eros. Then she bent to check the water's temperature, and he felt himself becoming aroused. He forced himself to control his randy member, saying, "Is it comfortable, madame? I do not like too hot a tub. The skin shrivels."

"I think the temperature perfect, my lord," she answered, "but put your hand in and see if it suits you."

"I will trust your judgment," he told her, stepping into the tub and seating himself. He held out his hand to her. "Come, madame. This tub was built for two, and I specifically instructed Toby not to fill it so full that two people would overflow it."

"You told your servant that we would bathe together?" Her voice was shocked. "Ohh, my lord, how could you! What will he think?"

"It is not his duty to think, Nyssa," the earl replied.

"Mayhap not, my lord, but nonetheless servants do think, and they gossip among one another as well. Why, half the gossip at court comes first from the servants. If one wishes to learn the latest bit of scandal, one has but to ask the servants. I cannot believe that you did not know it!"

He looked perplexed, as if such a thing had never occurred to him. Of course, she thought. Men were so damned dense when it came to the practical. They never noticed what was right underneath their noses. He probably never considered that all the information that his Toby passed on to him was but the latest gossip from Toby's fellow servants. Even dear loyal Tillie, far more discreet than many, was prone to exchanging gossip.

"Since you will be accused of deliciously wanton behavior, madame, whatever you do, come into my tub and join me," he said. "I need you to scrub my back for me."

"I can scrub it from outside the tub, my lord," she replied.

"But I cannot scrub yours," he said. "Come, Nyssa, though I know some people at court who do not bathe from one month to the next, I have not heard it said that bathing twice in a single day can harm you."

His eyes were twinkling at her, and she found she did not want to resist him. So far his games had brought her naught but pleasure. Besides, if she was to be honest, she had become sweaty during their lovemaking. Her skin did feel quite sticky. He waggled a finger at her, and with a small laugh Nyssa stepped into the tub, sitting opposite him.

"There," he almost purred, "is that not nice, sweeting?"

"I think you a most outrageous and possibly dangerous man," she told him. "How can I scrub your back from here, my lord?"

"I shall turn about," he told her, and proceeded to do just that before she might protest about water upon the floor.

Nyssa took a handful of soft soap from the stone jar by the tub and smoothed it over his back. Taking up a soft cloth, she began to scrub him. His torso was very long, and his shoulders broader than she had realized, but then she had had little time to observe him.

"Be gentle," he teased. "My skin is delicate, sweeting."

"Do not play the fool, sir," she scolded him. Carefully she rinsed off his back. "There now, you are done."

He turned so that once again they were facing each other. "Wash my chest now, madame," he commanded her.

"You are determined to be spoilt, I can see," she told him, but dutifully took up a second handful of soap and smeared it across his smooth chest. Her hands rubbed with a circular motion over his muscled frame. She rinsed him, saying, "Now, sir, are you satisfied?"

"I must wash you," he told her, and before she could protest, he was rubbing soap over her breasts, fondling them, squeezing them, playing mischievously with her nipples.

"That is not how to properly wash," she exclaimed breathlessly.

"No?" He feigned innocence as he rinsed her, and then bending his head down, he kissed each pretty breast in turn. "Now, madame, your back," he said, but instead of letting her turn about, he slid his hands beneath the water and, cupping her buttocks in his hands, lifted her slightly before settling her down upon his raging member. Then pulling her against him, he began to calmly wash her back.

Nyssa gasped, shocked by his action. She had never heard of people making love in a bath! His hands smoothed soap over her back, while at the same time she could feel him very distinctly deep inside her sheath. *He was throbbing.* She shuddered with a rising awareness of her own desire even as he drizzled water down her back. Then he was taking her face between his hands and kissing her passionately, his tongue foraging deep within her mouth, making her dizzy with her own longing. She realized that their legs had somehow become tightly wrapped about each other, yet she felt like she was going to fall at any moment.

"Lean back," he growled in her ear, and when she did, he kissed the slender column of her throat, her chest, and her breasts, all the while thrusting with sharp, little movements within her. He seemed almost deranged in his longing for her, and she felt a strange wildness coming upon her. Her nails clawed at his shoulders and back. "Vixen," he groaned, and his mouth fastened about one of her nipples, drawing hard upon it. He suckled her fiercely, and she moaned, her head thrashing. "*Varian!*" she managed to cry out. "This is madness!"

"I cannot get enough of you!" he half sobbed. "Dear God, Nyssa, why can I not be satisfied?" He was kissing her frantically.

She realized that she could not fight him, that she wanted his passion every bit as much as he wanted to give it to her. Passion, it seemed, was as addictive as sugarplums. She felt her body thrusting back at him, seeking the wonderful pleasure he had earlier given her. When it came, she wept in his arms, shattered by the tremendous lust that had overwhelmed them both, yet contented by the final outcome. She had never realized that married people made love so often and in such a variety of places.

He tipped her face up to him and kissed her mouth softly. "I adore you, Nyssa," he told her quietly. "You are magnificent."

She blushed. "I cannot help myself," she told him. "When you make love to me, I truly enjoy it. I do not want you to stop, I fear."

"We have gotten water upon the floor," he said, his face not quite as repentant as it should have been. "Shall I call someone to clean it up, or would you rather we dried ourselves off and found our bed, sweeting? A bit of wine to restore us, a little rest, and perhaps we may again this evening find paradise."

"The water will evaporate, and tomorrow Tillie can remove the stains it leaves," Nyssa said in practical tones. "God's bones, I am hungry again! Does lovemaking always make one hungry, Varian?"

Together they stepped from the tub and dried each other off. Then Nyssa cut several slices of bread, lavishly buttered a piece for herself, and placed a slab of rare beef upon it. Biting into it, she smacked her lips appreciatively, and then held it out to him.

"Would you like a bite, my lord? It is delicious."

"I shall make my own," he told her, "and afterward, I'll have a sweet. Pear tartlet."

"I had another treat in mind," she told him mischievously.

"Madame, I must have time to restore my vigor," he told her again.

"Can you not . . . well, is it not possible . . . ?" she attempted.

"Not at will since I was seventeen," he said with a laugh. "You will not be neglected, Nyssa, for I find you arouse me more than any woman I have ever known, but I am shortly to celebrate my thirtieth birthday, sweeting, and need a bit more time than when I was seventeen to regain my stamina. You are young, and I would have you well-satisfied lest you seek another lover and break my heart."

"Ohhh, I should never seek a lover!" Nyssa declared. "I am your wife, my lord. It would not be honorable to betray you."

Wonderingly he shook his head. "What loyalty do you have to me, Nyssa? A day ago my family entrapped you into marriage with me, and destroyed your reputation with the king. Surely such behavior is not deserving of loyalty. In time, I hope, you will come to fully love and trust me, but for now I should not blame you if you hated me."

She sat cross-legged upon their bed, munching on her bread and meat, but she answered him honestly. "Varian, did you not tell me yourself that when you refused to take part in your grandfather's scheme, he threatened to put me in another's bed, so you agreed to help him after all because secretly you loved me? Certainly such action on your part is deserving of my loyalty. You saved me from the Blessed Mother only knows what horrendous fate."

"But you do not love me," he answered her.

"Nay, I do not," she replied frankly, "but perhaps in time I shall. I cannot promise you that I will, but though we have been wed less than a full day, I find that I do like you. You are kind, and you have humor. I need to know you better, Varian."

"Then you are not angry with me?" he said.

"Nay, not at you, but at your grandfather. I regret the way in which we were forced to wed. I regret that the king should think badly of either of us, even though we may not be important to him. I value the king's friendship. I am saddened that he should believe that I betrayed that friendship by wanton behavior. We cannot tell him the truth, however." She sighed, then continued, "My mother did not know my father, Edmund Wyndham, when she married him. She had had but a single glimpse of him once from behind a hedge when he came to seek Grandfather's permission to marry one of his daughters. He did not even know how many daughters my grandfather had, or how old they were. It was most outrageous of him."

"And how was your mother chosen?" Varian de Winter asked her. He was fascinated by this tale of his unknown mother-in-law.

"She was the eldest," Nyssa answered him. "She was not quite sixteen. My grandfather's flocks had twice been wiped out by disease. He was left virtually penniless with a fine estate, but no gold to dower any of his eight daughters. When the Earl of Langford appeared, and wanted one of his daughters to wife, Grandfather at first was suspicious, but he had never heard any ill spoken of Edmund Wyndham. My father told him that he was newly widowed and that he had no children. My grandmother's fecundity was well-known in our region. My father reasoned that if my grandmother could bear healthy, living children, then certainly her daughters could as well. That is why he sought out the Morgans of Ashby.

"Still my grandfather demurred, but then Edmund Wyndham made him so handsome an offer he could not refuse him. My father agreed to take Mama without any dowry at all. Indeed he agreed to supply her with everything she needed. He would also dower Mama's sisters and help my grandfather to restore his estates. Grandfather, of course, consented. He could do nothing else and be considered a reasonable man. Mama was furious. She believed that she had been bartered into marriage. My aunts, however, were simply delighted by their good fortune.

"My father's nephew, Anthony Wyndham, came to marry Mama as proxy for his uncle, and to escort Mama to *RiversEdge*. She was furious, and says she detested Tony on sight, but I don't believe it. She was prepared to hate my father too, but his charm, she says, won her over immediately upon her arrival at *RiversEdge*. She fell deeply in love with him. When he was killed in an accident, she blamed Tony. I was not even two, and Mama was with child again. She lost the baby, a son, and she hated Tony even more.

"My aunt Bliss brought her to court, and that is when the king saw her and fell in love with her. Tony had been in love with Mama since the first moment he had seen her, and now he followed her to court, and was devastated to learn of her favor with the king."

"Like I love you," Varian pointed out to Nyssa.

A sudden comprehension dawned in her eyes. "Aye," she said slowly. "I suppose it is the same, but with Mama there was my father first. Tony would never have spoken up while my father lived. He nursed his passion in solitude, and no one was ever aware of it."

"What happened when my cousin Mistress Anne Boleyn came?" Varian de Winter asked his wife. "How did your mother come to marry Anthony Wyndham?"

"Tony was my father's heir, as there was no living son. When he finally came up to court, it was with a mad plan. He intended to tell the king that my father had asked him on his deathbed to marry Mama and protect us. It was a ridiculous scheme, Mama says, for my father was killed instantly when his horse threw him; but Tony decided the king would not know that. The king, of course, was delighted to have an honorable means of ridding himself of Mama, since he was so fascinated by your cousin Anne. They were married in the king's own chapel, as you and I were, and departed court immediately. Mama was outraged."

"To be supplanted by my cousin?" Varian wondered aloud.

"Nay," Nyssa told him. "She had never wanted to be the king's mistress in the first place, but how was she to refuse Henry Tudor? She realized that she would be but a diversion to him until another diversion came along. She is genuinely fond of his grace even to this day, however, and he of her.

"Mama was furious that Tony had been so bold as to claim her with a lie she dared not deny for fear of his life, when she was certain she hated him with all her heart. In time, however, he won her over. They are very much in love to this day.

"I have always called Tony 'Papa,' for indeed I cannot remember Edmund Wyndham. He and Mama always promised me that I should choose my own husband. It was a foolish promise to make, I fear. Marriages among people like us are not usually contracted for love, are they?"

"Nay," he agreed with her, "they are not."

"So I am your wife, Varian," Nyssa said quietly, "in the eyes of God, and in those of man. I know how a wife must behave, and I will endeavor to do my duty by you and any children with which we may be blessed. More than that I cannot, nay, I will not promise. I think despite it all that I am fortunate in you as my husband."

Her honesty charmed him. He could not imagine any other woman sitting cross-legged and naked upon a bed, in conversation with an equally

naked man, being so charming. "Every word you say, sweeting," he told
her, "and every action you take, endears you to me all the more. I am not
dissatisfied with this match, and I pray your parents will forgive me for the
way in which it was brought about."

"I think my uncle already approves of you, my lord. You still have to
deal with my aunt, I fear. Then there is the matter of how my parents are
to be told of this marriage between us."

"Can we not wait until we return to *RiversEdge?*" he asked her. "I
should prefer to tell them face-to-face."

She liked him for that. It was the action of an honorable man. "Aye,
that would be best, but we shall first have to win over Aunt Bliss. Lady
Marlowe has her yet convinced that you are a villain."

Varian's face darkened. "That woman's tongue should be tied in a
knot," he muttered. "She is the worst gossip at court!"

Nyssa giggled. "What a marvelous suggestion!" She chuckled. Then she
licked the few crumbs remaining from her meal off her fingers and smiled
seductively at him. "Come to bed now, my lord. You will catch your death
of cold, and I shall have to spend our brief honeymoon nursing you with
mustard poultices and herbal tea."

"Do you not wish a piece of tartlet?" he tempted.

"Perhaps later," she said with a small smile, and tossing back the covers
on their bed, she beckoned him to join her.

"What manner of woman have I married?" he marveled at her.

"I do not think I know myself," she replied, "but we shall enjoy finding
out together, won't we, my lord?"

He burst out laughing. "I said earlier that I should teach you to be
naughty, Nyssa, but I do not think it necessary that I teach you. You are,
I am pleased to say, quite naughty already."

"You think me naughty because I enjoy your attentions, my lord? I
would think you pleased."

"I am pleased, sweeting. Do not think I am displeased by your actions.
Nay, I am very pleased indeed," Varian reassured his bride.

"If you are pleased with me, sir, then why do you stand halfway across
the room by the fire?" she asked coquettishly.

He turned lazily and lay two more logs upon the fire. Then crossing the
room, he climbed into bed with her. "Now, madame," he said, his look a
smoldering one, "precisely what is it you want of me?"

Nyssa slipped her arms about him and drew him down so that their lips
were almost touching. "Make love to me again, Varian," she murmured
softly against his mouth. "I want your passion again."

Gently he caressed her face. He had awakened her to the pleasures of passion, but once the novelty of it wore off, he knew that she would find passion a hollow thing without love between them. She was so very young, and innocent, but he had learned this evening that her heart was a good one. He could but pray God that he could win that heart as easily as he had won her lovely body. Tenderly he kissed her, and then he said, "You may have my passion, Nyssa. It belongs to you even as my love belongs to you, my sweeting. It is yours forever."

Forever, she thought muzzily, giving herself over to his kisses. It was a wonderful thought.

CHAPTER 8

SHE does not look like a girl forced
into a marriage," Lady Adela Marlowe told her friend, Bliss FitzHugh,
the Countess of Marwood.

They were seated in the gardens of the Earl of Marwood's rented house
on a lovely spring afternoon, watching as Nyssa and Varian returned from
a picnic. About them the narcissus, daffodils, and primroses bloomed in
a riotous display of bright color. The young couple strolled arm in arm,
the basket in which their meal had been packed dangling from Varian's
free hand. Both were dressed casually, the bridegroom in dark breeches,
his white silk shirt open at the neck. Nyssa affected country garb in a dark
green skirt and white blouse. Her feet were bare and she carried her shoes
in one hand.

"Indeed," Lady Marlowe continued, "they do not look unhappy to me
at all. Why, your niece has the look of a cat who has swallowed a particularly tasty bird, my dear Bliss. And it is quite clear to anyone observing
them that Varian de Winter is absolutely besotted by Nyssa. How can this
be? They have only been married two days. All the gossip says it was an
enforced union due to Lord de Winter's bad behavior with the girl. I did
warn you about him, Bliss," she concluded in superior tones.

"It seems," Bliss replied, "that he has admired Nyssa from the first moment he saw her at Hampton Court last autumn. He was determined to make her his wife, Adela. Nyssa had nothing to do with him, as you well know. She was much too busy with her duties. I really know nothing more about it. The king summoned Owen and me to him the other night, and the next thing we knew, we were in the midst of a wedding. Ohh, I hope she will be happy!"

"She has made her bed, and will have to lie in it," Adela Marlowe said sourly. She was absolutely certain her friend was holding back some delectable tidbit of gossip about the matter. It was really quite mean of Bliss, considering their long-standing friendship. "I can only imagine what her parents will say when they learn of their daughter's outrageous behavior and this hasty wedding," continued Lady Marlowe meanly. "I'm sure the Earl of Langford would wish for a better match for his stepdaughter than the one she has so precipitously contracted."

Bliss's temper finally snapped. "God's bones, Adela!" she swore. "To begin with, my niece is certainly not guilty of any *outrageous* behavior. Her conduct has been exemplary. Both his grace and the queen have remarked favorably on it. As for Varian de Winter, I find him a most charming man. His estates match Nyssa's, and, most important, he is no fortune hunter. Besides, he is a member of the Howard family. Even you cannot be so dense as to not know who the next queen is to be. Catherine Howard's name is on everyone's lips, and Varian de Winter is her cousin. All the Howards will soon be very high in the king's favor. Will not my niece be sitting pretty then, Adela dear? By the way, have you found a suitable match for your little son yet?" Bliss gave Lady Marlowe one of her best smiles, knowing full well that her friend's lack of success in finding a prospective wife for her son was quite a sore point with her.

"Look at them," Varian murmured to Nyssa as they came across the chamomile-dotted lawn. "They are like two old village goodwives. I wonder whose reputation they are shredding today, sweeting?"

"My aunt looks very smug," Nyssa observed. "She has obviously bested Lady Marlowe somehow." Then she giggled. "I keep thinking about your remark last night about tying Lady Marlowe's tongue in a knot. Do you think such a thing possible, my lord?"

He waggled his bushy black eyebrows at her menacingly. *"Shall we try?"* he asked her wickedly, causing his wife to dissolve into another fit of giggles. "Do you think her tongue forked like a snake?"

Nyssa laughed harder. Her sides were aching. "Stop, my lord!" she begged him. "I will wear myself out laughing if you do not cease. Then you shall be left alone and filled with desire tonight. Surely you do not want that?"

"Nay, sweeting," he said softly, drawing her into his arms, covering her face with little kisses.

"My lord," she chided him helplessly, but she did not really want him to stop. "Remember, my aunt and Lady Marlowe can see us."

"So much the better," he answered her. "It will give them something else to chew upon, my adorable Nyssa. God's bones, I wish we could go home to Winterhaven now. This very day! I want you all to myself, and we have but tomorrow. Then you must report back to the queen."

"We will have most of our nights," she told him, her eyes growing soft beneath his passionate gaze. "I no longer have a place to sleep in the palace, nor do you, my lord. Each night we will meet here, and secrete ourselves away from the world, Varian. It is enough for now."

"Blessed Mother!" Adela Marlowe said, scandalized. "He is kissing her, Bliss! Why, he looks as if he would take her right there upon the lawn. 'Tis most shocking to say the least!"

"I think it rather romantic," Bliss replied softly. "They are newly wed, Adela, and learning to know one another. It is charming. I am so relieved! Nyssa's happiness will certainly reassure my sister and her husband. It will take some of the sting from the situation."

"Have you written to them about the marriage?" Adela Marlowe asked.

"Nay, Nyssa and Varian wish to tell them. When the matter of the king's marriage to the queen is settled, they will leave court, going to *RiversEdge* first, and then on to Winterhaven," the Countess of Marwood told Lady Marlowe. "They are right to do it this way. A letter is so impersonal when dealing with such a delicate situation."

Nyssa and Varian had now reached the seated women. They bowed, and then passed on into the house, still hand in hand, smiling.

"Where do you think they are going?" Lady Marlowe wondered.

"To bed, to make love, of course," Bliss said with a laugh. "I know that if I were Nyssa, married to that handsome devil, that is where I would be going. They both arrived yesterday afternoon, and did not come out of their bedchamber until after ten o'clock this morning. Tillie brought them a tray last evening. Nothing was left upon it this morning when the maid brought it back to the kitchen. Not a crumb of food, Adela, nor a drop of wine." Bliss chuckled. "He has the look of a man with stamina," she observed wickedly.

"Your niece is certainly behaving boldly for a girl who purports to have been a virgin two days ago," Lady Marlowe noted sharply. "Why, she barely knows the man, or at least so you all claim, yet her demeanor is that of an experienced woman."

"She was a virgin," Bliss said, suddenly angry. "The king insisted upon seeing the proof of the consummation. He required that Owen and I be there to see it too, so there would be witnesses to the validity of the union. The Duke of Norfolk himself brought the bedsheet from the bridal chamber. And Tillie told my May that she saw the blood on Nyssa's thighs when she helped her to dress that morning. Do not dare to even suggest that Nyssa was not a virgin. *She was!"* Then realizing what, she had in her anger, blurted out, Bliss continued, "And if you dare to tell *anyone* what I have told you, Adela Marlowe, I shall never speak to you again! Nor would the king be pleased to hear you gossiping about such intimacies regarding Nyssa."

"I just knew there was something you weren't telling me!" Adela Marlowe crowed triumphantly. "Do not fear, Bliss, I shall tell no one else. I just wanted to know all the details myself. Sometimes it is much more fun knowing what others do not know, don't you think so?"

The newlyweds spent another passionate night together, after their day picnicking in the woods. The following morning, however, Nyssa's two brothers arrived to meet their brother-in-law. Philip was plainly disturbed by the gossip he had been privy to, but young Giles, with his natural diplomatic tendencies, cautioned his elder sibling not to prejudge the Earl of March.

"You must discount more than half of what you hear at court, brother," Giles wisely told Philip, with the aplomb of a more seasoned courtier, "and even then you can believe only a small portion of the remainder. Surely you have learned that in our months with the lady Anne. The merest flutter starts a rumor racing."

"But Nyssa is married," Philip countered, tight-lipped. "The king and the lady Anne have told us it is so. I would know why! I fear for our sister. Lord de Winter's reputation is not a savory one."

"There is but one scandal attached to Lord de Winter's name," the more practical Giles said patiently to his elder brother, "and it happened years ago. Lady Marlowe and her friends simply refuse to allow the tale to die a natural death. Perhaps if the Earl of March were not such a handsome fellow, it would have done so."

"I want to know how this marriage came to be," Philip Wyndham repeated stubbornly. "If Nyssa had been planning to wed, she would have certainly told us. Besides, she would have wanted to go home to *Rivers-Edge* to marry."

Philip's first glimpse of their sister did not particularly comfort him.

There was something very different about her. Something he could not quite put his finger on; a new lushness. She did not look like an unhappy woman. Indeed she was more beautiful than he had ever seen her.

Philip, Viscount Wyndham, and his younger brother, Giles, made their most courtly bows to their sister and her bridegroom. "Good morrow, Nyssa," Philip said tightly. "Good morrow, my lord." His young face was serious.

"May I present my husband, Varian de Winter, to you, my brothers," she responded.

Philip exploded in anger, much to Giles's disgust. "And just how did this man become your husband, Nyssa? What am I expected to tell our parents? The gossip is not pretty, sister! What explanation can you offer me for your behavior?" He glowered at her.

"How dare you, Philip," Nyssa replied angrily. "You have no right to question me. I am your elder by four years. Have you forgotten it, or has your service at court gone to your foolish head?"

Giles snickered, and was glared down by both his siblings.

"Despite the disparity in our ages, sister, as heir to Langford it is my duty to oversee your behavior," Philip said pompously. "It is reported your behavior was wanton, Nyssa."

"By whom?" Her look was scornful. "Philip, you are a fool," his sister told him bluntly. "Being at court has done nothing to improve you, I fear. For your edification, I was married in the Chapel Royal by the archbishop and Bishop Gardiner. Uncle Owen and Aunt Bliss were there. There is nothing else you need know about it. Where, I should like to ask you, is the scandal in a lawfully contracted marriage?"

"They say he raped you and forced the match," Philip said furiously. "I do not care if he is a Howard, I will kill him if it is so!"

"I did not rape your sister," Varian de Winter said quietly, seeking to calm the boy's anger. "And although my mother was a Howard, I am a de Winter, my lord."

"I am Giles Wyndham, my lord, and right glad to make your acquaintance," the younger of the two brothers interrupted, holding out his hand.

The Earl of March shook the lad's hand and smiled gravely down at him. "How do you do, Giles Wyndham," he answered.

"Well, actually, my lord, I do rather well," Giles said chattily. "The queen has asked me to stay on with her after the matter of her marriage is settled. I quite enjoy the court, you know," he explained with an infectious grin. He was doing his very best to defuse a difficult situation. Philip had always adored Nyssa, and looked practically near to tears. My brother is making a damned fool of himself, Giles thought, disgusted.

"You are truly all right?" Philip anxiously asked his sister. She hugged him hard. "Aye, I am fine, Philip."

"Why did you marry him?"

"I will not tell you now, Philip, but you must trust me that everything is perfectly fine. The earl is a good man. He is most kind to me. I understand this is a shock to you, but never again take such a tone with me, brother, or dare to question my behavior. You should know I would never shame our name. Had I been born a boy, 'twould be I who was Earl of Langford today, *and not your father*. Remember it in the future, Philip. Now kiss me, and greet my husband properly."

Viscount Wyndham kissed Nyssa's cheek and then held out his hand to the Earl of March. "You have my felicitations upon your marriage to my sister, my lord," he said stiffly.

"Thank you, my lord," the earl replied. The boy was still obviously confused and angry. It would take a little time to win him over. Philip Wyndham's devotion to his sister was quite touching.

"Has anything exciting happened at court?" Nyssa asked her brothers. "It seems we have been away forever, and yet we have had really very little time to ourselves. I must report to the queen in the morning." She smiled at her husband, and then asked her brothers, "Will you go home with us when we leave court?"

"I will," Philip said. "I am not particularly enamored of the court, although I should not have missed the experience of coming."

"And I," Giles replied to his sister, "will remain in the lady Anne's service. Were you not listening when I told Lord de Winter?"

"You must call me Varian, Giles," the earl told him. "And you also, Philip. After all, we are family now."

"You asked for gossip, Nyssa," Philip said, ignoring his brother-in-law. "Mistress Catherine Howard was seen walking with the king in the Knot Garden. They were alone, and unchaperoned. Lady Ferretface could scarcely wait to spread the news to all the other ladies in the queen's apartments. The creature has missed her calling, I think. She would make an excellent pimp. Her instincts are quite base considering her bloodlines."

"*Lady Ferretface?*" The Earl of March was intrigued, and then his face lit up. "Of course! 'Tis Lady Rochford you speak of, is it not, Philip? What a perfect name for her. I have often thought she resembled a weasel, or a ferret." He chuckled. "Your eye is very sharp, sir. I congratulate you."

Philip softened. He said honestly, "I have never liked her. She is always lurking about, and listening."

"Nor do I like her," Varian de Winter agreed.

"Varian thinks we should tie Lady Marlowe's tongue in a knot to stop her gossiping," Nyssa told her brothers.

They whooped with laughter, and suddenly the tenseness in the room was dispelled. A servant brought in wine and cakes. The two boys remained with Nyssa and her new husband for over an hour before taking their leave of the couple. Each departed richer by a gold piece, pressed upon them by the Earl of March.

"What a pity we don't have more brothers-in-law," Giles noted.

"I suppose he is not as bad as I had anticipated," Philip admitted.

"You were very good with them," Nyssa told Varian when her brothers had finally gone. "Giles is a diplomat, but Philip is prickly."

"Philip adores you," he noted.

"Aye, I was almost four when he was born, and he was my baby from the beginning. Giles didn't come for another three and a half years. For that time it was just Philip and me. The bond between us is a strong one too. He is hurt I do not tell him the whole truth of our marriage, but I will not until we return home to tell Mama and Papa of it. Philip is very hot-headed. It would be just like him to call your grandfather out for his part in this matter. It could do no good, of course. Besides, now that the king has set his sights upon your cousin, he would not like to be denied his greatest desire, or find himself in the midst of a scandal caused by a thirteen-and-a-half-year-old boy. Philip could easily end up in the Tower, and then poor Mama would have to come to plead his case."

"This family I have gained by my marriage to you, madame, are they always involved in each other's business?" he queried her.

"Aye," she told him, nodding her head. "When you wed me, Varian de Winter, you wed the Wyndhams of Langford, and all their kith and kin. You are now related to Lord James Alcott, and his sons the Marquis of Beresford, the Marquis of Adney, and the O'Briens of Killaloe, and their wives. And of course there are my grandparents, the Morgans of Ashby Hall, Aunt Bliss and Uncle Owen, Lord and Lady Kingsley, as well as all my cousins. You will never be alone again, Varian, though I suspect there will be times when you wish you could be," she finished with a chuckle. "Oh, yes. Christmas is always kept at *RiversEdge*. Mama does it so well."

It would be a country life for them, he thought, not in the least displeased by the notion. His new relations would advise him on how to restore his estate to its very best. Nyssa's cousins would marry, and there would be hordes of children. A whole new generation to grow up surrounded by a large and loving family. Celebrating holidays together. Coming together for the weddings and the christenings. Sharing not just their joys, but the sorrows that were a part of life as well.

He remembered his step-grandmother, Lady Elizabeth, once saying to him, "Do not let Duke Thomas convince you that the power and the glitter are all important, Varian. Family is most important. We gain our strength in the hard times from the love of our family. Remember it."

He had not forgotten, although there had been little warmth in his grandfather's house. Now he had found that warmth that he had sought, and the family he had always longed for.

They returned to court the following day. Nyssa reported immediately to the queen, who told her privately, "He has gifted Mistress Howard with several substantial land grants, and a gold pomander ball. I think my time here grows short, Nyssa. If you vould like, you may return to your home vith your bridegroom as soon as you vish."

Nyssa shook her head. "I will remain with you, madame," she told her mistress, and then she smiled. "Giles tells me that you have asked him to remain in your service. He is very pleased."

"He is a goot boy," the queen said with a smile. "He and Hans get along quite vell. I vill need only two pages, as Hendrick has already told me privately that my household vill be considerably reduced."

"Will you mind, dear madame?" Nyssa asked her.

"Nein," was the reply. "I do not really enjoy all the pomp and ostentation of this court, although I vill admit to enjoying the dancing, the cards, and my new clothes. I haf chosen Richmond for my home. Hendrick has said he vill gif me another house or two as vell. I haf left it to him to decide. Richmond is a pretty place, and I enjoy the river. It reminds me of the Rhine River in my homeland. I vill be happy there. I vill entertain the Princess Mary, who has become my friend, and Hendrick has promised me that little Bess may come to stay vith me from time to time. She is such an intelligent child. I do luf her."

"You will be content then, madame, and are not unhappy to remain in England?" Nyssa asked her. "Will you not miss your family?"

"Vhen I came to ved the king, I left my family behind," the queen said. "I vould far prefer to remain in England than to go back to my brother's court. Our father vas a stern man, but he had a sense of humor about him. My brother Wilhelm is too dour a man. Once he is satisfied that I am happy, he vill let it be. I am freer in England than I vould be if I returned to Cleves. I vill never haf to marry again, Nyssa. I think I prefer it that vay. But vhat of you? Is your husband satisfactory? Despite the circumstances of your marriage, I vould hope that you could find happiness in it."

"Varian is a man of humor," Nyssa replied with a smile.

"And you enjoy his . . ." The queen stopped a moment, nonplussed.

Nyssa realized immediately what she was asking, and replied, "Aye, madame, I do enjoy his attentions. Although I am unable to make any comparisons, I will admit that he gives me great pleasure in our bed sport. I believe that I like him."

"Vell then," Anne replied, "it is a goot beginning."

The attentions now lavished openly upon Catherine Howard by the king removed Nyssa and her husband from the gossipmongers' minds. They had far better fodder to chew upon now than the impetuous midnight marriage of the Earl of March and Lady Nyssa Wyndham. Lord Lisle, the father of Anne and Katherine Bassett, had been arrested on Cromwell's orders. The sisters were terrified. Then Gardiner's ally, Bishop Sampson, was sent to the Tower. Every day brought a new revelation, and the king was behaving like a lad of twenty instead of a man facing his forty-ninth birthday.

The king and queen appeared together on May Day, and for the next five days at the jousts at Westchester. They were seen at the banquets following the jousts that were held at Durham House. These banquets were open to the public, who came to view the king, the queen, and their court. Anne of Cleves was very much liked by the common people, who saw in her a royal princess of charm and dignity. If Henry Tudor was uncomfortable knowing this, he hid it well. He entertained the victors of the jousts, rewarding them with purses of one hundred marks each and houses in which they might live. Henry and Anne were never again seen together at a public function as man and wife after the May Day week festivities.

The month passed quickly. Catherine Howard, officially still one of the queen's maids of honor, was seen less and less in the Maidens' Chamber, or in Anne's presence. It was a difficult situation. Anne pretended, as she had secretly promised Henry, to be in ignorance of her situation. The queen, however, saw that things were coming to a head when on June tenth Thomas Cromwell was arrested at the council table in the Privy Council by the Captain of the Guard.

Upon being informed of his arrest, the chancellor snatched the bonnet off his head and threw it angrily upon the table. "God help and save my master, the king!" he cried as a triumphant Norfolk, aided by the Earl of Southampton, stripped him of his badges of office and his seals. "You play at power, my lords, but you have no idea of how really dangerous a game it is you play," Cromwell warned as the Captain of the Guard took him in his charge, escorting him to the waiting barge that would take him down the river to the Tower.

Thomas Cromwell's arrest order was filled with allusions to his low background, and everyone knew that to be the work of the Duke of

Norfolk, who hated the fact that a man of humble background could have climbed so high. The chancellor was accused of treason. There were generalities about his maladministration and abuse of power, none of which was provable. It was said he had usurped the royal power by setting traitors free; that he had granted passports, and drawn up commissions without royal permission. Worse, he was accused of supporting heresy by two of his enemies, Sir George Throckmorton and Sir Richard Rich. The latter had perjured himself shamelessly at the trial of Sir Thomas More.

It was all a fabrication by Cromwell's enemies, and he had made many in both high and low places. The king chose to believe the allegations because it was convenient for him to do so. He was still angry at Cromwell for having gotten him into the marriage with Anne of Cleves in the first place. Cromwell wrote to the king, piteously asking forgiveness for his crimes and begging for his master's mercy. Henry ignored his faithful servant.

Archbishop Cranmer, knowing Cromwell for no heretic, bravely attempted to intervene on his friend's behalf. He was one of the few people at court who actually liked and completely understood Thomas Cromwell. He knew him to be the most loyal of all the king's servants. Everything Cromwell had done, he had done in Henry Tudor's best interests. The king would have none of it. Cromwell was guilty and must be punished for his alleged offenses. Bishop Sampson, the Bishop of Chichester, arrested earlier in the spring on Cromwell's orders, was freed, as were Sir Nicholas Carew and Lord Lisle, the Governor of Calais, the Bassett sisters' father. There had been five other bishops on Cromwell's blacklist, but he had not had the time to act against them before his own arrest.

Catherine Howard had moved across the Thames to Lambeth Palace, having left the queen's service. It was an open scandal among the common people who saw their king being rowed across the river on a daily basis to spend time with his ladylove. Even the queen could no longer pretend she was not aware of his behavior, but whatever she might have thought, she kept to herself. Publicly she would say nothing that would feed the gossip mills. To her ladies who attempted to bait her, she would say, "If it makes his grace happy, so be it."

On the morning of June twenty-fourth the king came to the queen's apartments and said for all to hear, "The weather is hot for June, madame. I fear the plague will soon break out. I would have you leave this day for Richmond Palace for your health's sake. I will join you in two days' time." Then he kissed her dutifully upon her cheeks and departed. They would never meet again as man and wife.

Word was soon speeding through the court that the king was sending the queen to Richmond for her "health." The queen went docilely, smiling and waving to all the people along her route who cheered Queen Anne gladly from their hearts. Shockingly, the king and Mistress Howard were entertained that very night by Bishop Gardiner, who gave a gala banquet in their honor at his palace. The court was abuzz. There was no longer any doubt that the king meant to replace Anne of Cleves, and quite soon—but how?

Five days after the queen's departure for Richmond, a Bill of Attainder was passed against Thomas Cromwell. As he was accused of treason, his civil rights were to be eliminated and his property confiscated. The king had not yet joined the queen at Richmond, and everyone knew now he did not intend to do so. In the first week of July, the House of Lords formally petitioned the king to investigate through the clergy the legality of his marriage to Anne of Cleves. Henry agreed, claiming that he had been "espoused against his will." This declaration caused some amusement among the court, none of whom had ever known the king to do anything against his will.

The Privy Council departed that same day in mid-afternoon for Richmond to see the queen. They would need her consent to the proceedings. They traveled the river, nervous, and unappreciative of the fair summer day and the beautiful countryside about them.

"Pray God she is no Katherine of Aragon," Lord Audley said to his companions in the first barge.

"Aye," Suffolk answered. "He's in no mood to be denied much longer, and like the other two, Cat Howard is dangling her virtue before him like a prize to be won. He'll not get between her legs without a wedding band and the crown matrimonial." Suffolk shook his head. " 'Tis the same game they all play, yet he does not learn. First the Boleyn, then Lady Jane, and now this girl."

"I believe you will find Queen Anne most reasonable," Archbishop Cranmer said quietly. "She is a sensible lady, and most wise."

The three barges carrying the Privy Council arrived at Richmond's stairs. The queen, who had not been forewarned, greeted them cautiously. What if Hendrick had changed his mind about the terms of the dissolution of their marriage they had secretly agreed to months ago? What if he had decided to send her back to Cleves? Anne eyed her guests nervously. Carefully, the Duke of Suffolk, who was the Lord President of the Privy Council, explained the situation, believing it would come as a complete shock to the young queen. He asked that young Hans von Grafsteen translate his words into the queen's native tongue so that she would be certain to completely understand him and fully comprehend what was involved. The queen's ladies were goggle-eyed at the proceedings. What a story they would have to tell after it was all over. Their heads swung between the Privy Council and the queen.

"So," Anne said to Hans in their own High Dutch, "it has finally come. He will take his new bride, and spend a summer of romantic love. God help the poor girl!" She wiped at her blue eyes with a lace-edged scrap of linen, thereby giving them all the impression she was saddened by her situation.

"What should I answer the duke, Your Grace?" Hans asked.

"I shall answer him, Hans," she told the boy. Turning to the Duke of Suffolk and the rest of the Privy Council, she said in English, "Because of the deep affection and respect that I bear his grace, I am content, my lords, to let this matter be decided by the Church, as my good lord the king vishes it." She curtsied to them, hands folded modestly.

"Are you absolutely certain she understands?" the Duke of Norfolk growled. He wanted no difficulties in this matter.

"Ya, my lord," the queen answered him, to his great surprise. "I understand completely. His grace vorries that our marriage is not a legal one. I trust his grace, and he vould not bring this matter to the attention of the clergy vere his conscience not troubling him, ya? Therefore, as a goot vife, I must accede to his vishes to haf the matter investigated further, and I will." She smiled at them.

"Thank you, dear madame," the archbishop said. "You are truly an example in wifely obedience to all women. His grace will be very pleased."

The Privy Council departed, delighted to have had so easy a time of it, but Duke Thomas was yet suspicious.

"What is that woman up to, I wonder? She seemed almost glad to give her consent. Surely she must know if the king wants the matter investigated, that she will end up without a husband, or a crown."

"Perhaps," the archbishop said smoothly, "that pleases her. I realize such a thing is difficult for you to imagine, Thomas, but some people are not interested in worldly power."

"Then they are fools!" Norfolk snapped.

The king was extremely elated by the success of his Privy Council. Anne had been so reasonable in their secret discussions, he had grown fearful that she had just been lulling him into a sense of false security; that when the matter became public, she would protest and attempt to hold onto her crown.

The following day Henry made a written declaration to the clergymen impaneled for the investigation into his marriage to Anne of Cleves. In it he stated that his intentions had been honorable, despite the fact he had not wanted to marry again. He had done it for the good of his kingdom, to ensure the succession by having more children. However, despite the good reports he had of the Princess of Cleves, one look at her when she arrived in England had convinced him that he should never be able to love or to make love to this woman. He had gone through with the marriage despite his deep misgivings because he could not learn of any honorable way in which to avoid the marriage without embarrassing the poor lady, who was after all but an innocent pawn in a political game. Still, this matter of a possible precontract with the son of the Duke of Lorraine, and his inability to consummate the marriage, nagged at his conscience. He wished the clergy's learned opinion in the matter. He had absolutely no ulterior motives for wanting to dissolve his marriage to the lady from Cleves, but was that marriage legal?

During the next few days witnesses were called to testify in the matter before the assembled clergymen. The Earl of Southampton, Admiral Fitz-William, and Sir Anthony Browne told the court of the king's immediate displeasure upon meeting the Princess of Cleves. Cromwell, from the Tower, swore to the king's instant unhappiness and his desperate desire to be free of the match. It was the last act of a loyal servant. The king's physicians were brought in to testify. Dr. Chambers swore that the king had told both him and Dr. Butts of his inability to consummate his marriage to the lady Anne.

"He said he was certain that he might couple with another woman, but that the lady Anne filled him with revulsion and he could not even attempt the act with her. I advised him to not try further, that being the case, lest he debilitate his sexual organs," Dr. Chambers said.

"The king has had many nocturnal emissions during his entire marriage to the lady Anne," Dr. Butts told the fascinated court. "This, my lords, is proof absolute of a lack of intercourse. Though he has shared the lady's bed, she is as good a maid as the day she arrived in England. I will swear to it upon my own immortal soul." He folded his fat hands across his rather substantial paunch in a pious gesture.

The House of Lords debated the matter, even as the clergy discussed it. The possible precontract with Lorraine had to be finally disposed of because the duke had married his son to the daughter of the King of France. He would hardly have done so had his son been betrothed elsewhere. Best not to open the matter up again lest France become offended. War was not desirable at this point. The king's declared lack of consent to the marriage, and his inability to consummate it, were considered valid enough reasons for ending the marriage. There was but one male heir to England's throne. More were needed. If Henry Tudor could not get those heirs on Anne of Cleves, then what good the marriage? The House of Lords agreed. The marriage must be ended.

On the ninth day of July the convocation of clergy from both the Canterbury and the York archbishoprics found that the king's marriage to Anne of Cleves was null and void on the grounds of nonconsummation and lack of consent. Both parties were free to remarry. Archbishop Cranmer, the Earl of Southampton, and the Duke of Suffolk went to Richmond to inform the queen of the court's decision.

"From henceforth on, madame, you will be considered the king's most beloved sister," the Duke of Suffolk told her. He then went on to tell Anne of the handsome yearly allowance the king had settled upon her. "You will also be allowed to keep all your jewelry, your plate, and your tapestries. Richmond Palace, Hever Castle, and the manor of Bletchingly are now yours. Only the king's daughters and a new queen will take precedence over you when you visit the court, madame. It is hoped that you will be content with these most generous terms afforded you by our gracious lord, Henry Tudor. God save the king!"

"I am most content vith my dear brother Hendrick's generosity," the lady Anne replied. "I shall write to him in a day or two declaring myself amenable to all that has passed this day, my lord. Vill that be suitable, do you think?" She smiled sweetly at him.

Why, she's absolutely delighted by this turn of events, thought the Duke of Suffolk. 'Tis a good thing Hal is not here to see her glad face. "Aye, madame, 'twill be most acceptable," he replied.

"Dr. Wotton is to be sent to Cleves, dear lady," the archbishop said, "to explain these delicate matters to your good brother, Duke William. If you would like to send a letter along to the duke, it might ease his mind even more."

"You vill help me to compose it?" the lady Anne asked. "I vould not like my unfamiliarity vith the English language to cause any confusion on Vilhelm's part. His mind can sometimes be like a dumpling."

Both the Earl of Southampton and the Duke of Suffolk chuckled at her remark, but the archbishop said, "Would you not prefer to write to your brother in your native tongue, dear madame? Will he not worry, and wonder if you address him in English?"

"I am an English voman now, my lord," Anne answered them, "but if it vill put your minds at ease, ve vill write the letter together in English, and then you may haf it translated into the language of my birth. Send Vilhelm both copies, however, so he vill see that the original is written in my own hand. I vill reassure him, and he vill be content, ya?" She smiled brightly at them.

"And would you have us take a message to the king, my lady?" the Duke of Suffolk asked her. "To reassure him that you are satisfied?"

"Ya," Anne said. "You may tell the king, my brother, that I am his most obedient servant, now and alvays." She curtsied to the three men.

"Incredible," the Earl of Southampton said, as they returned to London in their barge. "I have never known so reasonable a woman, but then from the beginning, when I met her in Calais, she was anxious, nay, eager, to please his grace."

"She has certainly pleased him this day," the archbishop said with great understatement. "I suspect we have lost a valuable diplomat when we lost this queen. I have never known a better tactician."

"She was delighted to be rid of him if you ask me," the Duke of Suffolk remarked. "Poor old Hal would be quite annoyed if he knew how well she accepted his will. I think I shall tell him she fainted at the news, but then you, Thomas, reassured her of his grace's goodwill. It will please his vanity. What think you, my lords?"

"His vanity needs no pleasing these days," the archbishop told them. "Mistress Howard delights him so that nothing else matters to the king, I fear, I am not sure this is good."

"Come now, my lord," said the Duke of Suffolk, whose fourth wife was many years his junior, "a young wife is a happy thing."

" 'Tis not Mistress Howard who distresses, but rather her voracious family," the earl murmured softly. "Duke Thomas fairly champs at the bit to regain the power he believes is rightfully his."

"Then perhaps you will speak out for poor Crum," the archbishop suggested. "He was never the easiest of men to get on with, I know, but we all realize these charges against him are feeble, and untrue."

"Your heart is good, my lord, but your wisdom fails you here," the Earl of Southampton told him. "Cromwell's fate is sealed. He is a doomed man, and no one save God Himself can help him. The king has set his mind to wed with Mistress Howard, and we must take the lady's family with her. We have no other choice."

"How did the Howard girl gain the ascendancy?" the Duke of Suffolk wondered aloud. "Was not the king's fancy also taken by the Wyndham girl as well? But then she married Norfolk's grandson so hastily."

His two companions shrugged and settled back. The archbishop said nothing, and the Earl of Southampton knew nothing. The royal barge sailed down the river, out of sight of Richmond, where the former queen was even now telling her ladies that they might depart for the court or their own homes. Most of the women were eager to get back to Greenwich in order to secure themselves places with the new queen. The king's nieces and daughter-in-law had not even come to Richmond. The Countess of Rutland would remain, but only until her husband, the former queen's Lord Chamberlain, was formally dismissed. Sir Thomas Denny, Anne's chancellor, and Dr. Kaye, the almoner, took their leave of the lady Anne and joined the departing women in a line of barges back to London. All were polite, but it was obvious that Anne was now considered a part of the past. Catherine was the future.

There was no room in the barges for the maids of honor.

"You will leave in the morning," the Countess of Rutland said to those who were going.

Nyssa bid her friends a fond farewell. Kate Carey and Bessie Fitz-Gerald both wept. The Bassetts were polite. Helga von Grafsteen and Maria Hesseldorf were going to remain with their mistress for the present. Young Viscount Wyndham bid the Princess of Cleves an elegant goodbye, sweeping his bonnet off and bowing quite low.

"I am honored to have been in your service, madame. I am always at your disposal should you ever need me," he said.

"You are a goot boy, Philip," the lady Anne told him. "I am grateful for your friendship, my lord."

"Are you certain that you do not want to travel home for a visit, Giles?" Nyssa asked her younger brother. "Our parents will be most anxious about you. Are you sure that you would stay?"

"I have to make my mark here at court, Nyssa," he told his elder sister. "You know 'tis the only chance I have. The Church is no longer a good career for second sons. There are three brothers behind me for our parents to match and worry over. Eventually I will move from Princess Anne's service up the ladder, but if I leave now, how will I ever get another place? No, it is best that I stay. Perhaps I will come home sometime in the autumn for a visit. My only regret at remaining is that I will not get to see Papa's face when you present him with a husband." Giles chuckled and his blue eyes twinkled mischievously.

Nyssa laughed. "You are very bad," she said, and bending down, she kissed her little brother. "God watch over you, Giles."

The budding courtier bowed to her and replied, "God protect you and Varian, sister."

"Lady de Winter," the Countess of Rutland called. "You are holding up the barge. Come at once!"

Nyssa turned to the princess, and almost immediately her eyes misted with tears. "I do not like to leave you, dear madame."

Anne of Cleves swallowed back her own welling emotions. "You are not to worry, Nyssa. I haf escaped the English lion's claws with hardly a scratch. I am now a vealthy and propertied voman, and I haf no man to answer to from this day forvard. No brother Vilhelm, so full of importance and so joyless; and no husband Hendrick, who from the first did not like me for a vife. Ve are better friends, he and I. Do not veep on my behalf, Nyssa. I finally haf vhat I vant. *I am free.* Free to live my own life as I choose. Nein, liebling. I am not unhappy."

"But what of love, madame? Who is there to love you?" Nyssa's eyes were full of her concern for the princess.

"For you, Nyssa," Anne told her, "romantic luf is important. You haf learned luf at your mama's knee, nein? I learned duty at my mama's knee. Vhat I know of luf is vhat you and a few others have shared vith me. It is enough for me. I vant no more." The princess then kissed the young Countess of March upon her cheeks and her lips, saying, "Go now. Go home vith your handsome bridegroom. You may write to me if you desire to do so. I vould velcome your letters."

Nyssa curtsied low. "It has been a privilege to serve you, madame," she said. Then arising, she hurried to get into the last barge leaving Richmond for Greenwich, where Varian de Winter was awaiting her. Soon she stood on the hot deck of the barge, watching as the palace and the waving women disappeared around a bend. It was over. Another chapter in her life had closed. What would her future hold?

Philip came and stood next to Nyssa. He said nothing, but he sensed her feeling of loss and reached for her. She turned and smiled at her brother even as he squeezed her hand.

"We're going home, Philip, and 'tis summer, and ohhh, I cannot wait to see Mama and Papa, and our baby sisters."

"I have abided by your wishes, Nyssa, but I believe our family will be greatly shocked by the news of your marriage, now almost three months ago," Philip said seriously. "Would it not be better if I rode on ahead with Uncle Owen to prepare them for this news?"

"Nay, Philip, it is not your place to tell our parents of my marriage. It is Varian's and my duty to do so. I know it will be a great surprise, but you must not interfere."

He sighed deeply. "I wish I were a man grown. I hate being in between. And I will miss Helga. Isn't she just the prettiest girl, Nyssa? And her heart is so good and kind," he finished with a blush.

"Why, Philip, I believe you have conceived a tendre for Helga von Grafsteen. Why do you not discuss it with Papa when we return to *RiversEdge*? I'm certain her dowry is a respectable one."

"Do you think he would listen to me, Nyssa?" Philip asked his sister. "He always makes me feel so young, though I shall be fourteen in October.

If the match could be made, and we waited until I was seventeen, Helga would be old enough by then too."

"Then speak with Papa, Philip. You don't want him to make a match for you with some girl you do not like," she advised.

"You were forced into a marriage," he said glumly.

"It is fortunate then that Varian and I like each other," Nyssa told him with a small smile, and then she grew silent again.

Their barge passed the soaring spires of Westminster and on through the city of London, sweeping southeast down the river to Greenwich. There was just the faintest breeze coming up from the sea past Gravesend, and then the towers and turrets of Greenwich came into view. She could see the other barges that had preceded them unloading their passengers. As the ladies and gentlemen who had been a part of Anne of Cleves's household swept up the green lawns, a lone figure remained. Her heart beat a little faster as she recognized that figure. It was Varian de Winter. It was her husband come to take her home.

CHAPTER 9

I SIMPLY will not let you go, Nyssa!"
Catherine Howard told the Countess of March. "You cannot leave me!
You are the only true friend that I have. All the rest of them! Pah!
Hangers-on, and greedy for what I can give them, but you are not like that
at all. I can trust you! *You must stay!"*

"Nay, Cat, I must go home," Nyssa told her friend. "My parents know
absolutely nothing of my marriage to your cousin. It is hardly something
I wished to elaborate upon in a letter. In all my whole life I have never been
away from *RiversEdge* until I came to court last autumn. I miss my family,
and they must meet and get to know Varian. If we do not go now, then
when?"

Although she was ostensibly staying with her grandmother at Lambeth
House, Cat Howard had rooms at Greenwich. Both she and her companion would have been fascinated to know that they were the very same
rooms once inhabited by Nyssa's mother, Blaze Wyndham, during her
brief tenure as Henry Tudor's mistress.

Cat pouted prettily at her friend's words. Her auburn hair caught the
sunlight streaming in through the windows that overlooked the river.

Nyssa thought how pretty she suddenly was. The dress Cat wore was obviously new, and of a very expensive material such as Cat had rarely seen. It was a deep rose silk with a low neckline that exposed a good deal of her pretty breasts. The gold pomander ball that the king had given her in April hung from her waist. About her neck was a rich gold chain studded with rubies, and every one of her plump little fingers had a beautiful ring upon it; and each of those rings had a fine gemstone set in it.

"If I ask Henry," Cat said slyly, "he will make you stay. He will do anything for me, Nyssa! *Anything!* I have never had a man so wild for me. It is quite astounding, considering his age."

"You have had other suitors? I did not know that." Nyssa was surprised. Cat had always presented herself as a complete innocent, although looking back upon some of their conversations, Nyssa realized now that that was not quite the case. And why wouldn't she have had suitors? She was a pretty young woman. Thomas Culpeper had certainly noticed her, although Cat said she had never bothered with him. If Cat was lacking in dowry, she was rich in powerful relations, which was almost as good in some cases.

Cat giggled. "You must not tell on me," she said. "Duke Thomas does not even know. The first man to pay me court was my music master, Henry Manox. He gave me my first kiss. Then when I was at Lambeth before I came to court, there was Francis Dereham, a gentleman pensioner in Duke Thomas's service." She giggled again. "My step-grandmother, Duchess Agnes, never knew what went on amongst her charges as long as we were mannerly in her sight."

Nyssa was shocked. "Tell me no more, Cat," she said. "But you had best tell the king of your harmless little romps. If you do not, someone else, jealous of you, surely will."

"If I tell Henry, and he grows angry with me, Duke Thomas will never forgive me. Nay, it is better I say nothing. No one will tell, for all were equally guilty of collective naughtiness. None will want to accept blame, and so all are safe from scandal," Cat said to Nyssa. Her little hands nervously smoothed her gown. "You will stay, won't you, Nyssa? I should be lost without you," she wheedled her friend.

Nyssa shook her head. "I must go home, Cat. Besides," she explained reasonably, "you will soon marry the king, and be off on your honeymoon. You will not want me along then. The king will want you all to himself. He is very much in love with you. Everyone can see it. It is quite the talk of the court."

"It is, isn't it?" Cat replied with a rather smug smile. "They say he has never behaved with any of the others as he does with me."

"You are very fortunate to have a man who loves you, Cat," Nyssa said. "Do be good to him. My mother says if a woman is good to her husband, he will always treat her well."

"Does she? How curious. I do not remember my mother for she died when I was very young, and I was sent off to the Howards at Horsham to be raised with my sisters and half a dozen others. I came to Lambeth when I was fifteen, and was put in Duchess Agnes's care. Do you think I will have children, Nyssa? I think I am afraid of it."

"The king wants other children, Cat. 'Tis one of the reasons he takes a young wife. We have only Prince Edward. There should be at least a Duke of York, and perhaps another Duke of Richmond."

"The king has two daughters," Cat answered sullenly.

"But a woman cannot rule England," Nyssa said. "Nay, you must give his grace at least two fine boys."

"And what of you? Will you not give my cousin Varian sons? You have been married for almost three months already. Is there no sign of a child? Varian likes children, you know. He would come to Horsham when I was a child to play with the little ones," Cat told her.

"Did he?" Nyssa was fascinated with this bit of information regarding her husband. He had certainly never said anything to her about children.

The two young women chattered for some minutes more, and then Nyssa arose, saying, "I really must go, Cat. Varian will be furious with me. I told him I was coming just to bid you farewell. I have been here for almost an hour. We have several days' travel ahead of us."

Catherine Howard stood up and hugged her friend. "Promise me you will come back to court when I am queen," she said, her cerulean-blue eyes boring into Nyssa's soft violet-blue ones. *"Promise!"*

"Some day," Nyssa said offhandedly. "I promise."

"For Christmas at Hampton Court," Cat persisted.

"Oh, not Christmas," Nyssa said, shaking her head. "Christmas is always at *RiversEdge*. I missed both it and my birthday last year because I was in service to the queen. *Not Christmas, Cat.*"

"Twelfth Night, then," the young queen-to-be commanded.

"I shall speak to Varian," Nyssa promised.

And I shall speak to Henry, Catherine Howard thought silently.

Nyssa went to take her leave of the king. She curtsied low to the monarch.

"It has been some weeks since I have seen you, my wild rose," Henry Tudor said. His love for Cat had made him benevolent again toward

Nyssa. "You bloom," he noted. "I must assume that your marriage to the Earl of March is not an unhappy one, then. What thinks your lady mother?"

"She does not know, Your Grace," Nyssa said. "We prefer to tell her together face-to-face. I think it better that way."

"Aye, you are very wise, madame." He smiled at her. "I have a wedding gift for you, Nyssa de Winter." The king lifted a fine filigreed gold chain studded with diamonds from about his own neck and placed it over her head. "You may come back to court when it suits you, madame," he told her. "You served well, and are much like your faithful mother."

"Your Grace!" She was astounded. Her hand went to the magnificent chain, and then she looked directly at him. "Ohh, thank you, my good lord! I shall treasure this gift all my life."

The king was pleased by her ingenuousness. "Go, madame, for you have a long journey ahead of you, I know. Perhaps next year we shall visit you, but this summer we have other matters to attend to, eh Will?" He turned to his fool, who nodded. "Tell your good parents that I send them my felicitations and praise the service that their daughter did render to the crown." He held his hand out to Nyssa, and she kissed it.

Then she curtsied a final time. "God bless Your Grace in all of his endeavors," she said, and backed from his presence. The king could be kind, but she had learned he was a gross monster who demanded his way in everything. She knew now the pleasures of lovemaking, and the thought of Henry Tudor as a lover sent cold chills down her spine. She most certainly did not envy Cat Howard.

When the door had closed behind her, Will Somers said to the king, "Once I chided you for letting her mother go, Hal, but nothing would do but you must have a Howard. I wonder if you do not make the same mistake again." His sharp brown eyes queried the king.

"This time it will be different," Henry Tudor said firmly. "My Catherine is a rose without a thorn, Will. I shall never be unhappy ever again. She will give me sons, and brighten my old age."

Will Somers shook his grizzled gray-brown head. The king was practically fifty years of age. He had walked this earth almost a half century, yet he was still a dreamer and a romantic. Will loved his master, and it pained him to see him hurt. How long would Catherine Howard make poor Hal happy before something or someone spoiled the idyll? Will Somers had seldom seen a happy ending here at court. He moved quietly to the windows and looked into the court below. The travelers were even now departing Greenwich.

Young Owen FitzHugh and his Kingsley cousin had been sent home earlier in the spring. They had seen the court, and there was no reason for them to remain. Nyssa and Varian would travel in the company of the Earl and Countess of Marwood, and young Viscount Wyndham. There was a coach along in the event the ladies chose to nap along the way, but for now both Nyssa and her aunt preferred to ride. A second carriage was provided for the upper servants, but Toby and Lord FitzHugh's body servants also rode. Only Tillie and Maybelle sat within. There were several baggage carts, and, of course, men-at-arms to guard it all.

The countryside was in full summer dress, but by mid-month there had yet to be any rain. In fact it had not rained since the end of May. The roads were hard, dusty, and dry as they made their way, moving west from Greenwich, and thereby avoiding the city of London. The Earl of March was impressed by the traveling arrangements made by his in-laws. There were fresh horses for them and for their coaches available all along their route. They stayed at the best inns, all of which had been notified ahead of time of their coming.

Marwood Hall and *RiversEdge* were located relatively near to one another, the boundaries of the two estates lying only five miles apart. Bliss and her husband would not, however, be going directly home. It would be necessary for them to accompany their niece to *RiversEdge,* where her parents would be told of Nyssa's marriage. Varian de Winter found himself nervous for the first time in his life. They traveled comfortably for several long days, and then suddenly one afternoon Nyssa began to recognize the landscape about her.

"We are near to home!" she said excitedly. "Look! There is the dear old Wye. Ohhh, see! The Mary's gold and the asters are already beginning to bloom." Her face was bright with delight. She knew she had missed *RiversEdge,* but not until this moment had she realized how much.

They descended from the London Road to what was called the River Road. It ran parallel along the Wye for several miles directly to *Rivers-Edge.* The land rolled gently on either side of the water.

Nyssa spurred her horse ahead of the others. " 'Tis Michaelschurch ferry crossing, Varian," she called to her husband. "Rumford! Rumford! 'Tis Nyssa Wyndham, and I'm home from court!"

The very elderly man seated upon a bench beneath a large oak tree arose slowly and turned to see who it was calling his name. His weathered face split into a wide grin as his eyes made out the rider. Reaching for his staff, he hobbled forward. "Mistress Nyssa! Yer home, and surely prettier than ever before," he told her as she came to a halt before him. Nyssa dismounted and hugged the old man.

"How is the ferry business, Rumford?" she asked him.

"Slow, mistress. Only the family and an occasional peddler to take across the old Wye these days," Rumford said. "Two of me three sons is now farming for yer da. Only the youngest helps me with the ferry. T'others say he can have their inheritance and good riddance. These modern times is different than when I was a lad, but what can I do."

"As long as there is a Rumford for the ferry, I can see no changes," Nyssa told him. "The Michaelschurch ferry is Rumford business."

The old man cackled with laughter. "Aye, and it is, mistress. Didn't I tell yer mama that all those years back when she come here as a bride for Lord Edmund, yer good father of sainted memory, God assoil him? Michaelschurch ferry and the Rumfords are one and the same."

Nyssa remounted her mare. "I will be needing your services shortly, Rumford," she told him with a smile. "You'll hear soon enough." Then she rejoined the others in her party, who were making their way to the house.

"Who was that?" Varian asked her. When he had visited Winterhaven, he had taken a road on the other side of the river.

"Old Rumford, the ferry keeper," Nyssa told him. "There have always been Rumfords to keep the ferry at Michaelschurch, or so they tell everyone. Frankly, no one can remember a time when there were not. My mother arrived at *RiversEdge* by crossing the Wye on that ferry. My grandparents and Kingsley relations live on the other side of the river. It is how we will go to Winterhaven, is it not, my lord? Oh, look! 'Tis *RiversEdge!*" she said excitedly.

Varian gazed in the direction in which her slender finger was pointed. A magnificent dark red brick house, covered in shiny green ivy and built in the shape of an H, lay ahead of them. About it were well-tended gardens, colorful with summer blooms. "I fear, sweeting, that Winterhaven is nothing so fine as your *RiversEdge,*" he told her. His eyes scanned the gray slates that roofed the house. There were a number of chimneys soaring upward above the roofs, which indicated to him a vast number of rooms with fireplaces.

"We will make Winterhaven every bit as grand," Nyssa promised him. He smiled at her, adoring her loyalty, for he knew how much she loved her childhood home.

As the horses and vehicles came to a stop before the great front door of *RiversEdge,* that door was thrown open and a very handsome couple emerged. The woman had Nyssa's eyes, but her hair was honey-colored. The gentleman was tall, with dark hair and very blue eyes. It was he who reached up and lifted Nyssa from her mount.

"Welcome home, my precious daughter," Anthony Wyndham said warmly, and he kissed the girl on both of her cheeks.

"Thank you, Papa," Nyssa said, and then turned to her mother.

The two women kissed, and Blaze knew instantly that something had changed. "Has the king dispensed with your services, my child? While I am delighted to see you home again, I am surprised. Until your uncle's outrider arrived yesterday, we had no idea that you would be coming. Is everything all right?" Blaze could see that her sister looked nervous, and who was this unfamiliar but most handsome gentleman?

Nyssa smiled at her parents reassuringly. "Let us go inside and have some wine, Mama. The road has been appallingly dusty. I shall tell you both of my adventures at court." She slipped her arm through her mother's and walked with her into the house.

Anthony Wyndham greeted his eldest son and heir. "So you've come home, lad, eh? Court not to your liking?"

"It is an experience worth having," Philip said, "but like both of my parents, I prefer the country. I did, however, meet a young lady I should like to speak with you about, sir. I realize that we are yet too young for marriage, but perhaps we could make those arrangements for the future before the year's end. She is one of the lady Anne's maids of honor. Her name is Helga von Grafsteen."

"A foreigner?" The Earl of Langford looked a bit disturbed. "She'll need a good dowry, lad, to make up for a lack of English lands. I had hoped one of the girls about here would suit you, but we can talk."

"Thank you, sir," Viscount Wyndham replied, and then he accompanied his father into the house.

Varian de Winter followed, his eyes reflecting his amazement at the warmth and charm of the Great Hall of *RiversEdge*. The room had a lofty, soaring ceiling with carved beams that were gilded and highlighted in a scroll design. Windows, set high, lined both sides of the hall, allowing in a wealth of bright sunlight. There were four fireplaces, none of which was now burning, as the day was so hot. The high board, at the far end of the room, was fashioned from golden oak. It was well-polished, and gleamed with the warmth that only age and loving care could give it. Behind the high board, and centered, were two thronelike chairs.

Well-trained, attentive servants were immediately in evidence, offering the guests wine and small biscuits. The servants were clean, as was their clothing. They were soft-spoken and mannerly. The Earl of March could but wonder what Nyssa would think of the elderly, creaking retainers she was going to find at Winterhaven.

Blaze Wyndham now turned to look at Varian de Winter. "And who is this gentleman, Nyssa?" she asked her daughter.

"Mama, may I present to you Varian de Winter, the Earl of March . . . my husband," Nyssa replied quietly. There! It was done.

"What!?" The single word was positively shouted by the Earl of Langford. "You cannot marry anyone, Nyssa, without my permission, and if you have, it shall be annulled immediately, girl. I will not have it! Do you understand?"

"Tony," his wife pleaded, "cease your outrage, and let me learn the truth of this matter." She turned to her sister and brother-in-law. "How were you involved in this matter, Bliss? Why did you not write to me about it?" She turned back to her daughter. "Indeed, Nyssa, why did you not write to your father and me about this?"

Owen FitzHugh spoke for them both. "This is Nyssa's story to tell, Blaze. Afterward, if either Bliss or I can add anything, we shall be happy to do so. We protected Nyssa as best we could."

"But obviously not well enough," growled the Earl of Langford. "My daughter's come home wed to some damn fortune hunter we don't even know! A fine state of affairs, and you'll answer to me for it, Owen."

Varian de Winter spoke up. "My lord, I am no fortune hunter, but your neighbor from across the river. Winterhaven is my family's home. You may have known my late father, Henry de Winter. I left my estates when I was six and was raised by my grandfather."

"And who the hell is he?" demanded Anthony Wyndham, red-faced with outrage. What the hell had possessed Nyssa to marry this man without their permission, or even their knowledge? She was not a flighty girl.

"My grandfather," the Earl of March said quietly, "is Thomas Howard."

"The Duke of Norfolk?" The Earl of Langford was visibly impressed, but he was still not satisfied.

"I would like to hear my daughter's explanation for her rash behavior," Blaze said quietly. Her husband noted the use of the word my.

"If you have all finished shouting, and posturing, and cross-examining each other, I will be happy to tell you how I came to be married to this gentleman," Nyssa said.

"Philip!" roared his father. "Where the hell were you in the midst of all of this? Could you not have protected your sister?"

"I knew nothing until it was an accomplished fact, my lord," Philip told his father bluntly.

"We were married in the Chapel Royal on April twentieth by the

Archbishop of Canterbury and Bishop Gardiner," Nyssa said quietly.
"The king was there. Indeed it was he who ordered my marriage to
Varian."

"Why?" Blaze asked her daughter.

"I must start at the beginning," Nyssa told her mother. "You have
heard the rumors that the king did not like his new wife, the Princess of
Cleves? They are true, though why he felt this way no one can really
understand. The lady Anne is a kind and good woman. Still, nothing
would do but that the king escape this marriage. He was granted an
annulment on the ninth day of the month on the grounds of nonconsummation."

"Nonconsummation?" the Earl of Langford snorted. "That damned
satyr will flourish his lance in any convenient sheath."

"Nay, Papa," Nyssa said. "He did not use the lady Anne. I know."

"But what has this to do with your marriage to this gentleman?" Blaze
pressed her eldest daughter. "I do not understand."

Nyssa quietly explained to her family what had happened on that
fateful night.

"And you lent yourself to this, my lord?" Anthony Wyndham said
scathingly to Varian de Winter. "I think little of you for it."

"What would you have had me do, sir?" the Earl of March said fiercely.
"My grandfather did not care with whom she was discovered. Better it be
someone who loved her than someone who did not." He glared at his
father-in-law.

The veins in Anthony Wyndham's neck stood out with his anger, but
his wife had understood the words that he had not. *Better it be someone
who loved her.* Looking at the Earl of March, Blaze saw that he did love
her daughter. He was as angry, and as protective of Nyssa, as Tony. She
put a restraining hand upon her husband's arm.

"He loves her, Tony. Can you not see it? Temper your anger and look
at him. *He loves her,*" she said softly.

"But does she love him? We always promised her that she could marry
the man she loved," Lord Wyndham replied. He looked at the girl. "Do
you love him, Nyssa? Tell me the truth, poppet. If you are unhappy, if this
is not to your liking, I will move heaven and earth to free you from this
man! I will not allow you to be unhappy for the rest of your life, Nyssa.
Neither your mother nor I want that."

"I do not know if I love Varian," Nyssa said honestly, "or if I will ever
love him. Is that not a chance people of our station take when we marry?
You did not know if Mama would ever love you when you married her.
Varian is a good man, and I do not think I can expect anything more than

that, Papa." She kissed her stepfather's cheek. "Now come, and give my husband your hand in friendship. Give us your blessing too."

"But," he protested, "I always promised you your choice of a husband, Nyssa. I feel that I have failed you somehow. I should not have allowed you to go to court. I knew it at the time, but I let you all overrule me because the king promised to watch out for you. Bliss, you swore to me that you would chaperone my daughter carefully. You failed, and now my child is trapped in a loveless marriage."

"Anthony," his wife said sternly, "Nyssa is not trapped in a loveless union. She is as loved by her bridegroom as I was loved by you when we were first married. Look at your son-in-law! He is calf-eyed over the girl. If you cannot see it, it is because you do not want another man in Nyssa's life but you. You never encouraged her to consider any of the young gentlemen hereabouts. Well, the matter is now out of your hands. Nyssa is a married woman, and if you will not, I will now welcome the Earl of March into this family." Standing upon tiptoes, Blaze kissed her son-in-law. "Welcome to *RiversEdge,* Varian de Winter. I met your father but once, at my wedding feast, when I married Nyssa's father, Edmund Wyndham. You favor him, except about the eyes. You have your grandfather Howard's eyes."

He smiled a slow, warm smile at her, raising her hand to his lips and kissing it. "I appreciate your kindness, madame. Let me assure you that I will care for your daughter with all the devotion I am capable of, I swear it!"

"Aye," Blaze said, returning his smile, "I think you will. You have my blessing."

"Hrrrumph!" Anthony Wyndham cleared his throat noisily, and they turned to him. He held out his hand to Varian de Winter. "You have my hand, my lord, and my blessing as well," he said. "But treat my daughter badly and you will have my enmity. I am not pleased with the fait accompli that you have presented me with, but since it would appear that I can do nothing about it, I will give you the benefit of the doubt."

"I thank you, my lord. I love Nyssa. I will not fail the trust you have placed in me," the Earl of March said.

"Then it is settled, and we can go home to Marwood Hall," Bliss said brightly, relief permeating her entire being. It had not been as bad as she had thought it would be. Anthony had been angry, and he had castigated her, but he was now resigned, thank goodness!

"Where is Giles?" Blaze asked her sister.

"The Princess of Cleves is going to remain in England," Bliss said. "She will now be called the king's sister, and only a new queen and the princesses will take precedence over her. She asked Giles to remain with her household, and he agreed to do so."

"He's a born courtier," Nyssa told her parents. "He thinks he has a future at court, and considers the lady Anne's household as a starting place. He will eventually be asked to join another household, Mama, I'm quite certain. He is very well-liked, and most clever for a boy so young."

Blaze and her husband nodded, satisfied. It was a good future for their second son.

"Will he come home anytime soon?" Blaze asked.

"He said perhaps in the autumn," Nyssa replied.

"We really must depart before dark," Bliss said loudly.

"Oh, very well, Bliss," her sister said. "Go home!"

The Countess of Marwood practically ran from the Great Hall, her husband following in her wake, chuckling quite audibly.

Anthony Wyndham could not prevent the smile that set the corners of his mouth lifting upward. "Poor Bliss. She was, I see, quite fearful of what I would say about this matter," he said.

"And with good cause, I think, Papa," Nyssa told him, laughing.

"You must be exhausted with your traveling," Blaze said. "Show Varian to your chamber, Nyssa. We will eat at the usual hour."

"Where are my brothers?" Nyssa asked her mother.

"Probably swimming in the river. Surely you have not forgotten? 'Tis summer, and all of you loved to paddle about the old Wye," Blaze said. "That is far more important than having an old sister return from court." She laughed, and Nyssa joined her.

"How old are your sons, madame?" Varian de Winter asked his mother-in-law.

"Richard will be nine in the late autumn. Teddy was just five, and wee Henry is three," Blaze told him. She looked at her daughter. "You will not believe how Jane and Annie have grown, Nyssa. Jane is already saying 'Da, Ma,' and she says 'Bo' for her brothers. They adore her. Annie, however, is quieter, allowing her sister to speak for them both, but she is close to walking on her own, and getting into everything." She looked at her new son-in-law again. "Do you like children, my lord?"

"Indeed I do, madame. I hope we will have as fine a family as you do. I was raised with my aunt and uncle, but I was some years their senior. I would have enjoyed a larger group of siblings."

"If you wish to remain here talking," Nyssa said, "I shall leave you, my lord, for I desire nothing more than a bath right now. I vow that all of the dust from England's roads is lodged in my hair and on my skin. The tub

I had at our house in Greenwich was nowhere near as big and as comfortable as the one I have here at *RiversEdge*. I shall insist upon taking it, Mama, when Varian and I depart to Winterhaven."

"Go then, my dear," Blaze told her daughter. "We shall be happy to entertain your husband while you bathe, unless, of course, he would like to bathe too."

"Perhaps I shall," Varian de Winter said, and he quickly followed his wife from the Great Hall.

"Must you encourage that licentious behavior, madame?" Anthony Wyndham growled to his wife.

Blaze laughed. "Ohh, Tony, do not be such an old fuss," his wife teased him. "You like to bathe with me sometimes."

"But Nyssa is just a girl, Blaze!"

"Our daughter is a married woman," she said. "You will simply have to accept it. She might even be with child already. They have been married almost three months, after all."

"Do not even think it," the Earl of Langford said. "Nyssa is far too young to be a mother. Besides, we are far too young to be grandparents."

Blaze laughed again. "I was seventeen when I had Nyssa. She will be eighteen shortly. She is certainly old enough. You refuse to see it because she is your daughter. Ohh, Tony, she will always love you. You have not lost her because she is married. But her husband must now be first with her, and then their children. Still, there will always be room for us, and the rest of the family." She kissed her husband.

"What happened, Blaze? She was just a little girl the last time I really looked," he said. "Suddenly she is a beautiful woman, a wife, the Countess of March. The time has gone too quickly."

"Children grow up, Tony," Blaze said gently to her husband. "I do not know what my daughter would have done without you to look to as her father. We have much to thank you for, and you know that Edmund, may God assoil his good soul, would bless you also for the love you have given his daughter. Now she is grown. We have two little girls of our own. Give Jane and Annie the love you have given Nyssa."

He nodded, and then said to her, "I do not suppose you would like to have a bath, Blaze." His blue eyes were hopeful and twinkling. "If Nyssa grows with age to be as beautiful and as wise as her mother is, my angel, Varian de Winter will be a fortunate man."

Blaze smiled and took his hand in hers. "Let us go and bathe, my dear lord," she replied to him.

Nyssa and her husband remained with the Wyndhams of Langford for
several weeks. Varian sent word to his servants at Winterhaven that he
would be arriving at the end of August with his bride. In the meantime he
became acquainted with his bride's family.

News of the king's marriage to Catherine Howard reached *RiversEdge*
the end of the first week in August. The marriage had taken place quietly
at the king's hunting lodge at Oatlands on the twenty-eighth day of July.
That same morning, quite early, the king's former chancellor, Thomas
Cromwell, was executed on Tower Green. The Howards were now triumphant.

"We must find a particularly nice gift to send Cat," Nyssa told her
husband.

The royal honeymoon progress moved slowly through Surrey and
Berkshire to Grafton in Northamptonshire, on to Dunstable, to More,
and finally to Windsor. The king, it was said, had become a new man. He
behaved very much like the young man he had been in his youth. He arose
between five and six in the morning, attended mass at seven, and then rode
until ten A M , when he wanted his dinner served. He played at bowls and
archery in the afternoon, and then danced the night away with his lively,
laughing bride. His leg seemed to have healed, and his temper was excellent.

The international situation seemed not to require his personal attention
for the moment. Cleves was content with the treatment he had meted out
to their princess. Indeed Duke William was reported to have said he was
glad his sister fared no worse than she had. France and the Empire fussed
at each other, but that was nothing new. Henry Tudor had nothing on his
mind but pleasure in that hot summer of 1540. Few other than the Dukes
of Suffolk and Norfolk could remember his ever having been so merry.

The Earl of March had to twice postpone their departure for Winterhaven, for Nyssa had not been feeling well. He was beginning to wonder
if he was ever going to get his wife to leave *RiversEdge*, and voiced his
distress to his sympathetic mother-in-law as the month of August ended
and September began.

"Wait until mid-month," Blaze advised him. "She will feel well enough
to travel then, Varian, and it will be less dangerous."

"Less dangerous?" He looked puzzled. "What has danger to do with
our traveling to Winterhaven? There is no danger."

"Has Nyssa said nothing to you, then?" Blaze was surprised.

"About what?" he asked her.

A strange look came over the Countess of Langford's face. "Oh, dear," she said. "I wonder if she even knows herself."

"Knows what?" the Earl of March demanded.

"Come with me, Varian," Blaze said, and she hurried off to seek Tillie. She found her daughter's tiring woman mending the hem of a petticoat in Nyssa's dressing room. "Tillie," the Countess of Langford said to her, "when was your mistress's last link with the moon broken? Think carefully, my girl."

" 'Twas June, m'lady. Is something wrong?"

"Did you not think it strange that she has had no flow since then, girl? Why did you not come to me about it when you got home?"

Tillie looked totally astounded. Why on earth would she have even bothered to mention such a thing to Lady Nyssa's mother? Then suddenly Tillie knew, and clapped her hand over her mouth, her eyes wide with comprehension. "Ohhhhhhh!" she gasped.

"Oh, indeed!" the Countess of Langford replied. "Where is your mistress now, Tillie?"

"You'll find her lying down, m'lady. She was took with one of them queer spells again," Tillie answered.

Blaze hurried into her daughter's bedchamber, followed by her son-in-law. Nyssa lay upon the bed. She was pale, and clutching a cloth scented with lavender to her nose. "How could you live in this house all your life and not know what is the matter with you, my child?" her mother began without any preamble. "You have seven siblings, Nyssa! Did you not even once suspect?" Blaze demanded of her daughter.

"Suspect what, Mama?" Nyssa replied weakly.

"I cannot believe I have raised such a doltish daughter!" Blaze fumed. "You are with child, Nyssa! It is as plain as the nose upon your pretty face. From what Tillie tells me, I would say you are to have a baby sometime in mid to late March. Ohh, I am so excited! I am to be a grandmother at long last!"

Nyssa grew even paler at her mother's words. Her poor stomach was roiling. Reaching for the chamber pot, she retched into it. Her forehead was riddled with tiny beads of perspiration. "Ohhhh," she moaned helplessly, setting the pot back upon the floor and putting the cloth back to her nose. "I do not remember you ever being sick like this, Mama, when you had a baby. I thought it was the fish we had at dinner today. I cannot be with child. It is too soon."

Blaze burst out laughing. "Considering the amount of time you and Varian spend in this bed, I am hardly surprised to find you having a baby, Nyssa. It would have been more extraordinary if you had not become enceinte. The women of this family are known for their fertility. Why, your grandmother produced your twin uncles just three months after you were born."

"*We are to have a child!*" Varian had been standing stock-still, astounded by their conversation. Now he managed to voice his happiness. "Ohh, sweeting, how can I thank you?" The Earl of March had tears in his eyes.

"I suppose Mama is correct," Nyssa allowed.

"Of course I am," her mother said firmly. "I am never wrong about these things."

"I had hoped to have my heir born at Winterhaven," the earl said slowly, "but I realize it will be impossible for Nyssa to travel in her delicate condition. We will have to rely upon your hospitality."

"Nonsense!" Blaze told him. "In a week or two Nyssa will have passed through this unpleasant part and will feel much better. There is no reason why she cannot travel in safety to Winterhaven. It is time that you went home, my lord. My daughter will have a great deal to do there, considering how long it has been since anyone has really kept their residence at Winterhaven. There will be servants to train, and the entire house will have to be refurbished. It is, I suspect, quite woefully old-fashioned. Nyssa tells me you have given her carte blanche to do whatever she would with the house."

"I have never had a baby before," Nyssa said nervously. "I will be all alone at Winterhaven. Ohh, Mama! Please let me stay!"

"When the time comes, I will come to you, Nyssa," her mother replied. "Besides, you are much nearer to Ashby at Winterhaven. No one knows more about birthing babies than your grandmother. You will be fine. Now, I must go and prepare Anthony for your happy news." She bustled from the bedchamber, her smile wide.

"You did this to me deliberately!" Nyssa accused Varian.

"My only thought, I swear, was for our pleasure," he told her. "Certainly my ignorance of your condition should have told you that I knew no more about it than you." He chuckled. "How could you not know?" he wondered aloud.

"I suppose I never paid a great deal of attention to Mama when she was breeding," Nyssa said, somewhat mollified. "We never really knew until suddenly one day her belly would bloom and she would tell us we would soon have another little brother. Philip and I never really cared, for we had each other to love and keep company. Giles was not born until I was almost eight. Puppies, kittens, my pony; these things were of far more interest to me than Mama having a baby, Varian."

"Aye," he said, remembering the duchess Elizabeth, his grandfather's second wife, when she had had her children. He had paid her scant mind, and if someone had asked him if she was breeding, he would have been hard-pressed to say if it was so or not. None of it mattered now. What mattered was that they were to have a baby.

Nyssa suddenly arose from her bed, a new light of determination in her eyes. "There are things I must ask Mama," she said. "I do not know if we dare to continue sharing our passion. I do not think I should like it if we had to stop altogether, but I do not know." Then her eyes twinkled. "One good thing has come of this, my lord. We will not have to go back to court! Whatever your cousin Catherine wants, the king would not allow me to endanger our child."

He laughed. "I agree, sweeting. In a few days, when you feel better, we will go home to Winterhaven and settle down like two mice in their winter burrow. No one but family shall come to visit, and we will never go to court again unless you wish it. Cat will soon forget about us amid all the wonders she will have as Queen of England."

"Ohh, Varian," Nyssa declared fervently, "I do like you so very much! I do not think I could have found a better husband myself." She flung her arms about him and kissed him passionately.

His heart almost broke with his happiness. It was the first time since they had married that she had voiced any strong emotion toward him. She was going to love him. One day she would love him every bit as much as he loved her. But for now it was enough. *She liked him very much, and they were to have a baby.* "I should like to call our son Thomas, after my grandfather," he said.

"Never!" Nyssa said. "I will never forgive your grandfather for his cruelty. Our son will be called Edmund Anthony de Winter, after my two fathers. I think it only fitting, and my family will agree."

"If you bring your family into this matter," he said, laughing, "then I am outnumbered, madame. We will call our second son Thomas."

"We will call our second son Henry after your father, and after the king," Nyssa declared firmly.

"Then our third son shall be Thomas," he said stubbornly.

"After our dear archbishop, if you wish it, my lord," she answered him sweetly, and smiled. *"But never shall I name a son of mine after Thomas Howard!"*

"I do not believe in beating breeding women," he said. "Are you certain you are breeding, madame?"

"My mama says so, and she is the expert, sir. Besides, you cannot beat me," Nyssa told him.

"Why not?" he retorted.

"Because you will never be able to catch me," she teased him, and slipping from his arms, she ran from the room.

His laughter followed her.

CHAPTER 10

WINTERHAVEN had been built in the thirteenth century. Despite the battlements crowning its four towers, which gave it the appearance of a small castle, its interior was that of a comfortable, well-to-do manor house. It was set upon the topmost crest of a hill. A small moat surrounded it. The moat was filled with weeds, for it had been many years since it had been necessary to flood it and fortify the house. The drawbridge had long ago been dispensed with. The Earl and Countess of March clattered across a pretty stone bridge, stopping directly in front of the main entry, which was already wide open to welcome them.

The house was built of pale gray stone. Nyssa was pleased to see that someone had modernized the windows in the recent past. Ancient buildings such as this one were usually much too dark. Everything was neat, but shabby. She could see that there was a great deal of work to be done. She wondered if Varian could afford it. It was not something that they had discussed. Her father had given her husband a very generous dowry, but he had insisted that Nyssa's house, Riverside, as well as the bulk of her inherited wealth, remain in her own hands.

"Nyssa seems fond of you, and you seem to genuinely care for her,"

Anthony Wyndham had told the Earl of March thoughtfully. "Still, I think it better for now, and perhaps for always, that my daughter retain a certain measure of her independence. Neither Nyssa nor I chose you to be her husband. When we know you better, we will reconsider the matter."

Varian had been surprised. The idea of a woman retaining her own property was an interesting one. Not that it was a new idea; it certainly was not. But he had never expected to marry such a woman. He understood Anthony Wyndham's position, however, and thought that had he found himself in the Earl of Langford's position, he might very well have done the same thing to protect his daughter.

"I am not a rich man," he told his father-in-law, "but neither am I a poor one. Now that I am to live again on my own lands, I must decide how best to utilize those lands."

"Have you tenants?" Lord Wyndham asked.

"Aye," Varian answered.

"Has your estate steward been collecting the rents from your tenants? Be certain that he has, and then find out what has happened to those rents," Anthony advised. "If they were not turned over to you for your living, they should have been used to maintain your property. You will have to visit each farmstead and see if it is being cared for properly. If it is not, then you will have to decide whether to evict the tenant or give him an opportunity to rectify his bad habits. You have lived at court long enough to be able to tell a man's worth. Common sense is all that you need.

"My in-laws breed horses, but once they raised sheep. If you have the means, try both. Sheep are a certainty every year, unless they get diseased and you lose the flock. That is what happened to the Morgans, but 'twas years ago. Wool is a valuable cash crop."

He chuckled at the look on his son-in-law's face. "The gold and silver have to come from somewheres," he told him practically. "You've spent so much of your life at court that you've forgotten, indeed if you ever knew, that wealth has to have a source, Varian. You've lived off your grandsire's bounty most of your life. He had to have some means to support the great family and the establishment that he has.

"Oh, he's in debt to be certain. Mighty men like Duke Thomas forget how to be truly frugal, but here in the country we don't live beyond our means. We cannot afford to if we're going to pay the king's taxes on time, see that our daughters are dowered, our sons outfitted, and our tenants fed. After all, poor Henry Tudor could not keep his magnificent court without us, and the taxes he gets from us." The Earl of Langford chuckled broadly. "No, indeed, he needs us."

Varian shook his dark head. "This will be more complicated than I had anticipated," he said slowly.

"Go with your instincts, sir, and trust Nyssa's," Anthony Wyndham advised him. "She's been raised in the country, and has a broad streak of good, common sense. My daughter is a country woman."

Varian remembered his father-in-law's words as he lifted his wife from her mare. "After *RiversEdge,* it must seem very old-fashioned," he said apologetically. He had not remembered Winterhaven quite this way, quite so down-at-the-heels as it now appeared to him.

"It will be so much fun bringing it up to date," she assured him sweetly. "As long as the chimneys draw well, my lord, and the windows are tight, we shall be cozy for the winter. There is time for us to renovate." Then she kissed his cheek reassuringly, and he loved her all the more.

An elderly couple hobbled through the front door, smiles wreathing their wrinkled faces. "Welcome home, my lord, my lady," they chorused brightly. It was obvious they were very happy to see their master and his new bride.

"This is Browning, and Mistress Browning," Varian said to Nyssa, "and this is the new Countess of March," he told the old couple. "She is the daughter of the Earl and Countess of Langford, and already carries the heir to Winterhaven. Have you assembled the other servants?"

"There are no others, my lord," Browning told his master. "Master Smale, the steward, says 'tis wasteful to hire servants to serve in an empty house."

"There is a chill in the air," Nyssa said. "Let us go inside and discuss this, my lord." She hurried past him, and the Brownings followed her.

Varian de Winter smiled to himself. He was impressed that his old servants immediately recognized in Nyssa the voice of authority. Bringing up the rear, he entered his house.

The Brownings led Nyssa into the Great Hall of Winterhaven. It was a cozy rectangle with two large fireplaces that were heaped high with burning logs. The room was more than comfortable. Nyssa removed her cloak, and handed it to Browning. "You are responsible for the kitchen, I presume, Mistress Browning? The morning meal will be served after mass each day. Nothing fancy unless we have important guests. Then you and I will go over the menus together. Cereal, hard-cooked eggs, ham, bread, cheese. I like stewed fruits, particularly now." She smiled at the elderly Mistress Browning. "No court hours here. Dinner will be at two o'clock in the afternoon. Then a light supper around seven."

"Yes, m'lady," Mistress Browning said, returning the smile. "I'll be needing help in my kitchens now, however."

"I will rely upon you to find it, for you know the families hereabouts. The girls you choose must be hardworking and of good character," Nyssa told her. "Pick as many as you need. I will see each girl myself, and determine who is fit to serve in this house. Those who are not suited to the kitchens will be considered for housework and the laundry. I am a fair woman, but know that I will tolerate neither immorality nor pertness in a servant. Now, please make my tiring woman welcome and comfortable."

"Aye, m'lady," Mistress Browning replied, curtseying. My goodness, she thought, her ladyship was very young to be so stern. It was clear she had been raised very well. Mistress Browning knew of *RiversEdge*. Its hospitality was famed, and its servants were the elite of the serving class. Her ladyship was obviously used to the very best. So much the better for Winterhaven, which had not seen a mistress in thirty years. It was going to be a new era. She could but hope she was up to it.

Varian de Winter watched proudly as his wife directed his two old retainers with a mixture of kindness and firmness. When she had finished speaking to Mistress Browning, he said to Browning, "I will want to see Master Smale immediately."

"I'll fetch him myself," Browning said. Now the fur was going to fly. Arthur Smale had been running the estate for over fifteen years. He was an honest man, but not one open to change. There would certainly be changes now that his lordship was home, unless, of course, they returned to court after the heir was born. "My lord," Browning ventured. "Have you and her ladyship come home for good?" He peered anxiously at them.

"Aye, Browning, we have. You may tell everyone," the Earl of March said with a warm smile. "We have come home to stay. We have come home to raise a houseful of children. Does it suit you, old friend?"

"Aye, m'lord! And 'twill suit all of yer people as well," the beaming old man told his master. "I'll go fetch Smale to you now, m'lord. He comes from the stables this time every day for his dinner in the kitchens. He's not changed his schedule in all the years he's been here as estate steward. He's a predictable man, is Smale."

"And I'll get ye some nice wine and biscuits, m'lady," Mistress Browning said, curtsying, her smile broad.

They hurried off. Nyssa looked about the hall. It was paneled. Both the paneling and the floors needed a good scrubbing and polishing. Poor old Mistress Browning was hardly up to such work. The high board and chairs were attractive, but they too needed attention. "Are there no tapestries?" she asked her husband.

"Packed away years ago," he replied. "My mother did two beautiful ones that hung in here when I was a boy, but when my father died, I stored them in the attics. I knew one day I should come home, and I did not want those tapestries ruined by dust and sunlight."

"Who on earth ever told you how to care properly for tapestries?" she wondered. " 'Tis not a man's province."

"My step-grandmother, Duchess Elizabeth," he said.

There was so much to do, Nyssa discovered in the next few weeks. Her early sickness past, she felt filled with vigor, and anxious that her new home be in order before her child was born. She sent to her mother for several older servants to train her new servants. Mistress Browning, though beloved and respected by all, was simply not up to the task. She probably never had been. Winterhaven had not been properly kept in years. Still, Nyssa diplomatically sought her opinion on a variety of matters, and the elderly housekeeper's dignity was preserved. Her daughter-in-law, known as Young Mistress Browning, began to gradually take over the old woman's duties, and proved quite satisfactory. The elderly housekeeper spent most of her days in the kitchens supervising the staff there, seated most comfortably in a large chair by the fire, a wooden spoon her badge of office.

To Nyssa's surprise, much of the furniture at Winterhaven was in good order, and that which was not was easily repaired. New cushions were made for chairs, along with bed hangings and drapes. Tapestries were brought from the attics and rehung. Carpets were ordered from London.

"Only the most backward of households still put rushes on the floor," Nyssa said. "We must have carpets."

"The king's houses still have rushes sometimes," Varian teased his wife. "Do you think the king is old-fashioned, sweeting?"

"Aye!" she answered without hesitation. "Besides, you were so frugal in your bachelor days, my lord, you have more than enough to cover the expense. It is a wife's duty to spend her husband's gold," she teased back.

On St. Thomas's Day a messenger arrived from the court. The day was icy, and the earl invited the king's messenger to stay overnight. "We will have an answer for you to carry back to his grace," he said.

The messenger was grateful for their hospitality. He was a younger son come to court to make his fortune, but there were so many like him also at court that he knew it would take a miracle to set him above the rest. One never knew, however, where a miracle would come from, and the queen had personally asked him to deliver her message into the hands of the Earl and Countess of March. If their answer pleased the royal couple, the messenger could profit.

"We are ordered to court by Twelfth Night," Varian told his wife in the privacy of their bedchamber, the scarlet bed hangings drawn about their oaken bedstead. "Will you be sorry that we cannot go, sweeting?" He caressed her ripening belly, thrilled to feel the child stir restlessly beneath his gentle hand.

Nyssa shifted her body so she might elevate her shoulders a trifle more. She was beginning to feel very uncomfortable with this child. Her body was swollen like a large marrow. Even the special gowns her mother had loaned her for this time were beginning to feel tight across her breasts and her belly. "I would hardly go to court looking like this," she muttered irritably. "I look like a cow about to calve. Besides, why would I prefer court to Winterhaven? Nay, my lord, this child of ours is providential. None of the king's wives, save the Princess of Aragon, has remained his wife for long. By the time our son is born, and I have recovered from the birth, and weaned him from my breast, your cousin could easily be replaced in the king's heart, and bed, by another pretty English rose," Nyssa concluded.

"Not if my grandfather has anything to say about it," the earl teased his wife. "Remember that Duke Thomas likes power."

"He could not prevent Anne Boleyn from losing her head," Nyssa countered. "He was, I am told, quick to disassociate himself from her once he saw the handwriting on the wall. He saved his own position while she sacrificed hers." She shifted herself again.

"You are just out of sorts, sweeting, because we cannot go to *Rivers-Edge* for the Christmas festivities," he reasoned. "You know I am sorry about it, Nyssa, but even your mother said it would not be wise to travel now. And so I shall tell the king. Smale has already drafted the missive. He is enormously disappointed that we are not returning to court."

"He is honest, but carries himself above his station," Nyssa replied. "He was his own master for too long, and believed it would always be that way. I do not think he will be able to change, Varian. Come spring you must replace him with his son. We have already sent most of the old servants to the cottages and replaced them with their younger sons and daughters and other relatives."

"Aye," he agreed. "I am tired of having to explain everything I wish to do. Winterhaven is, after all, mine to do with as I please. I value Smale's judgment, but the final decision must be mine." He had taken his father-in-law's advice in this and other matters. It had not failed him yet.

Early the following morning he entrusted the king's messenger with a sealed parchment in a leather pouch that would keep it dry in the inclement weather. The messenger rode with all speed, reaching Hampton Court on Christmas Day and delivering his message personally.

"Why can they not come?" demanded the young queen Catherine of the king. "Did you not order them to court, my lord, as you promised me?" She pouted at him prettily.

"The Earl of March begs our indulgence," Henry Tudor said. "His wife is with child and is advised against traveling. The baby is due in the spring. I can certainly understand his concern for her safety, my rose. I only wish that we shared the same predicament."

"But I wanted Nyssa to come," Catherine whined, ignoring his barb. "I miss her!"

"Have I not given you everything that your heart desires, my adorable wife?" the king crooned at her. He reached out to draw her into his embrace.

"Nyssa is my friend," the queen cried, pulling away. *"My only friend!* What fun is all of this without a best friend to share it with, Henry?" She stamped her foot at him.

He wanted to understand, but he did not. She was Queen of England. She had everything anyone could desire at her fingertips. Why was she complaining?

"You must make her come back to court after her child is born, my lord," the queen insisted. "I want Nyssa with me. I need her to be with me, Henry."

"But it will be some months before she can safely travel," the king told her. Catherine, of course, not having yet had a child, would not understand. He attempted to explain it to her. "She will need several weeks to recover from the birth itself. Then, as a country woman, she will want to nurse her child herself. It cannot be weaned from her breast for two or three years, Catherine. By that time, or before, she will surely be enceinte with another child. It is unlikely that you will see Nyssa de Winter in the near future, my sweet. But we will have to try all the harder to have our own children, won't we? If you are busy with your own family, you will not have time to think of Nyssa."

"If Nyssa cannot come to me, why can I not go to her?" the queen persisted. She did not easily relinquish what she wanted. "Are we not planning a progress through the Midlands next summer, my lord? Could I not see her then?"

Henry Tudor sighed, and then said, "You might be with child yourself then, Catherine, and unable to accompany me."

Children! Children! Children! 'Twas all men ever talked about, the queen thought irritably. Her uncle, Duke Thomas, was always importuning her to have a child. Another son for England, they all begged her. And Henry could not stop nattering on about it either, even in the midst of their most intimate moments as he grunted and sweated over her body. Was she to be allowed no time to be young? To have fun? "I want to see my friend," she told him stubbornly, "and I do not want to wait years to do so."

The king took his wife upon his ample lap and began to fondle her breasts. His bride, he had discovered, had a most prodigious appetite for lovemaking. Whenever she was angry, he had but to distract her in this delightful manner. Catherine would immediately forget whatever it was that had irritated her in the first place.

"Perhaps next summer it can somehow be arranged," he soothed her. "The hunting is good in that area. There are several great houses that could entertain us and our court. Next summer, my rose."

He kissed her hard, finding his own desire beginning to rise to the occasion. The Earl and Countess of March had been married but three months ahead of their king and queen. Catherine would soon begin to blossom with their own child, he was certain. He was still capable of siring a child. Why, he felt like twenty again.

On Christmas morning Nyssa awoke dispiritedly. The day was cold, yet absolutely beautiful. Tillie seemed unduly excited as she helped her mistress to dress for mass. But of course Tillie would be excited; everyone else was, but how could she be? A year ago she had been at court awaiting the arrival of the new queen. She had missed the wonderful Christmas celebrations that her mother always held at RiversEdge, but she had managed to bear her disappointment in her excitement over being at court.

Now she was a married woman, enormous with child, in a strange house that had no customs. *She wanted to go home!* She wanted to be Nyssa Wyndham again. Young and free to do as she pleased. The invader within her kicked and turned itself about, reminding her sharply that those days were over forever. Several tears slipped down her cheeks.

"Why, m'lady, what is the matter?" Tillie asked her.

Nyssa shook her head. Tillie would never understand how she felt. Why should she? She was young, and free yet. "Nothing fits," she muttered. "Practically everything Mama gave me is too tight now."

"You are carrying big," Tillie admitted. "I've seen me ma the same way, and then the baby is just the littlest bit of a thing. 'Tis all the waters, m'lady. As long as he's active, he's healthy."

"He is very active, Tillie," Nyssa grumbled. "As active as one of those tumblers one sees at the fair. I barely slept last night."

"Just a few more weeks, m'lady," Tillie soothed her mistress. "Why, spring will be here before you know it," she promised.

" 'Tis Christmas Day, Tillie," Nyssa said gloomily. "Spring is weeks and weeks away." She sighed piteously.

Tillie said nothing more. Carefully she brushed her mistress's lovely dark hair, braiding it into a single plait with a red ribbon through the strands. She helped Nyssa into a velvet breeding gown of dark green, noting the laces barely tied now. Her lady's bosom had greatly enlarged over the last few months, and swelled quite dangerously over the edge of the bodice. The skirt was divided, and the underskirt was of silver and green brocade.

Nyssa looked at her belly straining beneath the fabric, and fell into a fit of giggles. "I wonder if this is how a heifer would look if you dressed her up in a fine gown." She chuckled.

"She would be the best-dressed heifer in all of England," Tillie said, laughing, pleased to see Nyssa's good humor restored. One never knew these days if she would laugh or cry, or shout over some little thing.

The two women joined the earl in the chapel of Winterhaven for the morning mass. Nyssa grew weepy again. They were all alone, just the two of them. She wondered why she had even bothered to decorate the Great Hall with greens and candles. Who would appreciate them? There was no one. She sniffled softly.

When the mass ended, Varian de Winter took his wife's hand. "Let us go into the Great Hall and break our fast. Young Mistress Browning tells me that the kitchen staff have prepared a special holiday feast for us this day." He kissed her softly. "Happy Christmas, sweeting."

"I am not hungry," Nyssa said. "I think I shall return to my chamber to rest." She looked so woebegone.

"Nay, Nyssa, you shall not," he said adamantly. She glanced up at him, surprised. "You shall not disappoint the servants who have worked so hard to make this day a special one for you. I am sorry you cannot be at *RiversEdge*, sweeting, but it would not have been safe for you to go in your condition. That is no reason, however, to mope about and spoil Christmas for the rest of us at Winterhaven."

He had never spoken to her that way. He had always been so gentle, and so considerate of her. How could he possibly understand her feelings? He had never had the kind of family she had. But before the protest might even form upon her lips, he was leading her firmly from the chapel to the Great Hall. She could smell the pine and the bay as they approached. There was a low hum coming from the hall. What was it? She had certainly never heard that noise before. They entered the room, and she gasped with surprise, her eyes flying to his smiling face.

"Merry Christmas, Nyssa!" her family chorused as one.

Nyssa burst into tears. "Oh!" she sobbed. "Oh, I am so happy! Mama!
Papa! Grandmama Doro! Philip! Giles! Richard! Edward! Henry! And,
ohh, look at the girls. Annie and Jane have grown so since I saw them
last!" She turned to her husband. "Thank you, Varian," was all she could
manage to say before she began sobbing against his velvet-clad chest. How
could she have ever believed the terrible gossip surrounding his earlier life,
or his actions toward her? A man so thoughtful of his wife couldn't be
wicked or untrustworthy. How could she have ever thought it?

"She is just like her mother," Anthony Wyndham told his son-in-law
calmly. "They weep at the drop of a bonnet, these women. Do not look
so distressed, Varian. She is delighted with your little surprise."

"Ohhh, I am!" Nyssa sobbed. "I have never been happier in my entire
life, my lord." She reached for her handkerchief, wiping her eyes and
noisily blowing her nose. "Mama!" She and Blaze embraced.

"You are enormous," her mother noted. "Are you certain this baby is
not due until the end of March? Perhaps I was mistaken about the dates.
After all, you were married at the end of April. The child could be here
sooner. Sometimes a woman's flow does not stop right away. It is unusual,
but it has been known to happen.

"I had meant to return home in just a few days' time," Blaze continued,
"but I think now that I may remain with you until after the baby comes,
Nyssa. If there were to be a bad storm and I could not get back, I should
be most distressed. I shall keep Henry and the girls with me." She looked
to her son-in-law. "Will you mind, Varian?"

"Nay, madame, you are most welcome to remain as long as you desire.
Indeed I would be hard-pressed to help Nyssa when the child comes. I am
glad for your company, I assure you."

"You may not be glad for the company of these rascals," the Countess
of Langford said, a twinkle in her eyes, as she watched her twin daughters
toddling with determination after one of the hounds.

The morning meal was served, and Nyssa was astounded. Entirely on
their own the kitchen staff had set a menu and prepared it. There was a
large country ham, pink and sweet; dishes of eggs in a sauce of cream and
marsala wine, sprinkled with cinnamon. Hot wheat cereal with bits of
dried apple and pear was served up in fresh trenchers of bread. Trout,
poached in white wine with dill and lemon, caught the men's fancy. There
was a platter of large stewed apples floating in a mixture of hot honey,
raisins, and nutmeg, with a companion pitcher of thick, clotted cream.
There was a small wheel of sharp cheese, hot cottage loaves, silver dishes
of newly churned butter, and pitchers of both October ale and red wine.

Outside it was still dark, for the dawn came late at this time of year and the days were short. The family trooped to the high board and, seating themselves, began to eat with enthusiasm.

"How did you get here, and when did you arrive?" Nyssa asked her parents. "I did not hear you, and my ears are sharp."

"Old Rumford ferried us across early this morning. The road to Winterhaven is a clear one, and the moon was high," Anthony told her. "We traveled easily, my dear."

"And we arrived while you were at mass," Blaze said, taking up the explanation. "Our timing was quite perfect, I think." She smiled at her daughter.

It was suddenly the best Christmas Nyssa could ever remember. She was surrounded by so many who loved her—her parents, her siblings, *her husband.* Aye, he really did love her, and he never wavered in his devotion to her. Yet although she cared for him more than when they had first been wed, she still did not think she loved him. It was a puzzle, but she realized she was not unhappy, and surely that was all to the good.

Her family celebrated her nineteenth birthday with her, and they stayed until after Twelfth Night. Her Morgan grandparents, her aunts, her uncles, and her cousins all came to visit during those days. When they finally had all departed but for her mother and the three youngest of her siblings, she felt relief to have her home to herself again, though she had been so happy to see everyone.

The winter set in at last with the coming of February. Varian fretted about his flocks, for the lambing was upon them, and as always in lambing season, the weather was stormy. Old Lord Morgan rode over from Ashby to advise his granddaughter's husband, for he had once had enormous flocks of his own.

They had heard nothing of the court since the royal messenger's visit on St. Thomas's Day, when they had learned that the king and the queen would celebrate Christmas at Hampton Court. They had no visitors but an occasional family member. Nyssa was growing more and more short-tempered with her expanding girth. Nothing was remotely comfortable these days, neither sitting, nor standing, nor lying upon her bed.

February passed, and on the first day of March, Nyssa went into labor. "It is too soon," she fretted, frightened.

"From the look of you," her mother said with a smile, "it is none too soon. You are like a ripe peach ready to burst."

"I am bursting," wailed the Countess of March, "and it hurts!"

Her mother ignored her, instead ordering that the birthing table be brought into the countess's bedchamber and set by the fire, where it was warm. Kettles of hot water boiled over the fire. A large stack of clean cloths was prepared. The infant's cradle was brought, along with the swaddling clothes. The nursemaid was called to ready herself for her new duties.

Outside, gray, icy sleet was flinging itself against the glass windowpanes, and the wind was beginning to rise. Blaze made her daughter walk about until finally her waters broke. Only then did the Countess of Langford allow Nyssa to get onto the birthing table.

In the Great Hall, Varian de Winter paced nervously. His father-in-law, just arrived, sat calmly by the fire, sipping at his wine and chatting with his youngest son, who was playing with a puppy at his feet.

"Var, can I take puppy home with me?" little Henry Wyndham asked his brother-in-law. Henry would shortly be four. His big violet-blue eyes reminded Lord de Winter of his wife. The boy smiled up ingenuously at the man, his baby teeth like small freshwater pearls.

"Aye, 'tis yours, Hal. What will you call him?"

"Puppy," the little boy said with perfect logic.

The two men chuckled at the child, and he grinned good-naturedly back at them.

Blaze could not believe the ease with which Nyssa was delivering her child. She remembered how she herself had labored lightly for an entire day. Then her labor had become harder and harder, until finally, just before midnight, Nyssa had been born. Nyssa, however, was having quite an easy time of it. Blaze bent to peer between her daughter's legs, and saw that the child's head was quite visible.

"At the next pain, I want you to bear down as hard as you can and push," she told Nyssa. "It will take very little to birth this child."

The young Countess of March obeyed her mother, and as she was wracked by a hard pain, bore down, pushing with all her might. The child began to slip forth from her body. "Ohhh, I can feel it, Mama!"

"Push again, Nyssa," her mother ordered.

The young woman pushed, and suddenly a howl broke the virtual stillness of the room. Blaze Wyndham smiled broadly as she lifted her firstborn grandchild up and lay the wailing infant upon his mother's body.

"You have a son," she told her daughter, and then sought for the afterbirth. It had not yet emerged. Taking a small, sharp knife set aside for the purpose, she cut the cord and knotted it tightly in the baby's navel. Ohh, he was a fine boy!

"*Mama!*" Nyssa's voice was sharp. "The pain is beginning again."

" 'Tis the afterbirth," Blaze said, disposing of it.

"No," Nyssa told her. "I feel the same way I felt just a moment ago, when Edmund was born."

Blaze looked down again and gasped with surprise. "Heartha, take Lord Edmund and clean him up," she called to her tiring woman. "Tillie, I will want you to stand by. Your mistress is about to deliver another baby. 'Tis twins, Nyssa! Why did I not realize it before now? You come from a family known for its twin births! That is why you were so big, and that is why your babies are being born today instead of at the end of the month. Twins always come early."

Within a brief few moments Nyssa had delivered her second child. "What is it?" she demanded. "Do not mix it up with Edmund. He is the heir. I do not want him to lose his birthright."

"No fear of that," her mother said. "This one is a daughter. Ohh, I don't envy the poor little queen when Henry Tudor learns you have given Varian de Winter not just one, but two children. He will be so envious."

"Let me see her," Nyssa demanded, and Blaze put the baby on her daughter's chest. The infant's eyes were open, and she appeared to focus quite clearly upon her mother. She made small noises that absolutely fascinated Nyssa.

"What will you call Edmund's sister?" Lady Wyndham asked.

"I had not considered a daughter, but I think if it is all right with Varian, I shall call her Sabrina. Lady Sabrina Mary de Winter. What think you, Mama?"

" 'Tis a lovely name," Blaze said, "and now I think we had best cleanse Lady Sabrina free of her birthing blood so she may be swaddled and presented to her father, along with her brother."

The two infants were quickly cleansed with warmed, scented oil, and then swaddled in clean clothes. Heartha held the heir to Winterhaven, and Tillie proudly cradled his sister.

"Go and introduce them to their father and grandfather while I attend to my daughter," Blaze said, and the two servants hurried from the bedchamber while Lady Wyndham made Nyssa presentable for the husband who would surely be coming to visit her within a short time.

Slowly Tillie and Heartha made their way down the stairs and into the Great Hall.

"My lord!" said Heartha. "You have a son."

Varian de Winter leapt to his feet and strode toward her.

"And a daughter, my lord," Tillie told him.

The Earl of March stopped in his tracks. "A son *and* a daughter?" He looked nonplussed.

"Runs in the family," Anthony Wyndham said matter-of-factly, coming to look at his first two grandchildren. "Old Lady Morgan birthed four sets of twins, y'know. Two sets were girls. One was a mixed pair like these two, and the last set was boys." He peered down at the babies. "Which one's the lad?" he asked the two women.

"This one here, m'lord," Heartha said, beaming. "Lord Edmund Anthony de Winter's 'is name, Mistress Nyssa says."

"Is it?" Anthony Wyndham felt a bit misty-eyed. "Is that all right with you, my lord?" he asked his son-in-law.

Varian nodded, fascinated by the miniature of himself cradled in the tiring woman's arms. "Aye. I bred them, but according to Nyssa, I do not get to name them." He looked up with a grin and then said to Tillie, "What is my daughter to be called?"

"She's Lady Sabrina Mary de Winter, m'lord," Tillie replied.

"Is my wife well?" he queried her.

"Oh, aye, m'lord. My mistress is quite well. Lady Wyndham says her labor was a very easy one," Tillie informed him.

The earl left the hall and hurried to his wife's chamber. Nyssa was already newly bathed and in a fresh chamber robe.

"Did you see them?" she asked him impatiently as he entered. "Are they not the most perfect and beautiful babies, my lord?"

"Sabrina is bald," he noted, "but," he added, seeing his wife's outraged look, "she is the most beautiful little girl I have ever seen."

"And Edmund? I have given you an heir, sir. Are you not pleased with me? What is my reward to be? When I was born, my father gave my mother a manor, and I was but one baby. What shall I have for two?"

"Nyssa! Such greed," Blaze said, but she was laughing.

"This," the earl said, slipping a beautiful gold chain with a large pear-shaped diamond from his doublet, "is your reward for giving me an heir, madame. Since I was not expecting a second baby, I must beg your indulgence. What would you like?"

"I want a flock of sheep," she said. "I shall put aside the gold from the sale of their wool and invest it. By the time Sabrina is ready to wed one day, I shall have a fine dowry for her."

"The lambs born this spring are yours," he said. It was a highly practical idea, Varian thought. There would be other children, and some of them were bound to be daughters. Daughters needed fine dowries to obtain fine husbands. One day the king would die, and being related to a Howard queen would mean nothing then. Gold was the only thing that lasted. That never changed.

The babies were returned to their mother, and looking down at them, Nyssa felt a tremendous rush of love for her children. She was astounded to have two of them, amazed that they were finally a reality that she could touch, and caress. She looked at her mother. "How can you give both equal attention, Mama? I adore them both already."

"You cannot," came the wise reply, "but if you kiss one, be certain to kiss the other so neither will feel slighted. You will need a wet nurse now, my child. Twins are hard that way."

"Not yet!" Nyssa cried. "I have just had them. I want them to myself, Mama." She looked at her husband and smiled.

"A wet nurse will share the burden with you, Nyssa," her mother answered. "These grandchildren of mine will need all the food they can get. Look how quickly Jane and Annie grew in the last year. I have had a wet nurse to share my load. I favor neither of your sisters. When they cry for food, I pick one up, and Clara picks the other one up to nurse. Sometimes I have Jane, and sometimes Annie. It matters not to your sisters as long as their little bellies are filled."

"Listen to your mother, sweeting," Varian told her. "She has experience in these matters." He took his son from Heartha and smiled down at him before handing him to Nyssa. Then Varian removed his daughter from Tillie's arms. "They are perfect, and I thank you, madame, for giving me such fine children. They shall be baptized in the morning. Let Anthony stand godfather for Edmund and Sabrina both."

"Let us wait a few days, my lord, so that the rest of my family might be summoned. Anthony may stand godfather for Edmund, but I would have my brother Philip be Sabrina's godfather."

"And the godmothers?" he queried her.

"Aunts Bliss and Blythe, with your permission, my lord."

He agreed. "And the king must be notified, of course."

She nodded. "Aye. The sooner the better, and then perhaps Cat will realize that we cannot come back to court to play with her."

Several days later the king, at Whitehall, received a messenger from the Earl and the Countess of March. The messenger bowed low, and given permission to speak, said, "On the first day of March, in the year of our lord fifteen hundred and forty-one, Lady Nyssa Catherine de Winter gave birth to twin children, a son and a daughter, Your Grace. The heir to Winterhaven was baptized Edmund Anthony de Winter, and his sister will be called Sabrina Mary de Winter. Both the infants, and their mother, are well. The earl and his wife tender you their loyalty. God save good King Henry, and Queen Catherine!" He bowed again, and was dismissed.

"Twins," Henry Tudor said, his eyes narrowing to slits. "I would be content with one child." He looked at his pretty wife. "We must try harder, Catherine, my rose. Your cousin and his wife are already two up on us. It will not do, my pet."

"Can we see them this summer on our Midlands progress?" the queen said, ignoring him. "Will you order them to join us? She will have to have a wet nurse with two children, and so surely she can come to court for a short time, my dear lord. It would make me sooo happy to see Nyssa again. Perhaps I shall even be enceinte by then, and Nyssa could tell me all that I needed to know about babies." She smiled sweetly at him.

"Very well," he said, unable to resist her, and he pulled her down into his lap for a cuddle. "Would it truly make you happy, Catherine? You know I would do anything to make you happy."

"Aye, my darling, it would make me very happy," she told him, and kissed his mouth, her little tongue snaking unexpectedly over his lips. "Do you like that, my liege?" She pressed herself against him.

He fumbled with her bodice, pulling it open, handling her breasts with great familiarity. Then one of his hands slipped beneath her skirt and slid up her leg, past her thigh, and a single finger found its target. "Do you like this?" he growled at her, his finger working faster and faster against her little jewel.

The queen twisted her body about, unfastening her husband's codpiece loosed about his manhood, which was already well-aroused. Then seating herself upon his lap, facing him, she took him into her sheath. "Does that please you, my lord?" she murmured against his ear, biting down hard on it. Then she began to ride him.

He slipped his hand beneath her bottom, crushing the flesh of her buttocks with his finger. "I am going to mark you," he said.

"Yes!" she half sobbed. "Yes! Mark me! Make me your own, Henry Tudor." She moved faster and faster upon him, until finally they both exploded with their mutual pleasure. "Ahhhhhh," she groaned as his love juices filled her. "Ahhh, Henry!"

Perhaps they had made a child, the king thought, praying it was so. He wanted a child with this exquisite girl-wife whom he loved so very, very much. How had he gained such good fortune in his old age?

"You will not forget your promise to me, my lord?" she said sweetly. "You will order the Earl and Countess of March to join us on our progress this summer?" She kissed his ear and then licked it.

"I will not forget, Catherine," he told her. Ahh, the little russet-haired vixen was making him feel like a boy again! He found her mouth and became lost in their kisses.

PART III

THE QUEEN'S PAWN

COURT
Summer 1541–Winter 1542

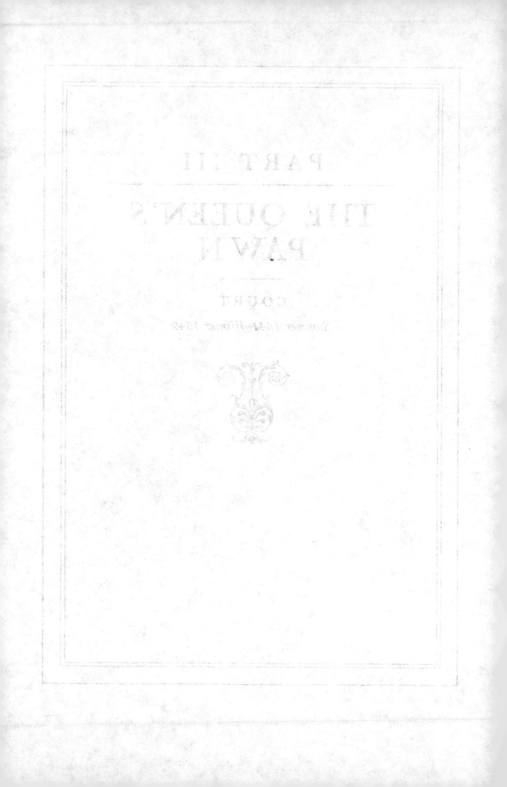

CHAPTER 11

THE king was ill. A difficult man when healthy, he was absolutely impossible when he was unwell. His ulcerated leg, which for the past few months had been fine, was suddenly painful again. The wound, always kept open for purposes of drainage, had suddenly closed. The leg grew inflamed and swollen. Henry Tudor ran a fever, and refused to follow his doctors' instructions once they had reopened the ulcer again.

"You need much liquid, Your Grace, to help us wash the fever away," Dr. Butts told the king sternly. As the king's senior physician he knew better than anyone how to handle his patient.

"Am I not drinking wine and ale aplenty?" growled the king.

"I have told you, Your Grace, that you must not drink ale, and your wine must be well watered," the doctor replied. "What we want you to ingest in great quantity is this herbal decoction that we have mixed with sweet Devon cider. It will ease the pain and chase the fever."

The king wrinkled his nose. "It tastes like piss," he said stubbornly.

Dr. Butts mightily struggled to control his temper. The king was without a doubt the worst patient any physician could have. "I would humbly suggest, Your Grace," he responded sharply, "that you overcome your childish aversion to your medication. The longer you are ill, the weaker you will become. It will be harder for you to regain your former strength. I am certain the queen would be very unhappy if your strength did not come back tenfold. You cannot fulfill your obligations to England if you do not get well."

Dr. Butts's meaning was crystal clear to the king. He glowered at the man, annoyed that he was so right in this matter. "I will meditate upon your advice," he said sullenly. How he hated being told what to do, but he had to admit that he felt like merry hell right now. He had even sent Catherine away from him. He could not allow her to see him in this sorry state. He looked so old. Every afternoon at six he would send Master Henage to his queen with loving messages and news, but he hardly wanted his beautiful young wife to see him in this disgusting condition. One good thing was coming of it, though. He could hardly eat a thing, and was rapidly losing weight.

He had been measured for a suit of armor just before his marriage last summer. He had been shocked by the measurements that had been called out. *"Waist, fifty-four inches."* That could not be right! He had made the fool armorer's apprentice measure his waist again, only to hear, "Waist, fifty-four inches," repeated. *"Chest, fifty-seven inches."* It was embarrassing.

After his marriage he had embarked upon a strenuous program of physical exercise. To his delight he had begun to see his muscles beginning to emerge from the fat in which they had been encased. He was watching what he ate, and now this sickness was aiding his endeavors. He did not, however, want to lose his sexual potency with the queen. He began to drink the doctor's disgusting potion, and to his further aggravation, he felt better almost at once.

Still, his temperament was terrible. He began to grow suspicious of the courtiers about him. They were all using him for their own gains, and his people were an ungrateful lot as well. He'd raise taxes. That would teach them! Henry Tudor thought about Thomas Cromwell. *Dear, devoted old Crum.* "He was the most faithful servant that we ever had," the king was heard to mutter darkly on more than one occasion. "Why is he not here for me now? I will tell you why," he shouted, and his gentlemen shifted their feet nervously. "Because my loyal and steadfast old Crum was convicted by false accusations, and on light pretexts!"

Once again the king was blaming everyone else for his actions. He wallowed in dark self-pity, and no one could oppose him in any matter whatsoever. It had been almost ten days since he had seen his wife, and he was not yet ready to be with her.

The queen was lonely. She sat amongst her ladies embroidering her motto, beneath a crowned rose, onto a square of brocade, which when finished would be set into a silver frame and presented to the king. Catherine had taken for her motto: *Non autre volonté que la sienne,* which when translated into English read: "No other wish but his." It was dull, tedious work, and she was bored with it. She gazed about her at her ladies: Lady Margaret Douglas, the Duchess of Richmond, the Countess of Rutland, Ladies Rochford, Edgecomb, and Baynton. *Same old faces.* When she had been married, her uncle, the duke, had told her the women he wanted her to include in her household. They were pleasant enough ladies, but they were the same old faces. She had had to tell Henry that she wanted her father's widow, her dull stepmother, Lady Margaret Howard; Lady Clinton, Lady Arundel, her sister, who she did not really get on with; Prince Edward's aunt, Lady Cromwell, who was the late Queen Jane's sister, Elizabeth, and married to Thomas Cromwell's son; and Mistress Stonor, who had been with her cousin Anne in the Tower. She is a cheerful companion, Catherine thought ironically, grimacing. There were others, of course, but few were young, and none were fun.

When she complained, her uncle had told her sternly, "You must remember that you are now the Queen of England, Catherine. You are a woman of property and position. Such women do not cry and whine for *fun* like unimportant little girls."

God's foot! *She was bored.* What good was it to be a queen when you could not have fun? She could almost wish she were not the queen; that the lady Anne was still the queen, and she just a maid of honor who could flirt with the gentlemen and have fun. Now it was the lady Anne, the king's dear sister, who was having all the fun. Gone was the slightly dowdy lady of Cleves. In her place was an absolutely fashionable woman who danced gaily into the night, bought whatever took her fancy, and was beholden to no man. It was not fair!

Still, the lady Anne must be lonely without a man. Catherine could not imagine life without a man. In that respect she found the lady Anne odd. Not that the gentlemen did not court her predecessor, but the lady Anne, while enjoying their attentions, would favor no man in particular. Still, she did enjoy leading them on; implying much, giving nothing. Princess Elizabeth, who was with her often, clearly admired the lady Anne.

When asked why she would not remarry, she would say with a twinkle in her blue eyes, "How could I choose another gentleman vhen I vas ved to a king like Hendrick? Who could compare vith him?" Then she would laugh merrily, and Catherine was never certain what she quite meant by her words, or why she laughed so happily.

Actually the lady Anne was a great deal more fun than any of the queen's ladies were. She came to court on a regular basis and was quite friendly with both the king and her pretty, younger successor. The first time she had come, Catherine was very nervous. But Anne had thrown herself facedown before the royal couple, and then rising up, wished them every happiness. She actually meant it, and had also brought magnificent gifts for them both.

The king had gone to bed that day with his leg paining him, but Queen Catherine and the lady Anne had danced together into the night, much to the court's amazement. The next day the former queen returned by special invitation to have dinner with the bride and bridegroom. They sat together laughing and toasting one another. No one had ever seen the king so genuinely affable toward Anne of Cleves. The court was goggled-eyed, which delighted both women.

At New Year's the lady Anne had presented the king and the queen with two great magnificent horses from her own stables. Identical yearlings, they were a fine dun color, with ebony fetlocks, and were caparisoned in rich mauve velvet edged in gold fringe with golden tassels. Their bridles were of heavy silver. They were led into the hall at Hampton Court by two handsome young boy grooms garbed in mauve, gold, and silver livery. The royal couple were enchanted, but some of the court sneered at the lady Anne for a fool.

"On the contrary," said Charles Brandon, the Duke of Suffolk, wisely. "She is an extraordinarily clever woman, I think. The only one of the king's wives to survive his displeasure, regain his favor, and lose nothing but a crown for her troubles."

And fun, thought the young queen. The lady Anne is far more fun than these proper ladies of mine. Unfortunately, it would cause talk if I kept her about me all the time, but oh, how I wish I could! If only Nyssa were here. The queen sighed so deeply that her ladies looked at her.

"What is it, Your Grace?" Lady Rochford asked solicitously.

"I am bored," the queen admitted irritably. "There is no music or dancing because the king is ill. I have not seen my husband in almost two weeks." She flung down her embroidery.

"There is no reason why we cannot have some music here in the privacy of your chambers, Your Grace," the Duchess of Richmond said.

"Let us call upon pretty Tom Culpeper to come and perform for us," Lady Edgecomb suggested. "He has a lovely voice, and plays both the lute and the virginals quite well."

Catherine considered the suggestion. "Very well," she finally agreed. "If the king can spare him, I should like it if Master Culpeper would come to amuse us for a time."

The queen's page was sent to the king to ask his permission, and Henry granted his young wife's request. He felt very guilty that she was beginning to chafe with boredom, and all because of his damned weaknesses.

"Go," he told Tom Culpeper, who was one of his favorite gentlemen. "And tell the queen I send her my dearest love. I will see her in just a few more days. Tell her that, Tom, and then when you return later, I would know in detail how she took the news." He grinned almost lasciviously and chuckled. "I know she has missed me."

Tom Culpeper was a handsome young man in his mid-twenties. His hair was chestnut-brown and his eyes a bright blue. He was fair of skin and had a most pleasing countenance, which he did not hide behind a beard. The king was very fond of him, and consequently spoiled him badly. It was something of which Tom Culpeper took full advantage. He had come to court as a boy to seek his fortune, and it would appear as if he were finally going to be successful in his quest.

Picking up his lute, he bowed to his master, saying, "I will bring your message to her grace. Then I will entertain her and her ladies, my liege."

The queen's ladies fluttered about Master Culpeper from the moment he arrived. Tall and slender, with a well-turned leg, he accepted their homage as his due. His charm, coupled with the twinkle in his eye and his easy smile, did not escape the women, most of whom were married. He amused them for two hours, singing and playing upon his lute. At one point he played his lute and sang while little Princess Elizabeth, up from Hatfield to visit her father, talented beyond her years, played upon the queen's virginals. Bess's fingers were gracefully long for a child of seven. Several of the ladies whispered that she had her mother's beautiful hands.

Finally the princess was escorted off to bed and the queen dismissed her women. Culpeper lingered a moment, and when Lady Rochford made to shoo him away, he said with authority, "I have a private message for the queen's ears, from his grace. I should like to deliver it now."

"Go along then, Rochford," Catherine said, "but stay near."

Lady Rochford curtsied, and backing from the room, closed the door behind her. Her pinched face was curious, but she dared not listen at the door.

Tom Culpeper bowed politely to the queen. He thought how very beautiful she looked. Her gown, in the French style, was quite smart. He had always known she would shine in the proper setting.

"Scarlet velvet becomes you," he said quietly. "I once tried to give you some, as I recall, and not so long ago."

"I accepted it," Cat reminded him. "I simply did not pay your price, Master Culpeper. It was far too high. Now, what message did his grace send to me?" Her look was imperious, but she was thinking how young and how very virile he looked right now. His hose hugged the curving calves of his long legs, and she wondered what it would be like to have those legs wrapped about her.

Tom Culpeper repeated the king's message slowly, watching her face as he did so. She was no great beauty, but there was an enticing sensuality about her.

"You may tell his grace that I miss him greatly and will welcome his return to my bed, and company," the queen said when Culpeper had finished speaking. "You may go now, Master Culpeper."

"Will you not call me Tom again, Your Grace?" he asked her. "We are cousins, after all, through our mothers."

"I am aware of our relationship, Master Culpeper. We are sixth cousins to be exact," she answered him severely.

"You are adorable when you are being stern, Cat," he said daringly. "Does the king like your mouth? I think you have the most perfect little mouth. It looks quite succulent."

"You are dismissed, Culpeper," she repeated coldly, but her cheeks were pink and her heart was beating quickly.

"I am always here for you, Cat," he told her. "I know that it can be sometimes lonely to be the wife of an older man." He bowed and left her presence.

What could he have meant by that? Catherine wondered. He was so handsome. Had he been flirting with her? Well, a little flirting never hurt anyone. Why could she not flirt back and still give her first loyalty to Henry? As long as no one else knew what she was doing. She giggled. Suddenly she felt happy again and she was no longer bored. The king returned to her bed two days later.

In April the queen thought that she might be with child, but either she miscarried early or it had been a false hope brought on by her natural anxiety to please the king. She wept, but the king had no time to comfort his wife. In Yorkshire a rebellion was being led by Sir John Neville, who wished to restore the more orthodox form of Catholic worship. The rebellion was fiercely put down. Henry Tudor would not have Rome meddling in his kingdom.

The king was now busy planning his summer progress to York and the northeastern counties. There was a small piece of business that he would take care of before leaving London. He would see to the execution of Margaret Pole, the Countess of Salisbury. She was an elderly woman, who had been lodged in the Tower for two years. Her father had been the Duke of Clarence, Edward IV's brother, and she was one of the last Plantagenets. She had always been loyal to the Tudors, indeed had served as Princess Mary's governess for many years; but her son Reginald, Cardinal Pole, had sided with the pope against the king. For this Margaret Pole would pay the ultimate price.

The queen pleaded desperately for the countess's life. Catherine hated injustice, and her husband was not being fair in this matter, though Cat did not say that. "She is no traitor, my lord, and she is an old woman. Let her live out her old age in peace."

Princess Mary also pleaded for her old governess's life. The tone she took, however, was more apt to anger the king than turn his heart and save the Countess of Salisbury. "Her death will be on your immortal soul, my lord," Mary told her father piously. "Do you not have enough sins piled up already? Would you really add the unjust death of Lady Margaret to that pile? Remember the last execution you personally ordered, my liege. You have come to regret it already in less than a year's time." She looked at him with her Aragonese mother's dark accusing eyes.

She is twenty-six, the king thought irritably, but she looks older. It is all that black she wears. "Dress in a gay color the next time you appear before me," the king said in answer to his daughter's plea.

"I am no traitor," the Countess of Salisbury declared when they took her to her execution.

The executioner was young and very inexperienced. He was unnerved by the fact the prisoner made him chase her about the block. Finally she was restrained. He hacked at her head, but his hands were shaking. Those who witnessed the execution later reported that he had butchered the poor old woman. It had been an awful death for a faithful servant. The court was secretly appalled by Henry Tudor's unnecessary cruelty. In Rome, Cardinal Pole publicly declared that he would pray for the king's black soul.

Plans for the progress proceeded in an orderly fashion now. France and the Holy Roman Empire were once again on the brink of war. They seemed to find it impossible to maintain a peace between them. François I, the French king, told his ambassador in England, Monsieur Marillac, to offer the Duc d'Orleans, who was the king's heir, as a husband for Princess Mary.

"What a fine idea," the queen enthused. "It is past time poor Mary was married. This is a perfect match! The French are as orthodox in their beliefs as are the Spanish. Mary will one day be Queen of France. Imagine! Your daughter! Queen of France!"

The young queen and Mary Tudor did not get along at all. Catherine believed that her older stepdaughter did not render her enough respect. The truth was that Mary did not. She thought her father's wife a frivolous, silly chit. What Mary refused to face was that her father loved his wife. When the princess was rude to the queen, she would suffer for it. Already two of Mary's maids had been removed from her household for a slight to the queen.

"I do not trust the French," the king told his wife. "Besides, we must keep the Holy Roman emperor as an ally if the trade links so important to us are to be kept open between England and the Low Countries. There will be no French marriage for Mary."

"She is no longer a maid with the first blush of youth upon her," the queen argued quite sensibly. "If not a French prince, then who? You have turned down almost every legitimate offer from every respectable prince and potentate in all of Europe, Henry. Who is left for Mary if you do not accept this offer? How many more offers do you think you will receive for her?"

"Mary could be Queen of England one day," Henry said bluntly. "England will have no foreign king."

"You have Edward!" Catherine cried.

"Only Edward," he growled at her, "and he is not even four. What if I were to die tomorrow? Will my son even survive to succeed me? I have no other sons, Catherine. For now Mary follows Edward."

"I am certain that we will have children," the queen consoled him. "I am going to ask Nyssa de Winter when I see her how she got herself with two babies. When I learn her secret, I shall have them two at a time. Two boys, Henry! One for York, and the other for Richmond!"

He laughed. She could be so naive sometimes, but then that was the absolute charm of his rose without a thorn. She was the perfect wife for him. He had never in his entire life been so happy as he was with her. He wanted to live forever.

They departed London on the first of July. Their train was absolutely enormous. This was an important progress, unlike most summer progresses that remained in and about the Home countries. Many in the court were traveling with the king this year, unlike other years, when they returned to their own homes. There were carriages to shelter the women, although many of them preferred to ride if the weather was fair. The baggage train was huge, for it carried royal pavilions that would be set up each night to house the king and his court, as well as all the equipment necessary for the field kitchens that would feed them.

While the pavilions were being set up, the court would hunt. Wildlife, wherever the king's train passed by, was usually decimated quite thoroughly. The game, however, was used to feed them and all their retainers. The scraps were given to the beggars who followed in the king's wake hoping for alms, or perhaps even the king's touch for their illnesses. The king's touch was said to be miraculously healing.

Dunstable. Ampthill, Grafton Regis. The king's progress moved with precision exactly on schedule. The Earl and the Countess of March were due to meet their royal master and his wife at Lincoln on the ninth of August.

Nyssa had been absolutely furious when the summons had come.

"I cannot leave my babies!" she shrieked. "I am barely recovered from my confinement. Ohh, I just hate Cat for this! I will never forgive her! You must go, Varian, and tell them that I cannot leave the children. The king will certainly understand. He will send you home again to us. You must do this for me!"

"The queen has specifically requested your presence, sweeting," he told her. "Your mother is coming from *RiversEdge* with little Jane and Annie to look after Edmund and Sabrina. We have two wet nurses, and the twins will survive nicely. They will not even know we are gone."

"I don't want to go back to court," Nyssa said mutinously.

"We have no choice," he told her patiently, but the truth was he did not want to go either.

"My milk will dry up. I have only had two wet nurses in the event that I became ill, Varian, and could not nurse our babies myself. Susan has helped me greatly, but Alice has a child of her own."

"A child who is ready to be weaned," the earl said.

"You want to go!" she accused him.

"Nay, but I know there is nothing we can do that will prevent Catherine from importuning the king to bring us back. So, we will go, and we will bore them all to death with stories of how wonderful our twins are and how marvelous country life is. They will soon grow tired of us. We will never be asked back to court again. I suspect we will be home by Martinmas."

"I pray you are correct," she told him. "I love nursing the twins. I will not be able to do it again once we leave Winterhaven."

There was so much to be done in order to join the court on a progress. Tillie was quite excited about it despite all the work that would be involved for her. Her mistress would need several hunting costumes, riding costumes, and gowns for the elegant entertainments that would be held in the evenings. It would be hard to keep everything clean and pressed. This would be far more difficult than just being at Greenwich, or Hampton Court. There would have to be a coach for their comfort, and a baggage cart for the clothing, as well as another baggage cart containing a small private pavilion, bedding, and cooking utensils. They would have to travel with a change of coach horses, and Lord and Lady de Winter would need at least three horses apiece for riding and hunting. Tillie would have an assistant, Patience. One of the undercooks from Winterhaven's kitchens, William, as well as Bob, a groomsman, would also travel with them. They would have to share quarters with Toby. It was a great undertaking to travel with the court in progress.

Nyssa's mother arrived several days before their departure, alone. "Your father does not like me being away for so long at this time of year," she said. "I have to agree with him, my child. There is soap to be made, fruit and conserves to be put up, fruit to be dried, ale and cider that will need to be brewed. There is no one at *RiversEdge* who can oversee these things for me if I am here at Winterhaven. It is also difficult for your sisters to be uprooted. I am going to take Edmund and Sabrina along with their wet nurses back home with me. They will be perfectly safe, and they are too young to be disturbed by a change of residence. The weather is fine, and the journey is but a short duration."

"With your permission, my lord?" Nyssa questioned her husband. "Mama is really quite correct. It is too great a hardship for her to be here when she can manage quite as well at *RiversEdge*. I know she will share the bounty of her harvest with us this winter since I will not be here to oversee my own household."

"I think young Mistress Browning is quite capable of doing some of your work," Blaze told her daughter. "You are very fortunate to have her. I will stay the night and instruct her myself. That will give Susan and Alice time to prepare my grandchildren and themselves for the journey. Jane, Annie, and Henry are quite anxious to have their niece and nephew come to visit for a time."

"It is obvious that you have everything well in hand, madame," Varian de Winter told her. "I think your plan an excellent one."

"Then it is settled," the Countess of Langford said, pleased.

Nyssa had to steel herself not to create a scene the next afternoon when her mother departed with her children. The twins were five months old this day, and they had, their doting mother thought, grown more beautiful with each passing month. Both now had headfuls of dark hair like their father. It was lustrous and raven-black. Edmund had his mother's violet-blue eyes, but Sabrina's eyes were already turning the dark green of her father's. The twins had very individual personalities, but they were both strong-willed.

Nyssa managed to hold back her tears as she kissed her babies farewell. Her mother could see how very hard it was for her.

"Now," Blaze said, "you know how I felt when I left you to go to court after your father died."

"Aye," Nyssa sniffled. "Oh, keep them safe, Mama! We will come home as quickly as we can. If Queen Catherine had a child of her own, she would surely understand how I feel!"

Varian did not bother to explain to his wife that queens did not raise their children. Queens birthed heirs to the throne, and having done so, their job was considered over. Royal children were raised for the most part by favored nobility and servants. He put his arm about his wife as the Countess of Langford's coach departed and Nyssa began to weep openly. There was, he knew, nothing he could say to comfort her. She would have to be sad for a day or two before her equilibrium righted itself.

Two days later, when they left Winterhaven in the coach, she asked him, "Do you really think the king will let us come home again soon?"

"We are not important," he said. "It is only because the queen wants us that he has summoned us at all. Between us we will convince Cat to send us home, but we will have to spend some time with her first before she grows bored with us. Then, if she still cannot be reasoned with, I will speak to my grandfather. He will make her behave herself." His eyes twinkled, for Nyssa looked rebellious at his suggestion. He knew that she absolutely hated the idea that she would have to ask Duke Thomas for anything. He could not help but chuckle.

"I will find a way to persuade the queen to let us leave court," Nyssa said. "I will not ask that man for anything!"

"Are you not happy with me, sweeting?" he asked her. "Do we not really have my grandfather to thank for our happiness?"

"You said yourself that your grandfather cared not what happened to me as long as I was discredited in the king's eyes. He would have put me in a groom's loft bed to gain his ends had you not agreed to his scheme. I would have been truly ruined!" Nyssa said furiously. No man could anger her more than the duke.

"But it did not happen. Instead it was my bed in which you were found. We wed, and now have two beautiful children. You cannot continue to hold this grudge against my grandfather, Nyssa. He is an old man with no one to love him. I pity him, sweeting. I know now that I should far rather be a de Winter, content in the country with a loving wife, than a Howard striding the halls of power."

She would not answer him, for the truth was she could quite easily continue to hold her grudge against the powerful Duke of Norfolk. She knew she would never be able to revenge herself upon him for what he had done to her. Her husband had asked her if she were not happy. The truth was, she was happy. She loved Varian and was proud of his newfound strength and pride in his family name. She loved Winterhaven. She loved their children. But the Duke of Norfolk had, with his ambition, taken control of her life away from her, and for that she would never forgive him.

Suddenly Nyssa's eyes grew round as she realized what she had thought. *She loved her husband!* She did! When had it happened? She had not been aware of any dramatic turning point in their relationship, yet she had just said to herself that she loved Varian de Winter. She could not imagine her life without him, or their children. She peeped at him from beneath her long lashes. He was so very handsome. Both Edmund and Sabrina had his long face and straight nose. Her mother had told her that love could grow, but she had thought Blaze foolish. Now she knew that her mother was right. Love could grow, particularly when a woman had such a sweet-natured, thoughtful husband as she did.

She touched his arm, and he looked down at her questioningly. "I love you," she whispered shyly to him, her cheeks turning pink as she said the words. The look that leapt into his eyes almost pierced her to the heart. It was a look of such joy that she was embarrassed to realize that she had caused it. She was not worthy of such love as he had for her.

His arm was about her shoulders, and now he took her hand in his, kissing the half-closed fist, even as he asked, "And when did you come to this most important conclusion, madame?"

"Just now," she said. "When I was thinking about how angry your grandfather made me, I suddenly realized that I could not bear the thought of being without you, Varian. My heart is so full of you."

He found her mouth with his, kissing her sweetly, deeply. She returned his kisses with more passion than she had ever felt. His hand slipped into her bodice, cupping a full breast, fondling it, teasing the nipple. "I know the pain it cost you," he murmured against her hair, "but I am glad you ceased nursing the twins. Now these little beauties are all mine again, my love."

"I think I am glad now too," she told him, blushing. Her fingers fumbled with the laces on his shirt, pulling them open so that her hand could slide in and rub against his broad chest. Beneath her fingers his heart beat a mad tattoo. She bent and kissed his chest, licking at his nipples and slipping her tongue across his flesh, down to his navel. Outside their moving coach the rain beat down.

He kissed her hard, his hand struggling to loosen his clothing. "Come upon my lap," he groaned to her. "I need to be inside of you!"

"The driver!" she gasped, shocked by his boldness. "What if he should see us?"

"The coach will not stop until we reach the inn," he panted, pulling her atop him. "He cannot see us."

She positioned herself upon his lap, feeling him slide easily into her sheath. Frantically she pulled her bodice open so he might have the freedom of her breasts. Then bracing her hands upon his shoulders, she began to slowly ride him, her eyes never leaving his. It was so wonderfully wicked, Nyssa thought. Coupling with a man in a careening coach, her skirts bunched up about her milk-white thighs, his hands crushing the soft perfumed flesh of her bosom, while she moved up and down upon his shaft. She wanted it to go on forever, but their excitement was such that it was quickly over. They lay sprawled together on the seat, their breath rasping with the ferocity of their shared passion.

Finally Nyssa said to her husband, "Did you ever do that with any other woman in a coach?"

"You should not ask a man such questions," he said, laughing.

"You did!" she accused jealously.

"I admit to nothing," he told her, "and besides, if I did, it was long before we ever met and married." Then he kissed her on the tip of her nose and began to fasten her bodice. "When we reach the inn, we do not want to cause a scandal."

"I think I shall ask Tillie to ride with us tomorrow," Nyssa said sweetly. Then she smiled up at him.

"You do, and I'll beat you," he responded, a dangerous light in his green eyes. "There are other games we can play to while away the tedium of travel, but I fear Tillie would be shocked."

She pushed his hands away. "See to your own attire, my lord," she told him, fussing with her hair, which had come undone.

"No Tillie," he growled, and she laughed seductively.

Suddenly everything had changed. Knowing she loved him now, Nyssa found herself growing jealous of any woman who looked upon her husband. Was this what love did to you? But she could find no fault in Varian, for his eyes were for her alone. If anything, her surprising and sudden admission of her love for him had only deepened his own feelings toward her. She found herself reveling in the love he gave her, which she had never been able to do before. She had felt guilty accepting that love when she had not been able to reciprocate it.

The journey to Lincoln became a real honeymoon for them. They were both reluctant to have it come to an end. They traveled across Worcestershire, with its rolling farmlands. There were great green fields filled with ripening corn ready for harvest, and grassy pasturelands of fat cattle. There were extensive woodlands for the maintenance of the deer; and some sheep, although the flocks were not as big or as extensive as in neighboring counties. The apple and pear orchards were near to harvest. The residents of Worcestershire made a country wine from the pears, which was called Perry. It was quite delicious, the Earl and Countess of March thought, when they were given it to drink their first night on the road. Nyssa discovered it was also far more potent than she had anticipated. Indeed she grew quite tipsy, to Varian's amusement.

The architecture of the region was very pretty. The town and the individual houses they passed were timber-framed. Their crucks, posts, and beams were painted black and white. Only the fine manor houses and the churches were of red sandstone, which was indigenous to the area. Gardens bright with color bloomed everywhere. When Nyssa commented on how pretty it all was, her husband agreed, but then he told her that they were fortunate to be passing south of the town of Droitwich, which was a foul place by virtue of its salt industry. Droitwich had three brine springs, and four hundred furnaces in which to dry its salt. The air for miles of the town was rancid and reeked.

They traveled on to Warwickshire. They were north of the river Avon, where the land was mostly woodland with common rights for the small landholders and the landless cottagers. The more powerful landowners in the district were constantly trying to enclose the forests and usurp their tenants' rights. There was much resentment in the area, and bandits could be a danger, but they were well-protected by their own men-at-arms.

They stopped in Coventry, which was a walled town. The Reformation had cost Coventry its cathedral, and had ended the cycle of Mystery plays for which the town had been famous. The loss of this industry had lost Coventry its prestige, not to mention a great deal of commercial income, for many small shops had done quite well selling their goods to the pilgrims. The town was in decline, but it was still beautiful.

"Why are there so few farmsteads?" Nyssa asked her husband.

"The land isn't good for farming. There are surface deposits of coal and iron, which are mined," he told her.

They moved across Leicestershire, and Nyssa was fascinated. She had never seen a landscape like Leicestershire's. There were virtually no trees, fewer hedgerows, and no deer to be seen at all. The fields were planted mostly in barley and pulses, although there was some wheat. They seemed to stretch on forever. Pastureland filled with cattle and black-faced sheep lined the roads for miles.

But there was much rural poverty because these lands were mainly in the hands of the nobility. The cottages showed neglect and were the poorest Nyssa had ever seen, single-room dwellings built of a mixture of clay, straw, and animal waste. Although the county produced wool, there was no cottage industry of weaving which would have brought the cottagers a better income.

They stayed a night in the town of Leicester. It was a center for the leather trade, and it was known for its excellent trade goods, cattle, and horse auctions. It was a prosperous enough town, but had not the happy air of the market towns in their native Herefordshire.

They were almost at the end of their journey as they crossed the boundaries from Leicestershire into Lincolnshire. This area's economy was dependent upon livestock. The fleeces of Lincoln's sheep were considered so fine that they were sold immediately upon shearing to outsiders, the prices being so high. The extensive fen and marshes produced reeds used all over England for thatching. Flax was also grown in the marshes, and woven into linen. Like Leicestershire, however, the great landowning families controlled everything in the region. The farther north one went, Nyssa realized, the more feudal everything became. The north, decimated in the time of William I for its continued rebellion, had never really recovered.

The town of Lincoln had lost its preeminence to Nottingham, but it was still a charming town, with a castle and a cathedral. The court had not arrived by the time they reached their destination, but the royal baggage carts had. The pavilions were being set up in the fields about the city. The Earl of March found the household steward who was in charge of setting everything up, and the steward directed them to a space on the very edge of the encampment.

"We have certainly not been given a prime site," Nyssa remarked, amused. "So much for being the queen's friend."

"At least we are not surrounded by a host of other pavilions, and we have a fine view of the countryside," he said with a smile.

The earl helped his servants set up their pavilions. They were placed upon wooden platforms, a larger one for the de Winters, and the smaller one for the servants. The little pavilion was divided neatly down the center by a heavy curtain so that the men and women could preserve their privacy. The Earl of March's pavilion was striped red and blue. His banner flew from the top of the tent pole, which would allow anyone looking for him to find him easily. Inside, fine carpets had been spread over the wooden platform. The living area and the sleeping area were divided by tapestries. There were braziers for heating the pavilion, for though this was August, they were in the north.

The living area contained a table for eating and several chairs. The sleeping area had a bed which was actually a large leather hammock fastened to four stout pegs set upon a rug-covered platform, with a feather bed atop it. The chests containing their personal effects were placed about. There were footed bronze candelabra and several glass lamps hanging from the ceilings for lighting. Outside the pavilion a small campfire was set up. These preparations would be repeated each time the royal progress moved on; sometimes every day, and sometimes every few days.

The servants drew water from the nearby river and heated it over the fire so that their master and mistress might bathe before the royal party arrived. Nyssa and Varian washed themselves in a small wooden tub, sharing the bathwater and toweling each other dry in the chilly air. Tillie and Toby had both been quite shocked when told that Nyssa and Varian would bathe each other.

"What is the world coming to, I should like to know?" Tillie huffed, annoyed. "The next thing you know, there will be no need for us servants. I never thought I'd see the day when my mistress would be so immodest as to bathe her own husband!"

"I don't like it any better than you do," Toby agreed, "but they ain't going to do away with the likes of us, Tillie, old girl."

"Tillie, come and help me dress," Nyssa called to her tiring woman. "I'm on the sleeping side of the pavilion. Toby is to help his lordship on the other side. Hurry now!"

"You see!" Toby grinned. "They couldn't do without us."

The Earl and Countess of March were elegantly garbed by the time the royal progress began to arrive at the encampment. Nyssa's gown was of deep blue velvet, its bodice sewn with silver beads and pearls. The under-skirt was of silver and blue brocade. The neckline was low and square, the sleeves wide and bell-like, turned back at the lower edge. About her neck Nyssa wore two fine ropes of pearls. Her dark hair was parted in the middle and gathered in a silver caul. A single sapphire on a silver ribbon was affixed about her forehead.

The earl was garbed in an elegant costume of wine-colored velvet. His silk shirt was ruffled at both the neck and the sleeves. His stockings were striped wine and gold. His doublet was sewn with gold beads and pearls. Atop his dark head he wore a flat bonnet with ostrich tips. A heavy gold chain was about his neck.

The progress was settling into the encampment. Protocol demanded that the Earl and Countess of March wait to be summoned into the royal presence. The Duke of Norfolk arrived to greet them, looking weary and travel-stained. It was a hard progress for a man of seventy. They had not seen him since they had left court over a year ago.

"Will you be seated, my lord? Some wine, perhaps?" Nyssa was the model of a perfect hostess. Only her husband noticed her cold tone.

The duke settled himself heavily into a chair and grunted his thanks as the goblet was offered him. He drank deeply. "You carry good wine with you," he noted. "How are my great-grandchildren?"

"Thriving, Grandfather," the earl said. He thought the old man looked a trifle worn.

"They would be better if their parents did not have to trek over half the English countryside following a royal progress because of the whim of a chit of a queen," Nyssa said sharply.

"Have you not yet beaten the high spirits out of her?" the duke said, not bothering to answer Nyssa directly, and thereby infuriating her even more. "At least she's a good breeder. Would God that your cousin Catherine proved as fecund."

Nyssa opened her mouth to respond, but Varian sharply reprimanded her. "Nyssa! Be silent, sweeting." He turned to his grandfather. "We heard that she had miscarried in late spring."

"Perhaps," the duke said gloomily. "She is very secretive about it. She has not the wit of a flea, and loves nothing but constant pleasure, but the king adores her. So far. She can do no wrong in his eyes."

He looked directly at Nyssa, and to her surprise, addressed her. "I am glad you are here, madame. The queen is restless, and she is bored. That is not good. I know not why she feels this way. She has everything her heart desires, yet she complains she has not her best friend. You seem to have that distinction, although I cannot comprehend why. Try to calm her, madame. Turn her to a more reasonable behavior."

"Cat cannot be turned if she chooses not to be," Nyssa said quietly. "How little you really know her, my lord; and that, I think, may prove dangerous for you both."

"The future of the family depends upon your success," the Duke of Norfolk told Nyssa.

"Nonsense!" she snorted. "Besides, we are not Howards, my lord. Varian and I are de Winters. We do not seek power and riches. We were content at Winterhaven with our children. If you fall from grace, my lord, it will not affect us."

He looked at her admiringly. "By God I could wish that you were a

Howard, madame. You look like a wild rose, but you are hard as iron."
He turned to his grandson. "Are you happy with her? You should be. She
is strong, and loyal to you. She loves you."

"I love her," the earl replied. "I have from the first moment I laid eyes
on her at Hampton Court. Nyssa is not of a mind to forgive you for the
way in which we married, but we both owe you a debt of gratitude,
Grandfather, for without realizing it, or even caring one way or the other,
you brought us together. For that we will attempt to help you, will we not,
sweeting?" His green eyes bore into hers.

We are one, she thought, triumphant. If she asked him to take her home
now, he would. *He loved her!* "We will remain, my lord," she said quietly,
"and I will try to be a good influence upon the queen." Her look was
imperious. She was granting him a favor.

The Duke of Norfolk grinned wolfishly at both of them. If I were
younger, he thought, she is just the kind of woman I would want for
myself. Clever and proud. He could but imagine, with envy, the pleasure
she gave his grandson in bed. She would be all fire and ice. A wild rose with
sharp, sharp thorns.

"The queen would see you," he told Nyssa. "I will take you to her; and
you, Varian, can make your presence known to the king. He is in an
excellent mood today. The hunting was good for a change."

They followed him through the encampment directly into its heart,
where the magnificent cloth-of-gold and silver-striped pavilions that
housed the royal couple were set up. Beneath a scarlet and gold awning
cooks were busily preparing a feast for the evening meal.

"The queen is there." The duke pointed to a slightly smaller pavilion.
"She is expecting you, madame."

Nyssa curtsied to her husband's grandfather, but there was nothing
subservient in the movement. Her eyes met those of her husband, and she
could see his mouth twitching with laughter. "My lords," she said, and
then moved on past them into the queen's pavilion.

Lady Rochford hurried forward. "Hurry!" she said to Nyssa. "She is
so anxious to see you, my lady."

The Countess of March followed Lady Rochford into the queen's
privy. Catherine Howard, gowned in the king's favorite rose velvet, arose
from her seat, and running forward, threw her arms about her friend, to
the shock of her ladies.

"Nyssa! Ohh, I am so glad you are finally here. We are going to have
such fun now!"

One look at Cat told Nyssa that something was very wrong. Could no one else see it? Her friend was like a lute string that was too tight and ready to break. Nyssa curtsied low, and when she arose, she smiled at Cat, saying, "You must tell me all about being a queen, madame, and I shall tell you all about my wonderful babies."

[LOVE, REMEMBER ME

CHAPTER 12

THE queen felt freer on progress than she had anywhere else since her marriage a year ago. Suddenly she was surrounded by a group of attractive young people whose sole goal in life was pleasure. Her best friend in all the world had arrived to keep her company and share her secrets. They would hunt all day along the route, and dance the night away. Henry was a fine companion in the mornings, but after his dinner, he usually wanted to sleep. She need only spend half the time pleasing him. The other half was her own time, and she would spend it as she pleased.

Nyssa hated the royal progress. It was the worst time of her life. Am I getting old? she wondered. Why can I not lose myself in the mindless pleasures that Cat does? Would it have been different if Varian and I were not wed; if we did not have children? But she knew that that was not so. There were many young married couples in the court, and they all seemed to be having a wonderful time. All Nyssa could think of, however, was that there was soap and perfume, jams and conserves to be made. Meat and fish had to be salted for the winter. How was this going to get done if she was not there to supervise? Oh, young Mistress Browning was capable, but Nyssa wanted to be home, overseeing her own household, not trekking all over England in the company of the court.

"Why can I not enjoy myself?" she asked her husband.

"For the same reason I cannot," he told her. "You and I are country people at heart. We are not courtiers who can while away their days in frivolous pursuits. I know Master Smale can oversee the harvest and the shearing, but I would prefer to be there myself."

"There is something strange happening with Cat," Nyssa told her husband, "and whatever it is, Lady Ferretface is part of it."

"What do you mean?" he responded.

"If it were anyone else but the queen," Nyssa said slowly, "I would say there was a man involved, but that cannot possibly be."

Varian de Winter felt a shudder ripple down his spine. Could his cousin be foolish enough to have taken a lover? Holy Mother! He prayed it was not so. The Howards had lost one queen to the headsman's ax. If Catherine were stupid enough to involve herself with a man not the king, she would eventually be found out. There was always someone watching when you least expected it. And a queen's adultery was considered high treason.

"Can you find out?" he said. "I do not want to speak to my grandfather unless you are certain of what you suspect."

"I will have to spend more time with her," Nyssa said, "and I have been avoiding it so we might be together." She leaned over and kissed him softly. "I prefer to spend as much time abed with you, my lord, as I can. Bed has ever been your strong point," she teased him, running a single finger down his thigh.

"If Catherine is silly enough to have taken a lover," he told her seriously, "we are all in danger of the king's wrath."

"We are not Howards," Nyssa said. "Why should the king hold us responsible if his wife's behavior is light? What have we to do with Catherine Howard, Varian?"

"You do not know how the king thinks, sweeting," he told her. "I was raised at court. He will accept no blame for anything. He seeks scapegoats whenever he finds himself liable for a fault. If Cat betrays him, he will not consider that part of the fault lies with him—that a man of his age should not have wed a chit so young and ripe to bursting, that Cat is not a rose without a thorn, but a flighty little girl, who thinks only of herself and of her own pleasures. The king will feel abused and ill-used by everyone about him if he runs true to form, and he will. He will blame everyone else for what happens. He will blame my grandfather in particular, and the Howards in general. My mother was a Howard, and I am Duke Thomas's only grandson. We will not escape his anger if Cat behaves badly."

"I will see what I can find out," Nyssa said, now genuinely concerned. "If there is another man, Varian, I am certain that it is just a harmless flirtation. Cat would never violate her marriage vows."

"I pray you are right, sweeting," he told her, and pulling her into his arms, he kissed her deeply.

To the queen's delight, Nyssa began to spend more time with her. She had also, to everyone's relief, ceased talking constantly about her twins. Other people's children were always so boring.

The progress moved on to the port of Boston so the king might indulge his naval fantasies. The queen and her court, however, boated on the waters of the river Witham past the elegant tower that soared above the church of St. Botolph. The boaters pelted each other with flowers, until the waters about them looked more like a field than a river. Then laughing and singing, they picnicked along the riverbanks.

The progress moved into Yorkshire and Northumberland, heading for Newcastle, the farthest north Henry Tudor had ever been in his kingdom. Varian de Winter left his wife to her own devices, attaching himself to the king's group of gentlemen in order to learn any gossip that might filter in from their wives or ladyloves. It was better that he and Nyssa not seem too close if they were to learn the truth.

Tom Culpeper, although a gentleman of the king's privy, was spending more time with the queen these days. One of his closest friends, Sir Cynric Vaughn, had singled out Nyssa and was pursuing her shamelessly.

"Now that you have stopped being an old goodwife," Cat said, "the gentlemen can see what a charmer you really are."

The two women were together in the queen's privy chamber of her pavilion. Kate Carey and Bessie FitzGerald had joined the progress, at the queen's invitation. But for their change in status, it was like old times, Nyssa thought.

"I do not think the gentleman should be so obvious in his attentions toward me," Nyssa said, almost primly. "After all, I am a married woman, Your Grace. Besides, I suspect he has earned his nickname, and not in a way any respectable woman would approve of," she noted. "A gentleman named 'Sin'? It sounds quite wicked."

Cat giggled. "He is wicked," she said, and she lowered her voice. "I hear he makes it a habit to seduce married women, and get them to fall in love with him. You had best beware, Nyssa, for Tom says Sin is madly in love with you, and means to have you!"

"How do you do it?" Kate Carey asked. "It seems every time you come to court, some gentleman desires you. I have not been so fortunate. I shall be married off to some dull fellow in due time without ever having known passion and mad abandon."

"Maybe when you are wed, the gentlemen of the court will feel free to indulge their passions for you," Bessie said mischievously. "They said it is dangerous for them to tamper with virgins unless they plan to wed them."

"True," the queen agreed wryly. "After all, if the road to paradise is already an open road, who is to know who has traveled it before? Still, the truth of the matter is that men are usually in such a hurry to couch their lances that they quite often do not even know if a maid is pure or not." She laughed. "Men can be managed, my dears."

Nyssa was shocked. This was a side of Cat Howard she had not seen before. It was cynical, and perhaps even a trifle dishonest. She had never before considered her friend in these terms. Wisely, she held her tongue, for they would just tease her about being a backward country lass even if she was a married woman.

"But if a girl is not a virgin, can a man not tell?" Kate Carey asked curiously. "When Nyssa married Lord de Winter, my uncle, the king, insisted that proof of the consummation be brought to him the following morning. That proof was a bedsheet with the stains of Nyssa's virginity upon it. If there is no blood, what can a man think but that his bride was not pure? I would be very afraid of such a thing."

"Do not be such a goose, Kate," the queen said. "Many a girl has gone to her marriage bed with a chicken's bladder of blood secreted beneath the sheets to give evidence of her purity."

"But a girl could become enceinte playing the wanton," Bessie Fitz-Gerald replied nervously.

The queen motioned them closer and said, "A girl can meddle with a man and not become enceinte if she knows what to do." She smiled knowingly, showing her small white teeth.

Her words disturbed Nyssa further. Why was the queen suddenly so knowledgeable? Was it because she was a married woman, or did her enlightenment stem from another time, a time prior to her marriage? It was a frightening thought.

"I want to dance!" the queen said, jumping up. "Kate, go and call the musicians. See if there are any gentlemen in the outer chamber, and tell them that we shall join them immediately."

The queen's musicians were summoned and began to play. The young men and women danced the spritely country dances. Wine was being served with small sugar wafers.

Sin Vaughn stood watching them for a time, contemplating his attack.

The Countess of March was without a doubt the most exciting woman he had ever met. Her very coolness to him, her air of respectability, enticed him greatly. Very tall, and slender, he stood head and shoulders above most of the court. The ladies adored him, and his charm was legendary. His oval-shaped gray eyes had the habit of narrowing almost to slits when he was considering some matter he deemed to be of importance. He had thick, wavy, ash-brown hair that was filled with golden highlights, and he was clean-shaven, unlike many at court. His chin was squared, and there was a deep cleft in it that set maidens to swooning when they looked upon him. His mouth was big, in keeping with the rest of him.

Snapping up a goblet of chilled wine, he was at her side as the dance came to an end. Her partner, seeing his rival, slipped into the background. "Madame," he said, handing her the goblet. She looked absolutely delicious, all flushed and breathless.

"My thanks, my lord," she said with a small smile. She was going to have to encourage him, she knew. He would be privy to all of Tom Culpeper's secrets, and Tom Culpeper was paying marked attention to the queen at all these little gatherings when the king was not present. Both he and Cat were quite proper in their behavior, but there was a tension between them that to Nyssa was almost palpable. Did no one else see it, or sense it? Was she imagining things? "You do not dance, my lord," she said to him.

"I have not the knack for it," he replied, smiling into her eyes and taking her free hand in his. "I have other talents, madame."

"Are you flirting with me, my lord?" she asked him.

He was amused. Usually women simpered at his attentions. "I believe I am, madame. Do you mind?"

"I am a married woman, sir," she said with an answering smile.

"Then perhaps I should ask if your husband minds?" he responded.

Nyssa laughed. He was witty, she had to admit. "Since the ladies all flirt with Varian," she told him, "I hardly think he can object if the gentlemen admire me. What do you think, my lord?"

"I think you are extravagantly beautiful," he told her.

"I think you, sir, are possibly very dangerous," Nyssa said, freeing her hand from his, handing him her goblet, and moving away from where they had been standing.

Cynric Vaughn burst out laughing. The quarry had been engaged, and the hunt was about to begin. She was the most intoxicating woman he had ever met. She was direct, and there was no artifice about her. He meant to have her, and he would.

"You stare at Lady de Winter too hard, I think, Sin," Tom Culpeper said. "You waste your time. Her grace says she is virtuous to a fault. Set your sights on an easier prey."

"No," came the reply. "She will be mine, Tom. I am not certain yet how, but she will. I want her as I have never wanted a woman."

"Beware, my friend," Culpeper warned him, "the king is fond of her. Lady de Winter's mother was once his mistress. How do you think she came to be wed to the Earl of March? He seduced the girl, and the king would not be satisfied until she was wed to him. He saw to it himself, and insisted upon proof that the marriage had been consummated so that de Winter could not legally repudiate the girl and keep her wealth. She is the daughter of the Earl of Langford."

"So it was no love match?" Cynric Vaughn said.

"There is no enmity between them that I know of, and they have children in common," Culpeper informed his friend.

"How fare you in your own hunt?" Sir Cynric wondered softly.

"You mistake my intentions," Tom Culpeper said. "I simply wish to climb high, as Charles Brandon did, but alas, that was thirty years ago. In those days one became the king's friend to advance a career, but the king is old now. One must become the queen's friend today in order to reach one's goals."

Cynric Vaughn laughed. "I do not believe that I have ever heard a better excuse for seduction, Tom," he told Culpeper. "But if you get caught, she will cry rape. The king will not let you off as easily as he did with that gamekeeper's wife. Besmirch his rose without a thorn, and you will find yourself without a head. Is it worth it?"

"My cousin the queen and I are just friends," Culpeper replied.

The king's progress moved across the soft rolling hills and moors of Yorkshire and Northumberland. Where the hunting was good, they would remain for a few days, and then travel onward. Nyssa did enjoy hunting, but more for the thrill of the chase than for the kill. Country-bred girls were usually good horsewomen, and she was no exception.

One afternoon her horse began limping even as a rainstorm caught her falling behind the main party. Looking for shelter, she espied the ruins of an ancient abbey and rode into the refuge of its walls. Dismounting, she took her mare's leg up and saw a stone lodged in its shoe.

"God's foot!" Nyssa muttered irritably, and then jumped at the sound of a male voice. Whirling about, she came face-to-face with Sir Cynric Vaughn.

"I saw you leave the hunt," he said. "Are you all right, madame?"

"My mare has caught a stone, and I've no knife with which to pry it loose," Nyssa told him.

"Which foot?" he asked, and when she showed him, he took the mare's hoof in one hand, removing the stone from it with his knife in the other hand. "There, madame. She will be fine now, but we, I fear, must wait for the rain to let up."

Looking past him, Nyssa saw what had begun as a shower was now a downpour. It was as good an opportunity as she would ever get to make friends with Sin Vaughn and draw him out. "Have you been at court long, my lord? I do not seem to remember you from my last visit," she began conversationally.

"I am here most of the time," he told her.

"You are Master Culpeper's friend," she noted innocently.

He laughed. "Aye, Tom and I are old friends, madame, but if you have set your sights in that direction, turn away. Culpeper has a most jealous mistress, I fear."

"Thomas Culpeper is of no interest to me," Nyssa told him. "I am a married woman, sir."

"So you have said, madame, on a previous occasion. Is it truly so, or do you say it to convince yourself?" He grinned mockingly at her. Reaching out, he entwined an errant lock of her hair about his finger.

"You are a wicked man, I am told," Nyssa said softly, looking seductively up at him. She was rather enjoying her little flirtation with him. He was outrageously handsome and he was going to kiss her. Oddly, she was not afraid. She was frankly curious, having never been kissed by any man but Varian. She should feel guilty, she knew, for such naughty thoughts, but it would only be a little kiss.

With his hand, he cupped her face, and lowering his own, he brushed his lips lightly across hers. "You are delicious," he said low. "I want to make love to you, madame. Here and now upon the grass beneath these walls. Think of the ghosts of the long dead monks observing us in our passion, and unable to fulfill their own." Releasing her head, he clasped his arm about her supple waist, his other hand fumbling at her breasts.

Nyssa pulled quickly away. "Fie, sir! You move too quickly to take liberties. I am not some shepherdess to be tumbled in the open. Look, the rain has stopped. We must get back lest we are missed." Without even asking for his assistance, she pulled herself into her saddle. "Are you coming, my lord?" she asked him, and then without waiting for an answer, kicked her mare into a trot.

Watching her hurry off, he smiled to himself. For all her protests of a husband, she was hot for loving. There would be time.

The progress moved on to Newcastle, visited the town officially, and turned south again for Pontefract Castle, reaching it toward the end of August. They would remain at Pontefract for a week.

On a rainy afternoon, as the queen and her women sat playing cards in her apartments, Lady Rochford came to tell Cat that there was a gentleman seeking an audience with her. He waited just outside the queen's anteroom.

"Who is he?" the queen asked Lady Rochford.

"He says his name is Francis Dereham, Your Grace. The dowager duchess, your grandmother, has sent him to you, and requests that you offer him a place as secretary in your household."

Catherine grew pale, and for a moment it appeared as if she would swoon, but then she said, "I will see Master Dereham in my privy chamber, Rochford. If my grandmother has sent him, then I must be kind." She arose and went into her private rooms. Her heart was hammering violently. *What did he want?* Was this to be another incident like those with Joan Bulmer and the others who had come to her requesting positions in her household, wondering if the queen remembered them and the dear old days they had all spent together at Lambeth Palace? Catherine had made them chamberwomen, and their service was faultless, but she resented the way in which she had been coerced, for their reminders of their time together at Lambeth had just stopped short of blackmail. Now *he* had come to request her favor.

The door opened and Lady Rochford escorted a man into the room. "Master Dereham, Your Grace," she said.

He doffed his cap to her, bowing elegantly as only he knew how. "I am honored, Your Grace, and bring greetings from the lady Agnes."

"You may leave us," Catherine told Lady Rochford, who withdrew. The queen glared at the man before her. She had remembered him as being more handsome. He was swarthy, with an elegant, tailored black beard, black hair, and black eyes that were dancing devilishly. There was a gold earring in his ear. "What do you want of me?" she demanded coldly. There was no welcome in her voice.

"What, little wife? No words of joy upon my return from Ireland?" he said, smiling toothily at her. His even white teeth had always been among his best features.

"Are you mad?" Catherine said angrily. "How dare you address me in such a manner, Master Dereham! *What do you want?*"

"Why, merely to share in your good fortune, Cat," he told her. "Should not a husband share in his wife's good fortune?"

"We are not man and wife," she said tightly.

"What, Catherine, have you so easily forgotten that we pledged our troth to one another at Lambeth just three years back? I have not forgotten," Francis Dereham told her.

"I was fourteen then," Catherine responded, "and nothing was formally settled. It was the silliness of an innocent girl. You can prove nothing, and should you attempt to cause a scandal, you will find yourself facing the headsman's ax, Master Dereham. The king dotes upon me, and will not be interfered with."

"Our troth was no secret, Cat," he replied. "Everyone at Lambeth then knew of it. I understand that Joan Bulmer and the other girls are now in your service. It was kind of you to find a place for them. I am certain that you can find a place for me as well. The dowager duchess, dear lady she is, thought I might suit you as a secretary."

"My household is full," she said stubbornly.

"Make a place then," he answered her threateningly.

"I must ask the king," she said. "Without his approval, I cannot appoint you. He is not an easy master."

"But he dotes upon you, my beauty. You have said so yourself," Francis Dereham said.

She hated him now with the same dark passion that she had once loved him. She was beaten, and he knew it. "You may lodge with the gentlemen ushers of my household temporarily until I have spoken with his grace," she said coldly. "You may go now, Dereham." She turned her back on him and waited tensely until she heard the door close behind him. Then Catherine Howard's fingers closed upon the nearest item she could find, and with a shriek she flung it against the stone wall. *"Nyssa!"* she shouted. "Come to me at once!"

The ladies in the queen's outer rooms heard her shout, and startled, looked at one another. The queen had never before shouted. Nyssa arose quickly and hurried to answer her friend's call.

"What is it, Cat?" she asked as she closed the door behind her.

The queen began to sob hysterically. Nyssa quickly poured her a goblet of strong red wine from the tray on the sideboard. She forced her friend to drink. When Catherine Howard had calmed a bit, Nyssa repeated her question.

"Oh, Nyssa," the queen said, "I am forced to take that rude fellow into my household. I hate him!"

"Why?" Nyssa demanded. "The truth, Cat! Perhaps I can help."

"His name is Francis Dereham. He was at Lambeth when I was there. He . . . he took liberties with me that he should not have. Now he is threatening to tell the king unless I take him into my household. My grandmother knows nothing of this, or she would not have sent him.

Indeed she would have seen he met with some unfortunate accident," the queen concluded.

"Did you not speak to me once about being courted by this Dereham, Cat?" Nyssa looked directly at the queen, who flushed.

"I was but bragging," she said sullenly.

"I warned you to tell the king," Nyssa said. "If you had done it then, before you were married, no one could blackmail you like this. He would have forgiven you, Cat. Now you are caught like an animal in a trap. You cannot tell him now. So you must suffer to have this Francis Dereham in your household."

"I know," Cat said despondently, and she drained the goblet.

"Dry your eyes, Your Grace," Nyssa said, handing her friend a handkerchief. "No one must see you like this lest questions be asked."

Catherine took the little linen square and mopped at her face. "Ohh, Nyssa," she said, "what would I do without you? You are my only friend! I never knew being a queen would be so lonely. You must never leave me! Promise me!"

"Nay, I will not promise you such a thing, Cat," Nyssa said. "If you love me, you will let me go home soon. I miss my children."

"If you went home, Nyssa, then you would never see Sin Vaughn again." She giggled, adroitly turning the subject away from what she considered unpleasant ground. "He is quite taken with you. Do you think he is handsome? As handsome as my cousin Varian?"

Nyssa laughed. "He is not as handsome as my husband, but he is a pretty fellow with winning ways. A notorious seducer, I am told. Neither of us should be seen in his company, Cat." She said nothing of the encounter she had had with Sin Vaughn. Cat would be unable to refrain from gossiping about it with the others; and she would read something more into it than there was.

"Was it Bessie or Kate who once said that handsome, wicked men are far more interesting than handsome, nice men?" the queen asked, and the two young women dissolved into laughter.

That night at the evening meal, the king was in a particularly fine mood, for he had personally killed six stags that day. When Nyssa and the queen danced together for his amusement, he was well-pleased. His little eyes followed their graceful movements as they pirouetted and twirled before him. His wife was wearing a gown of rose-colored silk. It was his favorite color on her, complimenting her lovely russet hair. Nyssa was equally lovely in a silk gown of pale spring-green, the bodice encrusted with pearls and peridots.

Afterward the king took both young women upon his lap, and said first to Nyssa, "I will grant you a boon for the pleasure you have given me with your dancing, my wild rose. What will you have of me?"

"I would be home with my family by Christmas, Your Grace," she said sweetly, and then kissed his cheek.

The king chuckled richly. "You are a wicked chit, Nyssa, for I know your desire conflicts with the desires of my queen, but I have given my word to grant your wish, and so I must."

"Thank you, Your Grace," she replied meekly.

The king laughed again. "You do not fool me, madame. You do not fool me one bit. Your good lord tells me how you have wrapped him about your little finger. I did not do so badly by you, Nyssa, did I? You are happy, are you not?"

"I am very happy, Your Grace," she answered him honestly.

The king turned to his wife. "Now what new extravagance will you have of me, madame? Another gown, or perhaps a new jewel?"

"Nay, sire, but one small thing," Cat told her husband. "The dowager duchess Agnes sent me a distant relative of hers, and begs that I find a place for him in my household. I could use another secretary, my lord. Will you allow me to do the lady Agnes this favor?"

"Aye," he said, "for by not coming on this progress and complaining constantly about the state of her health, she has done me a favor. Appoint this fellow if you will. What is his name?"

"Francis Dereham, my lord," the queen replied, and her eyes met those of Nyssa's in the shared conspiracy.

They left Pontefract Castle and traveled on to York, arriving in mid-September. The weather was becoming more autumnal, and it was raining more now, which made the journey uncomfortable at best. At York the king hoped to meet with his nephew, King James of Scotland. There had also been speculation that Henry might crown his queen at Yorkminster. The king, however, made it quite clear when queried that Catherine's coronation rested with her ability to produce another heir for him. She was obviously not with child.

The royal pavilions were set up in the grounds of an old abbey which was being refurbished for use as the site of the conference that Henry hoped to effect between himself and King James. The hunting was excellent. On one day the king and his huntsmen slew two hundred deer. The nearby marshes belonging to the river offered a bounty of ducks, geese, swans, and fish of all kinds. Nothing went to waste, and the cooks in the field kitchens were kept as busy as if they had been at Hampton Court, or Greenwich.

Nyssa had a headache and had not gone hunting that first morning in

York. She knew that the queen was also in the encampment. When her headache eased, she sought her out, knowing how easily bored Cat could become, and thinking to offer her a game of cards. The guards outside the queen's pavilion nodded and smiled to her as she passed by them unchallenged. Inside, Nyssa was surprised to find that the pavilion was deserted. There were no ladies hovering, waiting to do Cat's bidding, no servants bustling to and fro on a variety of errands.

"Cat?" she called softly. "Cat?" Nyssa passed through from the outer antechamber into the queen's privy. "Cat?" There was no one in the little room outside the queen's bedchamber. Perhaps Cat was asleep. Nyssa drew back the curtain gently, not wanting to waken her friend if she slept. Instead her eyes grew wide with shock.

The tableau before her was so sensual that Nyssa could barely breathe. For a moment she could not even move. She simply stared, mesmerized. The queen and Tom Culpeper lay sprawled and entwined amid the satin and fur coverlet of the royal bed. A single lamp, burning fragrant oil, cast a golden glow over them. Cat was naked as the day she had come into the world. Culpeper wore naught but a silk shirt that was open. Nyssa could see the queen's full breasts, round and lush as for a brief moment her lover changed position. Then he was between her legs, laboring mightily. Cat, her pretty face suffused with lust, was moaning her pleasure, encouraging him onward.

"Ohhh, God, yesss, Tom! Fuck me, darling! Ohhh, yessss! Don't stop! I need you, darling! Fuck me! Fuck me!"

"I won't stop, Cat," he growled quite distinctly. "I am not that sick old fool you're married to, my hot little bitch. I'll fuck you well this day, as I have before and will again!" He ground himself into her, and the queen groaned lustily.

Nyssa let the curtain fall, finally able to move. Then she fled the queen's pavilion.

She could not believe what she had just seen. Surely her eyes had deceived her. But she knew they had not deceived her. They had seen what they had seen, and now she was in a quandary as to what to do. She stopped in her flight, closing her eyes, and drew a deep breath to clear her head. The memory filled her brain, and her eyes flew open again. She needed time to think; to compose herself; to decide what she must do, or if she should or could do anything.

Reaching her pavilion, she called to the groomsman, Bob, to fetch her the gelding she liked to ride.

"Will ye be joining the hunt then, m'lady?" Bob said.

"Nay." Nyssa shook her head. "I simply wish to ride off this headache. I will not go far, Bob. You need not come with me."

Entering the pavilion, she called to Tillie to help her change her clothing. "Bring me the heather-colored riding skirt, and my boots."

"Yer as white as a ghost, m'lady. Are you all right?" Tillie's tone was one of great concern. "Perhaps you should lie down."

"Nay," Nyssa told her. "I need to get away from here, and be by myself for a little time. Ohhh, Tillie! I hate the court!"

Tillie helped her mistress out of her clothes and into a riding outfit consisting of the velvet skirt and a purple velvet bodice edged in gold braid. Kneeling, she fit Nyssa's boots onto her slender feet. "Are you joining the hunt then, m'lady?"

Nyssa shook her head. "I want to ride. Alone."

"Bob should ride with you, m'lady. His lordship won't like it that you've gone off alone. 'Tis dangerous," Tillie fretted.

"Living among the court is far more dangerous, Tillie," Nyssa told her tiring woman. "I will take my chances in the hills hereabouts. Besides, I will not go far, and his lordship will never know if you do not tell him, will he?" She patted the maidservant's shoulder and hurried from the pavilion, mounting the horse that Bob had saddled.

She cantered from the encampment, not really even heeding where she was going. The countryside about her was bleak. Outside the walls of York there seemed to be nothing but sky and hills. Here and there bits of autumn color were showing. She rode on and on until finally, as she topped a hill, she drew her horse to a halt, gazing out over the landscape below. Nyssa sighed deeply. She had caught the queen in adultery. *What was she to do?*

The king adored his young wife. He was unlikely to hear any ill about her from anyone. Particularly not from me, Nyssa thought. I cannot accuse the queen of light behavior without proof, and the mere evidence of my own eyes will not be enough. They will say that I am jealous that the king married Cat instead of marrying me. That I seek to turn the king away from her, and back to me. The question of my marriage to Varian will come up all over again, and my own behavior will be questioned. I can say nothing. I am forced to be silent in the face of this adultery and treason. I dare not even tell Varian, for he will go to his grandfather, and then Duke Thomas will go to the queen. Cat will not like it, and she will surely find a way to get even with me. I am no match for a reigning queen. I must remain silent to protect my family.

"I have never before seen such a serious look in any woman's eyes," a familiar voice said, amused. "What weighty matters do you ponder, my dear Countess of March? You are too beautiful to be so gloomy."

Nyssa looked up, startled to see Sir Cynric Vaughn beside her, mounted upon a fine black stallion. "I am thinking of my babies, and how I wish I were home at Winterhaven," she lied to him. "Surely, my lord, you know that I prefer the country life to that at court."

"When I saw you leave the encampment, I thought perhaps that you were going to meet a lover," he told her boldly.

"My husband is my only lover," Nyssa replied, irritated.

"How quaint," he drawled, "but surely dull."

It would be useless to bandy words with him, Nyssa quickly realized. He would not understand the love that she and Varian shared. "You do not hunt today, my lord?"

"Nor do you," he countered. "I am bored with this constant pursuit of game, which seems to amuse the king so greatly. Tell me, madame, what would you be doing if you were at home instead of here?"

"Harvesting apples and preparing to make cider," she said. "And then in a few weeks the October ale would need to be brewed."

He laughed, and his horse danced nervously at the sound. "Do you not have servants to do these things, madame?"

"The servants do the labor, of course, sir, but they must be overseen. Without direction, servants falter, my mother taught me."

"What about a steward, or a housekeeper?" he wondered.

"They can help, and in some cases take over for a master, or a mistress," Nyssa told him, "but they cannot substitute for them. Estates possessed by absentee lords are frequently poor ones. Their people lose heart when they do not have the direction of their true master."

"Hummmm," he considered. "Perhaps that is why my estate is not a profitable one, but I need a rich wife to restore it, and I cannot find a rich wife without a profitable estate." He laughed. "It is a serious conundrum, madame. So I remain at court."

"Where is your home?" she asked him, beginning to gently nudge her horse back in the direction from which she had come.

"In Oxfordshire," he said. "You would like it since all that is bucolic seems to appeal to you. I possess a tumbling-down old hall, a deer park, and a few hundred acres of overgrown fields." He moved his horse along with hers as they spoke.

"Are your fields not tilled?" she asked him, shocked. "What of your tenants? Have you no cattle or sheep?"

He chuckled. "You truly are a serious country woman. 'Tis no pose to make you stand out from the others, is it?"

"Sir, the land and its people are a trust. They are England. The king would tell you that himself," Nyssa said.

"I stand reprimanded, madame," he said with a smile. "You must teach me how to mend my ways and become a model landowner."

Now Nyssa smiled. "Sir, I think you mock me."

"Nay, madame, I should never do such a thing," he protested.

"Then perhaps, sir, you are again flirting with me?" Nyssa queried him lightly, thinking as she did that it was possible that Culpeper had confided his adultery with the queen to this man. The more people who knew, the more serious the situation had become. She had to find out.

"I think, madame, that it is you who flirt with me," Sin Vaughn said.

She laughed. "I thought you said it was Tom Culpeper I'd set my sights on," she said cunningly.

"Did I not warn you that Culpeper had a jealous mistress?" he growled, leaning over so that their faces were near.

"Why do you care?" she asked him daringly, and smiled into his handsome face. She was amazed at her behavior, but time was growing short. If Cat continued her dangerous course once they returned to London, she would surely be caught. The king's wrath would fall on them all.

"Because," Sin Vaughn said harshly, "I want you, Nyssa! The thought that you should want another infuriates me. Culpeper is a callow fellow. You deserve better!"

"I thought Master Culpeper was your friend," Nyssa taunted him gently, "and have I not told you, sir, that I am a happily married woman? I am aware of the direction in which your friend's interest flows. 'Tis a dangerous game he plays, my lord. You should tell him so."

"Do you think I have not?" Cynric Vaughn said. "He considers his lady a benevolent provider of all he desires."

They had reached the encampment. When they came to her pavilion, Sin Vaughn slid from his horse and, reaching up, lifted Nyssa down from her mount. They were standing very close. When she made to move away from him, his arm pinioned her hard, preventing her. Their lips were quite dangerously close for a brief moment. Then he smiled down into her eyes.

"You are really not experienced enough for this game, madame," he told her quietly, "but I will play it with you if you desire," and then he loosed her. With a quick bow he turned and led his horse away.

"Take yer mount, m'lady?" Bob was at her elbow.

"Aye, take him," she told the groom. "I've not ridden him hard. Just enough to get the kinks out of his muscles." She handed the reins of her horse to him and hurried into the pavilion.

What on earth had she been thinking of, trying to flirt with Sin Vaughn? The man was positively dangerous, a man without conscience or morality. She could sense it. I will not dally with him again, she thought. Now I know that he is aware of the queen's treason.

If Cat Howard fell, then all the Howards would fall, Nyssa knew. She remembered what Varian had said about it. *I am the duke's only grandson.* Surely the king in his anger would not strike out at the de Winters, but he could. Henry Tudor was a ruthless man. Everyone knew that he had slain Anne Boleyn when she could not produce a living son for him, and his eye lit upon Jane Seymour. Look how he had untangled himself from his marriage to the lady Anne of Cleves; had allowed Lord Chancellor Cromwell to be executed; had murdered the Countess of Salisbury. Nyssa shuddered. She had to know if anyone else knew of the queen's adultery.

The king issued an invitation to his nephew, James V of Scotland, the son of his sister Margaret, to join him at York. The ancient abbey stood refurbished and ready for the meeting between the two kings. James's queen, Mary of Guise, was enceinte with a third child. She must be brought safely to term, as their two young sons had recently died and Scotland had no heir. She did not want him to go. His council did not want him to go. James was no fool. Once he crossed over the border, putting himself into the lion's mouth, he could find himself a prisoner of his most dearly beloved uncle of England. He did not come.

Each day the English, stationed at vantage points on the border, sent word to Henry Tudor. There was no sign of the Scots. Indeed the border, usually a hotbed of activity on both sides, was unusually quiet. After five days the English king gave up and faced the truth. His nephew was not coming. Henry was not pleased by the slight, and those around him tread lightly until his temper had worked itself out. The queen was particularly clever at coaxing him. When finally his good humor was restored, the king gave the word that they were to move south. The time had come to return to London. Autumn was upon them, and the weather was beginning to turn colder, and wetter.

They crossed the Derwentwater moving southeast for the town of Hull on the Humber River. The emerald-green hills were almost treeless. The royal progress plodded on relentlessly. Its coaches and baggage wagons lurched over the gentle inclines, the court laughing and riding with it, the great packs of hounds barking excitedly, keeping pace with the horses.

Hull, a fishing port, had been granted a charter in 1299 by Edward I. It had originally been called King's Town upon Hull. Why the king wished to go there, no one really knew, but when he arrived on the first day of

October, the weather changed for the better, to everyone's relief. The blue skies were cloudless, and the sun shone down brightly. The air was mild. It blew fresh and salty from the sea beyond. The pavilions were set up overlooking the water. The king, it seemed, wanted to fish. His energy appeared to be inexhaustible. But at least one could sit in a boat or stand upon the beach when fishing. The ladies, excused from such activity, took the time to rest, bathe, and repair their clothing, for the king had announced they would remain five days.

Arriving to wait upon the queen one afternoon, Nyssa saw Lady Rochford in deep conversation with Tom Culpeper, standing in the shadow of the pavilion's awning. They did not see her as she moved quietly past them, and then, safe from their view, stopped to listen.

"You must be patient, Tom, my laddie," Lady Rochford said. "She is as eager for you as you are for her, but we are not safe here. Too many of the ladies are about, and there is no excuse to send them away from her without arousing suspicion. There are many who are jealous of her, but of course she will not believe that. Her heart is so good. It is beyond her ken to even consider that many would betray her. We must wait for a more propitious time for you to meet again."

"You know that I would not place her in any danger, Jane," Culpeper said. "God help me, but I love her, yet I can barely stand the time I must be away from her. When I hear the king brag of how he has used her, and how she cried out with his expertise, I want to puke!"

"You must not be jealous, Tom laddie, or you will spoil everything," Lady Rochford cautioned him. "The king is an old man. How much longer can he live? Then you will be free to pursue Cat without fear. For now, however, you must not place her in any danger."

Nyssa moved on. She did not want them to catch her, but she also did not want to hear any more. The whole situation was appalling. That they dared to speak of the king's death! Such a thing was treason in itself, but should she accuse them, they would deny it, and it would simply be her word against theirs. She was Nyssa Wyndham, who had once had the king's eye and lost it to Catherine Howard. Nyssa Wyndham, who was mysteriously married off to the Duke of Norfolk's grandson. It was an impossible situation. What was she to do?

Perhaps if she spoke to the queen. Reasoned with her. Were they not friends? Aye! That was what she would do! She would go directly to Cat and tell her she knew her secret. That she did not want to hurt her friend, just bring her to her senses. That she wanted to help. That Cat must not continue to betray the king, for she was sure to be caught in the end. That they would all fall victim to the king's anger and hurt. Cat was not stupid. Cat would see the sense of what she told her. She would realize that Lady Rochford was nothing more than a bawd, encouraging her to bad habits. Aye! She would speak to the queen.

CHAPTER 13

WHAT do you mean, 'you know'?"
Catherine Howard demanded nervously of her friend Nyssa de Winter.

The two young women were walking together along the sandy beach. Although the day was fair, the flat white horizon indicated that the weather would soon change. It was their last day at Hull. Tomorrow they would move on again, heading south for the capital. It had not been easy to get the queen all to herself, but Nyssa had made certain that Tom Culpeper would not be left behind today when the king went fishing. Last night at the banquet she had innocently told the king that she had heard that Master Culpeper was a fisherman par excellence, yet, she said, wide-eyed, she had seen no evidence of it to date. The king had absolutely insisted that Master Culpeper join him on their last day, much to Nyssa's delight. The handsome man had glared angrily at her.

Nyssa had coaxed the queen out into the fresh air, and Cat, her boredom beginning to settle in again, had gone willingly. The other ladies were just as glad to be left behind. Walking in the sunshine was not an activity most of them endorsed. Tomorrow they would be on the road again, and there would be no delightful interludes until they reached Windsor.

Now, Catherine Howard, her blue velvet skirts blowing about her, repeated her question. "You know what?"

"About you and Tom Culpeper," Nyssa replied.

"I do not know to what you refer," the queen said coldly.

"Cat, I saw you together." Nyssa's cheeks grew pink with the recollection. "There was no mistaking what you were doing. I did not mean to spy, I swear it! I came to fetch you one day in York when the king was out hunting and I had remained behind because I had a headache. When my head felt well enough, I came to ask if you desired a game of cards. I called to you, but you did not answer. I thought perhaps that you were sleeping, so I lifted up the flap to your sleeping area. It was then I saw you. I am sorry."

The queen ceased her denials now, saying, "What do you want of me, Nyssa? Gold? Jewels? A high position for your husband or some other relative? I will give you whatever it is you want in exchange for your silence. You are not the first to blackmail me."

"Your Grace!" The shock in Nyssa's voice was so genuine that it startled the queen.

"Well, you must want something," Catherine Howard said petulantly, "or you would not have told me that you knew. What is it?"

"I want you to cease this reckless behavior, Cat," Nyssa said to her. "You endanger not just yourself, but many others as well. What has driven you to such a thing? You have a husband who loves you and gives you everything. *You are Queen of England!*"

"It is not enough!" Catherine Howard said low. "Oh, Nyssa, I never knew it would be like this! The jewels, the clothing, the servants, the privileges of being a queen are wonderful, but I would give them all up in a trice had I but known the rest. Now I am caught like an animal in a net. I am the plaything of an old man, and I hate it. I want to love, and be loved as you are." She half sobbed. "Why has not love remembered me?"

"You are loved," Nyssa said quietly. "The king adores you, Cat. He can scarce keep his hands from you even in public. So much so that it is spoken about by the common people. He has not changed since the days he courted you. Surely you were not so blinded by the perquisites of being a queen that you overlooked the fact Henry Tudor was hardly in the first flush of his youth. I saw it. I lived in terror that he would favor me above you. Why could you not see it?"

Above them the gulls screamed and mewled as they swooped and soared above the two young women.

"You do not know what it was like to be born a Howard. My mother died when I was not yet five. My father's only interest was in finding another rich widow to marry, and in obtaining some position that would take him away from his five children. I was sent to the Howards at Horsham with my sisters to be brought up. We were raised like a litter of kittens or puppies. From the moment we arrived it was impressed upon us that though our lineage was the finest, we were poor relations. We must take what was given us and be thankful for whatever we got, no matter how coarse. I was given no education. I hid in the schoolroom where my brothers and other male relations were being taught so I might learn to read, and write my name. My hand is poor to this day, and I cannot spell to save my soul.

"Until I came to court I never had a garment made just for me. Everything I wore had been worn by someone before me. I handed my clothes, as I outgrew them, down to my little sisters. Sometimes the garments I was given were in such terrible condition I was afraid they would tear each time I put them on. Yet if I did not preserve them for Elizabeth and Mary, I was beaten for my carelessness and wastefulness."

Nyssa was astounded by Cat's description of her childhood. How different it was from her own pampered upbringing as the only daughter in a houseful of little brothers. She had been loved and cossetted from her birth by her parents, her grandparents, and all of her extended family. Her stepfather had spoiled her constantly. All of her siblings had been raised in the same loving manner. She was amazed that the powerful and wealthy Howards could treat their young so badly. But then, should she have been surprised? She knew what Varian's early life had been like.

Still, it was no excuse for the queen's adultery. "Under the circumstances, Cat, I should think, then, that the king's deep love for you would have made you happy instead of unhappy," Nyssa said.

"He does not love me," Catherine Howard said. "Oh, he thinks that he loves me, but what he loves is having a pretty young wife to flaunt before King François I of France and the Holy Roman Emperor. Everyone says so. A pretty young wife whom his courtiers envy—that is what pleasures him, Nyssa. As a lover he is horrendous, I assure you. Did your mother not ever speak about it to you? She was, after all, his mistress for a short time."

Nyssa shook her head. "It is not something a mother would discuss with her daughter, Cat. The intimacies, I mean."

"Well," the queen allowed, "perhaps he was not so gross in her day. He was still a young man then. But now, he is so fat, Nyssa, that he cannot mount me like a normal man. No! He must either sit me on his lap atop his manhood or I must kneel before him upon our bed, or stand bent over braced upon a table while he enters my female passage from the rear. If he lay atop me, he would kill me! Then he grunts and sweats over me until he has received his pleasure. Were I not able to quickly obtain mine, I should have none myself."

I do not want to hear this, Nyssa thought, shocked. And still Cat did not understand what was involved. "Whatever your difficulties or disappointments, Cat," she patiently explained to her friend, "you are married to Henry Tudor. You are his wife until death parts you. You have no other choice. If this adultery is discovered, you will lose your head, Cat. Your cousin Anne, for all her temperament, was innocent of the crimes with which she was charged. Everyone knew it, though no one would dare to speak the truth. And still she was beheaded. You are not innocent, Cat. If you fall, you will take the house of Howard down with you. Unfortunately my husband is Duke Thomas's grandson. If you hurt the king's heart and his pride, he will strike out with all the venom of a poisonous snake at anyone with Howard connections."

"But I love Tom Culpeper, and he loves me," the queen said plaintively.

"If Tom Culpeper really loves you, Cat, then speak to him. Tell him that his love endangers both your lives. If he wishes to squander his own life away, then he is free to, but if he truly loves you, he will want to protect you, Cat. Besides, what if you should become with child? Would you foist a bastard heir upon England?"

"Have I not said that I know well how to meddle with a man and not become enceinte?" the queen bragged. Then she shivered, drawing her cloak about her. "It is growing cloudy and cold, Nyssa. Let us walk back to the encampment."

"You have not promised me yet that you will give up this madness," Nyssa said. "If the duke learns of it, he will denounce you himself to save his own skin. He was the first to desert Anne Boleyn."

"He will not learn of it if you do not tell him," Cat said slyly. "Ohh, Nyssa! Tom is the only thing that keeps me happy."

"Who else knows, Cat?" Nyssa asked. "You could not carry on this liaison without help. And did you not tell me earlier that you were being blackmailed? The situation is already out of control. You have escaped detection only because we have been on progress. Once we have returned to London, it will be harder, and more dangerous."

"Rochford knows," the queen said. "You know how we always made fun of her and thought her silly? Well, she isn't, Nyssa. She has been so kind, and she knows how to keep a secret. I could not do without her. She understands how I feel. She does!"

"And the others? The ones who stoop to blackmail?"

"They do not know about Tom," Catherine Howard said. "They are

Joan Bulmer, Katherine Tylney, Alice Restwold, and Margaret Morton. Then, too, there's Francis Dereham, my secretary. I've told you about him. They were all with me at Lambeth. The old dowager did not keep as tight a rein upon her charges as she should have. We were sometimes very naughty. But by giving them places in my household, I have silenced their wagging tongues. They are not dangerous, Nyssa. You need not worry about them."

"Were there others, Cat? Others who knew you at Lambeth?"

"Aye," she said, "but I could not offer them places, for it would have seemed odd had I done so. I cannot employ everyone who knew me in my childhood, after all. They understood." The queen turned back toward the encampment. Their private interview was at an end.

Catherine Howard is teetering upon a precipice, and she does not even realize it, Nyssa thought, amazed. The whole situation was absolutely terrifying. She and Varian had to go home. They had to go home to Winterhaven before the king found out about all of this and wreaked his vengeance on them. She could no longer bear the burden alone. She must talk with Varian. They must leave the progress at Amphill. If they were out of sight, the king would forget all about them. Cat had not promised to give up Tom Culpeper. When she was caught in her misbehavior, and she would be, at least the de Winters would not be held responsible. Nyssa was almost frantic in her determination to flee the court now.

Because of the early departure planned for the next morning, there was no banquet or dancing that evening. For the first time in many days Nyssa and Varian had time alone together. A charcoal brazier warmed their bed space, its orange coals casting a faint glow about the chamber, the candles making shadows upon the walls. Propped up by pillows and bolsters, they sat naked in their camp bed sipping wine.

Nyssa knew this would eventually lead to lovemaking, and she needed to broach the subject of the queen before that happened. "I must speak with you on a serious matter," she told him.

"Hummmmm," he said, a finger trailing suggestively down her thigh and then back up again. "Why do you want to be serious now?"

"Because," she said with a small chuckle, "it seems to be the only time I have to do so. Do you realize that ever since we joined the royal progress, we have hardly been together at all except at night in bed? And some nights one of us has retired ahead of the other and fallen asleep. You spend your days with the king ahorse. I spend mine with your cousin. That, Varian, is where the problem lies."

"Has Cat been whining at you about her boredom?" he said. He reached over to take her in his arms and kiss her, but she pulled away.

"She is having an affair, Varian," Nyssa told him.

He stiffened and looked sharply at her. "Who the hell told you such a treasonous thing?" he demanded.

"No one told me, my lord. I caught them myself, but until today Cat did not know that I knew. Sin Vaughn is also aware of what is going on between the queen and his friend Tom Culpeper. I have been flirting with him in order to find out, Varian. Lady Ferretface knows too, I fear. She seems to encourage Cat to this madness."

Nyssa then went on to tell him the rest of the sordid tale of blackmail and adultery. When she had finished, she said, "Sooner than later, it will all come out, Varian. The king will be like a mad, wounded animal. He will strike out at the Howards for causing his pain. Your position is not safe. If we go home, however, then he is less likely to think of us in connection with Duke Thomas and the rest of the Howards. We have Edmund and Sabrina to think about. I can see no other way."

"Aye," he agreed with her. "We certainly cannot tell my grandfather, at this point. If it had not gone so far, we might have, and he could have exercised some control over Cat, but not now. The duke will protect himself first. The rest of the Howards and their kin will have to scramble for their lives. Damn! How could Cat be so stupid? I do not know why my grandfather chose her for the king. She is and will always be a heedless girl. She thinks only of her own pleasure. God help us all!" He ran an impatient hand through his dark hair. "You should have told me immediately, sweeting, and you should not have involved yourself with Sir Cynric Vaughn."

"I thought I could reason with Cat, Varian. I believed I could bring her back to her senses, but she simply refuses to understand how serious this is. She thinks if she can continue to please the king, all will be well. She will not accept the possibility that someone may expose her."

He shook his head. "Poor Cat. She does not understand that there is much more involved than just her marriage. The Church is divided between the more orthodox form of worship and the reformers. Each side thinks they have God's blessing on their endeavors. They will do whatever they have to do to gain their way, even if it means toppling a foolish little girl off her glittering throne. I do not want to be here to see that happen. You are right, Nyssa. There is nothing we can do. We must go home!"

"Oh, Varian, I feel so sorry for Cat, and for the king too," Nyssa said softly. She lay her head upon his broad chest.

He stroked her dark hair. It was soft and silky, and faintly perfumed. He had never before loved any woman until her. He knew that he would never love any woman but her. "We can do nothing for them," he said quietly. His voice was sad, and she raised her head up to look at him.

"What is it, Varian?" she asked him.

"Your sorrow is for the king and Cat. Mine is for my grandfather. I cannot help but wonder what kind of a life he would have had were he not so desirous of power. Why could he not be content with his lands and his family? His responsibilities are great, and yet he is constantly seeking more. Why could he not be happy with all that he has? He is so fortunate."

"He is a great man," Nyssa admitted reluctantly, "and great men are not like you and I, my love." Then she kissed him.

His head swam at the touch of her lips. He wrapped his arms about her and held her close. "I adore you," he told her softly.

She smiled seductively up at him. "You lust after me," she told him, caressing his cheek with a teasing hand.

"Aye, I do," he admitted, answering her smile. "I think we are wise to take advantage of this interlude, sweeting." A hand reached out to cup her breast, and her nipple puckered at his touch. "Such an eager little girl, she is," he crooned, stroking the firm breast beneath his fingers. Bending his head, he licked at her skin, faintly salty, yet sweet to his tongue. She murmured, and shifted against him so that they were closer. His mouth closed over the taut nipple, suckling hard upon it, making her whimper low. His teeth tenderly scored the tender nub, and she cried out softly. His hand cradled her head. His mouth now found her throat, and his hot kisses made her wild with her own deep longing for him.

"Oh, my darling," she whispered to him. "I do love you so very much! I can imagine no other life than as your wife and lover!"

He was almost ashamed of his eagerness to possess her, but her excitement was every bit as great as his. She sobbed with pleasure as he entered her, shuddering as he filled her with an incredible sweetness. There could be no more than this! It was so overwhelming that she could scarcely bear the pleasure of it. And afterward she lay contented in his arms, contented even as she knew he was contented. Later they would make love again, and the next time it would be long and drawn out. It was always that way with them. An insatiable hunger to possess each other, followed by a lengthier sweetness. She wondered as she did each time they made love if they had begun another child. She wanted more children, and knew that he did too.

Tillie awakened them before first light. Already outside their pavilion they could hear the sounds of activity as the encampment was dismantled about them. Their servants helped them to dress in warm, sturdy traveling garments, for the weather had turned wet overnight. Toby brought them food from the field kitchens: trenchers of hot oats, ham, hot bread, and cheese. They ate everything, knowing it would be late before they ate again.

"I've wrapped a loaf, some cheese, and apples for you, m'lord," Toby said, "and tucked 'em in your saddlebag. There's some in your bag too, m'lady. The king's groomsmen say he's anxious now to be home. He'll be riding everyone hard."

"You've scavenged for the rest of you too, I hope," the earl said. "This traveling is difficult for all of us."

"When are we going home, m'lady?" Tillie asked.

"We hope to have the king's permission to leave the progress at Amphill," Nyssa told her tiring woman. "He promised we could leave before Christmas. We are anxious to return to Winterhaven too, Tillie."

The sunny and warm respite they had had in Hull was over, and over too was the summer. It was October. The day was cool. The gray clouds lay low on the land, and the rain poured down. Here and there patches of bright color broke the bleakness as stands of trees, dressed in gold, showed off their autumn leaves. There was no hunting now. The court was eager to return south to lodgings with stone walls that the wind did not get so easily through.

The damp, cool weather was beginning to bother the king's ulcerous leg. He rode upon one of the great dun horses that the princess Anne had given him New Year's last, hunched against the rain, and with his pain. He could be approached by no one but the queen and his faithful fool, Will Somers. The Earl of March despaired, for they could not leave court without the king's permission.

"We must wait until we get to Windsor," he told his wife. "There is no getting to him at the moment."

Nyssa was disappointed, but she understood, and strove to be patient.

They stayed a day at Kettleby, where the queen was already excitedly planning for the Christmas holidays.

"We shall celebrate the Twelve Days of Christmas at Hampton Court," she told her ladies. "I do love Hampton Court! Nyssa, come and play cards with me. I must have a chance to win back what you won from me these past few nights." She giggled. "Henry says I should not gamble if I cannot win at least sometimes."

I should have said something when she mentioned Hampton Court and the holidays, Nyssa thought, but she decided that had she voiced a request to return to Winterhaven immediately, the queen would have said no, and then they could not have asked the king without insulting her. It was better not to encourage her enmity. I must be patient, Nyssa thought. She played

her cards carelessly, and allowed Cat to win back what she had previously
lost, plus a bit more.

"You must learn to play as skillfully at other games, Lady de Winter,
as you played at cards this evening," Lady Rochford said softly to Nyssa
as she prepared to return to her own pavilion.

Nyssa looked at the woman. Her dark eyes were fathomless. Her expression said nothing. "I know not what you mean, madame," she replied.
"You speak in riddles. I am not good at riddles." She fastened her cloak
about her and moved past Lady Rochford into the night. As the encampment was set up in identical fashion at each stop they had made over the
progress, it was not necessary for Nyssa to be escorted. The torches
outside of each pavilion gave enough light to show her the way. Moving
quickly along, she was suddenly aware of footsteps behind her. As she
turned to look about, two cloaked figures came up beside her, and taking
her by the arms, swiftly forced her from her path into the darkness beyond
the pavilions.

"Do not scream, madame, or I shall cut your throat," a voice warned
her.

Scream? How could she? Her throat seemed paralyzed by fear. Who
were these men, and what did they want of her? She wore little jewelry.
How bold these robbers were to accost her within the king's own encampment.

The pavilions had been set up tonight just beyond the ruins of an old
monastery. Nyssa's assailants half led, half dragged her into the shadow
of its crumbling walls. At the very moment they stopped, the moon slipped
out from behind a bank of clouds, revealing to her the faces of Tom
Culpeper and Sir Cynric Vaughn. Knowing her kidnappers immediately
eased Nyssa's fear; her throat relaxed and she drew a deep breath.

Then, yanking away from them, she hissed, "What do you mean by
your behavior, sirs? How dare you accost me, and frighten me half to
death!" She whirled about to return to the encampment, but cruel fingers
closed about her arm and roughly yanked her back.

"Nay, madame, we have business together, you and I," Culpeper
snarled into her face. "You have involved yourself in something that is not
your concern at all. You have deeply distressed and confused a lady of our
mutual acquaintance, madame. You must cease these actions. I will see
that you do so." He smiled at her, but the smile did not reach his eyes.

"You involved yourself in something that could cost that lady her life,"
Nyssa spat back. "If you truly care for her, you would not do it, but I
believe you to be nothing but a selfish, opportunistic bastard, Tom Culpeper! How can you believe yourself safe? Lady Rochford knows your

secret, for she foolishly encourages you both. Every day the danger grows greater, and the chances that the king will learn of your treason increases."

"*You will not tell him!*" Culpeper said fiercely.

"*I?* Are you mad? I should never betray Cat, nor would I be foolish enough to destroy the king's idyll of love. Nay, I will not tell him! Is that what this is about? You thought I would tell him of your perfidy?" She laughed harshly. "You are a fool, Master Culpeper."

"I do not believe you," he told her angrily. "If the king had not wed Cat, the chances are good he would have wed you. Cat told me how her uncle, Duke Thomas, arranged for your hasty marriage to his grandson to prevent the king from choosing you over Cat. If you betray my ladylove, the king would turn to you again."

Nyssa shook her head. This was precisely as she had thought it would be. "Tom Culpeper, listen to me, and try to understand what I say to you. I never wanted to marry the king. *Never!* My marriage was forced, but I love Varian de Winter, and I love the children I have borne him. I may even be with child again by my husband," she lied. "I think Cat wrong to behave as she does. I think you are wrong to behave as you do, but I will not be the one to expose your treason. My family would suffer for it. I will not do that to them just to satisfy a principle, particularly when the two people most involved in this disgraceful matter have no principles. Now let me go! My husband will wonder where I am, and you do not want him coming to look for me."

"Perhaps you are telling me the truth," Culpeper said slowly, "and perhaps you are not. Mayhap you say these things simply so I will release you, Nyssa de Winter. Before I do, however, I will give you a little taste of what will happen to you should you attempt to betray my ladylove and I." He moved swiftly behind her and, linking his arms through hers, hoisted her over his back so that she was quite successfully immobilized, her feet just off the ground. "She is all yours, Sin," he said. "Did you know, madame, that Sin lusts after you?"

"I will scream," Nyssa threatened them.

"If you do, we will claim you lured us here for immoral purposes, madame," he threatened. "Gag her, Sin, for good measure."

Sin Vaughn stepped forward and quickly tied a silk square about her protesting mouth. He caressed her face gently, but his eyes were cruel. Carefully, with skillful fingers, he unfastened first her cloak, which he lay aside, and then her bodice, which he fully opened. He ripped her chemise away and her breasts tumbled forth. His hands closed over the trembling flesh, and he crushed her breasts cruelly, his fingers imprinting themselves like scarlet ribbons across her skin.

Nyssa tried to struggle, but Tom Culpeper was quite successful in keeping her pinioned and helpless. She tried to scream, but the gag prevented her cries from being heard. Her attacker smiled, and holding onto one of her breasts, he bent his head and began to suckle strongly upon the other's nipple. When he had satisfied himself, he bit down hard on the nipple. Tears of pain slid down her cheeks as he moved his head to her other breast. Both rage and fear welled up bitterly in her throat, almost choking her. She fought strongly to escape these two beasts, but she could not. Her body arched as he bit upon her other nipple.

Sin Vaughn raised his head and stared lustfully into her eyes. "Let me have her, Tom," he said. "I know that I promised you I would wait, but let me have her here and now! God, she inflames me with desire!"

"Nay, you fool!" Tom Culpeper said angrily. "Cat will have my neck if I let you rape her now."

"A moment more then, and you can release her," he said. Gathering her skirts up, he tucked them in her waistband and tore her silk drawers off, tossing them aside in his eagerness. Kneeling, he leaned forward, pulling her nether lips apart, his tongue seeking her out.

Nyssa did not know how she managed to do it, but she could not allow him to perpetrate this further outrage upon her. She sagged her entire weight against Tom Culpeper, and when he stiffened himself to straighten her, she brought one knee up hard. The crunching contact she made with Sin Vaughn's jaw was extremely satisfying. He groaned, and collapsed on the ground at her feet. Hearing the noise, Culpeper released Nyssa. She tore the gag from her mouth, gasping for air and frantically drawing her skirts down to cover her nakedness.

Culpeper knelt by his friend. Sin Vaughn was quite unconscious. "What the hell did you do to him, bitch?" he demanded.

She gave him no explanation, saying instead, "If you ever come near me again, Tom Culpeper—you, or that animal lying on his back in the muck—I will tell my husband of this incident. Nay," she told him in answer to the unspoken question in his eyes, "I will not tell him now, for he would come after you to kill you. How would we explain his anger without betraying Cat? And I will not tell Cat, for she fancies herself in love with you and would not believe me; but be warned. Stay away from me, or you will regret it!"

"You have children, madame. Remember them, should you be tempted to any foolish behavior," he warned her.

"Touch my babies," she snarled, her eyes blazing her hatred, "and I will kill you myself! If you would feel safe from me, then see Cat does not importune her husband to prevent our leaving court to go home. Remember, the king promised we could leave before Christmas." Then she left him to attend to his fallen companion.

Nyssa hurried back to where the faint lights of the encampment burned. With shaking fingers she fastened her bodice up. Her cloak? Oh, God! She had left her cloak behind, but she would not go back for it. Only Tillie would know it was missing, and then when the tiring woman helped her undress, she would also notice the torn chemise and her lack of drawers. Nyssa knew that Tillie would have to be told, and indeed warned about Tom Culpeper and Sir Cynric Vaughn, lest they try to reach her the next time through her maidservant. Dear heaven! Did the queen have any idea of the kind of man Culpeper was? Nyssa doubted it. All Cat could see was a handsome young lover with bonnie blue eyes.

THE progress moved southward, passing through Collyweston and Amphill, arriving at Windsor on the twenty-sixth day of October.

Windsor Castle had been begun by William the Conqueror. Originally of earth and timber construction, it sat atop the ruins of an old Saxon hall. It had been erected to stand guard over the Thames River valley. Over the centuries, the English kings had favored it because of the good hunting in the vicinity. The wood defenses of the castle were redone in stone during the reign of Henry II. Henry III finished the stone walls and added towers. Edward III turned the castle into a magnificent residence, and there founded the Order of the Garter, which embodied the ideals of King Arthur's Round Table.

The original ancient chapel was tumbling down by the time Edward IV became king. He began its replacement, but it was Henry VII who saw that the nave was completed, and his son, Henry VIII, who built the choir. The king's beloved wife, Queen Jane, was buried in the chapel at Windsor. Henry himself intended to rest there by her side eventually. The king loved Windsor, and had loved it since his boyhood. The years had seen many changes since the young, handsome prince had come to Windsor to sport himself in all manner of athletic competitions. Still, at Windsor, particularly after a long and trying progress, Henry felt young again, despite the toll that time had taken on him. Many in the court watched amazed as the king's bed, eleven feet square, was brought into the castle. Henry himself could no longer manage the stairs easily, and used a rope and pulley system to haul himself up the steep steps.

At the banquet their second night at Windsor the Earl of March managed to gain the king's ear, and asked his permission to depart for his own home with his wife.

The king, mellow with good wine, and feeling particularly sentimental, said, "I know I promised Nyssa you might go before Christmas, but stay with us until Twelfth Night, my lord. Your wife loves to be at her beloved *RiversEdge* for the holidays, even as her mother did in her youth, but I realize that once I let you return, you will not come back to court again. Nyssa is a country mouse like Blaze was. It would seem that you, Varian de Winter, are every bit as much a country mouse as your wife. I could see it this summer on our progress. Your interest seemed to lie more in the species of sheep and cattle we traveled by, than in the deer we stalked." He chuckled. "I will not insist upon your coming again, but stay with us until Twelfth Night." Henry Tudor turned to his wife and asked, "You would like that, would you not, my precious sweetheart?" He placed a wet kiss upon her mouth.

"Aye, my lord," the queen said agreeably. "Please stay, cousin, and convince Nyssa not to fuss at me because I want her here awhile longer." Catherine Howard smiled sweetly at Varian, and he could see how easily the king was taken in by her. She looked so wholesome, and seemed so loving to him.

"Pray God she is not caught in her adultery until after we have left court," Nyssa said to her husband when he told her of his conversation with the monarch and his wife. She knew there was no use in railing to Varian that the king had broken his promise to her. One thing was certain. Cat obviously knew nothing of her lover's vicious attack upon her at Kettleby. Had the queen known, she would have not been so anxious for her to stay. At least Culpeper and Sin Vaughn had kept out of her way since that night. Sir Cynric had appeared the next morning sporting a rather nasty black and blue bruise about the size of a lemon just beneath his chin. He had, he claimed, fallen out of bed.

They hunted in the New Forest for the next few days. The king was in his element. There was nothing he loved better than being ahorse, chasing a stag. Each night the banquet hall rang with merriment as the court ate, drank, and danced. The lady Anne arrived from Richmond. Although she would have dearly loved to have gone on the progress, she had remained home in order that Catherine would not have to share the limelight.

She greeted Nyssa effusively, hugging her friend warmly. "Vas it a vunderful progress?" she demanded. "Ach! How I envy you."

"I would that you had been able to go in my place, dear madame," Nyssa told her former mistress. "I should have far preferred to remain at Winterhaven with my babies. When we left, they had each sprouted two little teeth on the bottom, and two top ones were beginning to come in as well. The king will not let us go home until after Twelfth Night. I shall miss

Christmas at *RiversEdge* again. It will be the third year in a row." She sighed deeply.

"One Christmas you must haf your Mama ask me to *RiversEdge,*" Anne said. "I am curious to experience this vunderful time you speak so happily of, Nyssa. But this year ve must content ourselves vith Christmas at Hampton Court. Last year no one knew quite vhat to do vith me. I am glad ve vill be together this year."

They would travel from Windsor to Hampton Court in barges upon the river. After four months on the road, everyone had spent more than enough time on horseback. Barge and living assignments were arranged by the king's household staff ahead of time so that everyone would know precisely where they were to go. To Nyssa's surprise, they found themselves traveling with the Duke of Norfolk.

As they entered his barge, he gave her a courtly bow and an amused smile. "I realize your antipathy toward me, madame, but I wish to visit with my grandson, and this opportunity cannot be overlooked. Besides, Hampton Court will be so crowded with courtiers that you will be forced to accept my hospitality there."

"After three months on the road, my lord, I should accept the devil's own hospitality," she said to him, knowing that he was really being very generous to them. Without him they might have ended up sleeping in a room with another couple, or separated into male and female dormitories.

"Are you certain, madame, that I am not the devil?" He chuckled.

"Nay, my lord, I am not," she replied pertly.

He laughed again, and his long face looked young again for a moment, free of all its cares. If he only knew what I know, Nyssa thought, but then he turned to speak with her husband. Nyssa settled herself comfortably back on the velvet bench with its high back, and watched the river go by. It was November first, and the day was gray and chill. Tillie and the other servants had gone overland to Hampton Court with the vehicles, leaving earlier that morning.

Nyssa smoothed an imaginary wrinkle from her orange-tawny velvet gown. She had had to dress elegantly because the king had announced that as soon as everyone reached Hampton Court, they would be expected to join him in the chapel for a service of thanksgiving for their safe return, and for his wonderful queen. He had told them this the previous evening, and the queen had beamed proudly by his side. Nyssa would have felt better if she had known that the queen had ceased her adulterous activities, but she knew that Cat had not. Lady Rochford was always hovering about her mistress, whispering words to the queen that no one else could hear, which usually brought a blush to her fair cheeks.

Tom Culpeper, it seemed to Nyssa, was growing more arrogant with every passing day. The queen's secretary, Francis Dereham, a man with a very black, nasty temper, had twice gotten into a match of fisticuffs with the handsome courtier. Fortunately the king had not been about, for fighting before the king was a serious offense. The higher in the queen's favor that Culpeper's star rose, however, the more openly jealous Dereham became. Several of the queen's ladies were heard to remark on it, for Dereham treated Catherine Howard with more familiarity than he should have treated his queen.

It was obvious to Nyssa that Cat was still seriously involved with Tom Culpeper. She was beginning to wonder if anyone else suspected the queen's wicked little secret. Her eye wandered to the barge just ahead. It was the royal barge, and the king and queen had entered it this morning smiling and cooing at each other like newlyweds.

They were close enough that Nyssa could see them through the glass windows of the barge cabin. They had not bothered to draw the curtains to ensure their privacy. She could see the queen seated upon the king's lap, laughing into his face, and Nyssa flushed, wondering if they were doing what she thought they were doing. Remembering what the queen had told her, and seeing the lustful look on Henry Tudor's face, she knew she was correct. Catherine Howard was shameless. She truly believed that as long as she did not get caught with her lover, and pleased her husband, it was all right. Nyssa turned away. She sighed deeply. It would be another two months before they could leave court. She prayed the winter would not be severe, and that the roads to Winterhaven would be open to them.

Along the riverbanks people stood waving to the court as they passed by. How glamorous and how exciting it must look to those good souls, Nyssa thought. How excited she had once been to come to London and be a part of it all. Familiarity with the dark side of the court certainly had dimmed her enthusiasm.

CHAPTER 14

THOMAS Cranmer, the Archbishop of Canterbury, was known to be a gentle man. He had not, to his immense relief, been required to go upon the king's summer progress. The archbishop stood more with the Reformation than with orthodox Catholicism. The young queen and her family espoused orthodoxy. The archbishop had looked forward to a quiet summer of prayer, meditation, and visits to little Prince Edward, who had also been left behind. The king's heir was considered too tender to be exposed to so long a trip.

And the summer had gone exactly as the archbishop had anticipated. There were no crises. There was no king suffering from a troubled conscience, which usually meant he wanted to rid himself of a wife. It had been absolute bliss until his secretary announced one day that a John Lascelles sought an audience with the archbishop to discuss a most important matter.

Thomas Cranmer knew all about John Lascelles. He was a fanatic. A reformer. A man who had absolutely no fear of the heretic's fire because he believed his view of God and the Church was the correct one. The archbishop sensed that Lascelles's visit portended trouble, but God only knew what he would do or to whom he would go next if Thomas Cranmer did not see him. The king and the court would be back within a few weeks' time. Better to get this over with and send Lascelles back to obscurity.

The archbishop sighed deeply and said to his secretary, "Is he waiting outside, Robert?" Of course he was.

"Aye, Your Grace, he is," the young priest replied.

Another sigh. "Very well, then, I will see him now."

The archbishop's secretary smiled sympathetically at his master, saying, "I will bring him in, my lord."

Lascelles bustled in, filled with great self-importance. "My lord archbishop, I thank you for seeing me so quickly," he said, bowing.

The archbishop's secretary discreetly withdrew.

"Sit down, sir," Thomas Cranmer said, "and speak your peace."

Lascelles seated himself and began. "I have information of a most delicate and possibly dangerous nature, my lord. It concerns the queen." Lascelles paused to take a breath, for his words had come out in a great rush with his eagerness.

I do not want to hear this, the archbishop thought to himself. The king is happy. Whatever this man says will make the king unhappy. Have we not had enough difficulties with wives, dear Lord? Must Henry Tudor and England suffer further? He looked directly at Lascelles. "Say on, sir, but be advised if this is merely tittle-tattle, or idle gossip, I shall have you beaten from my palace. I know the direction in which you go. I have not time for foolishness."

"I regret, my lord," Lascelles said, "that what I have to say is truth." Master Lascelles went on to tell the archbishop a tale told him by his sister, Mistress Mary Hall, a chamberer in the household of the old dowager duchess of Norfolk. Mistress Hall had known Catherine Howard since she came into the care of the duke. She had been very involved in raising the girl, and was deeply fond of her. The picture Lascelles painted of the young queen's youth was not, however, a pretty one.

"Is your sister a woman given to gossip, Master Lascelles?" Thomas Cranmer asked sternly when his visitor had concluded his tale. The charges made by this man were very serious indeed.

"My sister is a good Christian woman, Your Grace. It is not in her nature to lie. Besides, there were others in the dowager's household, now members of the queen's household, who were also privy to the lady Catherine's bad behavior. If asked under oath, they would testify to my sister's veracity and the queen's youthful misbehavior."

"I will hear no more from you today, Master Lascelles. I wish to speak with your sister, Mistress Hall. You but repeat that which you say she has told you. She is the witness to the facts of this matter. Bring her to me tomorrow, and I will examine her," Thomas Cranmer said.

John Lascelles arose from his seat and bowed to the churchman. "I will bring Mary to you in the morning, my lord," he promised.

When his disturbing visitor had departed, the archbishop sat back and contemplated what he had been told. It was a shocking story. Was it true? Though aware that the queen's Howard relations were not reform-minded, Thomas Cranmer never considered Catherine Howard or her family a threat to the Reformation in England. Duke Thomas had no violently deep religious convictions. He simply liked things done in the manner in which they had always been done. He did not like change, and resisted it where he could, but he also knew how to bend in a strong wind in order to survive.

John Lascelles, on the other hand, was fanatical, and determined in his desire to see Catholicism in its most orthodox form eradicated from England, from its Church, from the minds of its people. He was the sort of man who would dare, or do, anything to gain his way in the matter. *Was he to be believed?* Why had his sister suddenly come to him now and told him the secrets of the dowager duchess's household when the king had been married for over a year to the young queen? Did Lascelles believe that by slandering the queen he could engineer her removal and bring about the king's remarriage to a reformist? He was a fool if he thought he could manipulate Henry Tudor, or the see of Canterbury.

On the following morning Mistress Mary Hall arrived with her brother for her audience with the archbishop. She was a pretty woman, and had obviously dressed in her very best gown to meet him. It was dark silk with a more modest neckline than he was used to seeing. Her head was covered with a pretty French hood, and she curtsied to him most politely, dipping her head in respect.

"You will wait outside, Master Lascelles," he told the woman's brother. "Mistress Hall will be quite safe with me. Come, my daughter, and we will talk." He led her into his privy chamber and closed the door behind them firmly. "It is a wet and dank day, Mistress Hall," the arch-bishop said. "We will sit by the fire while we talk." He was doing his best to put her at her ease, for he wanted every detail that he could convince her to recall about this matter. With luck, it would go no further than this room, and he would not have to act on it at all. Lascelles, he had decided in the night, was naught but a troublesome fanatic who would eventually have to be dealt with.

Thomas Cranmer waited politely while Mistress Hall settled her skirts about her. He pressed a small cup of sweet watered wine upon her, then sitting back in his own chair, he said, "Tell me why you spoke to your brother regarding the queen's former life."

"I did not want to, Your Grace," Mary Hall said, "and I should never have said a word, for as naughty as Mistress Cat was, I hoped her marriage had changed her for the better. John, and my husband Robert, however, were constantly at me for not seeking a place in the queen's household. I said I did not want a place with the queen, but they would not let it rest. They persisted and they persisted. Each day I was told of another of my former friends in the dowager duchess's household who had sought and been granted a place with the queen. I can manage my husband, but John is a different kettle of fish. Finally I went to him, and I told my brother to leave me be, for I did not want a place with the queen. Indeed I felt sorry for her.

"'Why?' he asked. 'Because,' I said to him, 'all those women are demanding service with her. She dares not to refuse them lest they gossip of her former life at Horsham, and Lambeth.' I did not feel it was Christian of them to do so, Your Grace. If the queen had called upon me to serve her, I should have gone gladly, but I did not want to be like the others, implying a threat, demanding service.

"My explanation was not enough for John. He is worse than a rat terrier when he gets his teeth into something. He wanted to know exactly what the queen had done as a girl that would give others the opportunity to press her. Mind you, I think much of what went on was not really her fault. She was a young girl, an innocent. She was always being pressured by one or another of the gentlemen. I tried to warn her, but she is so headstrong, and I was but a chamberer.

"The dowager never saw what was going on. She did not want to see it. When there was a problem with her charges, she would act, but she rarely saw a problem unless it was pointed out to her. In this case the others did not want to bring to her attention what was going on beneath her roof, for they were as involved themselves in the wickedness, and having much too much of a good time."

"Tell me everything you remember," the archbishop said quietly. He had such a kind and gentle manner about him that Mary Hall felt completely at ease, which was just what the archbishop intended.

"I have known the queen since she was a wee bit of a thing, sir. I looked after her when she and her sisters first came to Horsham. Oh, she was such a naughty little thing, but her heart was good. You could not help but love her, and I did. The year before she went up to Lambeth Palace from Horsham, I told the dowager how much she loved music. My mistress sent a musician from her household, a handsome, feckless young man called

Henry Manox, down to teach my lady Catherine how to play upon the lute, and how to sing pleasingly.

"Young Manox sought far above his station. My poor little mistress thought he meant to wed with her when indeed all he really intended was to have her virtue. Oh, he was a bad one, was Master Manox! I warned him away from her, but they met secretly, I later learned. Then one day when the old dowager was visiting, she caught my mistress and Manox fondling each other's parts. She beat them both for their impudence, and sent Manox back up to London."

"Did your lady regret his departure?" the archbishop asked.

"Nay, not really," Mary Hall said matter-of-factly. "She had told anyone who would listen that she meant to wed with him, and that they were plight-trothed. It was not so, however. 'Twas but the dream of a maid with her first love. He could have been the love of her life, and she would have not been allowed to marry him. She is a Howard after all. He, a common musician."

"Of course," Thomas Cranmer agreed, nodding. "When did the lady Catherine come up to London, Mistress Hall?"

"Oh, 'twas a good year later, sir, and there was Manox waiting for her, eager to take up where he had left off, but she would have none of him then. She told him so in no uncertain terms. He was not happy about it, I can assure you, for I'm certain he had been bragging about his earlier adventure with her, and how she would come back to him."

The archbishop leaned over and refilled Mistress Hall's little goblet, smiling as he did so. "Go on, madame. Tell me about Francis Dereham. When did he meet the lady Catherine, and how involved with one another did they become?" He leaned back in his chair to listen.

"Francis Dereham was one of the duke's gentlemen pensioners. Like Manox, he was not her equal, but he did not let it bother him. Manox, of course, was pea-green with jealousy when he saw Master Dereham beginning to pay court to my mistress. She was totally entranced when the two men began fighting bitterly over her. She was the envy of every girl at Lambeth.

"Dereham gained the upper hand with Lady Catherine almost immediately. He was a great deal more dashing than poor Henry Manox, and had a better position. He could play the gentleman while the lutanist could not. Manox faded away, embittered, even as Francis Dereham rose in my young lady's favor. Still, he was not a true gentleman. He made far too bold with my mistress, but when I scolded her about it she told me, 'Francis has said we will wed one day.' 'What?' I replied. 'Is this the same silliness as 'twas with Master Manox? You do not have the right to pledge yourself to anyone, my girl! Your uncle, the duke, will choose a husband for you when the time comes, and that will be that.' 'I will have none but Francis Dereham,' she insisted.

"At that point, my lord archbishop, our long friendship began to wither away. I could not condone my lady's naughty behavior. Then Dereham threatened me. 'If you tell the dowager duchess,' he said to me, 'I will claim you are a liar and seek to harm me, for you are in love with me and I will not return your love. You will lose your position, and who will have you then?' What could I do but remain silent?"

"Do you know of any improprieties Master Dereham may have taken with the lady Catherine?" Thomas Cranmer asked her.

"Indeed, sir, I do, although my mistress excused them on the grounds that they were to marry one day. All the young people in the house believed that, for both of them constantly talked of it. At least Dereham's intentions were honorable, though Manox's were not. Many nights Dereham would creep into the dormitory where the young women slept and climb into Mistress Catherine's bed. I had been used to sleeping with her, but I would not do so any longer. I was a married woman. I well knew what all that puffing and blowing in the night was about. Several of the more chaste girls refused to sleep near her for such noises shamed them."

The archbishop was horrified. "Are you saying, Mistress Hall, that the lady Catherine was not a virgin when she married the king? That she gave herself willingly in carnal copulation to Master Dereham?"

"I cannot say for certain under God's oath, my lord, for the bed curtains were closed; but I believe that she was not a virgin when she left Lambeth for court," Mistress Hall told him.

"What else?" he asked her.

"They called each other husband and wife," she said. "Everyone heard them, and knew of it. Once he kissed her publicly, and so passionately that we remonstrated with him for fear the dowager would see them. Master Dereham replied, 'What? Shall a man not be permitted to kiss his wife?' The lady Catherine was somewhat embarrassed by him then. She was growing more aware of who she was, and considered his behavior a trifle coarse. I believe she would have been happy to be rid of him then, yet she continued to entertain him in her bed. Manox, angry that Dereham had succeeded where he had failed, began bragging to all who would listen that he knew of a secret mark on my lady Catherine's body. I warned him to silence, disgusted by then by what was happening, but unable to stop it.

"Finally the lady Catherine convinced Dereham that if he was indeed to marry her one day he would have to make his fortune, or the duke, her uncle and her guardian, would not even consider his suit. I know that she knew then that she was to go to court as a maid of honor to the new queen, the Princess of Cleves. The dowager duchess had just told her of her appointment, and had impressed upon her the honor involved. The lady Catherine was very eager to be rid of Dereham. He left her with his life savings, one hundred pounds, and went off to Ireland. The money, he said, was to be hers if he did not come back. He truly believed he was to be her husband, my lord. I heard the rumor that in Ireland he turned to piracy, but I cannot know for certain." She quaffed her wine.

The Archbishop of Canterbury felt as if a huge weight had been lain across his narrow shoulders. "Who in the queen's household was with her at Horsham and Lambeth?" he asked Mary Hall.

Mistress Hall considered a moment, and then she said, "There is Katherine Tylney, Margaret Morton, Joan Bulmer, and Alice Restwold, Your Grace. I do not think there are any others."

"Will they confirm your words, Mistress Hall?" he said seriously.

"If they are honest they will, my lord," she told him.

He nodded. "You are not to speak of this to anyone, madame. Not even to your brother. What you have told me indicates that the queen led an unchaste life before her marriage to the king. That in itself is not treason, but it might indicate that she has led an unchaste life since her marriage. Bad habits are often difficult to change. I must speak with these chamberers now serving the queen, however, before I make any decision in this matter, Mistress Hall. That is why I must request your silence. I may want to speak with you again." He arose. "Let me take you back to your brother, and I will instruct him as well in his behavior. Master Lascelles is sometimes overly enthusiastic in the pursuit of his cause. He is known for it."

The archbishop escorted Mary Hall from his privy chamber. Seeing them, John Lascelles leapt to his feet and hurried toward them. The archbishop held up his hand for silence before the man might speak.

"Your sister's speech with me is confidential and not to be discussed between you two, Master Lascelles. I intend to investigate the matter further, based upon what your sister has told me. I may call upon you both again in the near future to testify before me. Do you understand me, sir?"

Lascelles nodded. Taking his sister by the arm, the two left the archbishop's palace in Southwark. Behind them England's highest and most powerful cleric was left behind to mull over what he had been told. He could see no wickedness in Mistress Hall. Indeed, if anything, she was sympathetic to the queen, even if she disapproved of her former mistress's behavior. It was that behavior that troubled the archbishop.

There was no doubt in Thomas Cranmer's mind that Catherine Howard was a fickle young woman. She obviously fell in and out of love as easily as one changed one's linen. Henry Tudor's courtship had undoubtedly overwhelmed her. The king might be a corpulent, middle-aged man, but the power he represented, the wealth at his disposal, all must have been extremely heady and tempting to an unsophisticated young girl barely out of the country. He shook his head. Was she still in love with the king? Or had she already fallen out of love? Publicly she seemed a model wife, and God only knew the king was desperately in love with her.

What was he to do? the archbishop wondered. If the queen's behavior today was moral and decent, if she had honestly reformed her wicked ways, was there any advantage to bringing up her less than savory past before her marriage? The king would not be pleased to have the reputation of his rose without a thorn besmirched. I must pray on it, Thomas Cranmer thought. God will guide me. He walked slowly into his private chapel, and kneeling down upon his little prie-dieu, closed his eyes, folded his hands together, and prayed.

THE king returned to Hampton Court and ordered that on All Saints' Day a service be offered of special prayers of thanksgiving for their safe return and for his wonderful queen. Henry Tudor stood before his court in the Chapel Royal and publicly declared, "I render thanks to Thee, O Lord, that after so many strange accidents that have befallen my marriages, Thou has been pleased to give me a wife so entirely conformed to my inclinations as her I now have."

Nyssa de Winter's eyes met those of her husband's at the king's public declaration. Varian took her hand in his and squeezed it encouragingly. From his place on the archbishop's throne upon the high altar, Thomas Cranmer heard the king's humble words of thanks and knew what he must now do. John Lascelles was not a man to let go of this matter, having brought it to the attention of the proper authorities. The archbishop knew that if he did nothing else, he must lay the facts of this possible scandal, as he knew them, before the king. He retired after the service to write the king a letter.

At the mass the following day, All Souls' Day, Thomas Cranmer slipped a parchment containing his knowledge of the queen's early life into the king's hand.

"What is this, Thomas?" the king whispered to him.

"For your eyes alone, my liege. When you have read it, I will be at your grace's disposal," the archbishop replied.

The king nodded solemnly, and tucked the parchment into his vast sleeve. When the services had ended, he kissed his wife and hurried to his privy chamber to peruse what the archbishop had given him. He closed the door behind him, indicating to those who served him that he wanted to be alone. Laying the parchment upon a table, he poured himself a large goblet of rich, sweet red wine. He drank it down, and reaching for the missive, broke the archbishop's seal. He spread the parchment out and began to read. With each damning word his brow darkened. His chest grew tight as he attempted to draw a deep breath. For a brief moment the words on the parchment swam before his eyes. When his vision had cleared, the king raised his fist and slammed it down upon the table.

"*Lies!*" he ground out. "*Filthy lies!* I will not believe this foulness that the archbishop has presented me with, and I will have this man, Lascelles, arrested and clapped in the Tower!" He strode toward the door, and yanking it open, called to his personal page.

"*Fetch the archbishop to me this instant!*" he roared.

The page, white-faced, nodded and ran off. The king's gentlemen looked questioningly at each other but said nothing. Henry Tudor retreated into his privy chamber, slamming the door behind him so hard that it shook upon its stout hinges. Pouring himself another great goblet of wine, he drank it down in hopes of calming his nerves. He had never in his life been so angry. Even when the first Katherine had been so difficult, he had not felt such anger. For anyone to foul the good name of his darling young queen was outrageous. This Lascelles would suffer for his slander. When he was finished with this fellow, he would wish he had never been born. Henry's fist slammed down onto the table again in a white hot fury.

Thomas Cranmer had known that the summons would quickly come. He followed the king's page through the corridors of Hampton Court Palace, his robes swaying just slightly, his hands folded neatly into his sleeves. The boy sent to fetch him was pasty with his obvious fear. The archbishop had calmed the lad with gentle words, and then allowed the boy to lead him back to the king. The king whirled about as the archbishop entered his privy chamber, his face a mask of outraged anger.

"*This,*" the king snarled, shaking the parchment at his chief cleric, "this is filth! How could you pass it on to me? I want this Lascelles and his sister, Mistress Hall, arrested. It is treason to accuse the queen falsely, Cranmer. *Treason!*"

"There may be no treason, Your Grace," the archbishop said calmly. "Lascelles is a Protestant fanatic, 'tis true, but his sister, Mistress Hall, harbored a deep affection for the queen. She helped to raise her. Her brother nagged at her to seek a place with the queen, and she refused, for the queen's early behavior had disturbed her. She is a decent woman, my lord. She only told her brother of the queen's youthful indiscretions so that he would leave her in peace. She did not want the queen to feel she was pressuring her to take her into her household. 'Tis a pity others were not as scrupulous in their motives. At least four of the queen's women were with her at Lambeth. 'Tis curious, is it not?"

"This Dereham fellow arrived at Pontefract in August when we were there," the king told the archbishop. "Catherine made him her secretary. She said the old dowager sent him, and asked that we treat him with kindness. I let her have her way, although I did not like him."

"Hummmmm," the archbishop said with understatement.

"If it happened before we met, there is no treason, nor is there any adultery," Henry Tudor said slowly, "but get to the bottom of this pot, Thomas. I want no scandals later on. If the queen gives us a Duke of York, the boy's paternity should not be in doubt over such a thing as this. Find the truth, and then we will decide what to do."

"I will be most discreet, Your Grace," the archbishop said.

"Thomas," the king asked him, "why does God keep trying me like this? All those years to get a healthy son, and if the truth be known, the boy is not that strong. I came back to learn that he was ill. The doctors say he is too fat, and overprotected. I have ordered a regimen of exercise and simple meals for him. No sweets. He is better already. God's foot, Thomas! There wasn't even a window open in his apartment so the boy could get some fresh air. They were treating him like a little idol! Do I ask for a great deal, Thomas? I want sons. I want a good woman to wife. I am so happy with my Catherine. Is she to be taken from me?"

The king was beginning to feel sorry for himself, the archbishop saw, but then every man was entitled to wallow occasionally in self-pity. Not only had the king returned to news of his heir's illness, and now this disturbing and possible scandal over the queen; but he had just received word that his sister Margaret, the Dowager Queen of Scotland, had died. It was not that he and Margaret had been close. He had been far closer to his late sister Mary. Still, it was one more link with the past broken; a grim but firm reminder of his mortality.

"This business may be nothing more than a fuss over naught," the archbishop soothed his master. "Many maids are not quite what they seem to be when they marry. It is not the way I would have it, but it happens. If the lady Agnes was as lax in her guardianship, as it would certainly appear, it seems to me the fault lies with her, not with poor Queen Catherine, who was, after all, an unsophisticated girl. I will delve carefully into this business, learn the whole truth, and then as quickly inform your grace of my findings."

The king nodded. "Whatever you need, Thomas."

"I have your grace's permission to question certain individuals?"

"Aye. Do what you have to do. Ahh, God, I miss Crum!"

"God assoil his soul," the archbishop murmured piously.

"Thomas."

"Yes, Your Grace?"

"See that the queen is confined to her apartments until her good name is cleared. She may have only Lady Rochford to attend her. I shall not see her until this matter is settled in her favor."

"I will give the order, Your Grace," Thomas Cranmer said softly. He put a comforting hand on the king's shoulder. "Courage, Henry," he said. "God's will be done."

"Amen," the king answered, but he did not turn his face to the archbishop, else his friend see the anguish there, and not be able to do his duty. Thomas Cranmer could be trusted, and few others around him could be. They all looked to their own advantage.

The archbishop departed the king's privy chamber. In the anteroom outside, the king's gentlemen looked to him for some sort of explanation as he passed, but he gave them none. He simply raised his hand in blessing as he moved by them.

Nyssa was with the queen when the household guard arrived. She and the other ladies had been practicing a new dance just brought to court from France. The women were at first frightened by the armed men.

The captain of the guard stepped forward and bowed politely to the queen. "Madame, on the king's orders, you are to be confined to your apartments. Your women are all dismissed, and only Lady Rochford may remain with you."

"Captain," the queen said, her tone imperious, "what mean you coming to my chambers in such a fashion? Can you not see we are learning a new dance for the Christmas festivities?"

"Madame," the captain replied, "there is no more time to dance." Then without another word he began shooing her servants from the apartments. The queen's ladies needed no further encouragement. Picking up their skirts, they fled their mistress, each eager to be the first to spread the news that something terrible was about to happen.

"Nyssa!" Catherine Howard's tone was suddenly frightened. "Do not leave me! I am afraid."

"I am afraid for all of us, Cat," Nyssa replied. Then she lowered her voice and whispered to the queen, "Say nothing, Cat, until you learn what they know; and precisely what this is all about." She then curtsied to her and departed after the other women.

"Captain," the queen said. "Why am I being confined like this? Can I not see the king?"

"Madame, I regret that I do not know," the man replied honestly.

"I will go and speak with his grace, dear madame," Lady Rochford told the frightened young woman. "I will ask him why you are imprisoned." She moved to the doors of the apartment, but the captain blocked her way.

"I am sorry, Lady Rochford, but you are to be incarcerated with the queen, and not allowed to come and go at will. Food will be brought to you. You will want for nothing."

"Send me my confessor!" the queen demanded. "If I am to be denied my freedom, and access to my husband, then I must be allowed a priest, sir. Surely the king will not deny me a priest!" Her voice was high and beginning to border on the hysterical.

"I will ask, madame," was the captain's noncommittal reply. He bowed again, and backed from the queen's chambers.

Both she and Lady Rochford heard the key turn in the lock behind him. Wordlessly the two women ran to the other exits to the apartment, but they were all locked. Even the hidden door to the secret passageway that led to the king's apartments was bolted from the other side. Lady Rochford peered from the windows of the apartment, and it was as if an icy hand had gripped her heart. Below, at ten-foot intervals, were yeomen of the guard standing armed.

"*He knows!*" the queen whispered frantically. "What else can it be, Rochford? *He knows!*"

"Say nothing until you are accused," Lady Rochford whispered back. "You cannot be certain what the king has been told."

Lady Jane Rochford could feel herself slipping back in time, back to a similar situation in which her sister-in-law, Anne Boleyn, found herself accused. Anne had been guilty of nothing, but to save her husband, George Boleyn, Lady Jane had agreed to testify against her. Her sole evidence had consisted of the fact that Anne and her brother had spent an afternoon in a closed room together. Jane had told the court in a pretrial hearing that she believed Anne desired to conspire against the king, but that her husband, George, had sought to dissuade her. Just tell of how they were closeted for that afternoon, she was instructed. The rest will come out through others.

Jane Rochford had done as she was told. But Cromwell and the others had betrayed her. She had testified, and then listened in horror as her words were interpreted to imply that Anne, the queen, had committed incest with George, Lord Rochford.

"Ahh, God, no!" she had cried out, and been forcibly removed from the courtroom. They had not let her see her husband again. She had not been able to tell him that she had said no such thing; that she had been tricked; that she did really love him. She had never told George that she loved him. Instead she had been sent away from court with thanks for her loyalty and the promise of reward one day. Her appointment to Anne of Cleves's household was that reward, and later she had been appointed to Catherine Howard's service, which was far better. The king had had no love for the German princess, but he loved and adored Cat Howard.

Jane Rochford had waited for what seemed like many years to revenge herself upon Henry Tudor. In her exile from court, she had thought often of how she would hurt him as she had been hurt. She wanted him to feel the pain that she had felt when they had entrapped her into betraying her husband; when her husband was executed so cruelly. That she risked her own life meant nothing to her at all. She had no husband. No children. The king had to pay for killing George. He would lose the one he loved most in all the world, even as she had lost the one that she loved most in all the world.

That was why she had encouraged Thomas Culpeper and Catherine Howard into adultery. It had not been hard. The queen was a flighty, silly girl with ridiculous romantic notions. She had not the wit of a flea. She had honestly believed as long as she kept the king content, she could play her wanton little games and get away with them. As for Culpeper, he was a proud young man with a great opinion of himself, and he had fallen in love with Catherine Howard. She did not know which of them was the greater fool. How could they not see their foolish love was doomed?

Who had told on them? Lady Rochford wondered. She had intended to expose them herself, but not until the queen was well along with a bastard child. The king, she knew from the queen, had not been able to perform satisfactorily of late. He would know any child got on the queen was not of his making. He would either have to expose her or accept the bastard as his own. Either way, he would suffer the tortures of the damned. But now, Lady Rochford realized, something had happened. Some new unknown element had been introduced. Someone else had informed on the queen. Who was it? And why? What exactly did they know? She was a little afraid. If they knew about the queen, did they know about her?

Taking the queen's cold little hand in hers, she patted it, saying, "Remember, Catherine Howard, admit to nothing. You do not know what anyone has said, and for now it is just their word against yours. The king loves you best of all his wives, even your cousin Anne. He will believe you, but you must not panic."

Cat shuddered. "Do not mention *her* name to me. I cannot help but remember how she ended up. *I do not want to die, Rochford!*"

"Then say nothing, and when accused, deny everything," Lady Rochford said silkily. "Naught can happen to you if you are clever. There is no proof of anything untoward in your behavior." At least no proof that they can find, she thought, but if they can find nothing, they will manufacture it. That is how the king ridded himself of Anne Boleyn, but then he was out of love with her by then, and enamored of the Seymour chit. He is still in love with this girl. Ohh, I wish I could find out what it was they knew. Perhaps we can bribe one of the servitors who brings our food. I must know what is going on!

Nyssa had been frantically seeking her husband, and finally found him with the Duke of Norfolk. "The queen is confined to her apartments under guard, with only Rochford to attend her. The others have all been dismissed!" she told them breathlessly. "The archbishop, I learned from one of the guards, is in charge of the investigation."

"Jesus Christus!" Norfolk swore volubly. "Could you learn anything else, madame? Why is Catherine confined? There is no other woman, I know, and the king absolutely adores her. What has gone wrong?"

"Do you really care?" Nyssa demanded of him. "Is your distress for Catherine Howard, or for yourself, my lord duke?"

"Your wife's tongue could easily lose her her head," the duke said sourly to his grandson.

"My lord," Nyssa said angrily, "I have addressed you, and yet you ignore me. You do it all the time, and I resent it. Varian and I are here at court at the request of your niece, the queen. We would far prefer to be home with our children. If this queen you set up is tumbled down, are we not all in danger?"

Thomas Howard looked directly at Nyssa and said a single word, "Aye." His long face was grave, his eyes, usually fathomless, worried.

For a brief moment Nyssa felt sorry for him. Her voice dropped and she beckoned him closer to her. "The queen may be caught in adultery, my lord," Nyssa told him softly. "I cannot be certain, but why else would the archbishop be involved in this matter?"

"What do you know?" he asked quietly.

She told him, even as Varian put a protective arm about her.

"Why did you not tell me before this?" the duke asked her.

"Because," Nyssa said bluntly, "you would have exposed her to save your own self. I knew eventually she would be found out. I hoped when that day came, Varian and I would be long gone from court, and forgotten by a vengeful king out to destroy the Howards."

A wintry smile touched the duke's lips. He nodded, understanding her rationale. Like him, she had an instinct for survival. Her family came first in her life, even as his had always come first in his. "You will not be able to flee to your Winterhaven now, lest it look like you run to escape some guilt or culpability," he told her. "You will have to ride out whatever storm there is here with the rest of us."

"I know that," Nyssa told him, "and I will never forgive you if harm comes to Varian or our children through the Howards."

"I know that," he responded. "You are a woman with a long memory for a fault, madame. Keep silent on what you know, for what you know may not be at the root of the problem at all. I will go to the archbishop myself and ask him what this is all about. He will tell me."

"And will you tell us?" she asked him. "Or will you husband the information and leave us to wonder?"

"You will be kept informed," he said, and left them.

"What else could it be?" Varian asked his wife when they were alone again. "What could she have done to merit house arrest?" He went to the sideboard and poured them each a small goblet of wine.

Seated together before the fire, they sipped their wine and spoke in soft voices so as not to be overheard.

"Before her marriage Cat spoke of a rather unorthodox childhood in the old dowager's house," Nyssa told her husband. "The maidens were left badly supervised, if looked after at all. She told me of two men who tried to seduce her. I told her to tell the king these things so that one day they could not be used against her, but she would not. She was afraid that he might not marry her if she did."

"It is possible, then," he said thoughtfully, "that this unchaste life may have been dragged up to discredit her with the king, but who would do such a thing to poor Catherine? She has not the brain of a peahen, I fear, but her heart is good. Who seeks to harm her?"

Nyssa merely shook her head.

"We must behave as if we know nothing," Varian told her. "We cannot draw attention to ourselves, sweeting, lest we be dragged into whatever sort of scandal is brewing."

"Aye," she agreed. "With God's good luck, this matter will soon be settled and we can go home to Winterhaven."

CHAPTER 15

THE archbishop questioned John Lascelles and his sister, Mary Hall, once again. He allowed the Duke of Norfolk to sit with him in silence when he did. When they had departed, he turned to the duke, asking him, "What think you, my lord duke?"

Thomas Howard was slightly gray in color. He was genuinely disturbed by Mistress Hall's account of life in his stepmother's house. Most of the young women in the family had been entrusted to the dowager duchess's care at one time or another. They would have been better raised by the hounds in his kennels, he thought, but he was very circumspect in his answer to the cleric. "I cannot rely upon only the word of a servant in such a serious matter, my lord," he said gravely. "I must speak with my stepmother to learn what she has to say in her defense."

"Aye, I shall want to speak with the lady Agnes myself," Thomas Cranmer said quietly. "I am appalled she did not exercise better control over those young innocents in her charge."

"As am I," the duke replied grimly. He hurried off to Lambeth to speak with his stepmother.

The Dowager Duchess of Norfolk had already heard the news of the queen's confinement. Rumors were flying regarding the matter. If the misconduct had taken place in her house, she would be blamed. She was frantically searching the house for any incriminating evidence left behind by Catherine when she departed to go to court. Her stepson's arrival did not do anything to ease her mind. "What news, Tom?" she asked him nervously.

"Why, madame, did you not tell me of Catherine's misbehavior prior to our dangling her before the king's nose?" he demanded of the old woman.

"I did not know," Lady Agnes admitted, and then defended herself, "Why should the blame be on me alone? These girls came to me for polishing before they went to court. I should not have had to be responsible for their morals."

"Then it is true what they are saying? That you let the girls in your charge run loose like bitches in heat? God's boots, madame! Where was your good sense? Surely you must have known that a scandal of this nature would erupt eventually! With the others it would not have mattered, but this was the girl we singled out to be queen!"

"You are panicking, Tom," his stepmother said. "If the offense took place before the marriage, indeed before Catherine even met the king, she cannot lose her head for that. What is the worst that can possibly happen? He will put her away and marry another wife. The Howards will be out of favor again, as they were in the time of Anne Boleyn's fall. But, we will survive to play the game another day, I think." She smiled encouragingly at him.

"Perhaps," he said. "I have just come from the archbishop. I sense he seeks something more than has been given him. I do not believe he will find it, but if he does, then the situation will be far worse, madame."

The Archbishop of Canterbury pondered his second interview with Lascelles and his sister. They had not deviated a whit from their stories. Then there was the new knowledge he had just obtained from the king: that the queen's former lover, Francis Dereham, was now in her household. Why had Catherine taken this man into her service if she did not mean to take up with him again? He was young, and handsome, and undoubtedly vigorous in bed sport, unlike the aging, overweight king.

He had not proof as of yet, but could there possibly be adultery involved? That would mean treason. He shuddered. He had been given a mandate from the king to get to the bottom of the pot, but now it would seem that the pot was far deeper, and possibly dirtier, than he had ever anticipated. Still, there was no going back now.

He met with his fellow members of the Privy Council and laid the facts he had gathered to date in the matter before them. It was agreed that there was a basis for proceeding further in the investigation. The king was summoned and told of the council's suspicions, particularly the new ones regarding Francis Dereham. He groaned unhappily.

The archbishop told the king, "She has betrayed you in thought, and if she had an opportunity, would have betrayed you in deed."

The king put his head in his hands.

"Your Grace, I have no substantive evidence to date that would prove the queen has been unfaithful, but we must seek for such evidence if for no other reason than to clear her grace's name," the archbishop explained gently. "No stone can be left unturned."

The king looked up bleakly at his council, and then to their great amazement, Henry Tudor began to weep openly. "How could she betray me when I have loved her so greatly?" he cried, and then he slumped back in his chair sobbing bitterly.

They were shocked. They were astounded! Every man on the council knew in that moment how deeply the king had loved Catherine Howard. The more cynical among them wondered, however, how long that love would have lasted. They were embarrassed nonetheless that a man of his personal courage would have given in so to his emotions, yet they admired him for it. They could see their sovereign become an old man before their very eyes. It was a terrifying experience, for it touched on their own mortality.

The king arose heavily from the council table. "I am going hunting," he said, wiping his eyes with the back of his big hand.

Henry Tudor departed Hampton Court for Oatlands within an hour of his departing the council chamber. He took only half a dozen companions. He needed time to nurse his wounds. He did not want to have to face the public at this moment. He did not want to be there when the queen was officially informed of the charges that were to be lodged against her. Earlier, before he had left Hampton Court, he had gone to his chapel to pray, and to calm himself. Suddenly, outside, he had heard the sounds of scuffling, and Catherine's young voice desperately shrieking his name.

"Henry! Henry, in the name of God speak with me!"

Afterward they told him that the queen had pushed past her startled guards when food was brought and raced to his private apartments, past his own personal servants, in her effort to seek him out. They had not wanted to lay hands on her, but finally had no choice. He was glad he had not seen her. One look at her pretty face and he would have forgiven her. She did not deserve his forgiveness. Cranmer had but hinted at her crime, but in his heart of hearts Henry Tudor knew that his wife was probably very guilty. Little incidences kept coming back to him. Why had she really insisted upon giving a place in her household to that Dereham fellow? The man looked like a pirate. He had wretched manners. The king had once been witness to his arrogance, and nasty temper, although Dereham had not been aware of Henry's quiet presence.

The Duke of Norfolk felt very responsible for the disaster that had befallen the king in his fifth marriage. When he saw Henry Tudor's unhappiness regarding Anne of Cleves, he had deliberately sought among the women in his own extended family for a substitute the king might favor. Thomas Howard had been so eager to place Catherine Howard on England's throne that he had not investigated her youth thoroughly. If he had, he would have quickly found that the girl was unfit to be queen. Instead he had been as taken in by her plump prettiness as had the king. Now this girl had placed him in worse danger than Anne Boleyn had ever done. Still, Cat was his responsibility. He would do his duty.

The queen was visited by the council, and the charges against her were laid forth. Thomas Howard stood by his niece's side. Catherine's reaction was to have immediate hysterics. All she could think about was her cousin Anne. Like Anne, she was surely going to end upon the block. Still, they had not mentioned Tom Culpeper. It was just possible that they did not know. The charges, after all, did relate to her unchaste life *before* she became queen. And Duke Thomas was at her side. The Howards were not abandoning her. She struggled to calm herself, but it was not easy. She was very afraid.

By the following day, when the archbishop came to visit her, Catherine's hysteria was again high. He could not reason with her, nor even make sense of the words she was babbling in her fear.

"She will neither eat nor take drink," Lady Rochford said.

"I will return tomorrow," Thomas Cranmer said. "If she calms, tell her that I mean her no harm. I am here to help her."

The archbishop returned the following day to find the queen still frenzied. This time, however, he would not retreat. He sat quietly with her, speaking gently, endeavoring to reach through her blind terror. Finally, when she had grown a little less agitated, he said to her, "Madame, you must not disquiet yourself so. There is hope, I swear to you. See?" He drew a parchment from his sleeve. "I bring you a letter from the king, your husband, offering to treat you mercifully if you will but admit to your faults." He held it out to her.

She took it from him as if it were afire, then breaking the royal seal, read it, the tears pouring down her plump cheeks. "Alas, my lord, that I have caused such troubles to the husband who has been so kind and good to me," she told the archbishop.

"Madame, the king's heart may be broken by the grievous nature of these charges against you, but he would offer you mercy from the love he bears you. You have but to admit to your wickedness."

"I will answer all your questions, my lord, to the best of my ability and recollection," she promised him. "Will the king, my dearest lord, truly grant me his benign mercy? Do I even deserve it?" She could not cease weeping, and her eyes were red, but for the time being her hysterics were eased, and gone. She was struggling very hard to keep her composure.

"Our sovereign lord will deal gently with you, dear madame. All he would have of you is the truth in this matter," Thomas Cranmer assured the terrified woman. "You may confide in me, Catherine. I will do my best by you, I promise."

Her cerulean-blue eyes were swollen with her weeping, her lashes matted into spiky points. Her auburn hair, usually so neatly coiffed, was unkempt and undone. She wore no jewelry, he noted, but the wedding band upon her finger. It was a departure for a woman who loved all of the royal jewels and was apt to deck herself in as many as possible each day. Catherine Howard was Thomas Cranmer's picture of a fallen woman. She had guilt written all over her. Her very fear betrayed her.

The queen held up her hands. "Thank God for the king's goodness to me, although I am not worthy of it."

"Will you trust me then, Catherine?" the archbishop said.

She nodded, but then fell to weeping again for a long moment. He waited for her sorrow to subside, and then she said to him, "Alas, my lord, that I am alive! The fear of death did not grieve me so much before as doth now the remembrance of the king's goodness, for when I remember how gracious and loving a prince I had, I cannot but sorrow. But this sudden mercy, more than I could have looked for, maketh mine offenses to appear before mine eyes much more heinous than they did before. And the more I consider the greatness of his mercy, the more I do sorrow in my heart that I should so misorder myself against his majesty." She wept again, great gulping sobs of grief.

He could see that she had taken all she could for the moment, and so the archbishop left her, promising to return in the early evening.

When he had gone, Lady Rochford crept from the corner where she had been sitting. "Say naught to him, you little fool," she warned the queen. "He seeks to convict you, and surely you will end on the block like your cousin Anne. Admit nothing! Where is their proof but in the idle tongues of jealous servants?"

"The king will grant me mercy if I will admit my faults," Catherine said softly. "I am afraid, Rochford. I do not want to die. If I admit to my liaisons with Dereham before my marriage, then I will be forgiven. I will not die!"

"Admit to anything, Catherine Howard, and you will no longer be Queen of England. Is it not better to die a queen than to live in ignominity and disgrace? If you admit to Dereham, the king will cast you off. Knowing that old satyr, he is probably already casting about for a new rose without a thorn to warm his bed and to be his queen."

"Henry would not do such a thing!" the queen protested.

Lady Jane Rochford laughed bitterly. "Jane Seymour was primly waiting in the wings as they readied the accusations against your cousin Anne. Did the king not let his eye wander between you and Lady Wyndham even when he was still wed to the Princess of Cleves? Perhaps it is your dear friend Nyssa who will replace you in the king's affections."

Catherine Howard slapped Jane Rochford. "Do not dare to slander my cousin's wife," she said in a hard voice. "Nyssa de Winter is probably the only person in the entire world that I can truly trust. I pray God that my actions have not endangered her, my cousin Varian, or their children. I will do what I must to protect the family. It is all I can do now." She glared at her companion. "You had best pray, Jane, that the king does not discover my relationship with Tom Culpeper, or your part in fostering that relationship. If I go to the block, you will go with me. And if my real crimes escape the king's notice, I will spend the rest of my life being a good wife to him, if they will let me. If they will not, I will accept whatever portion I am allotted, and be grateful to be alive."

"How noble you have suddenly become in the face of danger," Lady Rochford said, rubbing her cheek. "Are you certain that letter came from the king? When has Henry Tudor ever been known to be merciful when betrayed by a woman? Perhaps the archbishop forged the letter, and used the king's seal in an effort to trick you, madame."

Catherine Howard blanched. "Surely the archbishop would not do a thing like that," she said. "He is a man of God!"

"Men of God who are servants of Henry Tudor are more apt to do the king's bidding than follow their conscience. The king is a certainty they must live with every day. God is but a nebulous eventuality."

The queen began to weep again. Was it possible the archbishop was going to betray her? She struggled to maintain her composure while behind her back Jane Rochford smiled to herself.

The many members of the Howard family, always in evidence at court, were suddenly not so evident. No one really knew what was going on, but everyone knew that the queen, adored yesterday, was today suddenly out of favor. How serious was it? There was no one to tell the court. All entertainments had been canceled. The king spent all his time in those first days of November hunting with just a few chosen companions, or closeted with his Privy Council. The queen was allowed no visitors. Those bringing food to her could only say that her grace was pale and not eating.

In the Duke of Norfolk's apartments, Nyssa sat quietly by the fire in the dayroom embroidering her husband's initials upon one of his shirts. She looked serene, but she was not. Thomas Howard, watching her, silently admired his grandson's wife. He had known absolutely nothing about her other than the fact that she was standing in his family's way when they had first met. Now that they were more or less trapped within these close quarters, he was discovering that she was a very intelligent, clever, loyal young woman. He also saw how very much Varian was in love with her. Well, at least something good had come of all his machinations, he considered bitterly.

Suddenly Nyssa looked up and her eyes locked onto his. "What news, my lord?" she asked quietly.

"Nothing yet, madame," he answered her. "The archbishop continues to press Catherine. It is as if he seeks something other than he has. If he does not learn anything more, my niece will retain her pretty, vacuous head. If he does find something, she will die as she deserves to, I fear. There is still hope, I think."

"Poor Cat," Nyssa said. "You should not have stressed all of the delights of being queen, my lord. You should have also told her of the difficulties involved, and the responsibilities, but you did not. She was ill-prepared to be a queen, but then I wonder if any girl is well-prepared."

"She should have been prepared," he told her. "Catherine was born a Howard after all."

Nyssa laughed. "Is there something magical in being born a Howard, my lord? You make it sound as if being born a Howard endows a person with not just beauty and grace, but wisdom and the ability to meet any challenge. Your name is an ancient and honored one, but God did not give the Howards any more ability to struggle through life with than He gave the rest of us. It is past time you realized that."

"Impudent chit!" he growled, and stamped from the chamber.

With a small smile of triumph, Nyssa returned to her embroidery. Besting Duke Thomas was very satisfying.

A servant entered the dayroom to announce that the king's sister, the lady Anne, was here to see her. Anne of Cleves hurried in behind the man. Putting her needlework aside, Nyssa arose to greet her former mistress.

"Welcome, dear madame. Come and sit by the fire with me."

"Ach! Such troubles for poor Hendrick and little Catrine," Anne said. "Vhat a surprise to learn of her life before court! The old Dowager Duchess of Norfolk vas certainly not a goot influence. Imagine allowing men to run about her house at night vith all those little girls in her charge. Is she dotty, then?" Anne settled herself, spreading her fashionable yellow velvet skirts about her. She accepted a silver goblet of wine from the attending servant, who then withdrew from the room.

"We are fortunate to have had good mothers and fathers to watch over us; to guide us; to see we learned morality," Nyssa replied. "Poor Cat was really quite badly brought up, I fear."

"Ya," Anne said sympathetically. "God help her now, for who else vill? It is not a goot thing to be a qveen."

"I have already heard a rumor that the king is considering returning to you, madame, should his marriage to Queen Catherine be over and done with," Nyssa told Anne, who blanched.

"Gott und himmel, nein! I vill never marry vith that rutting old boar again! Once vas more than enough! I vould tink that Hendrick vas through vith marriage now. He does not seem to be able to find a voman who can suit him, and the only one he claimed did, died, Gott assoil her goot soul. He is an old man. Vhy vould he vant another vife?"

"You know he does not see himself as an old man," Nyssa said. "Besides, the council will insist he remarry, and attempt to father other children. Little Prince Edward is his only legitimate male heir. What if something should happen to him?"

"Nyssa, when vill you see that a voman is just as capable of ruling a country as a man? Hendrick has two daughters, and both of them are very bright. Especially my darling little Bess. Bess vould make a vonderful qveen, but it is unlikely she vill ever haf the chance. Poor child. She is very upset about Catrine. They are cousins, you know, through Bess's mutter. Catrine has alvays been kind to her, and Gott knows few others haf. They hold the sins of the mutter against her little daughter. It is not kind.

"That is vhy I come to you today. Vhat is going on, Nyssa? Ve haf all heard the gossip about the qveen's early life, but vhat else is there? Catrine's behavior prior to her marriage to Hendrick cannot, my confessor tells me, be held against her as long as she has been a goot vife to Hendrick. Vhy do they continue to press her? Vhat do they suspect? Or is there some secret the court does not know? You vill know, for you are in this nest of Howards, and their safety depends upon the qveen's fate." She took a great draught of her wine.

"The Howards are just as mystified and frightened as the rest of us.

Duke Thomas, to his chagrin, did not know of the queen's early bad behavior. He is frantic the king will hold him responsible for all his unhappiness relating to the queen," Nyssa said.

Anne of Cleves snorted. "Duke Thomas is a vicked old man. He dangled that poor little girl beneath Hendrick's lustful nose, and look vhat he did to you, my sveet Nyssa."

"Ahh, but there, despite Duke Thomas, Varian and I have had a happy ending, madame. He loved me from the beginning, and I have come to love him. We were so happy at Winterhaven with our babies, until the queen demanded our presence on the progress. God, I hate the court!" She looked at Anne. "Why did you not come this summer?"

"I am too vell liked by the people. They still are angry at poor Hendrick for replacing me. I tink that may be the reason for these silly rumors you mention that Hendrick vants me back. The king asked that I stay home this summer so he might present his young vife to his people. I vas happy to comply vith his vishes. I enjoyed being by myself. Bess came to visit vith me, although poor Mary vas forced to go on the progress. Mary does not like Catrine."

"Princess Mary was hardly in evidence at all on the progress. She hunted with her father, but other than that, she only appeared on those special occasions when the king wished to present a united family front," Nyssa said. "She and her women were rarely seen, and kept to themselves."

The two women sat chatting about a variety of things, of the coming holidays and how this distressing matter of Catherine Howard would affect them. Nyssa told Anne how they had wanted to leave the progress at Amphill, but that the king, in an effort to please his frivolous wife, had reneged on his promise to them.

"You know how I love the holidays at *RiversEdge,*" Nyssa said. She did not tell Anne of the real reason behind their desire to leave.

Finally the Princess of Cleves departed, and Nyssa returned to her embroidery. It was already dark outside with the coming winter, but with her young eyes she was able to see her work in the firelight. What was going to happen to poor Cat? Would they learn of her adultery, or would she somehow escape the revelation of her treasonous behavior?

The archbishop had gone again to the queen, and cajoled her into making a written declaration of her scandalous premarital adventures. Catherine firmly believed that her liaison with Dereham was no true contract, but the archbishop thought otherwise. He believed that he now had enough evidence to prove a precontract had existed between the former lovers. It was possible under such circumstances to invalidate the marriage. Catherine had not been a virgin when she came to the king. There were no children involved to be harmed. A potentially explosive situation could easily be avoided under these conditions, yet Thomas Cranmer was still not satisfied. He sensed that there was something else.

"You did what?" Jane Rochford's narrow face was filled with rage. "You stupid little fool! You have given the archbishop the very weapon he needs to see that your marriage is dissolved!"

"But the archbishop said the king would forgive me if I admitted to my wickedness," the queen said. The fact that her lady-in-waiting had addressed her so disrespectfully went completely over her head.

"Aye, why should he not forgive his *whore?"* Lady Rochford was pleased to see that Catherine grew white with shock. She continued, "For that is all you will be to the king if you admit to this willing liaison with Francis Dereham. *The king's whore.* Not the Queen of England, but a royal mistress. Even your cousin Anne was never considered that, but then Anne Boleyn was an intelligent woman. You, poor child, have not the wit to know what you have done, do you?"

"Ohh, Rochford, what can I do?" Catherine whined. "I do not want to be known as a common whore! Tell me what to do!"

"Call back the archbishop," Lady Rochford said. "Tell him you were so frightened that you did not make clear to him that Dereham came into you with force. Say he raped you, damnit!"

"Will the archbishop believe me?" the queen quavered.

"Why should he disbelieve you?" Lady Rochford said impatiently.

But Thomas Cranmer did not believe the queen when he was recalled and fed this new piece of information. Now he was quite certain that the queen was lying. What else was she lying about?

"Be careful what you say to me, madame, lest your life be forfeit. His grace is prepared to grant you mercy, but only if you speak the truth of this matter to us."

"It is true!" Catherine insisted. "I swear it! Dereham forced me!"

"Every time?" the archbishop said disbelievingly.

She nodded vigorously. "Aye! I was never a willing party to his lustful intentions, I swear it! I wasn't."

"Your only hope, dear madame, is in the king's forgiveness. I warn you again to take a care as to what you tell me and swear to."

But Catherine Howard was now foolishly convinced that if she claimed rape, she would not be held responsible for her premarital conduct. Why should she not be believed? She remained adamant, and Thomas Cranmer could not sway her for the moment. In her confession she had said that Dereham asked her to marry him any number of times, but that she had refused him. When faced with the information that the chamberer, Mary Hall, had heard Catherine promise Dereham that she would love him always, unto death, that she indeed loved him with all her heart, the queen denied ever having said such a thing. It was Mary Hall's word against hers, and the king loved her. He would believe her over everyone else, Catherine convinced herself. Had Rochford not said so? And Rochford was wise in the ways of the court.

The Duke of Norfolk despaired to his grandson over Catherine's stubborn and childlike belief that if she admitted to nothing, nothing could be proved of her. "Does she not see that by admitting to a precontract with Francis Dereham, she may save her life?" he said. "If she says she was pledged to him first, then her marriage to Henry Tudor is invalid, and no adultery can be proved of her."

"They have no proof of adultery?" the Earl of March replied.

"Cranmer suspects," the duke answered his grandson. "He thinks, of course, it is Dereham. That is why he is pressing her so. Catherine and our family represent the old form of worship. The archbishop is no fanatic, but he is a reformer. He would see someone more like-minded as Henry's queen. Surely you know Prince Edward is being raised in the reformed faith. I have heard rumors that they would restore Anne of Cleves to the king's side, and the people would be very pleased if he went in that direction, Varian. They always liked her, and could never understand why a king would put aside a royal princess in favor of a mere English maid. Aye, Cranmer and his cohorts seek Catherine's death. Only if she is dead can they be certain she will not creep back into the king's good graces. Even as a mistress, she would be dangerous to them, or so they believe."

"You need have no fear that the lady Anne would remarry the king. She will not have him, Grandfather, or so my wife says. Besides, the lady's mother was of the old church, and the princess Mary has drawn the lady Anne back to that way of worship. It would do the reformers absolutely no good to restore her, for she would be of no use whatsoever to them," Varian told his grandfather.

"The Privy Council is having a secret meeting tomorrow," the duke said. "I will know more then. In the meantime be careful."

Francis Dereham, Henry Manox, and several others in the dowager's livery were arrested and confined to the Tower. The queen grew quite hysterical at the news. She was terrified at what they might say, and realized that she must say her piece first, before they were questioned. She begged that the archbishop attend her once more. Thomas Cranmer came to listen to her admission that, aye, she had indeed given Dereham gifts, and even received gifts from him. She had had a silk shirt made for him, but not satisfied, he had stolen a silver bracelet from her. He had in return had silk flowers made for her by a little woman in London, and given her some sarcenet which she had made into a quilted cap by the dowager's embroiderer, who had decorated the cap with friar's knots, a symbol of true love. When she had first worn the cap, Dereham, according to Mistress Hall, had said, "What, wife, here be the friars' knots for Francis!" To the archbishop all of this was indicative of a precontract, although the queen continued to vehemently deny it.

" 'Twas naught but in fun," she said. Then she went on to tell the archbishop of how Dereham's behavior was beginning to embarrass her greatly. "I feared his behavior would come to the ears of my step-grand-mother," she said, "and then I should be sent back to Horsham in disgrace."

"Why did you not speak to the lady Agnes about this man's disturbing behavior, and his too-free manner toward you?" Thomas Cranmer asked.

"I suppose I should have," the queen admitted slowly, "but we were really having such fun. I did not want to spoil it for the others. If my step-grandmother had known, she would have locked us all up, and we would have never had any fun."

"Did you not realize that your own behavior was wickedly opposed to all that a good Christian woman is taught, madame?" he queried her.

"I did not know how far it would go," Catherine said, pouting. "I was just an innocent maid up from the country."

"The fellow knew you carnally," the archbishop said. "Tell me about it, madame."

The queen began to cry again. "I am so ashamed," she sobbed.

Better she had been ashamed then than now, the archbishop thought sourly. This silly girl is causing us all no end of trouble. However, he turned his most beatific gaze upon her. "Tell me, Catherine, my daughter. Unburden to me, and you will be free again."

"Most times he had on his doublet and hose, but sometimes he was naked, I mean without his hose," the queen said. "He came to me when the old dowager had gone to bed. He brought me all manner of little treats. Sometimes wine, or strawberries, or sugar wafers. Once the most perfect apple I ever saw."

"What if the duchess had come in while you were together?" the archbishop wondered aloud. "What would you have done, my child?"

"She did come in once." Catherine giggled inanely. "I had to send Master Dereham into the gallery so he would not be caught."

Her own words had convicted her, thought the archbishop. She cried rape, yet she sent her lover to hide when she was near to being caught.

"When the news came that I was to come to court," the queen said, "I was so excited. My uncle paid for a whole new wardrobe for me. I had three changes of clothes! I never had new clothing before."

"What of Dereham?" Thomas Cranmer pressed her. "Was he upset that you were to go away?"

"Aye, but I cared not. I told him that if he wanted to ask my uncle's permission to wed me, he must go to Ireland to make his fortune. I had no intention of marrying him, but this was the easiest way to rid myself of the fellow. He saw my eagerness, and he berated me for it. I was forced to tell him that I did not care what he did anymore. I would go to court, and my uncle would find me a good match. Then Dereham said to me that he had heard that I was to wed my cousin, Tom Culpeper. He was very jealous." She giggled again.

"When he said that, what replied you, madame?"

"I said if he knew such a thing, then he knew more than I knew," Catherine told Thomas Cranmer. "I suppose Tom would have been a good match for me, but that the king fell in love with me."

The archbishop knew that the queen and her cousin had known each other since childhood. They had always been fond of one another. Culpeper was highly placed in the king's affections. Was it possible? Could it be? Was the handsome Master Culpeper involved with the queen? The opportunity was there for him to take. *Had he?* When the archbishop left the queen, he ordered Tom Culpeper's arrest. He had proof of nothing yet, but he certainly wanted to speak with the young man.

Culpeper was an ambitious fellow. He had come to court as a child. He was handsome and had a quick wit. The king was deeply fond of him. It was likely that in order to save his own skin he would tell the truth. But who knew what the truth was? the archbishop wondered. Had the queen committed adultery with Dereham? And would Culpeper know? Would his cousin have confided in him?

"Tom Culpeper has been arrested and taken to the Tower," the Earl of March told his wife as he entered the Duke of Norfolk's apartments. He had been playing tennis with Lord Melton when he had heard the news. It was already all over Hampton Court, for Culpeper was very popular among his peers.

"On what charge?" Nyssa asked, pale-faced.

"No charges have been filed against him yet. He has just been brought in for questioning," Varian de Winter said.

"If I found out, then someone else may have found out," Nyssa told her husband. "God help Cat Howard."

He took her in his arms and held her close. "It may be nothing, sweeting. You know that Cranmer has been prying hard. So far he has found nothing that would convict Catherine of anything but bad judgment in men, and a naughty itch she must have scratched."

Nyssa giggled. "You make it sound so bawdy," she said, "and it is very serious, Varian. You know it is!"

He smiled into her dark hair. "Fate has already set into motion whatever will happen, Nyssa. I cannot change it, and so if I do not see the humor in the situation, I will find myself in a depression from which it will be difficult to emerge. My grandfather's plans are about to be foiled for good and always. I am sorry for him, but we have our own lives to live, my darling. How long has it been since we have had a quiet moment together? I think it is past time, don't you?"

"I have been so fearful for Cat, and for us, that I have hardly thought about it," she said honestly.

"I know," he said, his voice rich with laughter. "I am afraid, madame, that like my cousin, I too have a naughty itch that must be scratched." He kissed the top of her head. "Don't you?"

Her soft body shook against his. "You are very bad, sirrah," she told him, but her fingers were unfastening his doublet, reaching past it to unlace his shirt. Her palms flattened themselves against his bare chest. She rubbed her cheek against his warm skin, inhaling his masculine fragrance. Spreading his shirt wide, she licked at his nipples teasingly. Then, sliding to her knees before him, she started to unfasten his top breeches buttons as he removed the upper garments that she had already undone. "Your boots," she said, realizing that they would impede her further progress.

He drew her up, and pulling her over to a chair by the fire, sat down. Her back to him, Nyssa took his leather-shod foot between her legs as he braced the other foot upon her bottom. "Push!" she commanded him as she pulled his boot off. Then repeating the process, she removed the other boot. Turning about to face him, she began to slowly divest herself of her own garments; first her bodice, and then her skirts. Her little pointed tongue flicked across her lips as she slipped off her petticoats, one silk, one woolen, and one cotton. Reaching up, she removed the caul about her hair and shook the soft, dark tresses loose of their confinement.

He watched her appreciatively, sprawled in his chair, his chest bare. "What if someone comes in?" he said.

Nyssa drew her chemise off, and cupping her breasts in her palms, she fondled them before his eyes. Naked but for her stockings, which were gartered with silk rosettes, and her elegant, bejeweled shoes, she walked across the chamber to turn the key in the lock of the dayroom. Silently he admired the long line of her back and her dimpled, rounded buttocks.

When she turned about, the sight of her saucy, upturned nipples thrusting up from her marvelous young breasts set his blood boiling. Sliding to her knees again, she began to place small, hot kisses across his lean torso. She licked at his belly, burrowing into his navel. The tight, hard bulge in his breeches was growing more evident with each passing minute. She cupped a palm over the protuberance and squeezed him teasingly. "I want you too," she said softly to him. Then she lay upon her back before the fire, her legs up and spread.

Her wanton behavior almost took his breath away. Fascinated, he watched as she spread her nether lips with her hands and began to play with herself. Her eyes never left his. Somehow he managed to get to his feet. With equal restraint he removed the remaining garments he wore. Then he stood for a long moment above her, watching as she teased her own flesh into creamy readiness. He slid to the floor next to her, drawing her naked form against his. Her skin was burning with her desire, and when their lips met, she sighed deeply.

He kissed her slowly, feeling the texture of the lips beneath his, enjoying their softness, their passionate response. When he knew that her mouth ached as much as his did, he pressed soft, butterfly kisses across her face. Her eyes were closed in her ecstasy, the thick dark lashes fluttering against her pale cheeks. He nibbled upon an earlobe, licking about the shell of her ear, pushing his tongue suggestively into it to tickle her.

She arched against him, reaching for him to stroke his turgid manhood. "Please!" she whispered urgently.

"Not yet," he murmured back to her. Turning her upon her belly, he let his lips and tongue explore the line of her backbone. His teasing kisses swept across her buttocks and down her legs, then back up again. Pivoting her onto her back again, he nuzzled between her breasts, feeling her wildly beating heart beneath his mouth.

He was driving her wild with his deliciously erotic attentions. His pent-up desire for her should have made him anxious to possess her, but this time he seemed willing to wait, to tease her with sensual games. She liked it, yet she was hot to have him. "Now!" she demanded, sinking her teeth into his shoulder and biting him fiercely.

"Impatient little bitch," he growled at her, slapping her lightly. Then his mouth closed over a nipple and he began to suckle hard upon it even as he plunged two of his fingers into her hot sheath, thrusting them hard, making her whimper with pleasure.

After the first brief release, she realized it simply was not enough. She wanted him deep inside of her, filling her full of his throbbing passion. Angrily she struggled against him. "Now, damn you! Now!" she hissed. Her fists beat a tattoo on his back. In answer to her pleas, he fiercely pushed her down again upon her back. Eagerly, Nyssa opened her legs to him, but to her shock he grasped her, yanking her limbs over his shoulders, burying his face between her thighs, his tongue with unerring direction finding her little jewel. Slowly he flicked back and forth over the angry pink nub of excited flesh. She couldn't draw a breath for a long moment. Her whole being was suffused with a glowing heat that seemed to blossom from deep within her.

"Varian!" she moaned. "Oh, God, you are killing me!"

Relentlessly he continued the torture, until she was near to expiring with her own lust, and then as suddenly as he had attacked her, he released her, sliding his hard body over her, his manhood entering her slowly, then pistoning her with deep, slow strokes. *"Now!"* he breathed into her ear. *"Now, sweet wife!"*

She seemed to explode inside, but as he moved on her, the excitement began to build again, until she was unable to tell the real from the unreal. She was soaring, yet melting away. She clutched at him, her legs wrapping themselves tightly about his torso. They seemed to go on forever, and then suddenly he was groaning even as his loving tribute burst with a rush into her hidden garden. They shuddered simultaneously, clinging to each other as the passion eased away and they were both left gasping for breath.

Overcome by her emotions, Nyssa began to weep wildly. "Oh, God," she sobbed, "it was never like that before, Varian. Our passion for each other has always been wonderful, but never like this." She wept against his shoulder, her hot tears slipping down his skin.

"I know," he whispered to her, his voice shaking. What had just happened between them was as surprising to him as it had been to her. He had never loved her as much as he did in this moment. He held her close, his loving arms comforting her.

They lay together before the fire in silence for some minutes, and then Nyssa said softly, "I think perhaps we should put our clothing back on, my lord. What if someone comes to get into the room and finds it locked? I will wager that such a thing has never before happened in your grandfather's apartments at Hampton Court."

He chuckled. "Probably not," he agreed. "We will dress ourselves in enough garments to reach our bedchamber, madame, my love."

"Oh?" She turned her tear-washed eyes to him. They reminded him of wet bluebells.

"I have not yet finished with you, wife," he said with a small smile. "Besides, what else is there to do now that the king is gone, the queen imprisoned, and the court shaking in its boots wondering what the hell is going on? I think we are very lucky, my darling. We have a cozy bedchamber, and we have each other. I think we should retire to it this very minute to while away the hours as pleasantly as possible. We cannot leave, and I should far rather play sensual games with you than stand about with the others, fearfully casting about for answers."

"Few will associate with us now anyway," Nyssa agreed. "We carry the Howard taint. There is, I fear, nothing else to do, my darling husband and lord, but lock ourselves away." Reaching out, she grasped at her chemise and pulled it on over her head, then turning back, she beckoned him seductively. "Are you coming, my lord?"

CHAPTER 16

Those on the Privy Council who were in sympathy with the Howards came to the queen and helped her to write a letter to the king, begging his forgiveness. Catherine was not the most intelligent woman, but she realized now that her only hope lay in her husband's love for her. If she could move him to forgive her, then he would stop the archbishop from digging further into her activities after she became queen. Her uncle had carefully explained how explosive the situation really was. This had enabled her to pull herself together. If she stayed afraid, she could not possibly hope to act to save herself, and her family. Dereham was jealous of Culpeper. She had rejected Dereham. Dereham, she sensed, knew what was going on between her and Tom Culpeper. She had to get Dereham and her lover released from the Tower before they were tortured and succumbed to confessing their involvement in her life.

I, Your Grace's most sorrowful subject and vile wretch in the world, not worthy to make any recommendations unto Your Majesty, do only make my most humble submission and confession of my faults. And where no cause of mercy is given on my part, yet of your most accustomed mercy extended to all other men undeserved, most humbly on my hands and knees do desire one particle thereof to be extended unto me, although of all other creatures most unworthy either to be called your wife or subject. My sorrow I can by no writing express, nevertheless I trust your most benign nature will have some respect unto my youth, my ignorance, my frailness, my humble confession of my faults and plain declaration of the same, referring me wholly unto Your Grace's pity and mercy. First at the flattering and fair persuasions of Manox, being a young girl (I) suffered him at sundry times to handle and touch the secret parts of my body, which neither became me with honesty to permit, nor him to require. Also Francis Dereham by many persuasions procured me to visit his vicious purpose, and obtained first to lie upon my bed with his doublet and hose, and after within the bed, and finally he lay with me naked, and used me in such sort as a man doth his wife, many and sundry times and our company ended almost a year before the King's Majesty was married to my Lady Anne of Cleves, and continued not past one quarter of a year, or a little above. I humbly beseech you to consider the subtle persuasions of young men, and the ignorance and frailness of young women. I was so desirous to be taken unto Your Grace's favor, and so blinded with the desire of worldly glory, that I could not, nor had the grace to consider how great a fault it was to conceal my former faults from Your Majesty, considering that I intended ever during my life to be faithful and true unto Your Majesty after, nevertheless, the sorrow of mine offences was ever before mine eyes, considering the infinite goodness of Your Majesty towards me from time to time ever increasing and not diminishing. Now I refer the judgement of all my offences with my life and death wholly unto your most benign and merciful Grace to be considered by no justice of Your Majesty's laws but only by your infinite goodness, pity, compassion and mercy, without the which I acknowledge myself worthy of extreme punishment.

This sad little plea was brought to the king, and when he read it, he felt a good deal better than he had in days. His poor little Catherine, led astray by these wicked and dissolute young men. There would have to be an annulment, of course, for he could not continue his marriage to an unchaste woman who might have been precontracted, but at least he would not have to execute her as he had her cousin. He smiled. He might even keep his little Catherine as a mistress. She was a great pleasure to him in bed.

The archbishop was announced, and glided in quietly.

"Well, Tom?" the king demanded.

"There is no doubt, Your Grace," the archbishop said, "that Catherine Howard was precontracted to Francis Dereham. Your union with her will have to be annulled, I fear."

The king offered his cleric the queen's letter. "Aye, she admits to it here. I am relieved, although I shall be sorry to lose her. She has been a most agreeable wife, the most agreeable of all my wives, in fact. I cannot, however, remain wed to an unchaste woman."

"There may be more," the archbishop said.

"Nay, Tom, no more," the king told him. "I am satisfied with the results. I loved my Catherine, my rose, as I never loved any woman, but my love has now abated. Let it be." Then the king returned to Hampton Court, and threw a dinner party, sitting at table with twenty-six of the handsomest ladies at the court. He was suddenly at his gayest, and flirted as of old with all the women. He did not see his wife.

Two days later the king rode off as if to go hunting, but in reality he rode to London, going to Whitehall, where he met with his Privy Council until early the next morning. He rested briefly and ate, returning to the council for most of the day.

Thomas Cranmer was certain that given time, he could discover evidence of the queen's adultery. The thought that Catherine Howard could possibly have foisted a bastard prince on England horrified him. He convinced the council, for on the council those who were not allies of the Howards were in the majority. They felt the archbishop should be given his time; that the queen should not escape their justice. The king, not wanting to be embarrassed further, argued against it, but he finally gave in to the Privy Council's demands.

The court, arriving from Hampton Court, saw the council as it broke up, coming from their chamber. The Duke of Norfolk looked very unhappy. The queen had been left at Hampton Court still under house arrest.

Aware that the court had departed, leaving her behind, Catherine Howard grew frightened again. The following morning the archbishop came to Hampton Court to see her.

"Why have I been left here?" Catherine demanded with a touch of her old queenly imperiousness.

"You will not be here long, madame," he replied. "It has been decided that you will be removed to Syon House in Middlesex for the interim."

"Syon? 'Tis in the country! Why can I not return to court? Will the king, my husband, not forgive me? Is this to be my punishment—to be exiled to some dreadfully dull country house, my lord? For how long must I stay there?"

"Madame, I am not at liberty to give you any explanations, excepting that you are to be removed from Hampton Court to Syon. You will be allowed four attendants and two serving women. You will be served as befits a queen. Prepare yourself to depart in two days' time."

"I cannot pack in such a short time," Catherine complained, stamping her feet at him. "You have taken all my servants from me."

"A new wardrobe will be given you, madame. You will have need for little in your new circumstances. Sir Thomas Seymour will remove your court clothing and seal your chests. They, along with your jewels, will be returned to the king, from whence all your good fortune has come."

Lady Rochford gasped. The queen was frozen with shock, and could not speak for a moment.

The archbishop fixed Jane Rochford with a hard look. "You are to be sent to the Tower, Lady Rochford, for you know far more of your mistress's behavior, I think, than you have told," Thomas Cranmer said sternly. "You must be thoroughly questioned."

"If you take Rochford from me," Catherine cried, her speech returned, "who will I have to keep me company, my lord? Surely you will not leave me to be alone?"

"You will have your gentlewomen and chamberers, madame. They will be your company. They will serve you," he answered her.

"May I choose my own ladies?" the queen asked.

"Nay," he replied, shaking his head.

"Just one of the four, sir," she pleaded. "My cousin's wife, Nyssa de Winter, the Countess of March. Oh, please, my lord!"

"I will think on it," the archbishop promised. In the end, however, he allowed her to have her choice of three of the four. The fourth lady would have to be Lady Baynton, whose husband, Edward, was to be the queen's chamberlain at Syon. Catherine asked for her two old companions—the king's niece, Kate Carey, and Bessie FitzGerald.

Varian de Winter was furious at his foolish cousin for involving his wife, but Nyssa said gently, "They seek to find a way to kill her, Varian. And they will find it even if they must bend the truth, or stretch it a little. One thing I have learned at court is that when the mighty desire something, they will always discover a way to get it. Your grandfather and Bishop Gardiner wanted a queen who was more Catholic than Anne of Cleves. They managed to obtain their wish. Now the archbishop wishes to pull down this queen and replace her with a more reformed one.

"Poor silly Cat has given him the ammunition he needed. They will seek until they find evidence of adultery. Then they will kill Catherine Howard for her foolish, romantic notions. If the king were to divorce her, or find a way for an annulment, there would always be the chance he would forgive her. He has loved her more than the others. The reformers do not want him to forgive Cat. She is a doomed woman. She may not admit to it yet, but she knows it. That is why she wants her few friends about her. I go gladly, even if I am still angry at Cat for her stupidity."

"What am I to do without you?" he asked her. "We have never been apart since our marriage. I do not think I shall enjoy sleeping alone again." He drew her into his arms and kissed the top of her head. "Once you are at Syon, I shall not see you until it is all over. Who knows how long that will be, Nyssa, my darling love?"

"The king's intentions toward the Howards and their kin is still a dangerous and dark thing, Varian," Nyssa told her husband. "You must be as quiet as a rabbit in its nest, outwaiting the fox, my lord."

"I will escape the fat old fox," he promised her, "and I will be waiting for you, Nyssa, to come back to me."

The Duke of Norfolk joined them with new information. "You will be allowed to take little," he told his grandson's wife. "The queen is only being allowed to have six changes of clothing, and nothing can be sewn with jewels. A bit of gold or silver, but that is all. Choose your own clothing with equal discretion. If you want, your tiring woman can go with you. They may allow the servants in and out, but I cannot promise you that for certain," he said.

"If anything should happen to Varian, or me," Nyssa said, "you must promise me that you will send Tillie home to *RiversEdge*, my lord."

"You have my word," he agreed, "but I do not think you need fear for yourselves, madame. You and Varian are de Winters, after all, and not Howards." He smiled grimly at her.

She curtsied to him, saying, "I had best go and ready myself."

"You are a brave woman . . . Nyssa," he said, using her name for the very first time. "I did not intend it, but I seem to have done my grandson a favor when I managed his marriage to you." It was the closest he would ever come to apologizing to her.

"I shared in the favor, my lord," she answered him, "for love remembered me when I found myself matched with Varian. I have learned to love in return." It was the closest she would come to telling him she accepted his apology.

Varian watched this exchange between the two people he loved the most in all the world, excepting his children; marvelling at how alike and yet how dissimilar his grandfather and his wife were. In time, he thought, these two might even become friends, providing they all survived the debacle of Catherine Howard.

Nyssa went to their bedchamber and told Tillie her news. "You need not go with me," she said. "If you choose, I will send you home, and hold no grudge against you for going."

Tillie pursed her lips. "I'll not leave you, m'lady. Why, me aunt Heartha would have me hide if I did. Besides, this new adventure will give me something to tell my grandchildren one day."

"You must have children to have grandchildren," Nyssa teased her tiring woman. "Have you a husband in mind, Tillie?"

"Aye," she admitted. "That Toby of his lordship's will do me nicely when we get back to Winterhaven, m'lady. He's shy, and a bit slow, but I see 'im eyeing me. It's time we both settled down."

Nyssa chuckled. Poor Toby, she thought. His fate was already sealed, though she would wager he did not yet know it. Still, he and Tillie would make an excellent pair. She explained to her servant that she could have but six changes of clothing, as that would be all the queen was allowed; and her garments must be plain, without adornment. Together they chose velvet skirts in black, a rich golden brown, deep blue, forest-green, violet, and orange-tawny. The matching underskirts were of plain satin and satin brocade. The duke found a seamstress among his household who helped Tillie remove the magnificent adornments from Nyssa's bodices, rendering them simple, with naught but gold or silver embroidery about the neck-lines. There were petticoats and chemises of cotton, lawn, wool, and silk; knitted stockings, and a single fur-lined cloak. Nyssa took no jewelry with her, wearing only a small gold and pearl crucifix about her neck, and her wedding band.

"You'll be needing French hoods," Tillie said. "You know the queen likes her ladies to wear them."

"They can't be jeweled," Nyssa said.

"We'll make them up new with just a bit of gold, m'lady," the seam-stress said helpfully.

"Thank you," Nyssa told her.

Within the two days' time, her wardrobe was ready, and on the morning of the thirteenth of November, Nyssa joined Kate Carey and Bessie FitzGerald for their trip to Syon House in Middlesex. They would go by barge from Whitehall. The queen would travel in the same fashion from Hampton Court in the company of Lord and Lady Baynton. It took all the courage she had to kiss her husband good-bye, but Nyssa managed to keep her composure. Then Varian and the Duke of Norfolk escorted her down to the Water Stairs, where her two companions waited. She did not look back as the barge moved upriver, making its way into Middlesex.

The three young women sat within the comfortable cabin. A small brazier heated the space. Kate and Bessie were very quiet as they traveled along. The two girls did not know what to say under the circumstances. Finally Kate said, "Do you think she really cuckolded the king?"

"I think she may have," Bessie said low, then turned to Nyssa. "Remember how she was always disappearing from her bedchamber at night when we were on progress? She would not come back for hours."

"How do you know that?" Nyssa asked her. God's boots, Cat had been appallingly indiscreet. Obviously everyone knew, but no one dared to say anything. She felt better about withholding her own knowledge.

"You were with your husband, I forgot," Bessie said. "Several nights she would disappear about eleven o'clock, and not return until three or four in the morning. I was always awakened by her return."

"I have heard," Bessie continued, "that Lady Rochford went mad when they took her to the Tower. They say she cackles, and babbles to herself all the time. I even heard that she talks to her dead husband, George Boleyn, and to his sister, Anne. They have taken everything from her, for they fear she will harm herself before they may hear her testimony."

"What good will testimony be from a madwoman?" Nyssa wondered.

"She has some lucid moments," Bessie replied. "I think they plan to question her during one of those times."

"You realize that the queen will be found guilty," Nyssa said.

"What do you know?" Kate demanded.

"I know nothing," Nyssa answered. "But it is obvious from the way things are going that Cat's reign is over. The question remains as to whether they will kill her, or not."

"If the king is angry enough," Kate said, "he will show her no mercy at all." Kate's mother was Mary Boleyn, who before her sister, Anne, had been the king's mistress. It was believed that Kate's eldest brother, Henry, was the king's son, but the king had never acknowledged him.

The young women fell silent again. The cityscape had given way to the rural landscape of Middlesex. The leafless trees were silhouetted black against the gray November sky. There was no wind, and the Thames ran dark and smooth. Rounding a bend in the river, they saw Syon House. Until recently it had been a convent. There seemed to be a macabre humor in incarcerating Catherine Howard here. The barge nosed its way into the quai serving Syon House. Upon landing they learned that the queen had not yet arrived.

The majordomo assigned to Syon led them to the apartment assigned to the queen. It consisted of three rooms, and was furnished modestly. There was a bedchamber for the queen, with a small dressing room, as well as a dayroom and a small dining room where they could eat.

"Where will we sleep?" Nyssa demanded of the majordomo.

Recognizing the tone of authority in her voice, he said politely, "A single chamber has been set aside for the ladies, madame."

"I am the Countess of March," Nyssa told the man. "Is there a dressing room for us to store our garments in and where our tiring women may sleep, sir? I realize our purpose here is serious, still, we must have some small comforts." She favored him with a smile.

"The room is spacious, with its own fireplace for warmth, m'lady, and there is not just a dressing room, but a smaller interior room for your servants." He bowed, and then asked, "Might I know the identities of the other two ladies?"

Nyssa nodded graciously. "This is the king's niece, Mistress Katherine Carey, and Lady Elizabeth FitzGerald, sir."

The majordomo bowed politely to the trio. "May I welcome you to Syon, my ladies," he said. "Allow me to show you your own quarters."

He led them from the queen's small apartments down the hallway and opened an oak door, beckoning them into a large square room, the walls of which were done in a linen-fold paneling. A bowed window with leaded panes and a window seat looked out upon the river. There was a fine fireplace in the room, and opposite it, a good-sized bed hung with tapestry curtains, dark green on natural linen. The draperies at the windows were heavy, dark green velvet.

"The bed will sleep two comfortably, m'lady," he addressed Nyssa, as the senior in rank of the three. "There is a fine trundle beneath that can be pulled out to sleep a third person."

"Excellent," she said to him. "I assume there is a trundle beneath the queen's bed as well, for one of us will always be with her."

"Aye, m'lady, and Lord and Lady Baynton have their own bedchamber."

"Very good, then," Nyssa answered him. "Since the queen is not yet come downriver from Hampton Court, will you have our baggage brought in so we may settle ourselves? Please notify us the moment the queen's barge is sighted. We must be at the quai to welcome her."

"Yes, m'lady," he said, and departed.

Kate and Bessie had elected to share a single tiring woman between them. Her name was Mavis, and she was a motherly, older woman. She and Tillie had hit it off immediately. The two women chatted amiably as they unpacked and stored away their mistresses' clothing and other possessions. They were pleased with the tiny room, and with the good-sized bed that they would share. They considered their quarters quite luxurious. It backed up on the large fireplace, and consequently would always be quite warm as long as the fire was going.

While the servants worked to make their small quarters comfortable for them all, the three young women went out into the gardens of Syon House. Wandering about, they found some late roses, not yet touched by frost, blooming pink against a south-facing wall. They gathered the fragile blooms and brought them indoors to arrange in the queen's dayroom, for they knew how much Cat would appreciate the little touch.

The majordomo came to tell them that the queen's barge had been sighted. They hurried down to the quai to greet their old friend.

"I wonder how she is feeling," Kate said.

Nyssa wondered too. She did not know whether to be shocked or surprised when Catherine, stepping from her barge, greeted them as if there were nothing wrong at all and she was not in a fight for her very life. She kissed and hugged each of them in turn, expressing her delight that they were to be with her.

"I suppose you are most put out with me, Nyssa," she said with her most winning smile. "I know that you hoped to be home at your beloved *RiversEdge* for the twelve days of Christmas."

"I am not in the least distressed, Your Grace. I am honored that you would ask me to serve you in your trying hour," Nyssa replied.

"Henry is most put out with me," Cat said, linking her arm in Nyssa's and walking up to the house with her. "I wrote him a very beautiful letter. I am certain that he will forgive me eventually. In the meantime he will isolate me here in the deep country to punish me, but," she laughed gaily, "we will make ourselves a most marvelous twelve days of Christmas, won't we? It shall be like when we were all children. No cares, and no gentlemen to worry us."

Nyssa could hardly believe what she was hearing. Did not Cat understand the seriousness of her position? Obviously she did not.

"Lady Rochford, they say, has gone mad," she said quietly.

"I am so relieved to be rid of her," Cat exclaimed. "She was always badgering me. I thought she was nice, but she is really quite nasty. 'Tis no wonder she never remarried. Who would have her?"

They entered the house, but when the queen saw her apartment, she immediately complained. "This really will not do! I cannot be expected to live in such cramped quarters. Oh, damn Henry! He is just doing this to be mean!" She whirled about and said to Edward Baynton, "My lord, you must write to the king and tell him I need more space."

"The king believes he has provided generously for you, Your Grace," the chamberlain answered the queen stiffly. "I cannot complain to him."

"Oh, very well," Cat said. "I shall write him myself."

"Perhaps we shall not be here very long," Nyssa said gently, attempting to cajole the queen. "By the time you write to the king, and he thinks it over and then answers you, your circumstances may have changed for the better, Your Grace."

"That was very nicely done," Lady Baynton said to her afterward.

"You know how to handle her, and I am most grateful for it, Lady de Winter. Despite it all, she is imperious, and very difficult."

"She is afraid," Nyssa said.

"You would not know it," Lady Baynton replied.

"No," Nyssa answered the good woman. "She does not show it. She is a Howard, after all."

HENRY Manox, the lutanist from the dowager duchess's household, was the first person to be questioned by the Privy Council. He readily admitted to attempting to seduce Catherine Howard when she was but twelve and a half years of age. "She was very well-formed for a girl of her tender years," he related. "She had the breasts of a maid of sixteen, I'll vow, my lords."

"Did you know her in the biblical sense?" the Duke of Suffolk questioned the man. "The truth now! Your life is at stake," he warned.

Manox shook his head. "I was the first man ever to handle her. With an untried maid, one must go slowly," he explained to them. " 'Tis like introducing a mare to the bridle for the first time. By the time I had her accustomed to it, she bolted and threw herself at that bloody Dereham. For all my trouble, and time, he was the one to have her maidenhead, damn him! Even so, I'd have liked a bit of her. She had a great taste for passion, did Cat!

"I tried to rid myself of the Dereham fellow so she would have to come back to me, but I failed, alas. I told the old dowager that if she were to pretend to retire at her usual time, and then an hour later visit the dormitory where Mistress Catherine Howard slept, she would see something that would both displease and shock her."

"And did she go?" the Duke of Norfolk asked sharply.

"Nay," Manox said. "She smacked my face, and said I was nothing but a troublemaker, and I would lose my living and her patronage if I did not cease my wicked and scandalous innuendo. I could do nothing more."

The Duke of Norfolk's narrow lips stretched themselves narrower in a grimace of disapproval. His stepmother had behaved very, very stupidly.

The Privy Council debated. They decided that Henry Manox could be of no real help to them. He was obviously not important in the scheme of things. To the musician's great relief, he was released from custody and sent on his way. He disappeared from London soon after, and was never heard from again.

The Privy Council next called Mistress Katherine Tylney, the chamberer who had been with the queen both before and after her elevation. She was a very distant relation of the queen's, a plain young woman with nothing special to recommend her.

"You have been with Catherine Howard for some time, is that not so?" the Duke of Suffolk asked the woman.

"Aye," she said. "Since we were girls at Horsham. She, of course, being a Howard, was of better birth than I was. I considered myself fortunate to go up to Lambeth with her."

"What kind of girl was she?" the duke queried further.

"Headstrong," came the blunt reply. "Catherine Howard must always have her own way in everything. Not that she wasn't pleasant about it, for she was. And she has a good heart, but she is headstrong."

"What happened on progress this summer, Mistress Tylney?"

"Please be more specific, my lord," she asked him.

"Tell us about the queen's behavior," Suffolk gently prodded her. "Was she all that a good wife should be to her husband, or was she perhaps duplicitous in her conduct toward the king?"

"Actually, she began behaving strangely in the spring," Katherine Tylney said, now given the direction they required her to go in. "At Lincoln the encampment was set up complete with the royal pavilion, but the king and queen stayed in the castle. Two nights during our stay the queen left her room late, usually after eleven o'clock. She did not return until four or five in the morning."

"Do you know where she went?" Suffolk said, and his companions on the Privy Council leaned forward to hear what the young woman would say.

"Lady Rochford had rooms two flights up from the queen's own apartments. The first time the queen left, she took Margaret Morton and me with her. When she reached Lady Rochford's chambers, she sent us away and then entered. I heard the door's bolt thrown. The second time she went, she only asked me to come with her. I was required to sit outside of Lady Rochford's chamber with Lady Rochford's servant that time. Again we did not return until five o'clock in the morning. I was most uncomfortable, for the hallway was quite damp."

"Was Lady Rochford in the room with the queen?" Bishop Gardiner asked Mistress Tylney.

"I do not know, my lord. The queen liked me, and so I think she trusted me more than some of the others. I was always taking odd messages to Lady Rochford, and returning with odder messages. It was not that the words were funny, it was just that I could make no sense of them at all."

"Was it possible that the queen was with Master Dereham?" Suffolk wondered aloud.

"Master Dereham did not join the progress until Pontefract, my lords," Katherine Tylney said. "That would have been impossible."

"Why did you not speak with someone about the queen's strange behavior, Mistress Tylney?" the Duke of Norfolk asked her.

Katherine Tylney looked at Duke Thomas as if he were mad. "Who was I to go to, my lord? The king perhaps? And what was I to say, sir? That his wife's behavior was odd, and secretive? I am a simple chamberer in the queen's household. I am a servant, not gentry. I had not the right to criticize the queen, and had I done so, neither the king, nor even you, my lord, would have believed me," she said.

"Thank you, Mistress Tylney, for your cooperation," Suffolk answered. "You are now dismissed, but we may ask to speak with you again."

She curtsied to the Privy Council and was escorted from the hearing room back to her confinement.

"Well, gentlemen," Suffolk said, "what think you?"

"It would appear that the queen was engaged in some sort of nefarious conduct," the Earl of Southampton replied.

"Aye, but exactly what, and with whom?" Lord Russell wondered.

"I do not think there is any doubt as to what she was doing," Lord Audley answered him. "The question is, with whom?"

"I may have the answer to that question, my lords," the archbishop told them. "I believe Thomas Culpeper is our miscreant, but I have not yet the proof I need. The queen seems very fond of him. He was on the summer progress for the entire four months. He would know her schedule as well as the king would know it, since he is a king's man."

"My God, Cranmer!" Duke Thomas said. "Culpeper was practically raised in the king's chambers. He came to court as a little lad to be a page. The king is deeply attached to him. It cannot be."

The archbishop shrugged. "My suspicions have been aroused."

"By whom?" demanded Norfolk.

"Your niece herself, I fear," Thomas Cranmer answered.

"I think," Suffolk said, "that we had best continue our questioning. We are next to speak with Margaret Morton, another chamberer." The duke signaled to the guardsman by the door. "Bring in Mistress Morton."

She entered, plump, and plainer than Katherine Tylney, if such a thing was possible. She was very excited to be testifying, and filled with self-importance. She curtsied to the Privy Council.

"How may I serve you, my lords?" she asked, without waiting to be invited to speak. She seemed not to realize her error.

"Mistress Tylney has testified to the queen's odd behavior on the progress, her nocturnal wanderings and such. Did you notice anything you wish to tell the council about?"

"Oh, aye," Mistress Morton said. "Her grace and the Rochford woman were up to something all right, 'tis certain. All those whispered conversations, the messages back and forth, and not one of them intelligible. Then there was the letters that Rochford was always getting from the queen and running off with, as well as those she brought back to her grace."

"You went out late with the queen, in secret, at Lincoln," the Duke of Suffolk encouraged the witness.

"Aye, and at York, and Pontefract too, my lords. We serving women are always used to running in and out of the queen's chamber, but at Pontefract her grace got into a shouting match with Mistress Lufflyn for coming into her bedchamber without knocking. She chased her right out, and forbade any of us to enter her bedchamber ever again without her express permission. Later that night the queen locked herself in the room with only Rochford in attendance. That in itself was very odd, my lords," she said with heavy meaning. "The door was not only locked, 'twere bolted from the inside to boot! Well, my lords, didn't the king himself come to visit his wife? He obviously expected to spend the night in her bed. There he was, no disrespect intended, sirs, in his dressing gown, his nightshirt, and his nightcap, and the door was barred to him." She looked about to see what effect her story was having, and obviously satisfied by what she saw, continued.

"Well, my lords, we banged upon the door, and Lady Rochford's voice finally asks us what we want. The king is here to see the queen, we told her. Then, for I was nearest to the door, I could hear a fierce scuffling going on inside, and Rochford saying she was having trouble with the lock, and the king getting more impatient by the minute. Finally, at long last the door is opened a crack, and Rochford's face pops out. The queen, she says, is suffering with a tremendous headache, and begs the king's leave to continue her rest alone that she might be well enough to join the hunt the next day. Of course, his grace acquiesces, being the kind gentleman that he is. God forgive me for saying it, my lords, but I thought to myself at the time, there's a man in there with her."

The room was very still. Here was the thing they sought, yet had feared, finally voiced aloud.

"Did your suspicions, Mistress Morton, perhaps give you an idea of who might have been with the queen?" Suffolk asked her.

"I would stake my life that 'twas young Tom Culpeper, my lords," she told them frankly. "It could be no one else."

"Not Dereham?"

"What, that bad-tempered, crude blowhard? Nay! 'Twas Tom Culpeper if it was anyone, my lords. I knew last spring, April, it was, that she was drawn to him. At Hatfield she stood in her window and cast loving looks upon him standing below. He too looked with love upon her, and blew kisses to her with his fingertips. Once, at Hatfield, she was alone with Master Culpeper for some six hours, locked in her privy chamber. When they emerged, they each looked like the cat who had swallowed the canary. You did not have to guess to know what they had both been about," Margaret Morton concluded archly.

"And you told no one?" Norfolk growled, as he had with Tylney.

"I am a chamberer," Margaret Morton said. " 'Twas not my place to inform upon my mistress. If I did such a thing, I should never be able to get a good place in a decent household again."

"Thank you, Mistress Morton," Suffolk said smoothly. "You are dismissed. Your testimony has been most helpful to us."

She bustled from the room under guard, and when the door closed behind her, the Duke of Suffolk said, "That was most enlightening, my lords, was it not? It seems, my lord archbishop, that your hunch is about to pay off quite handsomely."

"This is a great tragedy, my lords," the archbishop said quietly. "I take no joy in any of this. The queen is barely eighteen. If these charges are proved further, then she will end her days shortly on Tower Green as did her relative, Anne Boleyn, God assoil her soul." Thomas Cranmer had greatly admired Anne Boleyn, and tried to save her.

"Why should you care?" Norfolk snapped at him. "If my niece is convicted, then you can find a good reformed churchwoman to place by the king's side. Is not that what you and your allies really want, sir?"

"If you had not been in such a hurry to get your niece married off to the king so the Howards might be all-powerful, Thomas Howard," the archbishop thundered, "the king should not have been joined with such an unsuitable wife. None of this would have happened but for your ambition. This girl's death will be on your conscience forever."

"You would believe chamberers over a Howard?"

"Do you think it, then, a plot by the queen's chamberers to discredit her, and why would they do such a thing?" Cranmer asked.

"Women are difficult creatures at best," Norfolk muttered. "Who knows why they do any of the things that they do?"

"My lords, this bickering is getting us nowhere," the Duke of Suffolk interposed. "We have other witnesses to hear today."

Mistress Alice Restwold was brought in, and she was follwed by Joan Bulmer. Both of them said essentially the same thing that Katherine Tylney and Margaret Morton had said. Each added small details that the others had perhaps forgotten, overlooked, or not been privy to, but basically their testimony was identical. They were thanked and dismissed to go back to their confinement in the Tower.

The final piece of evidence that day was a letter found among Tom Culpeper's possessions. It had been written in the spring of the year in the queen's own hand. It was dreadfully composed, badly spelt, and ended with the tender words, *Yours as long as life endures, Catherine.*

There was now no doubt in any of the Privy Council's minds that Catherine Howard was involved in an adulterous relationship with Thomas Culpeper. No one wanted to tell the king, but Charles Brandon, the Duke of Suffolk, knew that the duty would fall to him. He was not only the king's best friend, but Lord President of the Privy as well.

The king was wild with anger over the discovery of his wife's infidelity. Suffolk tempered the blow as best he could, but there was really no gentle way in which to impart such news.

"Give me a sword!" Henry shouted. "I will go to Syon and kill her myself, Charles! Ahh, the false bitch, and I loved her! *Never again!* Catherine! Catherine!" Then he began to weep.

The council took it upon themselves to issue communiqués to their ambassadors in key courts in Europe explaining the latest events in the king's ongoing marital woes. The queen's behavior was referred to as *abominable.*

François I, France's king, and a renowned lecher, sent his dear brother Henry a most sympathetic letter of condolence.

I am sorry to hear of the displeasure and trouble which has been caused by the lewd and naughty behavior of the Queen. Albeit, knowing my good brother to be a prince of prudence, virtue and honor, I do require him to shift off the said displeasure and wisely, temperately, like myself, not reputing his honor to rest in the lightness of a woman, but to thank God of all, comforting himself in God's goodness. The lightness of women cannot bend the honor of men.

Privately François I said to the English ambassador, Sir William Paulet, of Catherine Howard, "She hath done wondrous naughty," and then he chuckled with a great appreciation of the queen's sexual behavior.

On the twenty-second day of November the Privy Council voted to take away Catherine Howard's title of queen. She was now simply Mistress

Howard again. Two days later she was indicted for "having led an abominable, base, carnal, voluptuous, and vicious life before marriage, like a common harlot with divers persons, maintaining however the outward appearance of chastity and honesty." She was further accused of having led the king on, and having married him under false pretenses, and for having imperiled the crown with the possibility of bastards.

The indictment, read to the former queen at Syon House, elicited far less response than the knowledge that she was no longer queen. When the members of the council had gone, Cat looked to Nyssa and asked, "Will they kill me?"

Lady Baynton looked startled by the young woman's frankness, while Kate and Bessie began to cry.

"If you are found guilty," Nyssa said, "aye, I think they will. For a queen to cuckold her king is treason."

"Oh," Cat replied, then she grew more cheerful. "They have but the word of my chamberers," she said. "Surely they will not believe them if I deny it? I am a Howard."

"They have others to question, Cat. There is Lady Rochford, and Masters Dereham and Culpeper as well. How could you trust old Lady Ferretface, Cat? Particularly after what she did to your cousin Anne. I never understood why Duke Thomas tolerated her after that."

"Because she was vulnerable, and he could use her," Cat said bluntly. "Lady Ferretface." She giggled. "Is that what you called her? She does look rather like a ferret, doesn't she?"

"My brothers called her that," Nyssa said.

"Is that adorable cherub Giles still with the lady Anne?" Cat was once again turning the subject away from the unpleasant.

"Aye, he is," Nyssa told her.

"We must really begin to think of Christmas," Cat said. "There is a most marvelous stand of trees just beyond the house to the north. Lady Baynton, do you think we will be allowed to gather branches? And we must have candles, and a Yule log as well."

The subject of death, of treason, of all things unpleasant, was now closed. And why not? thought Nyssa. She understands even if she will not admit to it. This may be her last Christmas, and she wants to make it merry. Why shouldn't she? "We must have a wassail bowl, and roasted apples too," Nyssa told Cat. "We always have them at *RiversEdge.*"

"Do you think we will have a boar with an apple in its mouth?" Kate Carey wondered aloud. "I always love it when the boar is brought in!"

"And will there be music, do you think?" Bessie asked.

"Oh, I hope so!" Cat said.

"She is mad to be planning for a festive Christmas," Lady Baynton told Nyssa softly. "Does she not care that her reputation is gone? That her marriage will be dissolved? That she is ruined?"

"She cares, but she will never allow you to see her innermost thoughts and feelings. She is too proud," Nyssa answered. "Besides, it is all unpleasant, and Cat has never been one to bravely face that which displeases her. She will not change now. So she plans for Christmas. Who knows what will lie beyond Christmas?"

"They say," Lady Baynton said confidentially, "that the king will go back to the lady Anne. 'Twould be a good thing if he did. She is a most charming and gracious lady." Lady Baynton liked Nyssa. She too was a married woman with children, and certainly more than sensible. Besides, there was no one else to talk with, for the other two girls were so young.

"I would not count upon the king and lady Anne reuniting, madame. They are the dearest of friends, and have the greatest respect for one another; but they do not like being married to each other, I fear."

"What a pity," Lady Baynton replied. She accepted Nyssa's opinion on the matter, for she knew that Nyssa was friendly with the lady Anne, and that her brother was one of the princess's pages.

"Do you know when Lady Rochford will be examined?" Nyssa asked

"The council told my husband they will do so tomorrow," Lady Baynton said. "I cannot understand why a woman of her years and her experience, particularly given her past background, did not guide the queen better. It would almost appear as if she encouraged her in her perfidy, if indeed the chamberers are to be believed, and I do not know why they wouldn't be. If I were in her position, I should be terrified."

Lady Rochford, however, was not terrified. Solitude had helped her to regain her senses, if only for a brief time. She came before the Privy Council in the Tower wearing her finest gown of black velvet. Her French hood was encrusted in pearls. She stood stiffly before them, her back straight, her eyes staring straight ahead.

"She is drawn as tightly as a lute string," Lord Audley whispered to Sir William Paulet, who had returned to England with the King of France's letter for Henry Tudor. Sir William glanced at Lady Rochford and nodded his agreement.

"To the best of your knowledge, madame," the Duke of Suffolk began, "when did this intrigue with the queen start?"

"In the spring," she answered him calmly.

"And was it the queen who approached Master Culpeper, or was it Master Culpeper who approached the queen?"

"At first 'twas he who pursued her," Lady Rochford said. "He had always been mad for her, since they were children. He thought to marry her, but then she wed with the king. Still, he was a bold young man, and he wanted her. The queen was very put out with him for his pursuit of her, but he persisted. Then the king put himself away from her, and she succumbed to Master Culpeper's charms."

"You are certain this was in the spring, madame? I would get our dates correct."

"Aye, in the spring. April, I believe. Aye, 'twas April."

"Where did they meet?" Suffolk inquired.

"In my rooms," Lady Rochford said with a smile. "They knew that they were safe there. I stood guard outside myself."

"She is totally mad," the Earl of Southampton said softly.

"But she is calm, and speaks the truth," Suffolk said. "It is as if she is eager to tell us her part in this matter. As if she is proud of it." He looked at Lady Rochford. "What else, madame?"

"I carried letters and messages between them, but then, of course, the chamberers have already told you that. Did you know that the queen called Master Culpeper her sweet little fool?" She laughed bitterly. "She was surely the bigger fool, but she was clever. Whenever she wanted her own way, and Culpeper would not give over to her, she would remind him that there were others waiting for her favors; behind the door, she would say. It drove him wild with jealousy."

"To your knowledge," Suffolk said, "did Catherine Howard have carnal intercourse with Thomas Culpeper?"

"Aye," Lady Rochford replied. "I was generally in the room when it took place on the progress last summer. She could not send me away when she was in my rooms without arousing suspicion. I was witness to their passion on many occasions."

The Duke of Norfolk felt as if he had been dealt his death blow. "Why did you not try to stop her?" he demanded of Lady Rochford. "To turn her from her dangerous folly? Why did you not come to me if you feared coming to anyone else?"

"Why should I have stopped her?" Jane Rochford said coldly. She fixed them with a fierce look. "Do you remember the last time I appeared before this council, my lords? You took my testimony, and twisted it. Then you executed my husband. You did so in order that the king might be rid of his wife so he could marry another." She laughed, and the sound had a hysterical edge to it. "Now, let Henry Tudor's heart be broken as my heart was broken! Nay, I did not stop that silly child, Catherine Howard, as she blithely tripped down the path to her own destruction. Why would I have done a thing like that? Even had I not been there to encourage her in her naughtiness, she would have betrayed the king. She is a trollop at heart."

For several long moments the Privy Council sat stunned by Lady Rochford's vitriolic words, and then, to their combined horror, she began to laugh. The laughter had the strong ring of madness to it, and sent a chill up the spine. It rang out, filling the chamber, growing in its intensity, seeming to have a life of its own, its evil sinking into the very walls of the room.

"Take her away," the Duke of Suffolk wearily told his guards, and when they had led the madwoman from the place, he turned back to the council and said, "Other than the testimony needed to convict the former queen of adultery, nothing else of what Jane Rochford said is to be repeated, my lords. I think we can all agree to that, can we not?" He glanced about at the others, and they nodded.

The Duke of Norfolk, not a man to show what he was thinking, looked gray with weariness and disillusionment. It was over. It did not matter what anyone else said. Lady Jane Rochford had hammered the last nail into Catherine Howard's coffin. Indeed she had hammered the last nail into the coffin of the House of Howard, and Thomas Howard was too beaten for the moment even to fight back.

"I think we have heard enough for today," the Duke of Suffolk said quietly. "We will meet here tomorrow at the same time to take the testimony of Thomas Culpeper. Are we agreed, my lords?"

They nodded, and leaving the chamber, hurried to gain their barges. Thomas Howard was quick to note that no one wanted to be near him, or to share his vessel. He smiled grimly to himself, and ordered his bargemen to pull hard for Whitehall. Arriving, he went quickly to his own apartments, and finding his grandson there, he said, "It's over. Rochford has finished it." Then he went on to tell Varian everything that had happened, even Rochford's claim of revenge on the king.

"How long does Catherine have?" the Earl of March asked.

"Culpeper has to be heard from, and then he and Dereham must be arraigned and tried. They will be found guilty, of course, and will be sentenced. They'll be executed as quickly as possible, and then I think everything will be quiet for the holidays. After Twelfth Night, however, it will begin again. It will not end until Catherine is slain upon Tower Green. Rochford will die too."

"What of my wife, and the others with Cat?" he asked.

"They'll serve her until her death, Varian," Duke Thomas said.

"Do they know what's happening here?" he wondered.

"Catherine and the others will only know what they are told," the duke answered him.

"I want to see my wife," Varian told his grandfather. "I realize that the Howards do not stand high right now with the king, but is it possible for me to somehow see Nyssa?"

"Wait until this business with Culpeper and Dereham is settled, and then we will see. I think I can persuade Charles Brandon that there is no harm in allowing you to visit your wife for an afternoon," the duke replied.

"What will happen to the Howards?" the earl asked.

The duke laughed harshly. "We'll be out of favor again, perhaps forever in this king's reign. Two Howard queens, and neither of them a good one. It does not recommend us, Varian. I think you may finally be grateful that your name is de Winter and not Howard."

"I will always be proud of my Howard mother," the earl said.

Thomas Howard's eyes grew moist with unaccustomed tears. "I must go and rest while I can," he said gruffly.

His dreams are crumbling about him, Varian realized. Then he thought of his wife. Nyssa had once told him that Duke Thomas had taken her dreams from her. Would she think it just retribution that the head of the House of Howard had just had his dreams taken from him? He thought she would. He would tell her when he saw her, but he somehow knew she would not gloat over the downfall of the Howards.

CHAPTER 17

THOMAS CULPEPER stood straight and tall before the Privy Council. He was dressed in black, his garments singularly plain, as befitted the occasion and a man in his position. His blue eyes stared straight ahead, never wavering.

"Are you in love with Catherine Howard, formerly Queen of England?" the Duke of Suffolk asked him.

"I am," came the bold reply.

"For how long have you loved her, sir?"

"Since we were children, my lord."

"You deliberately sought out this woman to seduce her despite the fact she was married to your king. A king who loved you, and helped to raise you. A king who trusted you. Is this so, Thomas Culpeper?"

" 'Twas naught but a game. I pursued her for my own amusement," he answered. "I certainly never thought that she would respond to my overtures. Indeed for some months she did not. It seemed the harder I pursued her, the more she rebuffed me, and the more determined I became to have her. Then the king grew ill last winter, and for many weeks refused to see his wife. She grew bored and lonely. I am not quite certain how it happened, but suddenly the queen was languishing with love for me. I could not believe my good fortune. The woman I had always loved finally loved me."

"And what form did this love take, sirrah?" Suffolk demanded to know. He stared hard at the young man. Thank God the king was not here to listen to this shameless recitation of perfidy and betrayal.

"I was fearful that the king would discover our secret," Culpeper continued. "I labored hard to be discreet, but Catherine sought every opportunity to be alone with me. It was madness, but it was wonderful!"

"Did you kiss her?"

"Aye."

"Fondle her parts?"

"Aye."

"Did you have carnal knowledge of each other, sir?"

"My lord, if I did or did not, I should certainly never admit to it," Thomas Culpeper said. "It would not be honorable."

Norfolk exploded with anger. "You call yourself honorable, you hopped-up piece of turd? You admit to kissing and fondling my niece, a married woman, the wife of your king, and you dare to call yourself honorable? If you address this council thusly in the belief that you are protecting Catherine Howard, be advised that Jane Rochford has already testified that she was a witness to your foul and disgraceful fornications!"

"Lady Rochford, I regret to say," Culpeper responded stiffly, "has all the morality of a London Bridge bawd ingrained into her soul. It matters to me not a single whit what she said to you. I will admit to nothing that would harm a hair upon the queen's head, my lords. You are, I fear, wasting your time questioning me further." He stared defiantly at them.

Thomas Culpeper was immediately removed from the hearing, for it was obvious that for now they would not get what they wanted from him.

"A little torture would wring the truth from him," said Lord Sadler sternly. "We need his confession."

"You can torture him to the point of death," Lord Russell remarked, "but you will not get him to say he committed adultery with the queen."

"His very silence, this arrogant refusal to admit to it, is in itself an admission of his guilt," Lord Audley noted.

"Aye," the Earl of Southampton replied. "He is in love with her, poor fellow, and men in love are more often the fools than not."

"May God have mercy on both their souls," Bishop Gardiner said piously.

"We might interrogate the queen again," the archbishop said.

"What good will that do?" Norfolk growled. "Catherine does not have two beans worth of sense in her pretty head. She refuses to accept the seriousness of any of this. She believes the king will forgive her."

"We could try," Suffolk said slowly. "What harm would it do to try? If we fail, they are still condemned by the testimony of the others. Culpeper is attempting to protect her, but she need not know that. What if she thinks he turned king's evidence to save his own miserable skin? She might tell us what we need to know in an attempt to revenge herself on him, and in an effort to save herself."

"We need not all go," Norfolk said, "but I should like to be among the party that does. I have to accept responsibility for her as a family member."

"Very well," Suffolk replied. "I will, of course, go. Gardiner, I will want you, and Southampton, and will you come also, Richard Sampson?"

Richard Sampson was Dean of the Chapel Royal. He had never been known to miss a single Privy Council meeting. He held the bishopric of Chichester, and was considered a fair man.

"Aye, I will come, my lord," he now answered.

The five members of the Privy Council were rowed upriver to Syon House. There they found Catherine Howard among her women, strumming her lute and singing sweetly, a song the king had once written for her ill-fated cousin, Anne Boleyn.

"Alas, my love, ye do me wrong, to cast me off so
"discourteously: for I have love-ed you so long,
"delighting in your company. Green Sleeves was my
"delight, and Green Sleeves was all my joy.
"Green Sleeves was my heart of gold, and who
"but my Lady Green Sleeves?"

Catherine Howard looked up at them as they entered, smiled and continued on.

"Thou couldst desire no earthly thing, but that I gave
"it willingly. Thy music to play and sing, and yet,
"thou wouldst not love me. Green Sleeves was my delight,
"and Green Sleeves was all my joy. Green Sleeves was my
"heart of gold, and who but my Lady Green Sleeves?"

They listened to her, entranced, and when finally the last note of the plaintive ballad had died and the spell was broken, Suffolk bowed politely to the young woman and said, "We have come to examine you further, Mistress Howard, based upon the testimony of the others that we have heard."

"Who has spoken ill of me? Lady Rochford? She is not important," Catherine Howard said imperiously. "You could not believe her over me."

"Master Thomas Culpeper has testified that he is in love with you, and has had intimate relations with you since last April," Suffolk, Lord President of the Privy Council, told her. "Lady Rochford confirms this."

"I have nothing to say to you gentlemen," she told them regally.

Bishop Sampson took the former queen's plump little hand in his. It was very cold, he noted. How frightened she must be, although you would never know it from her attitude. "My child, for your own soul's sake, I beg you to confess to all of your faults so I may shrive you."

"Thank you, my lord bishop, for your kindness," Cat said, "but I will not speak with the Privy Council again." She took back her hand, and reaching for her lute, began to tune it.

"You are facing death, you little fool!" Norfolk growled at his wayward niece. "Do you not realize it?"

Catherine Howard looked up from her lute. "We face death from the moment of our birth, Uncle. We are all facing death, even you."

"Do you deny then that you had carnal relations with Master Thomas Culpeper, Mistress Howard?" the Duke of Suffolk again demanded of her.

"I deny nothing. I confirm nothing," Catherine said stubbornly.

They departed Syon House defeated.

"She is protecting him, or thinks she is," Southampton said.

"It is a great tragedy for all parties," Bishop Gardiner replied.

On December first Thomas Culpeper and Francis Dereham were arraigned, and tried together. Dereham was tried for Presumptive Treason; for joining the queen's service with ill intent; for traitorously concealing his precontract with Catherine Howard. He pleaded not guilty.

Thomas Culpeper was tried for having had Criminal Intercourse with the former queen, Catherine Howard. Realizing now that there was nothing he could do to save either one of them, and anxious to clear his conscience, Thomas Culpeper, who had originally intended pleading not guilty, changed his plea to guilty. With the strong testimony of the chamberers, and of Lady Rochford, there simply was no other honorable choice.

It was Thomas Howard, Duke of Norfolk, who pronounced them both guilty. "You are hereby sentenced to be drawn on the hurdles to Tyburn, and there hanged. You will be cut down alive, disemboweled, your innards burnt before your eyes. Finally you will be beheaded, and quartered. May God have mercy on your souls," he intoned, his long face grave, his eyes sad.

On the sixth day of December, Francis Dereham was tortured in an attempt to wring a confession of adultery with the queen from him. As an already condemned man he had nothing to lose by confessing. The fact that he did not seemed to satisfy the Privy Council as to his innocence in that matter.

The families of both men were desperate to get their sentences commuted to a more merciful death. Culpeper's family succeeded. His full punishment was remitted because he was a gentleman. Although he would be dragged to Tyburn on a hurdle, once there, he would simply be beheaded. Francis Dereham would not be so fortunate. He was not considered a gentleman. His family had no influence, nor were there powerful relations to speak for him. He would suffer the full punishment.

The following day, December tenth, both men were taken to Tyburn. The day was cold and gray, yet the streets were full of people come for the execution. They pelted the condemned prisoners with garbage and offal as they were dragged along. At Tyburn it was discovered that there was no block. Thomas Culpeper knelt upon the hard ground, bowing his head, his lips moving in prayer. The headsman was swift and merciful.

Francis Dereham was not so lucky. He was hung upon the gallows until his face turned blue, and his tongue began to loll from his mouth. Cut down, he was stretched upon the ground, and held down as the executioner sliced his belly open, and dragged the long length of his innards from him. He shrieked in agony while the crowd that had come for his execution pressed around him cheering the gory spectacle. The smell of his burning bowels barely registered upon his dying brain. He was almost unconscious as they rolled him over, pulled him into a half-standing position, and lopped his head from his shoulders. Dead at last, it mattered not to him that his body was then cut into four pieces, each piece to be buried in unhallowed ground at each of the four different compass points. His head and that of Thomas Culpeper were then placed upon pikes, and carried in procession to the London Bridge where they were then set up, their eyes quickly plucked from their heads and devoured by the carrion crows.

At Syon House, Catherine Howard knew nothing of the executions that had taken place that icy December day, nor did she know of the arrests made in the following days of any Howard who could be found. Lord William Howard and his wife Margaret—her uncle and aunt—were taken, as were her brother, Henry Howard, his wife Anne, their children, and the aunt for whom Cat was named, the Countess of Bridgewater. All were incarcerated in the Tower of London, arrested for Misprision of Treason. The dowager duchess, remembering the Countess of Salisbury's unfortunate end but several months before, attempted to forestall the arrest warrant issued for her by pretending to be sick. The Privy Council brought a respected physician unannounced to Lambeth, and when he pronounced the lady Agnes fit, she was taken off, protesting mightily. Varian de Winter, Earl of March, Duke Thomas's grandson, was also imprisoned with his relations, although his wife did not know it.

Duke Thomas, however, had fled London after pronouncing sentence upon Culpeper and Dereham. Safe in his own stronghold, he sent the king an extraordinary letter in which he apologized for his relations, in particular his two nieces, Anne Boleyn and Catherine Howard. He begged to be allowed to retain the king's favor, telling Henry Tudor that he "groveled at the king's feet." As angry as the sovereign was with the Howards, he valued Duke Thomas, and grudgingly forgave him, although he never allowed the duke to regain his former preeminence. Henry Tudor was not about to be stampeded into losing a valuable servant, and Thomas Howard was an excellent Lord Treasurer. The lesson of Cromwell was still burned in his memory.

The Christmas season was now upon England. At court it was a gloomy affair. No one's heart was really in the celebration. The king was suddenly looking and behaving like an old man. There was no queen, and many of the court's most prominent people had either been jailed or had discreetly requested permission of the king's secretary to leave for their own homes. Each day was the same. The king would hunt in the morning in the New Forest, and spend the rest of the day into the evening sitting slumped in his throne on the high board, drinking, belching, and noisily passing wind.

At Syon House, however, it was a far merrier holiday. Lord Baynton, a kind-hearted man, could see no harm in allowing his prisoner and her ladies to go out into the wood near their abode to gather the traditional Christmas greens. The day of their excursion was gray. There was snow upon the ground, which was already hard with frost. Escorted by several men-at-arms, Catherine Howard, Nyssa, Kate, and Bessie made their way from the house into the wood.

"I hope the king does not learn of this," Lady Baynton fretted.

"What harm is there in it, my dear?" her husband replied. "She is not yet convicted of anything, though surely this is her last Christmas upon the earth. I have not the heart to deny her such a small thing as gathering greens." He watched the young women, their dark cloaks fluttering about them as they moved among the leafless trees which were silhouetted black against the gray-white sky. There would be snow again quite soon, he thought, watching the lowering clouds piling up on the horizon.

"I do not understand Catherine Howard at all," Lady Baynton said.

"Lady de Winter says she is aware of everything that is happening to her, but simply does not wish to face it. Do you really think it is so? I find the queen, er, Mistress Howard, quite a frivolous woman."

Her husband did not answer her question, but instead said, "Tell Lady de Winter that her husband has been arrested in the sweep and search for Howards. He is in the Tower, but quite safe, as are the rest of them. The king is seeking scapegoats, and Duke Thomas has quite prudently fled to Leddinghall. The duke is as sly as an old fox, and has as many lives, I'll vow, as a tomcat." Then he smiled at his own pun, which brought a small chuckle from his wife.

"Poor Lady de Winter," Lady Baynton said. "She is a fine young woman, and wishes nothing more than to go home. She has not seen her infants in over four months, my dear. Why, her husband is not even a Howard! Why would they arrest him?" She sighed. "It is really quite unfair."

"Duke Thomas is Varian de Winter's grandfather. The duke is very fond of him, and I suspect this is the king's way of getting at him. The duke's son, the Earl of Surrey, has fled with his father, and is as a consequence also out of the king's reach. Varian de Winter was at Whitehall awaiting his wife. It was inevitable that he would be caught up." Turning, Lord Baynton gazed back out the window to watch the greens gatherers.

Cat was exuberant in the chilly air. She frolicked in the snow like a little girl, her auburn curls unbound and flying about. Her girlish behavior brought smiles to the faces of her guards. "Look! Look!" she called to her companions. "There is a holly bush over there, and see! It is filled with berries." A guard held a basket while Cat cut several large branches of holly.

"There is everything that we need!" Nyssa cried excitedly. "Bay! Laurel! Boxwood! And over here a whole stand of evergreen!"

The greens were cut, and soon the baskets were completely full to overflowing. The guards gallantly took the heavy baskets from the young women as they walked back to the house. Below the slight rise upon which they stood they could see the river Thames. The banks were iced over, but the yellow river grasses made the wintry scene seem somehow less harsh. Snow began to fall again as they reached the house and hurried inside, eager for the fire in their quarters. Nyssa's toes were quite frozen.

"I wish to make candles," Catherine told Lord Baynton. "We cannot have a proper Christmas without candles aplenty. I will need the best beeswax, molds of all sizes, cotton wicks, rose oil, lavender oil, and bayberries, my lord. Tomorrow will be soon enough."

Lady Baynton swallowed her amazement when her husband replied calmly, "Of course, madame. I shall see to it myself."

"Are you mad?" she demanded of her husband as they lay abed that night. "Where will you obtain such items?"

"That, my dear," he said with a small smile, "you will leave to me. Catherine Howard will have what she needs to make her candles. Have you told Lady de Winter of her husband's fate yet?"

"I must find the right moment," she answered him.

The following day they made candles in all sizes and shapes, scenting them with rose and lavender oils, and with the bayberries they had been given. The candles cooled on a table set out in the kitchen gardens. Within a very few hours they were hardened and ready. In that time Cat Howard and her ladies decorated the three rooms assigned to the former queen with sweet-smelling pine branches and garlands of holly, boxwood, laurel, and bay that they had made up the evening before. The freshly made candles were then brought in and set about on every flat surface that could be found. When lit, the candles represented the Star of Bethlehem.

There were other customs that could not be observed. There could be no Lord of Misrule. Even Cat saw the inappropriateness of asking Lord Baynton to fulfill such a role. There would be no hunt for wild boar to be served at the Christmas feast. On Christmas Eve day, however, Lord Baynton suggested an excursion into the wood to find their Yule log. Lady Baynton feigned a minor complaint and requested that Nyssa remain with her.

When they were alone, she said to her companion, "My husband has had word from London, Nyssa. It seems the king has been rounding up all the Howards that he can find and clapping them in the Tower."

"Varian?" Nyssa asked, knowing instantly what the good woman was trying to tell her. Her heart beat a quick tattoo at the reply.

"Aye. I am sorry, my dear. Lord Baynton and I know that he does not deserve to be there. He is not even a Howard."

"Who else was arrested?" Nyssa asked. Oh, God! Why had they not fled without the royal permission when they had the opportunity?

Lady Baynton told her.

"But not Duke Thomas?" Nyssa observed, and there was humor in her tone, to Lady Baynton's surprise. "How did he escape the royal wrath? And what of Surrey?"

"Both fled from London," Lady Baynton replied.

"Of course," Nyssa answered. "I am not surprised. I warned Varian that his grandfather would bolt, given the chance. He is a master at his own survival."

LOVE, REMEMBER ME [331]

"Lord Baynton does not think the king will harm any of the Howards. He is simply very angry and heartsore right now. Eventually his sense of fair play will get the better of him."

"I pray that you are correct, Lady Baynton," Nyssa said. She did not know whether to believe the older woman or not. Perhaps she was just trying to be kind. If I think about it, Nyssa thought to herself, I will go mad. I must be strong for Varian, and for our children. Looking up at Lady Baynton, she said, "Do you know how to make frumenty?"

"Gracious!" the good woman replied. "You are a country woman, aren't you? Well, so am I! Indeed I do know how to make it! Let us go to the kitchens and see if we have all the ingredients."

Christmas frumenty was a very special treat. Made from finely hulled wheat, it was boiled in milk until it was soft, and then sweetened with a sugar loaf, a rarity which made it a delicious holiday dish. It was not served at any other time of the year. Finding what they needed, the two women made the dish, and then set it aside in a warm spot by the fire.

The small paneled room that served as their hall was prettily decorated, its candles burning brightly when the Yule log was dragged in by Cat, her ladies, and the servants. At Christmas most class distinctions were eased considerably. Cat sat impishly atop the log as it was pulled along, singing at the top of her lungs the traditional song used to ward off any evil spirits from the log, and from the fire it would give.

"Wash your hands or else the fire
"Will not tend to your desire;
"Unwash'd hands, ye maidens know,
"Dead the fire though ye blow."

Everyone in the household wanted to touch the Yule log for luck. Finally it was pushed into its place within the fireplace, and Catherine Howard lit the great log, her face bright with childlike excitement. It was oak, and well-dried, and sprang to bright, flaming life almost immediately.

A special supper was served to them. There was fish caught that very day in the river, broiled, and laid upon silver platters dressed with watercress. There was a fine country ham, and a leg of lamb; a fat capon stuffed with fruit and nuts; and a duck in a sauce of dried plums and sweet wine flavored with cinnamon. There was turnip with butter and nutmeg, carrots, and braised lettuce. The bread had been newly baked that morning, the butter freshly churned, and the cheese brought from a nearby farmstead. Wine and ale were served. Everyone ate heartily, their appetites increased by the time spent in the open air. Nyssa, however, picked delicately, for her appetite had deserted her.

They had no musicians, but Cat had her lute. As the Yule log blazed merrily in the fireplace, she played and sang traditional Christmas songs for them. Those who did not know her well found it hard to imagine that such a sweet-voiced girl possessing Cat Howard's pretty face could be so wicked and unchaste. Yet the servants knew, if the former queen did not, that two men had already died for their fornications with Catherine Howard.

After a time the Christmas ale, the cakes, and the frumenty were brought in and served to the little assembly. Cat Howard clapped her hands in delight.

"I have not had frumenty since my days at Horsham," she said. "Who made it? Ohh, I always loved it as a child!" She greedily spooned the treat into her mouth. "Ummmm, it's good!"

"Lady Baynton and I made it," Nyssa said. "While you were out this afternoon seeking the Yule log. We thought you would enjoy it."

Just before midnight Cat and her ladies went outside, accompanied by Lord Baynton. It was very cold, but the skies had cleared. Above them a quarter moon shone down, casting a silvery glow on the river below them. Then suddenly they began to hear the Christmas bells. All over England the church bells joyfully tolled in Christmas. The air was so clear that they could hear the great bells of Westminster several miles away as they pealed and rang, welcoming the Christ child, banishing the devil. Adjourning to the chapel of Syon House, they heard mass, as most people all over England were now doing.

Catherine Howard insisted upon celebrating each of the twelve days of the Christmas season. On the nights that followed, they danced with each other and played children's games like Hide the Slipper and Blindman's Buff. Some evenings were quieter. They simply played cards and diced with one another. There could be no mummers at Syon, nor village children come to sing and be given cakes and pennies. The poor who came with their wooden bowls for ale, however, were not turned away, at the request of the former queen. The king would have been very angry to learn that his disgraced consort was keeping a far better Christmas than he was. Indeed Lord Baynton worried a little about his master finding out, but he had not the will to deny Catherine Howard.

Nyssa finally told the others of Varian's arrest. Kate and Bessie were sympathetic and cried. Catherine Howard, however, said, " 'Tis so like Henry to behave in such a petty manner. None of those he has imprisoned is responsible for my bad behavior, nor were any of them involved. I suppose my uncle, the duke, is out of the royal reach."

Nyssa nodded. "Of course," she said dryly.

"Do you hate me for all of this?" Cat said. "You would not have ever had to leave Winterhaven and your children had I not begged the king for your company. Had I not done so, you would be safe with your husband at home."

"I do not hate you, Cat," Nyssa said quietly, "nor can I wish away what has already happened. It cannot be changed. But I am no saint, Cat Howard. I am indeed angry that your foolish actions have endangered my husband and my children. You cannot blame me for that."

"The king will release Varian," Cat said. "He is no Howard."

"Everyone keeps saying that," Nyssa told her, "but everyone identifies him with the Howards because of Duke Thomas."

There was nothing else to say about the matter. The twelve days of Christmas were over and gone. They waited at Syon for what was to come. On the twenty-first of January the government finally acted in the matter of Catherine Howard. Both houses of Parliament passed an Act of Attainder against her. When the king approved the attainder, Cat's fate would be sealed.

The archbishop came to speak with the queen. He wanted her written confession as to her adultery with Thomas Culpeper. He did not like seeing to her demise without this concrete assurance, although in his heart he felt that she was guilty.

"Thomas Culpeper has paid the ultimate price for his treason, Mistress Howard, and Francis Dereham for his presumption," he told her. "Will you not confess to me now, and clear your conscience?"

"I do not hold that to love a man is a sin," Cat replied to him, and refused to speak further on it. She was shocked to hear of the executions, but hid it well. She turned to Nyssa and said, "Please escort the archbishop to his barge, Lady de Winter."

Nyssa took up her cloak and walked from the house with the cleric. "Can you tell me, my lord, how my husband is?" she asked him.

"He is safe and well, my dear," Thomas Cranmer said, "but he, and the others, have been found guilty of Misprision of Treason by the Privy Council. Their possessions are to be forfeited to the crown."

"But that is not fair!" Nyssa cried. "My husband was never involved in any of the queen's misbehavior."

"I do not disbelieve you, my child, but the king is an angry, heartsore man. He wants revenge upon the Howards for his hurt."

"My husband is not a Howard," Nyssa said angrily. Then an idea struck her. Catherine Howard would shortly be condemned to die. Everyone knew it. She couldn't save Cat by remaining silent. But she might be able to save Varian. Nyssa could see the archbishop was troubled by Cat's refusal to confess to her misdeeds. He would always wonder if she had gone to her death an innocent, unless . . . Nyssa said to the archbishop, "My lord, I wish you to hear my confession. *Please!*"

Thomas Cranmer looked startled. "Here, madame? *Now?*"

Nyssa nodded vigorously.

Suddenly the archbishop knew that she wished to tell him something, but she also wished to be protected by the seal of the confessional. It had to be something very important. She was obviously using it to bargain for her husband's pardon and the reinstatement of their estates, now forfeit. "I can promise you nothing but absolution, my child," he told her honestly. "Absolution is the only thing in my power."

She nodded again, this time slowly. "I understand, my lord, but nonetheless I wish to confess to you. I will not kneel for fear of attracting the attention of those in the house." She put her hands in his. "Forgive me, Father, for I have sinned."

"What sins have you committed, my child?" he asked her.

"I caught the queen in the act of adultery at York, and I did not report it to the proper authorities. I saw her coupling with Thomas Culpeper while the king hunted."

The archbishop was staggered by her words. It was a moment before he could catch his breath again and ask, "Why did you not expose this sin, my daughter? By not doing so, you became a party to treason yourself."

"I feared I would not be believed," Nyssa said. "Remember that the king was once thought to be caught between the affections of Catherine Howard and Nyssa Wyndham. I honestly believed if I told what I knew, the king and others about him would say that I had said it out of jealousy. The king was so deeply in love with the queen, I knew he would not believe me. He would have punished me and my husband for lying. So I held my peace. I did not even speak of it to my husband at first. At Hull I finally told the queen that I knew of her illicit fornications with Master Culpeper. I begged her to cease and to be a true and loyal wife to her husband."

"You are to be commended for that advice, my daughter," the archbishop said approvingly. "What happened then?"

"The queen said she loved him, and could not cease. I reminded her that she endangered not just herself, but her family as well. I asked what would happen if she became with child? She would not heed my warnings. Then at Kettleby, Tom Culpeper and his friend, Sir Cynric Vaughn, accosted me one night as I walked from the Royal Pavilion to my own pavilion. They threatened me with violence, and Sir Cynric tore my bodice open and fondled my breasts. When he lifted my skirts, I kicked him, knocking him unconscious. Culpeper, who had been restraining me, released me to attend to his friend. As I made to flee, Culpeper warned me if I exposed him, my children would suffer. I dared not tell my husband, for he would have sought immediate satisfaction of the two men, and the scandal would have been out.

"What could I do, Your Grace? I am but a simple woman. I was afraid for my babies. Besides, Culpeper and the queen were being so indiscreet that I knew eventually they would be found out. That is why I was so desperate to go home, so we might be away from the trouble when it began. You need have no doubts, my lord, as to your own actions. Catherine Howard is guilty of adultery, and for my sin of omission in this matter, I beg God's forgiveness," Nyssa concluded.

"You have it, my daughter," the archbishop told her, making the sign of the cross over her. "You have done well to make your confession to me. I can promise you nothing but the absolution I have given you, but perhaps I shall be able to help you in that matter dearest to your heart, Nyssa de Winter. Thank you for the ease you have given my own conscience. I would not condemn the queen unfairly, but sometimes in matters like these, it is difficult to get at all the truth."

The Archbishop of Canterbury entered his barge and was rowed downriver to London. As she watched him go, Nyssa felt as if a great weight had suddenly been lifted from her shoulders. She realized now how terrible a burden her secret knowledge had been. Cat Howard's fate had been sealed long before her own confession to Thomas Cranmer. At least she knew now that Varian would be safe.

For the next few weeks they heard no news, and then without warning, on the morning of Thursday, the ninth of February, the Duke of Norfolk arrived with the other members of the Privy Council. They came unannounced. Only the warning of a serving maid who saw the barges on the river heading toward Syon gave them a brief time to prepare.

Catherine Howard curtsied to the lords crowding into her dayroom. "I had heard you were at Leddinghall," she said to her uncle.

"I was," he answered her sourly, "but since I am first the king's good servant, and he asked me to return, I did."

"And how are my aunt of Bridgewater, and my uncle William and his wife; my brother Henry, his wife, their children, and my cousin Varian? And, oh yes! How is the dowager?" she asked him pointedly.

"You are too pert, girl, and particularly under the circumstances," he answered her harshly.

"I am no girl, my lord, but a woman," she told him.

"Too many times over, it would seem," he snapped angrily. "Now be quiet, Catherine, for I have been sent to deliver to you most serious news.

The Act of Attainder, passed originally against you on the twenty-first day of January, has now been read twice more, on the sixth and seventh days of this month. You have been condemned to death, as has Lady Rochford."

"Has Henry signed my death warrant?" she asked him.

"Not yet," Norfolk said quietly.

"Then there is hope!" she cried softly.

"There is no hope," he said coldly. "Dissuade yourself of that fantasy, madame. You are condemned to die."

"When?" Her face was pale, as were the faces of her women.

"The date has not been set yet," Norfolk answered.

"If I must be slain," Catherine Howard said, "can it please be in secret? I do not wish to be an entertainment for the people."

"You will die on Tower Green, as did your cousin Anne. There will be just a few witnesses for posterity, and to satisfy the law," he told her gently. "Despite your cruelty to the king, he does not wish to be cruel to you, Catherine. Now prepare yourself to leave Syon one day in the near future. You should not be in residence in the Tower for more than a day or two." He bowed to the assembled household, and then, with the rest of the council, he departed, escorted out by Lord Baynton.

"Henry will not kill me," Catherine Howard said desperately, refusing to believe her fate. "I know him. He is just angry. He has the right to be, but he will not kill me."

Kate Carey wept softly in Lady Baynton's arms afterward. "There is little mercy in my uncle," she sobbed. "Why does Cat believe that the king will spare her? Does she really know him so little? She is guilty, and my aunt, Queen Anne, was not; yet Queen Anne died on Tower Green. I am so afraid for Cat. What will happen when she can no longer hide from the truth?"

"She will have no choice but to face it," Lady Baynton said.

"She hides from it now," Nyssa comforted Kate, "because it is the only way she can keep from going to pieces. We must be brave for her, Kate, because we are all she has to help her through this ordeal."

Lady Baynton prepared the small wardrobe Cat would need in her last few days of life, while the others kept the former queen entertained so that her mind would not dwell upon the inevitable. None of them were prepared, however, when the Privy Council arrived the following morning to remove Catherine Howard from Syon House.

Cat had not slept well the night before, and was just arising from her bed. Informed that her uncle and the rest of the council were there to escort her to the Tower of London, Cat shrank back amid her pillows. "No! It is too soon! I cannot go today! *I cannot!*"

Struggling to keep from weeping, the serving woman prepared her tub, all hot and fragrant with damask roses, Cat's favorite scent. They bathed her, washed her hair, then dried her and dressed her in clean undergarments.

"How long is this all going to take?" grumbled the Duke of Suffolk.

"My lord, you sent no warning of your coming," Nyssa said gently. "She had a bad night, and slept ill, so arose late this morning. It is her custom to bathe first. Surely you would not deny her such a small thing? We know her time is so very short."

Charles Brandon, Duke of Suffolk, knew himself to be rebuked, but it had been done with such sweetness, he could find no anger in himself to respond to her.

"Will she then eat?" demanded Norfolk.

"Aye," Nyssa said, looking directly at him.

He turned away from her. Her look had been accusatory, and he knew exactly what she meant by it. She was holding him responsible that her husband was locked in the Tower among that unfortunate lot of his relations. The truth was, he did feel guilty, but would never admit to it. Why should he?

A small meal was brought into the former queen's bedchamber, but Cat could not eat this morning. She was simply too afraid. She sent the food away. Now they were dressing her all in black velvet, and putting her fur-lined cape with the gold frog closures about her, the French cape with the gold trim over her head. She was handed a pair of leather gloves lined in rabbit fur.

When she was led out into her dayroom and saw the grim faces of the men who had once deferred to her, Catherine Howard was overwhelmed with a terrible fear. "*I will not go,*" she said in a tight little voice.

"You do not have a choice in the matter, madame," the Duke of Suffolk said. "Come along now." He offered her his arm.

Catherine shrank back. "Go away!" she said, her voice high.

"Try to remember you are a Howard, madame," Norfolk growled angrily at her. "Try to behave with some dignity."

"Get away from me, Uncle!" she shrieked, and flung her gloves at him. "I will not go! I will not go! You cannot make me go! If I am to be killed, then do it here and do it now, but I will not go with you! Do you understand me? I will not go!"

The archbishop, Bishop Tunstall, Bishop Sampson, and Bishop Gardiner tried to reason gently with the terrified woman, but to no avail. They could neither bully nor cajole her into leaving Syon willingly. Suffolk finally did the only thing he could. Signaling to two of the soldiers who accompanied him, he ordered them to take the queen to the waiting barge; and so, screaming and shrieking, Catherine Howard was bundled into the black, sealed barge brought for her transportation.

"If either of you goes to pieces now," Nyssa warned Kate and Bessie, "I will smack you both. One hysterical woman is enough. If we cannot manage to control ourselves, they will not let us remain with her. Do you want her all alone in the Tower?"

They shook their heads, then followed Lady Baynton and Nyssa out of Syon House and down to the sealed barge, where they could hear Cat's pitiful screams. Norfolk, Thomas Cranmer, and Stephen Gardiner were inside the vessel with the queen. The four women joined them and managed to calm their mistress. The Duke of Suffolk, Lord Baynton, and the rest of the Privy Council were in a larger barge, which also contained a number of soldiers. A third barge held the household's female servants, the queen's confessor, and more soldiers.

The barges made their way downriver, passing beneath the London Bridge, where the heads of Francis Dereham and Thomas Culpeper were still on display. Fortunately the curtained windows of the queen's barge obscured the unpleasant view of the rotting heads of her former lovers. On the steps of the Tower, its constable, Sir John Gage, waited to greet Catherine Howard. His demeanor was most respectful. It was as if nothing had changed, and the queen was simply coming for a social visit.

Catherine Howard was helped, weeping and shaking, from the barge. She was brought to the queen's apartments in the lieutenant's house. The knowledge that her cousin Anne had once been in these very rooms was of no comfort to her. That evening the Bishop of Lincoln came to hear the former queen's confession, but though Catherine made a confession, it did not bring her any comfort.

In the meantime the Privy Council, seeking to ease the king's heartache and make certain that Catherine Howard met her just fate as quickly as possible before the king relented, attached the Great Seal to the top of the Act of Attainder, and wrote the words, *Le Roi le veut,* which in English meant: "The king wills it." This way the king did not have to put his signature to the document, which was then read in both houses of Parliament, and the royal assent formally announced. The executions of Catherine Howard and Jane Rochford would now take place. Everything was official.

No execution could take place on a Sunday, of course, and so Catherine

Howard was granted one more day of life. On Sunday evening Sir John Gage requested permission to see her, and it was granted.

He bowed politely to her and said in as gentle a voice as he could, "You will be executed tomorrow morning, madame. We will come for you at seven o'clock. If you wish to unburden your soul at this time, I would advise you to do so with your good confessor. If there is anything that I can do for you, madame, and it is in my power, you have but to ask me." He bowed again.

Her women waited nervously, expecting another outburst of hysterics. Instead Catherine Howard said softly, "I should like it, sir, if you would bring me the block upon which my most unhappy life is to end. I wish to practice laying my head upon it, for I would not make a bad impression at last. There is nothing else I require. Thank you for asking, however."

He was stunned by her request, but he said, "It shall be brought to you immediately, madame." Then he bowed again and left.

"How can you?" Bessie FitzGerald whispered. Her blue eyes were wide with fear. She found it hard to believe that by this time tomorrow her friend would be dead. They were young, and the young were not supposed to die!

"Anne died with elegance and dignity," Cat said. "She was a Howard, and I am a Howard. I cannot do any less."

"What will happen to us when it is over?" Kate Carey asked Lady Baynton. "What is to become of us?"

"Why, you will go home, my dears," Lady Baynton said. "The court will no longer be a fit place for young girls. The court always becomes a rough and dull, masculine place without a queen."

"Henry will not be long without a wife," Cat said knowingly. "He is not a man to live long without a woman. I hear he has already been celebrating his soon-to-be freedom. They say he has enjoyed himself with Elizabeth Brooke, and favors our old friend Anne Bassett greatly."

"Where on earth did you hear such things?" Lady Baynton demanded.

"The servants at Syon knew everything," Cat said, "and they would tell our serving women, who would gossip to me if I asked."

"Elizabeth Brooke is notorious for allowing any man who so desires to sheath himself within her," Lady Baynton said indignantly. "As for Mistress Bassett, I think little of her, accepting gifts from a married man! She will find herself in trouble one of these days, mark my words." Lady Baynton had become very fond of Cat Howard, despite it all.

"She was always so proud of the horse and saddle the king had given her," Nyssa remarked. "She thought it set her above the rest of us. She really is a dreadful snob, although her sister is pleasant."

Catherine Howard smiled at the woman she called her best friend. "Soon you will be home in the country again," she said. "I know how much you will like that. How old are your babies now? They will have grown some since you saw them last. Who is looking after them now? I could never see myself having children." She sighed ruefully. "Perhaps it is better that I did not. Look at poor little Bess, Anne's child. She is all alone. Never sure whether she is in favor or out of favor. I wonder what will happen to her when she is grown."

Nyssa laughed. "So many questions, Cat. Edmund and Sabrina will be a year old on March first. They certainly will have grown, since they were just five months old when we left them. Mama is still taking care of them. I would trust no one else. I often wonder what they look like now. I shall be glad to be home in the Wye valley again. We shall be there just in time for spring, if I can first convince the king to release Varian, and then return Winterhaven to him."

"I have caused you much difficulty," Catherine said regretfully. She looked suddenly sad.

"Aye, you have," Nyssa agreed with her, and the others looked horrified, but then Nyssa continued, "yet, Cat, I love you dearly, and I am proud that you would call me your friend."

The queen's cerulean-blue eyes teared and she said, "You will not forget me? You will pray for me?"

Nyssa embraced her friend, saying, "Aye. I will pray for you, and how could I forget you, Catherine Howard, after all the adventures you have involved me in?" She laughed shakily. "I regret none of it."

"The Howards did find you a wonderful husband, and in doing so, saved you from Henry Tudor," Cat replied. "You found love, Nyssa. I know you realize how fortunate you are. Sadly, love did not remember me. Even the king, for all his professed passion for me, only desired me, and liked having a pretty young wife to show off. Manox and Dereham sought the triumph of seduction. Perhaps Tom Culpeper loved me a little, but I think his quest was also a dangerous game he but hoped to win. I wonder if I ever knew what love truly is, Nyssa."

Before Nyssa might answer, the block was brought into the queen's chambers and set down in the center of the floor. Catherine Howard stared at it. Upon that piece of wood she would end her life. Bending, she ran her hand over it. It was smooth, and cold. She shivered, then turned about. "Lady Baynton and Lady de Winter will personally attend me tomorrow morning. Kate, Bessie, though you must come, I will not burden you with this task, though I know if I asked, you would gladly serve me in my final moments." She then looked to her two chosen ladies. "Help me to practice now," she said.

They helped her to kneel before the block. Catherine Howard lay her neck upon it for the first time. It was really not so terrible, and it would be over in a moment's time. She raised herself up and then leaned forward again. She did this several times, and then, seemingly satisfied, she arose to her feet. "I want beef for my supper," she said. "And a pear tartlet with Devon cream, and the best wine the king's cellars have to offer me. Send to Sir John and tell him so!"

The meal brought to the former queen that night was simple: prawns poached in white wine, a capon in a lemon-ginger sauce, the beef she had requested, artichokes braised with butter and lemon, bread, butter, and cheese. The tartlet was large, and the clotted cream sweet. Despite all the cups of wine they drank, they could not seem to get drunk. Instead they sat about telling tales of when they were maids of honor to Anne of Cleves, making Lady Baynton laugh until she was weak.

The night passed too quickly, and suddenly it was six o'clock of the morning. The serving woman brought the queen her tub, and Cat bathed. She was then helped into her undergarments and the black velvet gown with its black and gold satin brocade underskirt. The standing collar on her gown was carefully removed. Catherine Howard's lovely auburn curls were carefully pinned atop her little head. She slipped her feet into a pair of round-toed shoes. She wore no jewelry.

Her women were as somberly dressed, each in a black velvet gown with a slightly decorative underskirt. Lady Baynton wore a French cap, encrusted with pearls and gold, but Bessie and Kate elected to wear small flat velvet caps edged in pearls with small egret tips. Nyssa, however, put her hair in a golden caul because Cat had always liked it that way.

The queen's confessor came and heard Catherine Howard's final confession. They closeted themselves in the queen's bedchamber, but they were not there for very long. Finally there was a ceremonious knocking upon the door. Nyssa opened it slowly to find the king's Privy Council, minus the Duke of Suffolk, who had been taken ill in the night, and the Duke of Norfolk, who later admitted he could not bear to be present at the execution of Catherine Howard.

"It is time, madame," the Earl of Southampton said.

Nyssa felt her heartbeat accelerate, but Cat simply nodded, saying, "I am ready." Escorted by the Privy Council, her four women, and her confessor, the queen then went out onto Tower Green.

Lady Rochford was already there, and they were shocked by her appearance. She was disheveled and unkempt. Her dark eyes were wild, and she was babbling nonsense. The king had ordered a special act passed by the Parliament, allowing him to execute an insane person.

Catherine Howard was asked if she had a final statement to make, and she said in a clear, young voice, *"I ask all Christian people to take regard unto my worthy and just punishment with death, for my offenses against God heinously from my youth upward in breaking all of His commandments, and also against the King's Royal Majesty very dangerously.*

"I have been justy condemned," Catherine continued. *"I merit a hundred deaths. I require that you look to me as an example, and amend your ungodly lives, obeying the king in all things. I pray for his grace, our sovereign lord, Henry Tudor, and beg that you all do so as well. Having done so, I commend my soul to God, and His infinite mercy,"* she concluded.

Catherine's two chosen women helped her to mount the gallows where the block, so lately in her chamber, now waited, set amid a pile of straw. There the hooded headsman awaited the queen, leaning upon his great ax. Nyssa wondered what the face beneath the hood looked like, and whether he felt any remorse in doing his duty.

Catherine Howard smiled quietly at the man and said, "I forgive you, sir." Then, as custom also demanded, she pressed a gold piece into his hand, in effect paying her own death tax. Turning to the two women who had escorted her up to the gallows, she thanked them for their faithful service, taking time to bid Kate and Bessie, already weeping below her, a tender farewell. Holding out her arms to Nyssa, she embraced her. "Do not forget that love remembered you in spite of it all, Nyssa Wyndham. Be good to Varian, and do not think too harshly of Duke Thomas." She kissed her friend's cheek, and then turning, said to the headsman, "I am ready, sir."

Lady Baynton and the Countess of March helped the queen to kneel down before the block. Catherine Howard looked heavenward, her lips murmuring a soft prayer, then crossing herself, she leaned forward, her arms gracefully outstretched. The headsman struck swiftly and mercifully, the thunk of his ax severing the queen's head neatly and burying itself for a moment in the block below.

Nyssa had not been able to tear her eyes away from the horror. It had taken no time at all, and yet the ax had seemed to hover above its victim for an eternity before descending downward. In one moment Catherine Howard's life had been snuffed out. The sound of her voice still echoed in the icy morning air. Disoriented for a moment, Nyssa looked about her. The day was gray and somber. Lady Baynton, her hand shaking, slipped her arm through Nyssa's, and together the two women descended the gallows while the queen's remains were wrapped in a black blanket and laid in a coffin.

At the bottom of the gallows Lady Baynton tenderly gathered the sobbing Kate Carey and Bessie FitzGerald to her motherly bosom. Nyssa looked about her again, this time her eyes focusing upon the scene. There was the Privy Council, Sir John Gage, and a detachment of Yeomen of the Guard. A small huddled group of people she did not recognize, legal witnesses, obviously, stood upon Tower Green. The ground beneath her feet was hard and, she saw, covered in frost. Jane Rochford was now led past them up to the gallows to be executed. Nyssa was past caring. The sound of the ax told her the deed was done.

Four of the guards brought the queen's coffin down from the gallows, and following the weeping women, they brought it into the Chapel of St. Peter ad Vincula, where a place for Catherine Howard had been made near to her cousin, Anne Boleyn. They stood quietly in the dim chapel as Cat's confessor said the prayers for the dead. Then together the four women left the chapel, passing the coffin of Jane Rochford, which was being brought in to be interred in a far, dark corner. Outside, the four stood confused for a moment in the gray and sunless morning, not quite knowing what to do now. Then Lord Baynton was by their side.

He put an arm about his wife and said to them, "Come, my dears. It is time for us all to go home now. I have a barge waiting." Then he smiled at Nyssa. "Not you, however, Lady de Winter. There is a gentleman over there who wishes to speak with you." He pointed.

Nyssa turned to look, and her heart leapt in her chest. For a long moment her voice would not cooperate, and then she managed to say, "Varian!" forcing her legs forward until she was running into his outstretched arms. He was pale. He looked haggard. But he was alive, and he was running toward her also!

He wrapped his strong arms about her, their lips met in a kiss, and she was weeping. To her amazement, he was too. "I thought never to see you again, sweeting," Varian de Winter told his wife honestly. "Yet I am free! Free to go home with you to Winterhaven again, Nyssa. Home to our son and our daughter!"

"How can this be?" she sobbed into his doublet.

"I do not know," he said. "For two months I have been kept in a filthy cell, told I was guilty of concealing treason, and that my estates were forfeit for my crime. Then this morning Sir John Gage came to me and told me that the king had decided an error had been made in my case. That I was a de Winter and not a Howard. I was to be released, and my estates restored immediately. The only requirement to my release was that I must be a witness to the queen's execution. After that I was free to go. There is a barge waiting for us at the Water Stairs."

The archbishop. Somehow Nyssa knew that Thomas Cranmer was responsible for her husband's release. He was a just man, and she realized that he had somehow convinced the king of the inequity in allowing the arrest of the Earl of March.

Putting her arm through her husband's, she hurried with him from the Tower to where their barge was waiting. Tillie was already in it with Toby, smiling broadly. They were rowed to Whitehall. Within the hour their carriages were packed and ready to depart.

As they made ready to leave the apartments of Duke Thomas, he appeared before them and asked Nyssa politely, "Did she make a good end, madame?"

"You would have been proud of her, my lord," Nyssa said. "I could not have been half as brave as Catherine Howard was."

"You will not be back to court," he said. It was a statement.

"Never again," his grandson answered him, "but should you need me, Grandfather, I will come to you. Do not be so overweening proud, Thomas Howard, that you do not ask."

The duke nodded in the affirmative. Like the king, his age was showing now. He looked at Nyssa. "And will you come if I call you, madame?" he asked her.

She waited a long moment before answering him, but then she said, "Aye, *Grandfather,* I will come."

"You have forgiven me then," he said gruffly.

"Once," Nyssa told him, "I thought that you had taken all my dreams from me, Tom Howard, but I am older and wiser now than I was then. You did not take my dreams from me, you gave them to me. I just did not know it at the time. Aye, I forgive you for me, but I will never forgive you for Cat. I know that you can understand that."

"I do," he said.

Nyssa stood upon her tiptoes and placed a kiss upon the grizzled cheek of the Duke of Norfolk. "Good-bye, Grandfather," she said to him.

The two men embraced, and then the duke hurried from his apartments, but Nyssa had seen the tears in his eyes and heard the catch in the old man's voice.

Together she and Varian left Whitehall. There was no need to take their leave of the king. He was aware of their going. It was Monday, the thirteenth day of February in the year of our Lord, fifteen hundred and forty-two. With luck they would be at *RiversEdge* in time for the twins' first birthday, and then they would go on to Winterhaven. The weather held, and within just a few days' time the Wye, silver-green in the winter sunshine, stretched below them as they viewed it from the London road. *Almost home. Almost home.* The horses' hooves seemed to drum that cadence as they cantered along the hard, snowpacked road.

"We will be at *RiversEdge* in just a little bit," Varian de Winter told his wife. "We will have to think of some wonderful gift for the twins. They will not even know who we are."

"They are young, and will never remember that we were away from them for so long, except that we will tell them the tale one day when they are old enough to understand it," Nyssa replied. "As for a gift, I already have it."

"You have a gift for the twins?" He was surprised. "How could you have a gift for the twins?"

"Because, my lord," she said, snuggling against his shoulder and nibbling upon his ear, "you and I made them their gift last autumn before I joined poor Cat at Syon. I was so wrapped up in serving her in those last awful months that I only just realized it a few days ago myself. I am going to have a baby, my darling! We shall give Edmund and Sabrina a brother come Lammastide!" And she laughed happily.

"And this son is to be Henry, is he not?" the Earl of March said to her.

"Nay," she answered him. "I am not pleased with the king's behavior as of late. Besides, there are too many Henrys in England."

"It could be another daughter," he teased her. "What shall we call a daughter, madame?"

"It is a son," she said firmly. "A woman knows these things. This child is a son, Varian, and I shall give him my estate at Riverside for his own. He shall be a propertied gentleman."

"But what is his name to be, madame?" her husband demanded.

"Why Thomas, of course," she told him, surprised he had not known it. Then leaning forward, Nyssa de Winter spied *RiversEdge*. "Look! Look!" she cried excitedly. "It's Mama and Papa before the front door, and ohhh, Varian! They have the twins in their arms! Dear God! I do not even recognize them. Oh, my darling, I shall never leave our children or our home again!"

Varian de Winter looked at his wife, and then pulling her into his arms, he kissed her. He had never loved her as much as he did now. "Love," he said, "has remembered me, Nyssa, and I am so thankful for it!"

"Why did you say that?" she asked him, startled as their coach came to a stop.

"Say what, sweeting?"

"Love, remember me," she answered him.

"I do not know. It was just a thought I had, my love."

The doors to their vehicle were pulled open, and stepping out, Nyssa felt a shiver run up her spine. *Love, remember me.* The words echoed in her head. Godspeed, Cat, she thought to herself. May you find that love with God that you could not find on earth. Then, smiling at her family, she hugged them and gathered both of her children into her loving arms, looking up at her husband happily even as she did so. They were so fortunate in each other. This was what was really important in life. Love had indeed remembered them all. She would be grateful for it as long as she lived.

AFTERWORD

HENRY VIII was not expected to marry again, although his Privy Council importuned him to for the sake of the succession. Both he and they, however, knew better. He would father no more children. Still on July 12, 1543, seventeen months after Catherine Howard's execution, the king married Katherine Parr, the widow of Lord Latimer. Although the conflicting religious powers that were attempting to gain the ascendancy in England tried to pull this queen down too, she survived the king, who died on the twenty-eighth of January, 1547. She was a devoted and loving wife to Henry, bringing his family back together and convincing him to restore his daughters, Mary and Elizabeth, to the rank of princess, wiping out the stigma of their bastardy.

As for the Howards, Henry forgave them all, and restored their possessions to them within a few months' time. The old dowager duchess Agnes was released from the Tower on the fifth of May, 1542. She died three years later. Duke Thomas managed to keep his position as Lord Treasurer, but he never again really regained the king's favor or trust. He died in 1554, at the age of eighty-one.

Anne of Cleves remained a good friend to the royal family. She lived out the remainder of her life in England, enjoying her personal freedom and her generous income. She died in 1557, a year before her favorite of Henry's children, Elizabeth, ascended the throne.

Bishop Stephen Gardiner became Lord Chancellor under Mary I. He had spent most of Edward VI's reign in the Tower. He died in 1555.

Thomas Cranmer, the gentle Archbishop of Canterbury, was burned at the stake on March 21, 1556, during the reign of Mary I. He was in his sixty-seventh year.

Henry VIII was succeeded by his only son, Edward VI. Edward was nine and a half years of age, and lived into his sixteenth year without marrying or producing issue. On his deathbed he was convinced to alter the succession as his father had ordered it, and settled it upon his very Protestant cousin, and former playmate, Lady Jane Grey, the granddaughter of Charles Brandon, Duke of Suffolk, and his wife, Mary Tudor, Henry VIII's sister. Jane Grey reigned nine days before being ousted by the angry English, who considered Henry's daughter by his first wife, Katherine of Aragon, Princess Mary, the true heiress.

Mary I became Queen of England in 1553. Popular upon her ascension, she lost favor quickly by first marrying her cousin, Philip of Spain, and then bringing the Inquisition to England. Her fanatical passion for her faith was marked by soaring intolerance and the never-ending smell of the fires from Smithfield, burning those condemned by the Inquisition. She died in 1558, childless, abandoned by her husband, who had returned to Spain. She was forty-two.

Of all Henry VIII's children, the second surviving child, Anne Boleyn's daughter Elizabeth, was a long shot to become queen, and yet on November 17, 1558, she did. She died in 1603, in her seventieth year of life, having reigned forty-five years, longest of any British monarch.

As for the Wyndhams of *RiversEdge*, and the de Winters of Winterhaven, they are my own creation. Rest assured, however, that they lived happily ever after, and may one day appear in the pages of another of my novels.

A Message to My Readers

I hope that you have enjoyed *Love, Remember Me,* the account of *Blaze Wyndham*'s daughter, Nyssa. Next year Ballantine and I will bring you the story of *The Loveslave,* a sensual tale of 10th-century Moorish Spain. Its heroine, Regan MacDuff, is forced to sacrifice her virtue in an act of stunning revenge, in order to protect her identical twin sister. Her adventures take her from a convent on the west coast of Scotland, to a rough, half-primitive Dublin, to the elegance of the Moorish city of Cordoba, where Regan is reborn in the persona of Zaynab, the loveslave. You will meet Cordoba's famed caliph, Abd-al Rahman III; his equally celebrated Jewish courtier, Hasdai ibn Shaprut; and the one man whom the loveslave cannot forget, the dashing sea captain, Karim al Malina. This is the one for all those readers who have been begging for another sexy harem book. Trust me. You're going to love it!

Until next year I remain your most faithful author, still longing for that Carolina moon. . . .

—BERTRICE SMALL
SOUTHOLD, NY

ABOUT THE AUTHOR

BERTRICE SMALL lives with her husband, George; Deuteronomy, the long-haired Maine Coon Cat; Checquers, the fat black and white cat with pink ears; Nicky the Cockatiel; and Gilberto, the cranky Half-Moon Conure. The family heir, Tom, is now a college man. Bertrice Small is the author of *The Kadin, Love Wild and Fair, Adora, Skye O'Malley, Unconquered, Beloved, All the Sweet Tomorrows, This Heart of Mine, Enchantress Mine, Blaze Wyndham, Lost Love Found, The Spitfire, A Moment in Time, A Love for All Time,* and *Wild Jasmine.*